SONG OF
THE LEGIONS

MICHAEL LARGE

To Kalpa
best wishes
Michael

BAYONET BOOKS

SONG OF THE LEGIONS
BAYONET BOOKS LIMITED

www.songofthelegions.co.uk
Copyright © Michael Large 2011

ISBN Number 978-0-9568853-0-2

Published by Bayonet Books Limited
Registered Office: Unit 36, 88-90 Hatton Garden, London EC1N 8PN

Correspondence Address: Bayonet Books Limited
PO Box 364 Loughton, Essex IG10 9ET

Front cover image and map by Michael Large

Printed in Great Britain by Ruddocks

For My Wife Joanne

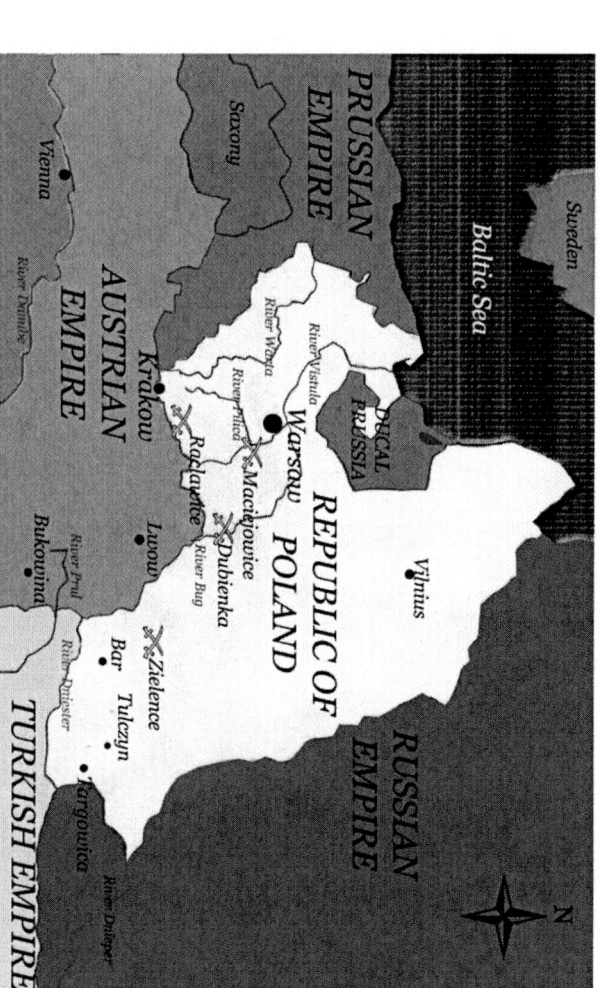

THE REPUBLIC OF POLAND, 1773

5

AUTHOR'S NOTE

Historical notes, a chronology, a glossary, and a short note on pronouncing Polish words, can be found at the back of this book.

I have used the shortest and simplest English versions possible for all Polish names and words.

A full guide to the Polish names and words used in this book, their alternative spellings, and to Polish pronunciation, can be found on the author's website www.songofthelegions.com.

PROLOGUE
ITALY, THE THIRD OF MAY, 1798

We were marching on Rome, for General Napoleon Bonaparte. We were Poles, in the French army. We fought alongside our French allies – or masters. Our flag was the White Eagle. We fought against the Black Eagles – Prussia, Austria, and Russia, the Satanic Trinity.

We were the Polish Legion – a wandering nation of twenty thousand men, women, and children. Betrayed by our King, our country destroyed, we fought on. Our enemies called us the *Foreign Legion*. They would not even speak the name of our Motherland, for the shame of their crime.

If they would not speak our name, then we would *sing* it. So we sang as we marched through Italy. We sang the Song of the Legions –

> *"Poland is not dead, as long as we live,*
> *Our lands, that the invaders have taken,*
> *We with our sabres will retrieve!"*

This fine song was written by Jozef, the lawyer. I knew Jozef. I first met him twenty years ago, when he was hiding in my mother's barn. I was but six years old...

CHAPTER ONE
PODOLIA, 1779

I was born in The Year of Our Lord 1773, one year after the First Partition of Poland. Our enemies had cut great swathes from the Republic, devouring it leaf by leaf, like an artichoke. Russia stole land to the East, Prussia stole land to West, and Austria stole land to the South. Our land – Podolia.

Podolia, land of the black earth, lies in the southern wilderness betwixt Muscovy and Tartary. It is a poor, savage place, riven by war and banditry, where water is drunk more often than coffee or vodka. We are a tough border people, proud, and nobody's fools. This Polish land, now an Austrian province, was ruled by a treacherous Pole named Felix Potocki, a scoundrel in the pay of Russia. A fine state of affairs!

None grieved the dishonour of the Partition more keenly than my mother. Our milksop king would not fight. Had my mother worn the Polish crown, it would have been a different story indeed, I can tell you. My mother Angela was a pious and learned lady, the brightest and the most beautiful in the whole province. She had the wisdom of Solomon and the strength of Sobieski. As a young maiden, she was the darling and delight of her parents.

Those same parents, though of the noblest line, were poor as the meanest serfs. They wore wooden swords and pulled their ploughs by hand. They lived in a walled village with other penniless nobles, locking themselves away like lepers. The pride of their nobility was their only possession, and they guarded it jealousy. Their wretched hovels were distinguished only from the peasants' huts by wooden porches, proudly displaying mildewed coats of arms. In those sad days, there were hundreds of such places in Poland.

Even there my mother shone like a diamond in a pile of ashes. And the gleam of a diamond will always attract magpies. How my parents came to be wed I know not, for they never spoke of it. My father had a strong sabre arm, and pocketfuls of gold, and the rest can be imagined. It was not a good match. Our house was unhappy, for it was a house divided against itself. A house divided against itself cannot stand.

My father's home was no peasant hut. It was a grand nobleman's mansion, the most splendid stack of firewood you ever saw. It was single-storied, in the baroque style, with a grand colonnade flanking the massive iron-bound door. From walnut floor to oak beams, every last splinter of that damned house was wood, aye, all save the glass in the windows.

Beyond the vast entrance hall lay the library, where I studied at my mother's knee, the trophy room and the armoury, where I played among muskets and the stuffed heads of wild beasts, and the dining hall, where I ate prodigiously and grew at an alarming rate. I quickly grew to be a tyrant and a bully, the terror of the other children. For all that, I was good at my studies, a quick learner. My mother was strict, and fear of the strap made me study hard and master my books.

"He's an able scholar and a strong hand. We'll make a general of him," crowed my proud father. My mother, scowling, said nothing.

Close by my father's house there was a stone bastion for defence, a gun tower with loopholes for muskets and cannon. We often had good cause to take shelter in that tower, for my father was notorious – he was Felix Potocki's henchman. Tulczyn, Felix's stronghold, was only a few days ride from our village. It was a dread place, dreary amid the black steppes, built on pyramids of unquiet bones.

Throughout my childhood my father was generally absent. My ageing grandfather, who also lived in the house, spent his days out hunting, or in his cups. Thus my mother ran the estate herself, controlling servants and serfs with an iron hand.

One day I came running in from childish play. I was six years old. My footsteps clattered across the yellow walnut floor. That fine polished floor, burnished to a glorious sheen by the servants, shone gold as honey. I must have marched my toy soldiers across that battlefield to victory a hundred times.

My mother was in the library, which had ceilings with coffers of gilded wood, decorated with intricate carvings. After she had settled the many affairs of the estate, she would attend to my studies, or tell me a story. That day, as the evening shadows drew in, and my books had been set aside, she told me the story of Pan Twardowski, which was my favourite.

You will know the story, for both the Germans and the English call it *Faust*. Pan Twardowski was a great nobleman. He made a pact with the Devil to give him wealth and power, in exchange for his immortal soul. Twardowski signed in blood, as is usual with these satanic pacts. However, as a Polish nobleman, he was not in the habit of ever paying his bills, whether they be to Jews, innkeepers, or the Devil himself. So Twardowski included a *special clause* in the pact, whereby the Devil could only take his soul to Hell if he visited Rome. Then Twardowski swore he would never go there.

Using the Devil's magic, Twardowski became rich. He built splendid castles and held sumptuous revels. One night he summoned the spirits of the dead, using the Devil's magic mirror. Word spread until he was notorious throughout the land. All the while the Devil bided his time.

"After cheating his fate for twenty years," my mother said, "Twardowski stumbled blind drunk into an inn – an inn called 'Rome'. For there are hundreds of inns of this name in our Poland. Waiting with the other drinkers at the next table was the Devil, and all his hideous demons. With a great bloodcurdling cry, the Devil pounced. Grabbing Twardowski in his bloody claws, he dragged him off to Hell, to be damned. Halfway to Hell, in the depths of his despair, Twardowski prayed to the Blessed Virgin Mary for deliverance. He glowed red hot, like a burning coal, and the Devil dropped him, with a great howl!

"So Twardowski fell a thousand leagues, twisting over and over in the void, and landed with a dusty thump on the Moon. There he lives still, to this very day. His only companion on that cold and lonely sphere is a spider. Every so often, Twardowski lets the spider descend to Earth on a silken thread, to bring news from the lost world below."

That day, I piped up – "Mamusia – that man in the barn, is *he* Pan Twardowski, fallen to earth?"

My mother's face was all consternation. It was as if a thunderclap had fallen over the spring sky. "What man in the barn, Ignatius?" she said, taking my hand in a grip of iron.

"Why, I saw him today," I said, "a gentleman from the city, with fine clothes – and a sword!"

"Have you told anyone, Ignatius, my son?" she said, her voice urgent but calm.

That fine gentleman with his silver hair had made a deep impression on me. I had been hunting for mischief amongst the bales of straw, chasing the chickens with my dogs, when I found him.

"Hello, young sir," the gentleman had said, tipping his hat, and looking up from his book. Although surprised, I was unafraid. I spoke with this fellow, who seemed to me as old as Methuselah, but as gentle as a lamb. He bade me bring him a red apple, and in exchange had given me a zloty, and told me to go directly to my Mama, and no other. I had given my word as a gentleman to do as much.

I was accustomed to such strange comings and goings as these. My mother led a secret life. She held clandestine meetings in our house, under my father's very nose. All my young days I had been dimly aware of it. Now, on this warm, intoxicating summer's evening, I finally spoke of it to her.

"I have not told a soul, Mamusia," I said, truly, "upon my word as a gentleman!" I said, proudly.

"Good boy," my mother replied, and smiled, for she regarded danger with contempt. In this nest of traitors, my mother was a true patriot. She was an agent of the Confederates of Bar. The Confederates were a band of brave men who had fought on against the Russian invaders long after our own King had surrendered. These rebels had their base in Podolia. The man I had met was one of their soldiers. My mother gave them food, shelter, money – and guns.

On her finger, my mother always wore a diamond ring decorated with a cross of rubies. We sat alone together in the library. The rubies caught my eye, for they were shining as red as blood in the flickering light of the fire.

"Mamusia," I said, "that silver-haired gentleman wears such a ring as yours. What does it mean?"

"It is a ring of mourning for the brave men who died for our freedom," she said.

"May I wear it, Mamusia?" I asked, eagerly.

She shook her head. "No. Only those who fight for our freedom can wear a ring such as this," she said. "Brave men like the gentleman in the barn. Some day, not in my lifetime, but perhaps in yours, Poland will be free. Do you want to fight for freedom, my son?" my mother said.

"I do!" I said, without hesitation.

"Do you swear it?"

"I swear it," I said, enthralled by the power of her voice. She drew me towards her, caressed me, and placed the ring on my finger.

"Now run along, my little soldier. But not a word. Don't tell a soul."

CHAPTER TWO
PODOLIA, 1787

At fourteen, I was bound for the profession of arms. My father's family were all soldiers. *O'Bloomer*, my warlike Irish forbear, was a colonel in the English army. Upon his discharge, being a younger son with no estate to inherit, and having drunk and gambled away all his army pay, he followed the profession of arms to Russia. Mother Russia, in spite of her naturally peaceful and pacific nature, is constantly having to fight endless wars. These are always provoked by, and always entirely the fault of, the tiny nations that border Her vast lands. Mercenaries therefore being in great demand in Moscow, my grandfather became Peter the Great's artillery instructor, and in due course became rich.

Eventually the old mercenary retired and settled down in Poland. When asked why he had not stayed on in Russia, he would indignantly reply that only a fool would do such a thing, to live under a tyrant, when he could live in liberty! Poland was a democracy, where a man could say and do as he pleased. A man need not fear the dungeon, the knout, nor the gulag. This was my grandfather, the old hypocrite. Compared to my father, however, the man was a paragon of virtue.

My father, the Count Peter Blumer, was named after the self-same tyrant that my grandfather served. His career was even more disgraceful. For my father served in Felix Potocki's private army. By his ruthless conduct and rapacious greed, he quickly rose to a high rank, becoming the chief rent-collector for the Potocki clan.

By treaty, the Austrians had ruled Podolia, this land they had stolen from Poland, for the past fourteen years. But it was Felix Potocki, not the Hapsburgs, that ruled our roost. Podolia was after all far enough away from Vienna for them not to care what went on, so long as they were paid their dues.

Felix was Our Lord Brother. He was a *krolik*, a petty king or warlord, and the head of the powerful Potocki family. Their emblem, the Pilawa cross, a *double cross*, was everywhere. It hung from the door of his castles and palaces, from our door, on the uniforms of Felix's soldiers, and above my father's heart. Felix had a formidable private army. Naturally it had its own officer corps, in which my father was numbered as a general. My father commanded regiments of Cossack and Tartar mercenaries, whose primary duty was to police – that is, terrorise – the peasants.

A magnate, a great landowner, and the richest man in Europe, Felix owned so many castles and palaces across Poland, Austria and France that he scarcely had time to remember them all. He had a magnificent palace in Warsaw that stood right beside the King's own palace (and was bigger than it, to boot) that he rarely ever visited. On Felix's rent roll were hundreds of towns, cities, farms and villages. He was so fabulously wealthy that it was rumoured he was an alchemist, and had discovered the secret of turning lead into gold. Of course this was nonsense. The source of this vast wealth was very simple to anyone with eyes to see – my father and his Cossacks were the very devil at collecting those rents!

Felix himself was a cultured and learned man of letters, a pious God-fearing man, a patron of the arts, a philanthropist, always doing great charitable works, a senator, and a politician. In short – a scoundrel!

At fourteen I was old enough to decide my fate for myself – so long as my father approved of my decision, of course. Although I wished to be a soldier, I preferred to enlist in a military academy, for the sake of my education, rather than to serve Felix. My father, much to my surprise, declared this an admirable choice.

Now it was time to cut me loose from my mother's apron strings. I had grown into a great bull-necked youth, with scarcely more sense than a horse, and as great a thirst for drink and mounting. I could bend two iron horseshoes in my great fists. My bulky frame cast a black shadow over the old wooden house. I stomped around the house like a golem, or a wild beast. I could ride, and shoot, and handle a sword.

For all that, I was apt at book learning, and a keen scholar. Raised a true gentleman, I spoke French like a Frenchman and Latin like a priest. From my grandfather I learned every English oath and curse. At my father's insistence I spoke tolerable German. I had read the Greek poets and the French philosophers, and I always ate fish on a Friday.

"God bless you, Ignatius, my son," my mother said, holding my hand, on which I wore the ring with the cross of rubies. The red stones shone in the white morning sunlight. She embraced me for the last time. Then I took my leave of the world of women.

My father and grandfather were waiting for me outside, in the shadow of the stone tower. They were mapping out my career.

"Only the cavalry is fit for a gentleman," my father was saying, "I'll not have my boy foot-slogging like a peasant – how would that look?"

"Nonsense!" roared my old grandfather. He spoke Polish badly, but his Russian was good, and the languages are enough of a kin that the speaker of one may be understood by the speaker of another. "The cavalry is good for nothing but parades and chasing women!" my grandfather spat. "Isn't that right, Ignatius? Haven't I told you that a thousand times? Join the artillery! Guns are the future! Guns and firepower! Not piddling wooden lances!" My grandfather, of course, was in the artillery.

"Yes, grandfather," I replied, "you have told me so on no less than ten thousand occasions. The cavalry swan about all day in their fancy uniforms, drinking champagne, and going to balls with ladies tarted up to the nines. The real hard work is done by the artillerymen, salt of the earth, up to their necks in muck and bullets. Your wise words have made a deep impression, sir."

They had indeed!

"Good lad!" beamed my grandfather. Both my father and grandfather, laden with ill-gotten gold, and being of a fierce and mercenary disposition, envisaged my honourable (and lucrative) future in the profession of arms, following in their family footsteps. As I set out to serve my military apprenticeship, they spared no expense, procuring the finest horses and weapons that money could buy. Thus they furnished me with my sturdy horse, first among a gentleman's possessions, and a string of remounts. Hanging from my belt was a hussar sabre, and in the breast pocket of my kontusz were a good German compass, a gold watch, and a snuff box, also in gold.

My father and grandfather made me display my swordsmanship. We fought two bouts of parry and counter, and I disarmed them both, one after another. They roared with delight, clapped me on the back, and poured bison-grass vodka down my throat. After we had downed this vodka, my grandfather produced his old guns – a pair of good English pistols, and a great piece of iron taller than I was.

"This is Brown Bess," said my grandfather, "the only true female you shall ever meet."

These English muskets were greatly prized as the finest to be had anywhere in the world. Gleefully I turned it over in my hands. The great barrel was Sheffield steel, engraved with the maker's name. It had a silver fore-sight, brass-lined touch holes, a bevelled lock with safety-catch, iron mounts, and a horn-tipped ramrod. The walnut stock was figured with a deep red feather grain at the butt, which held a small spring-loaded box for storing greased linen patches and tools – the wad cutter, powder flask, and capper.

"Fire it," the old man ordered. I drew a bead on a chicken clucking harmlessly in the yard. My eyes spun with vodka. I pulled the trigger. My head rang with the awful bang. Brown Bess kicked my shoulder like a mule. I staggered and nearly fell. The hen vanished in a puff of feathers. My father clapped me on the back again, laughed, and cheered.

"Here, my boy," my father said, giving me a hefty purse of gold, "spend this as soon as you can, make a good splash, and send me word for more. I'll not have those Austrian bastards look down their noses at an honest Blumer. Watch yourself in Vienna – it's a damned expensive place. Borrow not from the Jews. Be disciplined. Obey orders. If you must fight a duel, make sure it is over cards, and not a woman."

"Thank you for your good advice, sir," I replied. Unfortunately, whilst I wholeheartedly concurred in all this, affirming that nothing would please me better than a life of sword and saddle, and gladly accepting these good gifts, I had entirely neglected to inform my honoured and beloved kinsmen of *which army* I had decided to join.

Naturally, they assumed that I would join the army of the House of Hapsburg. Podolia was after all a part of the Austrian empire. In those days Austria had the largest army in the whole world, greater even than the army of Russia. Austria's hussars were the finest to be had anywhere, not least because of the number of Polish mercenaries and conscripts in their ranks.

"Fine prospects, and a great deal of money, await an officer of the Imperial Army," my father pronounced, and I swear there were tears of joy springing from his money-purse.

"I have no doubt that what you say is true, father," I replied to the old man. I had not spoken a word of a lie.

"Serve your lawful sovereign, boy," my father snivelled, "make us proud."

"Have no fear, I will faithfully serve my lawful sovereign, sir," I replied, as I swung myself unsteadily onto my horse.

My kin waved me a fond farewell from the farm, on a warm sunny day, and I rode westward, for Krakow. At Krakow, the road turns south for Vienna.

Podolia is a naked ocean of wilderness, half-tame, half-wild, under an endless sky. Painted cornfields spread out like a jewelled tapestry – golden fields of wheat, and silver fields of rye. Over the years, our people had slowly begun to tame this wilderness, to make it a garden of man. We bred fine horses, cattle and sheep. We grew tobacco, potatoes, hemp and flax. The forests sang with bee hives. Here were a million Poles, slaves under a Hapsburg flag, serfs of a lackey of Moscow.

At Krakow, I rode north – for Warsaw.

CHAPTER THREE
THE THIRD OF MAY, 1791

Such a day! It was dawn, on The Third of May, the Feast of Our Lady, in the Year of Our Lord, Seventeen Ninety-One. Old Poland was on her last legs – again. Surrounded by enemies without, and honeycombed with traitors within. We few boys had rallied to her tattered flag. We were the King's cavalry, waiting for orders.

We were in the courtyard of the Poniatowski Palace in Warsaw. It reeked of horses and leather. The air sang with hoof beats ringing on flagstones. Sunlight shone on the red walls and roofs of the city, picking out the white spires and domes on the horizon. Our grand old city was red and white, just as Canaletto painted it, the same colours as our flag.

The front rank of riders lowered their lances. Red and white swallow-tailed pennants fluttered in the breeze, and lines of steel spearpoints glittered in the morning sun. We cut a great dash. I sat on my old brown stallion, wearing my crisp new cavalry uniform of blue jacket and red trousers, with shiny silver epaulettes and buttons, and a red fur-lined czapka, our square sided cavalry cap, on my head. My comrades and I were newly enlisted that very day, having graduated as officer cadets together, and we were as happy as priests in a nunnery. As much as we loved the cavalry, we had less respect for its commander-in-chief, His Majesty the King. A herald announced His arrival.

"Stanislaus-August Poniatowski, by the Grace of God and the Will of the People, Elected King of the Republic of Poland and Grand Duke of Lithuania, Ruthenia, Prussia, Mazowia, Samogita, Kiev, Wolyn, Podolia, Podlasie, Livonia, Smolensk, Sever and Czernihov..." Et cetera!

This was Stanislaus-August, not a Pole but a Saxon – that is, almost as bad as a German, if anything can be. Amongst his subjects he was called 'the Bullock,' so named for his emblem, a red calf, on his coat of arms. Lamentably, he is known to history as the Last King of Poland. Poor, foolish Poniatowski! An empty, windy creature, redolent of macassar, with a soft stomach and a head full of French books and nonsense.

The Bullock was the cast-off lover of Catherine, Tsarina of Russia, Satan's illegitimate daughter, herself. She had forced us to elect him as our king – at gunpoint – as a payment for services rendered, after terminating their carnal affair. That tells you how much our throne was worth in those grim days!

The Tsarina considered him her puppet. And so did we, until that day. On that day, the greatest of his life – and ours – he was in high spirits. Our Saxon King and his nephew, the General, passed down the line, talking amiably to the cadets whose names, and whose parents, they knew. These were well-heeled boys from rich clans and noble families – Dabrowskis, Czartoryskis, Sulkowskis, Jablonowskis, Tarnowskis, Zamoyskis, or any number of other illustrious families, whose names invariably ended in *ski*.

Our General, the King's nephew, was Prince Joseph Poniatowski. He was known by his nickname, Pepi. Pepi was a tall, slim cavalier, a charmer, with a magnificent set of moustaches and a killing gleam in his eyes. We all adored Pepi. Many thought that the wrong Poniatowski sat on our throne. By birth and by blood, Pepi was a mixture of Austrian, Saxon and Czech. Even his nickname, 'Pepi', came from the Czech abbreviation of his Christian name, Jozef. Pepi had served the Austrians in the Turkish Wars, with great distinction, and been showered with honours by the Hapsburgs. But when his uncle came to our throne, he had joined him. Since then, by some strange alchemy, Pepi had become a truer Pole than any of us.

21

When the pair of them reached me, the King eyed me suspiciously through his monocle, noticing my red hair, and my pale skin. "What is your name, soldier?" He demanded.

"Ignatius Alexander Blumer, Majesty," I replied, and saluted. The King's eyes widened.

" '*Blumer*'? " he exclaimed, appalled, for I was clearly not one of his bluebloods. "Is that an *Irish* name?"

"It is a POLISH name, Majesty!" I retorted, angrily.

The King glanced sideways at Pepi. "What an impudent fellow! I don't like the cut of his saddle."

"On the contrary, uncle," Pepi grinned, and winked at me, "young Blumer*owski* here is perfect for what we need."

Perfect for what? I wondered! I had not been chosen for the cavalry for my name. I was chosen because I was six feet and two inches tall in my stockinged feet, broad as an ox, with a neck like a bull. I was armed from head to foot with sabre, pistols, and my English musket. In short, I was a fearsome sight! I was indeed perfect – perfect for dirty work.

There was a silence, broken only by the snorts of the horses. The King was going to speak. We craned our necks to listen. Stanislaus-August was nervous. He reddened to his boots, fiddled with his cuffs, coughed, and then began to talk. His speech was, as always, on his pet subject, the Constitution that he had written – or at least put his name to, no doubt having had some lackeys do the actual scribbling. This Constitution would reform our archaic laws, he told us. It would give the King the power he needed, and give the Citizens the rights they wanted. Above all, it would strengthen the army.

When the King had finished, Pepi spoke. "As you all know, the final vote is due to be held on the fifth of May," Pepi said, "but with something this important, why wait?"

We all laughed. Our swords were going to do the voting. The King made a sour face, for he had no stomach for the rough side of this business. Pepi drew his sabre, with a rasp of steel and a flash of silver in the sunlight, and he cried – "For the Motherland!" – and we cheered him to the echo.

Pepi caracoled his horse, and spurred it out of the courtyard. It was a fine Polish charger, pure white, caparisoned in silver and gold. We followed him, on our own, lesser, steeds, hard on his heels, hooves clattering. As we swept out through the gates, we passed by one of Felix Potocki's many palaces. It stood opposite the King's Palace, less than a pistol shot away across the street. The Pilawa cross – the double cross, Felix's emblem – hung above the wrought iron gate. It reminded me of home, the home I had not seen in four years.

Pepi, ever the gentleman, tipped his czapka to Felix's guards as they gawped at us through the iron railings. I was right behind him.

"Is Felix there?" the King asked his nephew.

"No," Pepi replied. "Our Lord Brother Felix is in Moscow, with the Empress."

The King laughed, delighted. "What a shame! He'll miss the vote!"

CHAPTER FOUR
THE MAZURKA

"The Bullock is right – anyone can get in the cavalry nowadays!" taunted the next man, a tall, dark haired, slim lad, who spoke with a drawling Warsavian accent. "It's full of country hicks from the provinces!" he teased me, loudly. This was my comrade Kasimir Tanski.

This lancer rode a dappled grey horse, a mare, with a glossy grey coat like pearl satin. She danced lightly on her feet. My own stallion had taken a distinct shine to her. He, by contrast, was a huge, clumsy brute, with shaggy fur more like buffalo hide than horse hair. Nevertheless, my stallion let out a great amorous bellow, bared his awful yellow teeth, and lurched towards the mare. She, alarmed, bared her own white teeth and sank them into his neck.

Kicking and bucking wildly, the two horses clashed. It was all I could do to keep my foolish beast in hand, and I dug the rowels of my spurs mercilessly into his flanks. He let out another great bellow, and the mare released her grip and pranced away sideways, spitting and hissing like a wildcat.

"Damn this crazy mare!" Tanski exclaimed. "A thousand apologies, comrade!"

Everyone in the army called each other 'comrade', whilst the nobles, in those days, referred to each other as 'My Lord Brother'. By our ancient laws, every nobleman was equal – 'My Lord Brother' – but the greatest of the gentry were the grand magnates. When I say the greatest, naturally I mean the *richest*. The greatest of these magnates was of course Felix Potocki, warlord of Podolia. As my Irish kin were foreign nobles, (and therefore not real gentry) I was an anomaly. So 'comrade' suited me well enough.

Tanski could not help but smile as he regarded my horse's grotesque appearance, the shaggy brown and orange hair, huge red eyes like a bear's, a mangy mane streaked with silver, and horrible stained and rotten teeth. The beautiful mare stared at him with contempt.

"This romance is over before it began, Blumer."

"Nonsense! Your mare is merely playing hard to get."

Tanski laughed. We disentangled our horses and rejoined the line as the regiment trotted down the street. We had been in Warsaw now these four years in Poniatowski's cadets, studying drill and tactics – when our punishing schedule of drinking, gambling and wenching allowed it. All four of those long years, the Sejm (which was what we called our Parliament) had been in session. Four long years of angry debates about the Constitution.

The whole nation was in a fever for this Constitution. Crowds marched through Warsaw on a daily basis, with black banners, demanding this or that, whipped up into a patriotic fervour. In the taverns and coffee houses they spoke of the rights of man, religious toleration, kindness to Jews, the education of peasants and women, and other nonsense.

Along with my fellow cadets I had spent days and months on the back of my horse, arse aching, on guard duty, policing these crowds of whingeing peasants. Our constipated Sejm had sat all this time, like a hen trying to lay a goose egg. Who should have a vote? What privileges should the townsfolk have? How much tax should the workers' guilds pay? How much land should the peasants be given? All questions of great import, no doubt, but they bored me to tears. I cared not a grosz for the small print, but I wanted the Constitution. With no money or connections, I needed a war to make my name.

"When the Empress gets wind of this," I said to my horse, "there'll be war all right."

What a pretty picture we made that fine day, like a neat rank of toy soldiers marching across a child's nursery floor. Our standard fluttered joyfully in the breeze behind the King, the crowned white eagle on a red field below a white sky. Above us, three black crows wheeled lazily over the city. An ill omen. Poland's enemies – Russia, Prussia, and Austria – all have black eagles on their coats of arms. Three black eagles circling the white.

Remember the herald who announced the Bullock's arrival? Who called out that long list of the places of which His Majesty was King – Lithuania, Ruthenia, Prussia, Mazowia, Samogita, Kiev, Wolyn, Podolia, Podlasie, Livonia, Smolensk, Sever and Czernihov? Well, all those lands and provinces were gone. Lost, or as good as lost. The herald may as well have proclaimed that the Bullock ruled the Moon with Pan Twardowski as his Prime Minister.

Lithuania was still with us, more or less, but hanging by a thread. Prussia, once our vassal state of Teutonic mercenaries, created by us to fight our enemies, had become a monster, and run amok, like the evil golem in the story told by the Jews. Of Podolia, my homeland, you know already.

As for the rest – Ruthenia, Samogita, Kiev, Wolyn, Livonia, Smolensk, Sever and Czernihov – they had long since been taken by the icy hand of Mother Russia, in the grisly and murderous business that the Tsarina called 'gathering in the lands'. We still had Mazowia, the great cities of Warsaw, Krakow, and Vilnius, and a few others. But for how long? The Bullock held them only by the grace and favour of the Empress of the North.

We rode past the churches, the coffee houses, the taverns, and the theatre house, and the green and red and white and brown stone houses of the old town. A great swirl of excitement rose up around us like a storm on the steppes.

"Strike up a tune," came Pepi's order. "Play something merry – play 'the mazurka'!"

Our drummers and trumpeters struck up the mazurka, and the song rang out – the Song of the Legions. This mazurka had no words and no author. It sprang from the heavens like a friendly spirit in that golden spring of the Third of May. A fife player in a regiment of loyal Cossacks and a Jew harpist by the roadside joined in.

It spread like forest fire and soon the air was alive with it. By now the street was thronged with citizens and peasants, staggering from the alehouses and churches. All of the citizens had realised, by some magic, exactly what was afoot. They began to gather together. Slowly at first, then faster. As we advanced the trickle of people became a deluge. Faces pressed to every window. Men, women, children, young and old, gentile and Jew. Men waved their hats and women their scarves. They cheered, sang, and rejoiced. Every inch of pavement was thronged with people. We pushed slowly through the press.

We slowed our horses to a walk. Rose petals and cherry blossoms seemed to fill the air. Girls pressed flowers and laurels upon us. Bells rang. Doves fluttered to the heavens. By now the street was so full that people were clambering onto the green roofs of the red and white houses, waving flags and banners. No Roman Emperor ever had so splendid a triumph as the Bullock received from our Warsaw folk – but in this excess of delirious joy, we all quite forgot that the barbarian hordes of our enemies had not yet actually been conquered.

As we were swept along in this sea of joy, there was even a priest, to bless our voyage! A bishop, no less, intoning prayers, making the sign of the cross and spraying the Bullock, Pepi, and the rest of us cavalrymen with holy water as we rode by.

"One of these damned priests is on our side, anyway!" Tanski sneered. "Mostly they hate the Constitution. At Mass last week, my priest called it a pact with the Devil."

"I have heard the same slanders," I agreed, "my priest says there are Jacobins hiding under every bed in Warsaw, ready to set up guillotines on every street corner, close the churches, sell our women to the Jews, and so on. Lies and nonsense!"

Tanski considered himself an authority on the dark rumours that were swirling through the taverns and coffee houses, and was greatly given to talk of plots and conspiracies.

"I'll tell you where this treachery comes from – from Felix Potocki. He's a Freemason, of course," Tanski tapped his nose. "Upon my soul, Felix put the priests up to this knavery."

Moments later we rode by the friendly bishop, who had been administering unctions and blessings to the Bullock by the dozen, kissing his hand and drenching him in holy water. We gaped at each other in amazement.

"Hell's teeth!" we both exclaimed, "that's the same priest!" Right under our noses, this crafty priest was fawning over the Bullock as if he were God's anointed, and not the Devil's disciple, as he had been saying only yesterday.

Abruptly, the column stopped, for it was but a short road to the Wawel Castle. This red brick fortress, as picturesque as a storybook castle, was brimful inside with politicians – the *karmazym*, the crimson ones. This was what we called the rich nobles and magnates, on account of their expensive crimson clothing, especially their boots. These politicians sat there all day long, squatting on their fat backsides, farting out great clouds of hot air.

We rode into the square to find that it was ringed with soldiers. There, at the head of his troops, surrounded by engineers and cannon, was the great man himself, General Kościuszko – known to all as the Commander – as great a son of liberty as ever lived.

Pepi and the Commander saluted each other.

"Would you be so kind as to lend us one of your engineers, my dear General?" Pepi drawled. "One never knows – the Sejm could be packed with gunpowder!"

The Commander grinned. "Private Sierawski!" he bellowed, and from the ranks of engineers, there was summoned a gangling boy of barely sixteen. He had a mop of unruly hair beneath his czapka, and long, finely tapered violinist's fingers on his clumsy hands.

"He's a crafty little sod," the Commander said, "he'll serve you well."

By this means we made the acquaintance of Jan Sierawski, from Krakow, as he never tired of telling us, engineer *extraordinaire*, by his own account. Sierawski took his place beside us. Puffed up as he was, he would be well matched with the preening bullfrogs of the Sejm who sat inside the Wawel Castle.

At the castle gate, the King doffed his three-cornered cap to the crowd, to a storm of applause. By now some persons amongst the mob had become greatly agitated. So much so that our men were obliged to link arms and drive them back, for fear that they might storm the Sejm. Thus, by a strange irony, we protected our adversaries from our friends.

Then the King stepped down from his horse and a groom took the reins. Stanislaus-August had a kind, nervous, intelligent face. A gold-handled sword hung at his hip. He wore a white powdered wig and a glorious orange robe emblazoned with eagles against the spring cold. Over his left shoulder hung a blue silk sash. At his neck was a golden clasp picked out in precious stones, bearing his coat of arms, a red bullock. For all our misgivings about him, the King cut a fine figure before the castle.

Crowds were still gathering, swelling the procession that had followed us from the Poniatowski Palace to bursting. A river of people, like a second Vistula running through the streets. The Constitution meant freedom. Freedom from foreign enemies, and from the tyranny of the nobility at home. We had to have this Constitution, one way or another, come what may, whatever the politicians said.

This King of ours was an intellectual, who lived in a world of books and fine ideals. He had fine words to sway the doubters in the Sejm into voting for his Constitution. His nephew Pepi was more practical. He had surrounded the Sejm with soldiers. For good measure, he was bringing a few of us along with him inside the senate house – including Tanski, Sierawski and myself – as his hand-picked jockeys. Under Pepi's orders we drew our swords and stormed into the castle.

CHAPTER FIVE
THE CRIMSON ONES

Let me explain the reason for our parlous situation. Our
nation's ruling dynasty, the glorious Jagiellons, died out three
hundred years ago. This left us without a royal family, so a
King was elected by the nobles of the Sejm. He acted as a
kind of glorified steward on their behalf. By these same
ancient (and downright insane) laws, any one noble senator
could veto any proposal made by the King. One senator with a
grudge, or who had been bribed, could paralyse the nation.
The King could get nothing done. If the nobles didn't want to
pay tax, well, damn it, they wouldn't pay tax – VETO! If that
meant we had no army to repel the Russians, or no roads, or
no schools in the villages, then so be it. *Nie Pozwalam! I will
not allow it! VETO!*

This was what the nobles called their 'golden freedom'.
The freedom of men such as Felix Potocki to do whatever the
hell they pleased, and damn the rest of us, over whom they ran
roughshod with the sword and the knout. We had another
word for it – *anarchia.*

"The Constitution will put an end to this madness of the
Veto," Pepi said, "unless somebody VETOES it first, that is.
A fine conundrum!" he frowned.

"We will veto the veto, General!" we replied, making the
throat-cutting gesture.

With that, we passed through the Marble Room, with its
twenty-two portraits of Polish Kings, painted by French
masters. Stanislaus-August paused for a moment, and nodded
at the sombre crowned heads in a mark of silent respect. His
predecessors stared back. His portrait was the last of the line.
The King gazed sadly at the gilded, marble-floored room.

"My famous Thursday Dinners were held in this very room, nephew," the King recollected. "The finest minds were there – artists, poets, intellectuals, scientists. We cooked up the Constitution over those feasts. It was a glad time, before the long shadows drew in." The King sighed sadly. After this morbid moment, we pressed on, stepping carefully to avoid tearing the furniture with our spurs, our scabbards scraping on the marble floor.

In the great hall the great lords had gathered, the karmazym, the crimson ones. The Sejm resembled a Turkish bazaar rather than a place of government. One could buy anything from a tasty snack to a position in the government with equal ease. Hawkers plied their trade selling beer, pastries, and candied fruits, stepping between the high benches and tables strewn with papers where the senators and their lackeys argued and bickered endlessly.

On one side stood the firebrands, the radicals – the men they called *Jacobins*. The Church said they were heretics and fanatics, who preached that even peasants and women should have rights – or even votes. Naturally I considered myself a liberal and enlightened sort of a fellow, but I was no Jacobin. That was taking things too far. Votes for peasants and women, by God! Whatever next?

There was Cyprian Godebski, playwright and poet, a staunch supporter of the Constitution, eating a pie wrapped in a copy of the *Warsaw Gazette*. As well as being a poet and a politician, he was a lieutenant in the grenadiers.

Beside him was Senator Jozef Wybicki, the white-haired lawyer. He was besieged by whingeing clients waving petitions (and complaining about their bills) even on that grand day. With a shock, I recognised him – he was the old man who had hidden in my mother's barn!

The King went around and around the hall, begging wavering Senators for their vote. There were a number of bishops in the senate. Almost all of these bishops were dead set against the Constitution – and the King conversed with each in turn, in vain, begging them not to use the veto.

"The arse speaks to the bishop, but the bishop just speaks to himself,"[1] I observed. Pepi, meanwhile, accosted a buxom young girl who was selling apple cake, vodka and beer.

"Make room for the young lady, there!" Pepi cried at a group of senators who were sitting at a bench, poring over a copy of the Constitution. They were busily crabbing and scribbling with their quills. These were our enemies. Traitors in the pay of Russia. Pepi swept their papers aside, then lifted the serving girl up with one arm and deposited her, blushing, upon the bench. The papers fell to the marble floor in a chaotic swirl.

"How clumsy of me! A thousand apologies!" he exclaimed in mock horror. "Comrades!" Pepi snapped his fingers at us, grinning, "clear up this mess, at once!"

We gathered up the fallen papers in a great balled-up mass, to howls of protest from the Senators, who scrabbled after them. In the mêlée, the papers were torn to shreds.

I ran into one of those fellows, who was on his knees, grabbing after his carefully worded objections that were now no more than ribbons. I knew him for Hetman Adam Severyn Rzewuski. He was a Podolian warlord, a henchman of Felix Potocki, a lackey of the Russians. I seized him by his crimson cloak and raised him roughly to his feet. His lordship was a great bear of a man, strong as a wrestler, but his body had run to fat, and a ponderous belly hung below his barrel chest. Hatred and contempt were writ on every inch of his hard, coin-counting face, from the tip of his bristling beard, to the top of his shiny head, which was as bald as an egg.

"A thousand pardons! Your papers, My Lord," I said, shoving the torn bundle at him.

---

[1] *Polish saying, roughly equivalent to 'you might as well talk to a brick wall' or 'you're wasting your breath'*

"Damn your eyes!" he cursed, snatching them, "you stinking Jacobin dog!"

"If you are not content with my apology, Your Lordship," I bowed, "you may ask me for satisfaction at any time," I replied, and casually tossed my glove onto the bench before him, a blatant challenge to a duel. He placed his hand on his sword hilt. Then he glanced at my comrades and, seeing himself outmatched, withdrew.

"I don't duel with peasants!" he sneered, by way of excuse.

"I am a gentleman, Sir," I said coldly, "and you are a scoundrel, a traitor and a coward."

Rzewuski's face turned red as a beetroot. He lunged at me, but his flunkeys seized him by the tail of his kontusz and held him fast.

"Unhand me, you damned serfs!" Rzewuski grumbled, thrashing about with his arms and floundering like a landed fish. He made a great show of anger, but I had the measure of my man – many's the time I've seen braggarts in the taverns dragged off by their friends thus, glad to avoid a fight. I watched with pleasure as Rzewuski's men led him away, with him pretending to protest all the while.

"Blumer!" Pepi called after me, "dear fellow, would you be so kind as to cut this cake?" It was a plump and delicious apple cake, with a pungent smell of cinnamon, almost as luscious as the girl who had brought it to us, who now, sadly, was nowhere to be seen. We cut the cake up with our daggers. Then the King returned, disheartened.

"Am I to do this alone? Won't you help me persuade the senators, Pepi?" He spluttered.

"On the contrary, Uncle," Pepi retorted, "my men are being *extremely* persuasive, as you see. Their very presence encourages these politicians to be reasonable."

Pepi gestured at us. We agreed, most vigorously, with cake on our lips, and swords in our hands. All around us, politicians shrank back, terror-struck. Nobody was talking about the veto any more. Nobody was saying very much at all, in fact.

"Perhaps you are right after all, nephew," the King conceded, grinning. "These are the men for such work as this!" With that he swept away, cape billowing, followed by a flock of servants and hangers-on to put clear air between us and his royal personage.

I am a big man, but Pepi was a hand taller, and he loomed over me like a tower of genial menace. "Blumer, my boy," he drawled, "I'd be obliged if you would keep an eye on My Lord Brother Baldy there, for he appears to be in a bad humour this fine day. I think you upset him."

Thus, under my watch, Rzewuski slipped out of the chamber. He went with one of the bishops. Perhaps he was only going to pass water, but, as I was bid, I followed him, with Sierawski and Tanski hard on my heels.

Rzewuski and the bishop were talking in the Marble Room. They were sharing a fortifying glass of vodka beneath the far window. I peered cautiously around the door. There was a round table pushed to one side, and a stack of gilt chairs gathering dust. The old kings in the pictures glared down, as if deeply displeased with the two conspirators who skulked amongst the velvet-covered furniture.

"Lord Potocki will be furious when he hears of this treachery!" Rzewuski said, gnashing his teeth. "He will ride here at the head of an army, to protect our ancient rights!"

"This reckless King will ruin our country," the Bishop agreed. "Our salvation can only come from Russia!"

Well, this bishop was a real turncoat. Only moments before he had been congratulating the King, dousing him with Holy Water, and kissing his psalter.

At this point we three burst in, falling over our own feet. We stared at them insolently. The Bishop put down his bottle of vodka and snatched up his mitre. Rzewuski glared back with contempt.

"You think to frighten us, you young ponces?" he snarled. "Bishop Massalski and I shall veto this damned Constitution, if no one else has the balls to. My duty is as clear as my conscience. I am going to the voting chamber, and damned if any of you little shits will stop me."

I blocked their path.

Rzewuski placed one hand on his sabre hilt.

"Stand aside, peasant!" he roared, "I was killing Turks for Holy Russia when you were soiling your nappy and sucking your mother's teats."

"My Lord," I said angrily, "I would thank you not to mention my mother again."

My wrath burned like a powder fuse. All present saw it, save for Rzewuski.

"F— you, boy," Rzewuski spat in my face, "and f— your whore of a mother, too," he added, for good measure. Then he hiked up his sword belt over his paunch and strode towards the door.

I met him halfway and, without ceremony, struck him across his bald head with the butt of my gun. It was a gentle enough tap, though it knocked a few teeth from his jaw. The unfortunate senator collapsed to the floor with a crash. There he lay, groaning and crying murder and treason, blood pouring from his gaping mouth.

My comrades stood open-mouthed and winced at the sight of this great crimson one laid low. Even they were shocked by my violence, and the alacrity with which I delivered it. Tanski whistled, impressed. I trained my gun next on the Bishop. "Your Grace, please administer the last rites to this fellow and to your Holy Self, while you're at it. If you take one step towards this door, I shall blow out your brains!"

The Bishop crossed himself, turned as pale as a plaster saint and prayed for deliverance. As the saying goes, the arse talks to the Bishop, but the Bishop just talks to himself!

Thus the Constitution was passed without a veto. There were a few 'abstentions' though. Joy was unbounded, and all fears banished. The King proceeded to Saint John's Church, across the square from the Wawel, to celebrate the Feast of Our Lady. There, the populace received him rapturously and acclaimed him to the rooftops. Our Holy Lord Brother, Bishop Massalski, was there again, with his ewer of holy water, anointing the crowd and the King, his loyalties swinging around like a weathervane in a storm.

Suddenly we heard that blessed mazurka again, and young Sierawski was beating a drum, three or four simple notes, beating time to the steps of the dance. We danced in a circle around the column of old King Sigismund, up on his pillar, sword and cross in hand. From the slow elegant steps of the dance, the men gliding sidewards, and the women elegantly stamping their heels and clicking their fingers.

Everyone was smiling, and Tanski leaned over a girl he had his arm around and said something dirty, and I found myself arm in arm with the girl from the Sejm. She smelled of apples and cinnamon, and she smiled at me, as we danced. We all seemed to float above the Wawel Square, a ring of laughing girls and soldiers, gentlemen and traitors, priests and philosophers, Jews and gentiles, magnates and madmen, over Warsaw, with poets in the cafés, and traitors in the Sejm – and our hearts soaring. We danced in that circle, where our past was full of failure and our future was full of suffering, but on that day we lit a torch to burn through the awful darkness that was to come.

Bells rang across the city, as far away as dirty old Praga, the seamy suburb of fleshpots across the river. My comrades and I reflected that there were sure to be a few taverns that would welcome three young heroes fresh from the Sejm, who had struck a great blow for freedom this day, this day of Our Lady the Third of May.

Such a day! We went to Neybertowa's Coffee House, in Wiejska Street, being the nearest coffee house to the Sejm, and one of the grandest in the whole town. We stood a few rounds of strong black Polish coffee, which we all agreed was the best in the world. Then we had a few glasses of bison grass vodka. A good many toasts were drunk and a good many songs were sung. Joy-shots rang out and wisps of powder-smoke curled up into the heavens.

Up above us the evil old man in the moon, Pan Twardowski, drooled and cackled, as he sent down his spider on its silver string, to hear our gossip, to stir poison in our vodka, whisper sedition in our ears, and weave webs of treachery in the shadows.

CHAPTER SIX
THE FEAST OF OUR LADY,
AND THE PODOLIAN POPE

Cyprian Godebski, the poet, invited the three of us to dine at the salon of Madame L, his inamorata. I have obscured her name from this memoir, and you will see why later.

Madame L was a woman of legendary and disgraceful hospitality. She was an heiress and a widow, he explained, with a fine estate and a good income, wildly rich, but more importantly, a staunch patriot. She was a passionate supporter of the Constitution. She held the rank of Castellan – that is, military governor of one of our cities in the east. Perhaps I should say military govern*ess* instead of governor.

It was rare but not unknown to find a woman Castellan in the Republic, although it was unheard of in the rest of Europe. Her duties as Castellan were onerous. She organised supply trains, ordnance, hospitals, militias, fortresses, garrisons, and a thousand other things from latrines to spying. Accordingly, she had great power. She issued orders like a general, and could have her soldiers clapped in irons, or court-martialled, if they gave her cause.

This formidable lady kept a large rambling mansion near the old city gatehouse. Her establishment was run like a French literary salon. It was a showy place of smoke and mirrors, intrigue and *amours*. Godebski explained that this most martial lady was very fond of the cavalry, and cavalrymen in particular, and that we would be made most welcome, and thus it proved.

"When a guest enters the house, God enters also," was her greeting, in the fine traditions of the nobility. She was a dark and handsome woman, gorgeously attired in Italian silks, her bodice picked out in pearls and sundry gemstones, her unruly hair piled up on her head in the fashion of the day. She was as sharp as a backsword, with sharp eyes, and a sharp tongue to match.

We were all much taken with her and the splendour of her household. After living for four years in spartan barracks and dingy lodgings, it seemed that we had spent a whole day in palaces – first the Wawel Castle, and now the beguiling palace of Godebski's pretty paramour.

Godebski was twenty-six years old, which to me, at eighteen, made him as old as Methuselah. As we sat down to eat, I caught him eyeing his grey hairs in the gilt mirrors on the walls. The poet took a drink of mead and stared glumly at the ornate wooden ceiling of Madame L's dining hall. He wondered aloud if the ceilings of her bedchamber were of the same intricate design.

"Lamentably, I have failed to be admitted into that sweet sanctuary, to see for myself!" he admitted, with a great pang of regret. "I have laid siege to that pretty citadel for a long while now. I have courted her in poem, in song, with gifts, and with my esteemed company. I have pledged her my undying love, and all my worldly goods. Admittedly I have no great monetary fortune to speak of, and a few trifling debts, but am I not wealthy in talent, and rich in my reputation? And yet, despite all this, despite my passionate advances, my fusillades of flattery, my sorties of sonnets, all my attacks have been in vain. I have made no breach in her defences!"

Madame L always had many good ladies at her house, which was excellent, and some bad ones also, which was even better. She presented Godebski with a beautiful gold pen and a walnut writing table, and similar gifts to the rest of us. All of these we lost, gave away, or broke, in our drunken stupor.

Our fame – or notoriety – had spread far and wide in the shortest possible space of time. We drank copiously to that, and to the health of our fair hostess, and her fair company. We shrewdly imagined that it should dissipate quite as quickly, too, for a guest is like a fish, and stinks after three days. Thus ensconced, we caroused and raised Cain. We knew not night from day.

Madame was certainly enamoured of the cavalry, for within some hours a young galloper, a lieutenant named Elias Tremo, came to call. With him was the faithful old warrior Jozef Wybicki, who I had already seen in the Sejm. Senator Wybicki and the lady embraced like old comrades, and they laughed and cried for joy.

Godebski reddened with anger as Elias Tremo stooped to kiss the lady's hand. Tremo grinned up at the lady through his cavalry moustaches. She did not smile with her lips, which were painted as red as our cavalry breeches, but her eyes flashed like spearpoints.

"Gentlemen! Ladies!" she clapped her hands and servants brought us drinks, tray after tray, glass upon glass, bottle following bottle, "a toast! To The Glorious Third of May!"

We all cheered and drank. Madame and this fine gentleman, their pale skin flushed with Spanish wine, began to talk nostalgically of the past, as the long dark evening shadows drew in around us.

Jozef was a good few years older than any of us, even Madame, and had been through a good deal more. We asked him about the Thursday dinners at the Wawel Castle, of which everyone had heard, but which had not been held for these ten years now. Thus discoursing, we took a further drink or two.

"The Thursday Dinners were held in the Marble Room," Wybicki recalled. "It is a grand round room, the very same room where you lads persuaded Lord Rzewuski how to vote, by appealing to his conscience with oratory, to his intellect with rhetoric, and to his skull with a musket butt."

Although we laughed heartily at this, by now it had begun to dawn on me that I had not heard the last of that bald-headed beast Rzewuski.

Jozef lit his pipe. "King Stanislaus-August would invite artists, scientists, poets, intellectuals and politicians to dinner on Thursdays, at the Wawel Castle. The wisest, the most learned, the most respected. I had the honour to be invited regularly – before the King and I had our small disagreement, of course," he chuckled. "We talked for hours," Jozef frowned slightly, "or, rather, come to think of it, the King talked for hours, and we listened to him blathering on."

I nodded, impatiently, in my cups. "Yes, yes, we know all that. What we want to know is, what did you have to eat?"

"Ah! The dishes!" Jozef waxed. "There were no sickly sugarloaves, oily Russian caviar, or liver-rotting Parisian champagne. None of that expensive foreign rubbish."

"The Bullock probably couldn't afford it," I butted in, for our army pay was in arrears again. Jozef ignored this.

"We ate simple country food," Jozef told us, "beef in horseradish sauce, game, mushrooms, poppy seed cakes, fruit, nuts, and white cheese."

Young Lieutenant Tremo, who had been lounging on a couch, spoke to the rest of us, to impress Madame. He was plainly Godebski's rival for her affections.

"I was at those glorious dinners!" he confessed, boastfully.

At this Godebski leaped up, as if stung. "Damned lies!" he roared, reaching for his sword. Swords were not put aside at dinner, or any other time, for that matter. Indeed we wore them to the privy.

"To sword, Sir! A pipsqueak like you would not have dined with those great and learned lords!"

Poor Cyprian Godebski, you will rightly gather, had never been invited to the Thursday dinners.

The young officer stood his ground. "I demand your apology, comrade! In fact I attended many of the Thursday dinners as a young boy. Indeed, I helped prepare them."

"Calumny! Lies upon lies!" Godebski was in uproar.

"Stay your hand!" Jozef intervened. "The lad speaks the truth, for this is young Lieutenant Elias Tremo, son of the father, Pawel Tremo, the King's Chef, and the finest chef in all Europe, back in those days."

Godebski was not happy, but when Elias offered to prepare one of these fine dishes for us, so that we might dine in imitation of the King and his Thursday guests, the uproar subsided.

"If you were at these dinners, Comrade Tremo," Tanski put in slyly, "then you can settle a question of mine. Never mind the food – what about the women?"

"Gentlemen," said Elias Tremo, with great solemnity, "I can assure you, there were none. The Senator has told me that no ladies – and certainly no 'women', for there is a difference – were ever present at the Thursday dinners."

All eyes turned to Senator Jozef Wybicki. Madame arched her eyebrows wickedly.

Flustered, the lawyer said hastily. "Um, ah, er, why, yes, the boy is absolutely right. None at all."

We all laughed, for when a lawyer denies a fact, one knows it for God's own truth! Then Elias Tremo repaired to the kitchen, to supervise Madame L's servants and cooks in preparing our dinner.

"The lad has his feet well under the table," I remarked to Godebski, "I fear you have a rival."

The poet bristled with rage. "Damn it! Damn that fickle woman!" he ranted.

In a short while, the dinner was served, under the direction of Tremo, the son of the father. Verily, the apple did not fall far from the tree, and it was excellent. We commenced with our traditional Polish soup – borsch with *uszka*, which are small dumplings shaped like ears – followed by roast hazel grouse, larded with a delicate sauce made from onion and pork fat. This was followed in turn by mutton and vegetables.

"At the Thursday dinners," Jozef reminisced, "we drank excellent Spanish wines, Hungarian Tokay and Polish mead, much as we are enjoying now from our gracious hostess. The King quenched his thirst with spring water. He does not drink and neither does he smoke."

"A man who doesn't drink or smoke, is good for nothing, as the proverb says," I observed, drunkenly.

"Indeed! Damn right! Damned Bullock," Jozef agreed, drinking a small glass of vodka to aid his digestion and smoking his pipe. The vodka was chasing the wine around the table. Years before, Jozef had of course fallen out with the King and his mood soured as he remembered it. He grumbled over his dessert. It was plums – just as it always was at the Thursday Dinners.

"The damned King always ate plums for dessert, plums, plums, always bloody plums, even in the dead of winter," Jozef recollected, bitterly.

"Why so many plums?" I asked.

"Because the King is full of shit!" Jozef roared, laughing but still angry. "Who are you, anyway, you great big oaf?" he demanded, turning on me with suspicion.

"Why, I am Angela Blumer's son, Ignatius," I replied. "My dear mother, God rest her soul, knew you."

He peered at me and then slowly began to smile.

"By God! So you are!" he took off his spectacles and shook my hand, delighted.

"Who is this old fool, Blumer? A friend of yours?" Tanski, bored, hissed at me from behind his hand.

"Senator Jozef Wybicki here was a Confederate of Bar in the last war," I told him. The others immediately fawned around him, impressed. He was no longer a drunken old fogey in a wig, but a warrior of legend.

"You fought the Russians?" Sierawski said.

44

"Indeed I did!" Jozef said, growing misty eyed, "and we lost!"

We listened as the old warrior remembered his glory days.

"It was in 1768 when the Russians invaded, on some pretext or other. The Bullock surrendered without firing a shot, the damned coward! It was a disgusting act of cowardly treachery. My comrades and I declared our Confederacy against him at Bar, and we fought on, for four years, against both the Bullock and his damned Russian mistress. Ha! That was one hell of a boundary dispute!" he cried, his eyes gleaming with nostalgia.

"Bar, of course, is in Podolia," he continued, "a good place to hide out. So there we hid, and from there we would ride out in sorties and raid the enemy. But I fear that even Podolia is lost to us now!"

Young Tanski, who was drunk, took the offensive against Podolia and Podolians, both of which he thoroughly detested. "Esteemed Sir," Tanski said loudly, so I could hear, "naught grows in the black earth of Podolia but weeds and stones. As for the Podolians themselves, they are a bastard race of dogheads, heretics, Jews, Tartars, traitors, sodomites, blackamoors, Cossacks and Irishmen. The loss of Podolia is no loss at all. The Austrians are welcome to it!"

Everyone laughed – with myself excepted. Tanski and Sierawski collared Elias Tremo and they disappeared together to the kitchen. They were whispering together and making mischief. We were all drunk by this time. Tanski's mocking of Podolians had angered me greatly. Fury boiled in my chest. The others, in their cups, and spoiling for trouble, encouraged him. As was common in those grand old days, the meal soon became a merry drinking bout. These often ended in quarrels, and since it was our fashion to go armed at all times, blood was often spilled.

"Comrades!" Sierawski staggered in, smirking through his moustaches, "one last course!"

A pig's head was brought on to the table. Tanski and Sierawski bore it aloft. They were wrapped in white tablecloths, in imitation of priestly vestments, with leather wine bladders set upon their heads for mitres. Tanski fell to his feet before the carcass, genuflecting, and flicking mead from a jug over us all, like holy water, and making the sign of the cross unctuously in the air with a knife and fork.

"*In nomine Patris et Filii et Spiritus Sancti! In the name of the Father, the Son, and the Holy Spirit!*" Sierawski cried. "To prayer, my Lord Brothers, and praise the Lord! For it is the Podolian Pope himself! With his communion wafers!" Tanski exclaimed, triumphantly, producing a plate of fried pierogi. They began solemnly intoning a nonsense doggerel song they had invented, and styled 'the Podolian Psalm.'

"*Ora pro nobis, sancti pierogi di Podolia, Amen!*"

The gentlemen and ladies, all in their cups, fell about laughing at this. There were cheers and jeers, and much drunken hilarity. In a rage, I ran at Tanski and struck him hard in the chest. Although he was a big strong fellow, he was thrown across the room, hit his head on a bench, and passed out cold. Turning next on Sierawski, I drew my blade and held the point to his throat.

"To sword, Sir! We came here to drink a toast to the Constitution, but instead you mock me!"

"No! Mercy, Comrade!" Sierawski yelled, throwing up his hands. We declared a truce. Godebski and I picked up Tanski from the floor by his ankles and tossed him into a horse trough to sober him up. Jozef Wybicki, being inclined to more intellectual pursuits than this, took his leave and went to bed. The dashing young chef de cavalry, Elias Tremo, had also vanished. As indeed had Madame.

Tanski staggered back into the dining room, trailing excrescences from the water trough. Various foul liquids ran unhindered over Madame's fine furniture, and dripped on the parquet floor and the Persian carpets. We tied a white linen napkin around Tanski's head so that he looked like a Turk. A dark red stain, like wine, gradually spread through the white cloth. After that, we fortified ourselves with more vodka.

We then had an arm-wrestling contest with the servants, thus reducing the few tables and chairs that remained unbroken to matchwood. We had made a wreck of the room. It was heaving with filth and bottles and littered with drunks lying as still as corpses, and groaning like damned souls.

"After the drink, comes the hangover," Tanski said, clutching his aching head.

"Best to keep drinking, then," I replied, opening another bottle.

At long last, when all four of us had been felled by vodka, the bell tolled for silentium.

CHAPTER SEVEN
THE BATTLE OF ZIELENCE, 17 JUNE 1792

Pepi took a letter from his pocket and read aloud to the army –

*"The desire of Her Highness Empress of Russia is to use
her armies to return to the Republic, and to Poles, their
security and freedom. Each true Pole knows our
Fatherland can only be saved by Russia, otherwise we will
be enslaved. I urge you, Prince Poniatowski – abandon the
Constitution. Join us.
Signed, Severyn Rzewuski, of the Targowica Confederacy."*

A great howl of derision rose from the ranks. The army sat
atop a hill beside a place called Zielence, which was near the
Russian border. It was a fine windswept sunny day at that.
From my seat in the saddle, amongst the lines of cavalry, I had
leisure to watch the birds chase heedlessly across the sky, the
sun lighting up the white bellies of the clouds as they billowed
there like great swollen pierogi. My abiding memory of the
day was of feeling ravenously hungry. Once the jeers had died
down, he continued.

"Comrades," Pepi said, "our Russian brothers are coming,
to save us! They are 'hastening to the aid of Poland's Golden
Freedom', in a spirit of brotherly love and affection. Here, on
this hill, we shall greet our dear liberators in the same friendly
manner."

This brought a great cheer, and laughter, and we all beat
our lances on the ground. While we had been making merry in
the taverns of Warsaw, Felix Potocki was in the Kremlin,
taking the Judas Kiss from the Great Whore Herself, the

Empress. Now the Empress hated two things most of all in this world – Poles and Revolutions. A Polish Revolution was not therefore a thing calculated to win her approval. Rather, it roused her to a rage that would terrify a horde of Cossacks. Such anger in women far exceeds that which mere men are capable of. She sent an army without even bothering to declare war.

Felix rode back across the border at the head of a body of Russian troops. On 14 May 1792, a year after the Constitution was signed, we were thunderstruck by a betrayal that lives in infamy to this day – *Targowica*. At the village of that accursed name, in Podolia, Felix and other traitors, under Russian orders, vowed to destroy the Constitution at any cost.

"Lord Rzewuski," Pepi told the army, holding up the letter, "not daring to show his face again in Warsaw, thoughtfully wrote me this letter, urging me, and all of you, to join the nest of Targowica traitors."

There were shouts of 'No!' and 'For shame!' Pepi stilled them with a wave of his hand.

"Comrades, here is my reply –

Mr. Rzewuski, I cannot follow your advice to betray the nation. As a sworn soldier, and a man of honour, my duty is to defend our beloved motherland to the death!"

There was another great shout of approval, and the letter was circulated through our camp, for our signatures. Tanski, Sierawski, and all the other fellows signed up. I paused as I put pen to paper. As sure as night follows day, the letter would pass directly to the desk of the Russian Ambassador.

During that same year since the Third of May, Tanski and I had been promoted to Warrant Officers. This puffed us up like peacocks. We were quite unjustified in our vanity and conceit, for the position of Warrant Officer holds less power and honour than emptying bed-pans.

Of course, Godebski had the best of it. With his rival, Lieutenant Tremo, away at the war, he was staying behind in Warsaw to guard the lovely widow Madame L from the depredations of any invaders. He was writing love letters by a warm fire, not huddled on that blasted windy hill, signing his own death warrant. I signed the letter anyway, and passed it on to the next man in line.

Targowica was the worst treason, of course, nothing less than civil war. With Potocki's treachery, Podolia had, in effect, gone over to Russia. The flood of Podolian volunteers slowed to a trickle. Few dared defy their overlord, to whom they owed clan allegiance. But still, there were a few of us here at Zielence, standing in the King's ranks, fighting for the Republic.

"Hey, look, Blumer," Tanski said scathingly, "why, another Podolian has deigned to turn up! That makes two of you! It's that bastard Zayonczek!"

It was indeed General Zayonczek, the chief of the cavalry, and our chief. We watched him as he came thundering past on a magnificent white stallion. He doffed his czapka and brandished his sabre in the air.

"For the Constitution, boys! For Poland!" he roared at us, as he hurtled by at breakneck speed. He was a dashing officer, known for two things – his beautiful wife, and his extremist political views, some of which were so insane as to put the French revolutionaries in the shade. It was said that *he actually believed women should be allowed to vote*.

"Mad Jacobin bastard," we spat after him. It was widely speculated that General Zayonczek's wife, a great beauty, and as rare a piece of womanflesh as ever walked the earth, had inclined him to such great lengths of folly. Tanski, Sierawski and I ruminated on this awhile as we sat our horses. Sierawski was idling with us, sharing a pipe, having excused himself from digging ditches, or whatever menial task it was his engineers were about.

"Perhaps there is something to be said about your Podolia after all, Blumer," Tanski reflected. "Whilst Podolian men are all ignorant hairy brutes, such as your good self, the women are reputed to be finely-made, feisty amazons."

"Soon enough we can find out for ourselves," Sierawski said. "After we lose this war, as we surely will, we can hide out in Podolia, as old Jozef Wybicki did when he lost the last one. For the place is so barren and Godforsaken our enemies will not trouble themselves to seek after us there, even if they vowed to follow us to the ends of the earth."

"Aye," said Tanski, "the only drawback to his splendid plan that I can see is that the food and the weather in Podolia are even worse than they are in Siberia."

"The arse speaks to the bishop," I snarled, "but the bishop just speaks to himself!"

We were not confident. We had our swords, lances and muskets, and our horses, but the King possessed no foundries for cannon, so we had a scant few of those. We lacked powder and ammunition. Our nation's entire army numbered barely forty-five thousand untried recruits, fewer than half the number that the Russians could put in the field.

So Felix's Podolian army would certainly have been welcome standing alongside us at Zielence that June morning, as allies, and not as yet another enemy. As it was we faced the Russians, outnumbered three to one, as they stared up at us from the bottom of that hill. A hill that seemed to shrink smaller and smaller with every minute that passed, and every endless detachment of Russians that arrived at the foot of it.

As it came to pass, Felix's army contented itself with some brigandry. They looted and burned several villages, hanged and murdered a few men, and raped any women they could lay their hands on. But they stayed in the south. They did not venture north to the Russian border to fight us. Wisely, they had left the actual fighting to the Russians, led by the infamous Suvarov.

Suvarov, in command of a Russian army of one hundred thousand battle-hardened and fanatical men, had marched north from the Ottoman Empire, where he had spent the last few years mercilessly butchering the Turks.

This was our adversary. Suvarov. We were enthralled and obsessed by this devil, this talisman, this sorcerer and harbinger of doom. Suvarov! Suvarov! Suvarov! Such magic in one man's name.

"If only we had such a man to lead us," we said.

"Suvarov is called 'the Invincible'," Sierawski, the know-it-all, said unhelpfully. "The common folks believe he has dark powers and the evil eye. They say he's a sorcerer, who sold his soul to the Devil. He can turn himself into a werewolf, or a giant vampire bat, and he feeds on the bodies of the dead."

"Damn it!" I snapped. "Don't you have a latrine to dig, boy?" Although Sierawski's story was stuff and nonsense, the worst village gossip, there was no denying that Suvarov was evil. Suvarov was, in truth, the diabolic emissary of the most swinish and degenerate tyranny to have been unleashed upon Europe since Attila the Hun.

But Sierawski was not finished. "They say this man Suvarov, the Invincible, has great vigour of character, and a nature bordering on insanity. He is a genuine barbarian, a fanatic, and his army, that you see at the foot of this puny hill, resembles him in its character, as dogs grow to resemble their masters," he concluded mordantly.

A ripple of fear was spreading through the ranks from all of this talk. Yet another phalanx of grey-coated Russians arrived at the foot of the hill and began setting up cannons, mortars and bombards.

"Suvarov is not here, Comrades!" I called, loudly. "His arse is too sore, from being f-cked by the Devil!" I announced. It was a wild and blatant lie.

Then, miraculously, Suvarov's spell seemed to break. For it was true. Word spread. Suvarov was not here. Suvarov was really not here. My words, spoken in jest, were true. Suvarov had left this day at Zielence to lesser generals. Nevertheless, with Suvarov absent, presumably in his cups, that still left three or four thousand of us facing ten thousand of them – the best odds we were likely to get in this war.

Thus, for all this idle talk, our little army ended the morning where it began. We sat at the top of the hill, and waited for the Russians to attack. Our infantry were in the centre, with the cavalry on the wings, as was the convention of war at the time. Our new, and untried, brigade of cadets was on the left-hand side – traditionally, the place reserved for the weakest units. Down in the valley, regiment after regiment of Russians had been gathering since seven in the morning – infantry, cavalry, cannon, and Cossacks.

Tanski rode off for news, and came haring back, his face grim, his horse's hooves throwing clods of earth into the air. His horse thundered in at such a speed that I feared he would ride me down, but at the last possible instant, he wheeled it around, turning on a tynf, and bringing the beast to an abrupt halt. I had to admit, it was done in a fine style. My own riding was good, but workmanlike. I rode well, but Tanski rode like a Sarmatian prince on the steppes of Arabia.

He brought bad news – more treachery!

"Our Lithuanian brothers have deserted us, the beet-eating bastards!" he spat from his saddle. "The Lithuanian army has gone over to the Russians, and Targowica! We've lost a third of our strength, at a stroke, before we've even fired a shot! Damn those cowardly, treacherous, sodomitical, beet-eating bastards to hell!" Tanski exclaimed. This drew angry looks, curses, threats – a number of the men in our Polish ranks were Lithuanians, including General Kościuszko himself, and, unfortunately for Tanski, our Lieutenant.

"God Damn it, boy!" the Lieutenant screamed, "I'm from Vilnius myself!" Tanski hastily apologised.

Discretion being the better part of valour, he rode back to his platoon as quickly as he came.

Over the hill, we could hear the artillery fire. It was a strange sound. Each cannon shot was like a giant beating a stone floor with a hammer, followed by a long roll of thunder. The echo lasted a damnably long time, rolling like the waves of an invisible sea. The roar of the massed batteries together sounded like a raging ocean.

Our horses' ears twitched at each rumble. Having been well broken in, they were used to the sound, and as for us, our nerve held. It is vital to treat a horse well at the sound of shot, whether musket or cannon. Coax it, comfort it, and cajole it. Never beat or threaten or chastise it. That will teach the horse fear, and fear breeds fear, until it becomes ingrained. Likewise, you must not allow your own fear to infect it, at which even the stoutest animal can take flight. If the master is a coward, how can the servant be expected to be brave?

A horseman's backside is in more or less constant contact with his horse, except at the gallop, and it is through the horseman's body – especially the backside – that the horse takes his orders. As is well known, unfortunately, the body communicates fear to the outside world through the medium of a man's backside, which is a treacherous trumpet indeed.

Any man who has seen a battlefield will see the men in constant procession behind trees and bushes, hastily responding to the call of nature. Honour dictates that one cannot admit to fear. So one blames over-indulgence in drink, or the local food, for the unruly actions of one's bowels. No one is fooled, but the pretence suffices. Honour is satisfied.

Pepi was holding our raw, untried brigade in reserve. There was nothing to be done but stand and watch the ebb and flow of our men, soldiers and cavalry going to and fro, dancing in step to the music of the battle, back and forth, and to listen for what news we could.

At first, a stream of our recruits ran past us, in flight, broken by panic under the Russian artillery fire. We stood our horses to one side to let them pass. When they reached the rear, some would rally and return, shamefaced, to the fray – others would not.

From our rear, hurrying past in the opposite direction, came the Potocki regiment, shoring up the breach, and leading a counter-attack. Irony of ironies, this infantry regiment of four hundred men had been gifted to the nation by none other than Felix Potocki himself – who else! That was in happier times, years ago when he dreamed of becoming the King. The man knew how to play off both sides all right.

A grand regiment they were too – naturally, since they were all Podolians! We Podolians could ride and shoot. We were tough border people, strong of body, simple of brain. We did what we were told and went to our deaths happily and without complaint. We therefore made excellent soldiers.

How treacherous was that war, then, setting kin against kin! These brave Podolians were led by Felix Potocki's own nephew, the infamous Jan Nepomucen Potocki. Another raving Jacobin, rabidly for the Constitution, he was a captain in the engineers, and a right queer fish, according to Sierawski. Still, here he was, and good for him. We glimpsed him that morning, through the smoke on that blasted hill, charging forward with his men.

My good Podolian countrymen threw back the Russians and gave them a sound beating – and gave the nation yet more cause to rue Felix Potocki's treachery. Oh for a few thousand more of us! Four hundred men was a mere cobweb against a deluge. The Russians immediately retorted with an infantry charge, securing the village of Zielence, which was on our flank.

Our brigade had not even drawn a sword yet. A rumour spread that Pepi had ordered cavalry to eject the Russians from the village – and so he had, but it was not our brigade. The honour fell to others. We stood by, bitterly cursing our luck, as another squadron flew by us – only to fly back again, leaving the village in flames, and the Russians also withdrawing from it, but in good order.

It was a stalemate, with the armies locked together like two wrestlers trying their strength.

When the Russian assault finally came, it came on the right. A massive bombardment fell on our elite cavalry. Simultaneously they were charged by massed ranks of Cossack horsemen. Our view of this was obscured by the hills and the pall of powder smoke. We heard all the evil sounds – the crack of gunshots, the random, disembodied shouts, the rattle of drums, and the call of the bloody trumpets. We heard first the barrage, then the hideous cries of dying men and the shrieks of stricken horses. Then, finally, we heard the Cossacks, and their bestial war cries –

"Pole-Jew-Dog – Die!
Die, Lachy, Die!"

'Lachy' is a derogatory Russian and Cossack term for Pole. This particular 'song' dated from the massacres at Uman, in the great Cossack rebellion in the last century.

"The Cossacks are splendid looking fellows, but they write very poor songs," I said, to try to steady my platoon's nerves. Inside my stomach churned like a milk pail, but I kept my face impassive and lit my pipe with a steady hand. Men are like horses. You must show them you are not afraid, and they will think you are made of iron.

Next we heard hoof beats and trumpets – shouts – and saw gallopers haring to and fro, carrying messages. A cannonball trundled past us, taking with it the leg of an unfortunate horse.

"Our right wing is retreating!" came a shout.

"We have no orders!" some laggards yelled. "Give us orders!" came shouts from all around, and pathetic cries of "Run! Save yourselves! Every man for himself!"

"Here's the order!" I roared, drawing my pistol, "the first man to run, dies!" I caracoled my horse, and trained my gun on my wavering comrades.

"Here we stand, here we die!" I roared, my voice hoarse but calm. "We hold the line! They shall not pass!"

The platoon, who knew that I was a man of my word, held. Still, it was pandemonium everywhere else, as we saw a line of our cavalry streaming past us in full flight.

"Bastards! Cowards! Traitors!" we jeered, shaking our fists at them.

"What do we do, Sir?" a soldier shouted.

"I told you! We hold the line, damn it!" I roared, brandishing my pistol. I remember that I felt oddly calm and happy, almost exhilarated, in that moment. By some miracle, the right wing held. More than that, it began a counter-charge, utterly decimating the Cossacks and the Russian cavalry.

It was General Zayonczek – he had rallied them. Zayonczek, my fellow son of the black earth, came hurtling back and forth, laughing like the wrath of God. A Podolian is worth ten ordinary soldiers, by God! The men began to recover their courage, and forget their fear. Thus is a battle fought, with the heart and mind swinging wildly from fear to bravery, and sometimes back again.

At that point, with the men starting to take heart, Pepi came ambling past us, as if on a summer stroll in the country. He was on foot, at the head of those of the Potocki regiment who were still alive, and two more battalions from other regiments. We cheered them to the heavens. The infantrymen were powder-blacked, covered in mud, bloodied, in tatters. How we envied them! Fools that we were!

Pepi was conversing with Zayonczek, who leaned over from his saddle to take his orders. The Prince was on foot, and armed with musket and bayonet, like an infantryman, as was his wont. Pepi was fond of quoting our enemy, Suvarov, who held to the dictum 'the bullet is a fool, but the bayonet is a fine fellow!' The army loved Pepi for many reasons, but not least because he would regularly dismount from his horse, roll up the silk sleeves of his gilded tunic, and wade into the trenches with the bayonet alongside the common soldiers.

Scurrying behind Pepi were two liveried servants, carrying some sort of collapsible bed or table. It was Pepi's harpsichord. As the cannon balls fizzed overhead and buried their noses in the Zielence mud, Pepi's servants unfolded his music box and a camping stool. Smiling serenely beneath his moustaches, the Prince settled before the instrument and, quite extempore, proceeded to perform a short recital of the marvellous, nameless, jaunty mazurka that we had heard on the Third of May. A great cheer rang out across our ranks as he concluded, and he stood to a round of applause. Behind him, a crew of artillerymen was desperately dragging a cannon into position.

"Ah!" Pepi cried with delight, "here is the percussion! Play well, boys, and don't miss a note!"

We could see Zayonczek haranguing Pepi as he played upon his keyboard. There was no love lost between the two of them. After a short and bad-tempered conference, Pepi reluctantly put up his instrument and the two generals made their way over to our line.

"Comrades," Pepi addressed us genially, "the right wing has held, after a small affair with the Cossacks, who have now been put to their heels." This brought a huge cheer of relief. A weight lifted from all our hearts. Pepi grinned and held up a hand. "However, the Ekaterinoslav Grenadiers are now on their way to meet us, instead. These Podolian fellows and I shall receive them warmly."

Grenadiers, as you will know, are the elite of the infantry. As one, our brigade begged and pleaded with him to let us run them down. We had not fired a shot or drawn a sword all day, and it was now late, so late, in the early evening. Pepi declined. "Thank you, comrades, but no. You are my reserve, and will await further orders."

It was more than we could stand. It felt like a gloved slap. Heartbroken, humiliated, we sat on our horses, cursing, fuming like caned schoolboys.

On came the Russian grenadiers, giant men, splendid in their blue and grey uniforms and bulbous fur hats. Rays of evening sun glinted off their shouldered muskets as they marched towards us in perfect order. As they marched up the slope, Pepi and his sharpshooters began to fire on them. At every shot a grenadier seemed to fall to the ragged crash of rifle fire. On they came, these brave fellows, the men in the second rank stepping over their dead comrades.

By now, our cannon had found its range, too. It scythed down ranks of these splendid grenadiers, and their advance collapsed, decimated.

Despite them being our mortal enemies, I felt a stirring of pity for them, and I felt pride at the wonderful spectacle of arms they presented, even as the bullets tore through their breasts. I thought of my Irish grandfather, a mercenary, who wore that same Russian uniform.

Finally it was our turn. General Zayonczek, boiling with impatience, rode up to our ranks. It was a warm day but he was wrapped in a thick fur over his uniform. Tanski, who had never seen him up close before, later remarked that this General should have had a sheep, rather than a pig, on his coat of arms, for the General's thick, curly blond hair was cut close to his scalp, like a ram's fleece. He had bushy blond cavalry moustaches to match it. Zayonczek was not one to mince words:

"*Szarza!* Charge!" he called, chopping down his flashing sabre. The front rank lowered their lances, the swallow-tailed pennants fluttering in the breeze. Then we hurled ourselves forward in a mad charge, a wave of furious cavalry emitting blood-curdling screams, spearpoints and brandished sabres glinting in the sun – szarza! Szarza!

We wielded those slim chivalric ashwood lances and wore a fine uniform – tight red trousers, a blue jacket with red or yellow facings, depending upon one's regiment, silver epaulettes, and a fur-trimmed red czapka. The front rank was a charging mass of beautiful Polish steeds, the descendants of the Arab chargers our Sarmatian forefathers brought with them from Persia.

It was a spectacle indeed, green grass beneath blue sky. Before us were the Russians on their stout, sturdy steeds, gaudily caparisoned, snorting, neighing, and prancing gracefully beneath their grim faced grey riders. The enemy cavalry were clad in varied grey costumes and greatcoats, with gleaming silver and gold cuirasses, many wearing bearskin hats decked with eagle feathers, others in helmets and wolfskins. They were armed with sabres and pistols.

Our lances were slim and graceful weapons, twelve feet long. The lance was difficult to wield but deadly in a skilled hand, and it could be handled almost as dexterously as a sabre. It was feather light, cut from ashwood, impregnated with linseed oil and tar, with a metal heel, and a red and white silk swallow-tailed pennant behind the steel spearhead.

The front rank held their lances between the looped forefinger and the middle finger of the right hand, before raising them high above their heads to deliver a powerful thrust at the enemy – this was called '*par le moulinet*'.

The sabres of the enemy cavalry met the lances of our first rank. The enemy may as well have been wielding dandelions as sabres. Our lances tore them apart, a flying wall of deadly spears. Many of the Russian horses had broken and run before us. They were transfixed and terrified by the fluttering swallow-tailed pennons on our lances, which were not merely for decoration, but terrorised the simple minds of the beasts. It was an unbelievable chaos – horses and cavalrymen falling together, felled like trees, men with their clothes on fire, set alight by the blazing wads from muskets and pistols, men impaled on lances like suckling pigs.

Only the front rank of the cavalry carried the lance, together with a pair of pistols. The second and third ranks, following behind, carried a musket into battle at the charge instead. I myself was relegated to the second rank, to make use of my English gun, for we were sorely short of firearms. Thus I arrived moments after this first great wave of devastation, and the front rank were already chasing the retreating Russian cavalry from the field.

Beside me were Russians, wounded, in a heap, burning, trying with their sabres to slash the legs of our horses. I realised then how fanatical and determined were our foes. Ahead, a distinguished boyar with a fine long beard was brandishing their Russian flag, sabre in hand, his reins tied around his wrist. A great slick of bloody foam ran from his horse's mouth. The boyar was trying to rally his regiment. They were in full flight from the field, to his great disgust and shame. He was bawling obscenities at the backs of his retreating comrades.

At the sight of this insolent invader I was overcome with anger. Bringing my steed to the gallop I broke out like lightning from the ranks and joined battle with this audacious boyar. With a lucky shot from my musket I knocked him from the saddle. He fell from his mount still clutching the flag, which trailed behind him in the mud. I had merely wounded him. He sat on the trampled grass, his long white beard running with blood, his sabre across his knees, wheezing for breath like an old grandad. Naturally I assumed that he wished to surrender, and, as an honourable man, accordingly extended my hand to accept his sword and flag.

I had underestimated him. The boyar jumped to his feet and lunged at my horse with his sabre. Cursing, I reined to one side to avoid these blows, and the boyar's sabre glanced wide. Furious, I slashed at him with my sabre, and fetched him a good downward cut.

He fell to the ground still clutching the flag.

Gasping with the exertion, I sat heavily back in my stirrups, and gulped down a good breath. Then and only then I took stock of the situation. Precisely no one had paid the slightest heed to this inept and bloody single combat, being much too preoccupied with their own pressing concerns. Blood ran from the boyar's wounded head.

But even then, the old boyar came back at me. He was on hands and knees, barely even moving now, wracked with exhaustion and sorely wounded. Sickened, I wiped the sweat and blood from my face and dismounted, in order to capture the flag. Suitably angered, and in no mood for any fresh treachery, I marched up to him and drew both my pistols. We were at point blank range.

"Now then, your lordship. Surrender that flag, and I will spare your life," I said firmly, "no sense in dying for a length of cloth, now, is there?"

Neither I spoke any Russian nor he any Polish, but our mother tongues are so very similar, that we could make ourselves plainly understood. Besides that I trusted in the eloquence of my pistols.

"Over my dead body, Lachy!" retorted the boyar, in peremptory tones. He was an aristocratic sort, hewn from Siberian rock, hardened by winters and vodka. This was madness. I frowned, and brandished my pistols again, and he merely smiled, trying to raise his sword in challenge. A religious medallion glinted at his neck. He clutched his Russian flag white fingered with his other hand. A hand that now shook, with fear or cold, I could not tell.

We both glanced at this battle flag, a blue flag streaked with mud, with a black eagle inlaid in gold emblazoned upon it. The double-headed eagle of the Tsars, a hideous, mythical beast. I thought of the horses transfixed by our pennants, hypnotised like rats before snakes. I turned back to the boyar.

"The flag, sir, or you die," I said, as I took aim with a shaking hand.

"My death matters not, Lachy," he shrugged, "*U nas mnogo ludei – We have a lot of people!*" With a last dying effort he made to run me through with his blade. I fired, and the ball entered his chest three inches below the religious medal, piercing his heart, killing him instantly.

Some hours after that, their right wing collapsed, and we took the flag from the dead boyar's hand and sent it back to Warsaw. But we could not dislodge the Russian infantry, try as we might, and we were in want of ammunition and food, as ever. As the evening darkness fell, we stole away like hunted wolves in the night. We followed the captured flag, and retreated back towards Warsaw.

This left General Morkov, the one Russian General who had deigned to actually turn up that day, in possession of an empty field strewn with corpses. Including, among their number, the bearded boyar, stretched out and growing cold on the ground.

CHAPTER EIGHT
DUBIENKA, 17 JULY 1792

Thus we fell back, and retreated towards Warsaw. It was a fighting retreat. On the way, the Commander had decided to make a stand at a place called Dubienka. For my part in taking the flag, Pepi rewarded me with a galloper's errand. Leaving my regiment behind, I rode hard across country with a bundle of papers and orders. I arrived at the Commander's headquarters filthy and spattered with mud. It did not matter, for the headquarters themselves apparently consisted of a huge dirty hole in the ground. Or as the engineers have it, a trench.

"Dispatches from General Poniatowski, Sir!" I cried.

The Commander glanced up from his desk, which was a plank across two barrels, before reluctantly putting down the book he was reading. I handed over the leather wallets, clicked my heels and saluted smartly, and then stared at this legendary man with a mixture of awe and fear. General Tadeusz Andrzej Bonaventure Kościuszko. Second string to Pepi he may have been at that time, but to us, Kościuszko was simply 'The Commander'. And he always will be.

When I met him at Dubienka he was about forty-five years old, and already a legend, for his feats both on the battlefield (where he enjoyed great success) and in the boudoir (where he did not). Though a gentleman, the Commander was from a humble background. His family had little money, but his prodigious talents were recognised in him as a student. He was educated abroad, at the expense of the King, to study artillery, engineering, naval tactics, and, somewhat improbably, fine arts.

Upon his return, the Commander became tutor of the youngest daughter of the Grand Hetman, the lady Ludwika

Sossonowski, with whom he fell in love. Having no hope of ever obtaining her father's permission, the lovers determined to elope together, for the Commander was not a man to be served black soup[2] by anyone. He crept into the house in the dead of night, but was taken by surprise by Ludwika's father's guards. A combat ensued. After fighting like a lion, the Commander was flung out into the street, covered with wounds, half dead. So much for marriage!

His next amour, it was equally well known, went much the way of the first, but with fewer deaths. After this second desperate faux pas, determining that discretion is the better part of valour, the Commander volunteered to fight for the colonists in the American War. There he built the fortress at West Point, fought in numerous battles, won a great and eternal victory for liberty, and suffered not so much as a scratch in the process. Clearly, his engagements in battle with the English were less hazardous than his engagements to the daughters of our Polish nobility.

It was said that the first paramour, Ludwika – now married, and a Princess, if you please – still burned for the old warrior, and had connived at court to arrange his career and promotion for him. Naturally I set no store by such idle gossip where my hero was concerned.

The Commander was a tall, fiery man, with strong handsome features, a great lion's mane of dark hair, dark eyebrows, wide, intelligent eyes, and a full fleshy nose. He wore a brilliant white waistcoat and a high-collared shirt. A dark red cravat was gathered at his throat and from it hung the Order of Cincinnatus, awarded to him by George Washington.

I had caught him in the middle of his lunch. A wooden board set across upturned barrels served for a desk and a table. On the board were water, vodka, cold veal, cucumbers, cold

---

[2] *An unsuccessful suitor would be fed black soup by the lady's family to signify that his proposal had been refused – see Pan Tadeusz by Adam Mickiewicz, the Polish national poem*

boiled eggs, and a pitcher of those cold beet soups of which the Lithuanians are so fond. I stood to attention, my bones aching from the ride. The Commander began leafing through the dispatches. He glanced up at me.

"Sit down, Comrade! Your regiment is following you here, so there is no need for you to go anywhere. All roads lead to Rome, as the proverb says! Sit, boy, take a glass, and eat. That's an order. For we are not going anywhere, and neither are they."

The Commander nodded casually over his shoulder, beyond the fortifications, to the river, where the Russians sat on the opposite bank. Twenty thousand of them faced four thousand of us.

I propped my musket against a wall and fell upon the food like a hungry dog. The soup was chlodnik, a cold, uncooked soup, slightly sour in a pleasant way and refreshing, made of fermented beet juice and finely grated raw beets. Perfect chlodnik is served with the cooked shelled tails of crayfish, although the Commander had none, a lack which he cursed vociferously.

As I ate, the Commander read the rest of Pepi's dispatch, unconcernedly, and lit his clay pipe from a fire burning in a brazier. When he had finished, and committed the dispatches to memory, he tossed them into the blaze and returned to his book. I had been desperate to know what the Commander had been reading whence I had interrupted him. Summoning all my courage, I asked him.

"Virgil – the Aeneid," he replied, gruffly. "What of it?"

The Commander had been reading the old Roman bugger's poem, rather than poring over the latest French artillery manual, or Marshall Maurice de Saxe's treatise on war, a copy of which I had myself.

It transpired we were both great readers, and each carted great stacks of books about with us on campaign, to fill the long empty hours encamped. Their subject was invariably war. It may appear odd that we should have spent our days and years at the wars, and then, for our leisure pursuits, buried our noses in books on the same subject. Yet, what could be more natural, than for a tradesman to read of his trade?

"So you know your classics. Excellent – exactly as a gentleman should. Have you heard of the Roman Cincinnatus?" The Commander touched the medal at his throat.

"Naturally," I replied. "After defeating Rome's enemies, the general retired to his farm, to the plough, the simple life of a country squire. But when a new plague of barbarians threatened Rome, the Roman Emperor called him back from retirement, to fight again."

The Commander roared with bitter laughter and slammed his great fist on the table. The food leapt into the air, then fell back again, the vodka bottle shaking perilously on its axis. The Commander stared at it as if to still it by sheer force of will, and it obeyed. One did not meddle with the man.

"George Washington has a grand sense of humour. For he awarded me this medal, and I retired to my farm, and my plough. Ha! Come see my fields! See my harvest!"

The Commander sprang from the trench and strode across the hillside. I snatched up my gun and followed where he led. The rude hill of Dubienka had been fashioned into a makeshift fortress. A line of wooden spikes traversed it like the spines of a porcupine, behind which soldiers crouched in hastily dug, shallow muddy trenches. Those few cannon we could muster had been dug in behind gabions, which was what the engineers called wooden boxes or wicker baskets filled with earth and stones. This was the Commander's creation, or, at least, the creation of his engineers, who numbered amongst them one Sierawski of Krakow.

In war, as in life, natural causes, outside our control, do much, the Commander explained. The great tacticians of any campaign are hills and forests, which you must be skilful enough to select for your encampments. Our defensive line was on the western side of the River Bug, with the Russians on the east. Our fortifications ran between the river and the Austrian border, stretching like a chain. In front of us there was a swamp, through which the Russians must pass before they could attack us. They would be obliged to wade through the river, and then the swamp, under our fire.

"It isn't much of a field for cavalry," I complained.

"You cavalrymen and your damned horses!" the Commander chided me. "Fie, boy! War is a serious business, not a sport for gentlemen." He pointed across the river at the Russians. "Do you think you can defeat that endless tide of fanatical soldiery with chivalry and piddling wooden lances? Cavalry wins battles, but it is the infantry that wins wars."

As we picked our way across this strange garden of death, I realised with horror that the Republic ended beyond the muzzle of my gun.

I had anticipated that we were on some vital errand at the edge of the Bug, the very edge of the frontline, the precipice. I had thought we were there to scout out the Russian positions, set the fuse on a powder mine, or take a few prisoners. Instead, the Commander searched about in the reeds until he found a small net secured there in the water. Trapped in it was a clutch of shrimp-like crabs, crayfish, like little knights in their black armoured shells, snapping their tiny claws.

Back in the trench, we roasted the crayfish over the embers of Pepi's dispatches. Their shells slowly turned from black to pink, and their sliced and skewered bodies butterflied open. The Commander smiled, dipping the hot fish in the cold beet soup. "Perfect chlodnik!"

As the Commander had said, I did not need to rejoin my regiment, they followed me to Dubienka to reinforce the Commander's men. There we had a fine battle with the

Russians, who waded through the river, and the swamp, to fight us. We shot them down in droves as they came.

Despite his genius as a sapper, the Commander's fortifications could not hold out against wave after wave of Russian attacks. On they came, rank after rank of grey uniforms, as he predicted they would. There were bearded moujiks and peasants waving religious icons, and there were boyars in gold epaulettes that ran down their arms from their shoulders to their wrists, and dismounted cavalrymen dragging their horses through the mire.

As the Russians say, 'we have a lot of people.' Men from every nation of the Russian empire seemed to be charging across that ford, as alien to each other as we were to them. Men from the steppes, men from beyond the Urals, from Georgia, Siberia, Kazakhstan, Tartary, and Samarkand, and the Cossacks, tribe upon tribe of them, advancing upon us across that humble ford. Suvarov's golden horde. It was as if we were fighting the workmen of the Tower of Babel. The ground was covered with grey coated dead, men from a dozen nations of an empire that enslaved half the world.

"The worst of this," I said to Tanski, as we reloaded our muskets, "is that the Tsarina sends all of her enemies to do her fighting – you know what I mean, the moaners and the malcontents. Rich magnates whose estates she wants to steal. Old boyars who grumble about her antics in the bedroom. Nobles who want a say in the government. Peasants who won't pay their taxes. Divide and conquer. Thus the cunning old whore kills two birds with one stone. Or rather, we kill them for her."

Tanski pulled the trigger and the bullet flew through the bejewelled eye of an icon of the Virgin Mary. This painting was being carried into battle by a Russian soldier. It was a strange sight, to see him carrying this beautiful icon that would have graced any altar. It was their battle flag. This standard bearer could not have been more appalled if the bullet had pierced his own eye. After a short, shocked, pause, his brigade began storming towards us, with redoubled efforts, waving their sabres and bayonets and howling fanatically.

"What the Devil are you doing, you fool?" we roared at Tanski, "Shooting at the Blessed Virgin? You've really done it this time!"

Tanski had turned pale with mortified embarrassment. "It's these damned French muskets, Blumer, you couldn't hit a barn door with them! Lousy peashooters!"

"Save it for confession," the Commander roared, grabbing him by the collar and hurling him bodily out of the trench. "We are retiring from the field. Sierawski – the powder!"

The Commander had a bunch of lit fuses stuck in the brim of his hat and the smoke was billowing around his head, so that he appeared to be the very devil. At the sight of him, soldiers on both sides fell back in a panic. He waded through us, chasing us out of the trench. Behind us, our trumpets were sounding the retreat. We rolled a precious barrel of gunpowder out of the dugout. We had so few, gunpowder was like gold dust.

"It's not a retreat, but a strategic withdrawal, as they say," the Commander said wryly. "Be not alarmed, comrades, but a second Russian army approaches from the rear. They have crossed through neutral Austrian territory to get behind us."

The Commander primed the taper on the powder barrel with one of the fuses from his hat. He had a lit cigar in his mouth and with this he lit a hand grenade which he pitched over his shoulder at the advancing Russians, without a backward glance.

Our horses were tied to a post near the opposite foot of that same hill, the hill that we were now relinquishing to our foes. None of our comrades had lingered, they had all ridden off, in accordance with the Commander's strict orders, which, in the circumstances, were naturally obeyed to the letter. We mounted our horses and set our spurs hard at their flanks. The horses ran like devils, their ears set along the sides of their heads, eyes bulging, foaming at their bits, sweat running down their flanks.

At a good distance we paused and the Commander vaulted from his horse, cautioning us to do the same. He wrapped the reins twice around his fist and set his hat over the beast's eyes. Our abandoned and forsaken battlement was seething with curious Russians by now, hunting for trophies and souvenirs. They probed at the trenches and dugouts with bayonets and sabrepoints, like a dunghill of curious ants.

"Let God have mercy on their souls!" the Commander said. The trench that we had lately vacated detonated in a great eruption of earth and noise. It was as if a meteorite had struck. My ears rang and my horse reared wildly – had I still been in the saddle, I should have been thrown a furlong up in the air. As it was, I found myself on my knees, with the Commander hauling me to my feet. His lips were moving, but all that I could hear was a great rushing noise in my ears, as if I were standing under a waterfall.

No doubt inured to this concussion by a lifetime of such explosions, the Commander set me on my horse again and we rode off after the rest of the army. The Russian regiments around us were closing in, like the drawing of a noose, and it would not pay to tarry here, with naught but a mountain of corpses behind us.

Presently, my ears ceased ringing, and I regained my wits. The Russians had left four thousand dead on that hill and their General had them buried post haste to conceal their number. Yet they could easily afford such a butcher's bill. The Commander informed us that about a hundred of our men had fallen, but, alas, we could ill afford even that. We would lose more in the days to come, from illness, injury, and desertion.

However, for all that it appeared that by the Commander's prudent orders, we had ridden out of the trap in good time, and we would ride back to Warsaw. Our corps was tired and battered, but it was still a formidable body of men.

"At Warsaw we rendezvous with the rest of the army, commanded by Poniatowski, and make our stand together there," the Commander informed us tersely, as we broke our march to hurriedly scavenge fodder for our horses.

The Russians had crossed into neutral Austrian territory to get behind us. We had been forced to retreat so that we would not be surrounded. In the smoking dusk our army rode back bloodied but unbeaten, with our muskets across our saddles, and our dusty standards furled. We were not like victors but a harried rearguard retreating across the plains, horses staggering, men slumped asleep in their saddles, pistols in hand, as the caissons and the wagons rattled in the ruts of the ruined roads.

The unhappy day revealed the same flat barren countryside all about and the smoke from the fires of the night before stood thin and windless to the east. There was nowhere to hide beneath that cold unmerciful sky, nothing for it but to ride on to Warsaw. And the silver circle of the summer moon peered down, the winking eye of evil old Pan Twardowski who sat above us drooling and cackling at our fate.

The grey dust of the enemy who were to hound us to the gates of the city of Warsaw seemed ever closer. We shambled on through the driving horizontal rain, and the vicious unrelenting Siberian winds, lashing our exhausted horses on. Swarms of Cossack riders were gathering at our rear like ravenous buzzing horseflies, settling on any stragglers. They were an endless and constant irritation, and did not allow us occasion for a single moment's respite. If challenged by our men in numbers, they would always fall back, wary as wolves, cowardly as jackals. They were always waiting behind the next rise or the last lonely copse of hanging trees.

Midmorning we watered at a shallow ford that had already been walked through by our horses and pack animals, the riders dismounting to drink from their czapkas and then riding on again down the dry bed of the stream and clattering over the earth, the plains running to the horizon, thickly grassed and grown with barley and corn. At dusk we sent riders west to Warsaw for news of Poniatowski.

At this ford the Commander set an ambuscade for the Cossack riders and we sat in the reed beds waiting for them with our czapkas doffed and our weapons wrapped in our cloaks lest the metal winking in the last rays of the evening sun betray us. We baited our trap with a string of hobbled horses and we did not wait long for the fish to bite, for the Cossacks greatly esteemed and coveted our fine Polish steeds.

When the next band of Cossacks forded the stream we met them with a resounding volley. They fell to their deaths in those same waters. They wore ragged dirty garments and filthy beards to their waists. They were armed with immense lances such as our forefathers used to fight against the Teutonic Knights in olden days, with wheel-lock muskets, and with bows and arrows. Their bodies bobbed in the water like corks. We saw the lice and vermin jumping from them in search of new and warmer habitations.

But no sooner had we dispatched these fellows, with the fresh gunsmoke still palling in the air, than another band of Cossacks appeared, greater still in number. This new warparty veered off, disdaining the gauntlet we had thrown for them. They did not come near us but rode down upon a small village or hamlet that lay nearby. We all knew what lay in store for the poor peasants of that village, for the men would all be slain, and the women raped and then slain. A few hotheads rode out after the Cossacks, and we knew they would not return.

The Commander angrily cuffed to the ground a lieutenant of the cavalry who asked for permission to pursue the Cossacks with his squadron. The lieutenant took up his czapka and set it back on his head, wiped the dirt from his tunic, and sat his horse with tears running down his face. We rode off after the rest of the army, toward Warsaw, abandoning the already burning village to its fate.

CHAPTER NINE
THE ROAD TO WARSAW, AUGUST 1792

On the road to Warsaw we met our comrades, Poniatowski's men. Our hearts rejoiced at the sight of the vanguard riding forward to meet us, the red and white swallow-tailed pennants on their lances dancing in the dusk. We were all angry, and we had all had enough of the Commander's fighting retreat.

"We've licked these bastards twice, so why do we run?" Tanski roared. "Now Pepi is here we shall stand and fight these barbarians! We shall win or die!"

Our spirits soared and we drained the last vodka in our canteens. At the sight of Pepi's horse we roared "Long live Poniatowski!"

The Commander, saluting, ran to embrace his fellow general. But at the sight of our beloved Prince, our hearts sank. Pepi's face ran with tears of sorrow and disgrace. Neither death nor defeat could have moved the Prince to such a state of despair. Something far worse had befallen us. A tremor ran through the army.

"My dear General Poniatowski," the Commander began. "What ails you? It is a fine day, is it not? Old Poland yet lives. Her armies are undefeated in the field. With our two forces united, we are outnumbered by a mere three to one by the Russians. I'll take those odds, by God!"

Pepi saluted. "My dear Lord Brother, I bring orders from the King. To avoid further bloodshed, His Majesty has joined the Targowica Confederation and abolished the Constitution. Go back to your homes, comrades. The war is over."

The Commander shook his head in angry disbelief. "The Bullock jests, does he not? This is treachery, by God!" and he spat from the saddle, in front of the Prince. A dead hush descended, broken only by the fluttering of flags and the nervous sighs of the horses. The Commander gripped his sword. Very clearly and evenly, the anger boiling in his voice, he said, "I'll serve this King no more. He is a coward and a traitor, and this is high treason." With that, Tadeusz Kościuszko tore his general's epaulettes from his shoulders, and hurled his general's baton and all of his insignia of rank into the dust, and rode off.

The Prince slumped in the saddle, alone, crestfallen, desolate. What foreign force from without could not achieve, treachery from within had brought about. A house divided against itself cannot stand. Before our very eyes the regiments drifted away, as the summer snows melt before the rays of the sun. Officers broke their swords in rage. Some took their own lives from the shame. Soldiers threw away their muskets and burned or buried their colours. Only a few hundred die-hards like us remained. A horseshoe of angry riders rallied around our tattered standards on the deserted plain. All the while the enemy grew nearer.

"God's nails!" Tanski railed, "The King wants to spare our blood, does he? I say it's our own blood to spill! We are all free men in this army. We have no conscripts or slaves here, as the Russians do! It's my right and my duty to die for the Motherland! A pox on the Bullock, and long live the Republic!" he cried, drawing his sword.

"We are in a fine pickle here, boys," Sierawski spat, "We are damned if we do, and damned if we don't. For if we ride on, we disobey our King, but if we surrender, we betray our oath and our country," he said. Then Sierawski shrugged, and he too drew his sword. "Well, the hell with it, to betray a traitor is no treason, and, more to the point, I'm damned if I'll run a step further from these blasted barbarians, who could not even read a constitution, let alone write themselves one. An oath is an oath!"

They eyed me expectantly.

"What say you, O'Blumer the Irishman?"

I cast a glance at the band of angry patriots that remained. "That's *Blumerowski* to you, comrades," I replied. "Well, here we are, vastly outnumbered, the army in pieces, betrayed by our King, our glorious Constitution trampled underfoot, without any hope of any foreign aid whatever. In short, without a dog's chance in hell. Against such odds, even Hercules is an arsehole. Why, I say we fight on, of course!"

When a Pole has made up his mind, nothing can shift him. "If we are to fight on," I added, for I always had an eye for the details, even then, "we shall need both a general, and a new king. And we will find both our new king and our general sitting there yonder."

I referred, of course, to Prince Poniatowski, who was sitting sulking, like Achilles in his tent, not ten yards away. As one man, our eyes were transfixed upon our Prince. He was bareheaded and his silk cravat, in red-and-white, hung crumpled at his breast. From it hung that hunk of silver that his uncle had awarded him, the Medal of the Virtuti Militari.

Pepi rode with a retinue of the greatest worthies in the land – crimson ones, princelings and lords from the noblest families in the Republic. They were dripping with money. Every pistol had an ivory handle, every sword a gold hilt. Many of them wore full-length sable kontusz coats, in the old style. But gold will bend before iron, as the corn bends beneath the scythe. These great lords of old Poland stood helpless and crestfallen. They were as broken and bereft as we of the ordinary soldiery. We watched them as they gathered around the heartbroken Prince like anxious parents around an invalid child.

So Pepi's servants brought him his tiny harpsichord. The Prince was wont to play this in times of great joy, which were rare enough, or, as was more common with us, in times of great sorrow. At Zielence he had played it as the Russian cannonballs rained down on our heads. Now he sat before the harpsichord, for all the world as forlorn as the Wandering Jew himself. Tears ran down his cheeks and fell on to the ivory notes of the keyboard.

Abruptly, the silence was broken as Pepi struck up our mazurka. In that moment we recalled that glorious Third of May in Warsaw, marching along to the Royal Castle with the crowds cheering and the pipes playing and the sun shining, and all the girls gazing at us adoringly, and the citizens doffing their caps respectfully. One and all we soldiers took this for a sign from the Almighty. We elbowed aside the venerable noble lords and courtiers who surrounded our Prince.

"Away with you, grandad," Sierawski snapped at a balding nobleman, "this is no time for handwringing like an old woman! Old Poland is on her last legs – again!"

"Show some respect, young man! I am the High Chamberlain of Lithuania!"

"I don't care if you're the Lord Mayor of Krakow himself!" Sierawski bawled, shoving the Chamberlain roughly aside. "Make way there old man!"

Pepi raised an eyebrow at me, but carried on playing.

"Good day to you, comrade. I see that you have something in mind for me. What do your men aim to do? Raise me up on a shield like a Roman Emperor?"

"These are your men, Majesty, not mine," I retorted bluntly, "and, if I read my history aright, you would not be the first Polish King to be elected on the battlefield by his troops, after the incumbent was found wanting."

At this, Pepi became angered. "I bid you, my good comrade, to remember that Stanislaus-August is our lawful King. He is more to me than a mere uncle. As you all know, upon the death of my father, I had the honour to be adopted by the King, as His ward – His son. Since that day, more than twenty years ago, I have lived in my uncle's household, and I have been the happy recipient of such love, affection and care, that His Majesty could not have been a better father to me than if I had been his own natural son."

No one heeded him. The spark caught root and blazed into a fire. A hubbub arose. The rabble of soldiers, invigorated with new hope, beat their lances on the ground and began loosing joy-shots in the air. Up went the cry –

"Long Live King Jozef! King Jozef of Poland!"

Oh, such sweet sorrow to have heard those words, and I should have given my very soul to have seen it come to pass. It was not to be, and it was never to be.

The assembled worthies fell to earnest debating. At last, after some politicking, they inclined to the view of the soldiers, and joined in the general acclamation. Even the old High Chamberlain was persuaded. Pepi ceased playing and gently closed the lid of his harpsichord. He waved his hands for quiet, and finding none, he mounted his horse. Standing upright in the saddle, he demanded silence. It was denied him.

He cried out, unheard, above the chaos and the din – "What would you have me do, Sirs? Depose my own uncle? Impossible!"

But we would have none of it, and bore him aloft like a trophy, in spite of his vehement protests, our reluctant king. For, is it not the truth, and a wise proverb, that only the man who does not want to be a king, is truly fit to be one?

CHAPTER TEN
MARKUSZEM, 26 AUGUST 1792

"Pepi should have taken the crown," I said, as the Russian soldiers lined up.

"We shall be lucky to have any crowns upon our heads at all by the end of this day, or any heads upon our shoulders, for that matter," Tanski replied gloomily.

No sooner had the Commander departed for exile in Leipzig, than the Prussians, our supposed allies, also hastening to our aid, had invaded us from the West – skewering the country in two. After them, the Austrian armies were lining up to provide further friendly aid from the south. With all of these friends hastening to our aid, Russians, Prussians, and Austrians, it was just as well we had no enemies!

Now all of the cities had fallen – Danzig, Vilnius, Warsaw, and finally Krakow. Sierawski noted that his home town held out longest with grim satisfaction. We last partisans, a few thousand of us under Prince Poniatowski, had fought on awhile. We were a ragged enough band of insane cavalry, and we paid court to the lady of death. Only her sweet kiss could cleanse the sins of defeat and dishonour.

We were run to earth at a dusty hole named Markuszem. We were holed up at one end of a valley. Sunset fell upon us from above, spitting red through the blazing white clouds. Ahead of us, the Russian cannon were wreathed in grey, with great gasping mouths like beasts. We had no reserves nor allies, we had only prayers and dreams. Against the cannon fire we matched our rosary beads. As the noose tightened at Markuszem gallows, Pepi lowered his lance with the swallow-tailed pennon and charged. He charged across the waste, with the storks and herons of those marshes squawking and clattering angrily into the air before him. As he disappeared into the midst of the Russians, they parted before him like a grinning mouth, with the cannon fire churning up the earth like a foaming ocean. Then the teeth of the beast closed in around him.

"The Prince must not die!" cried one of the officers. "To me, you men!"

Tanski and Sierawski and I exchanged incredulous stares before the Russian guns.

"He means you!" we all said, grinning, and pointing at one another, before setting spurs to our horses, and without further ado we three charged into the whirling maelstrom.

This officer spurred his horse hard, drawing blood. We did likewise, and our horses fairly flew, not Pegasus himself could have covered the ground so fast. In a trice we had caught up with him, and our dear Prince Pepi. Unnerved, the Russian infantry scattered before us, just as the birds had flown, moments before. Pepi was unhorsed and was assaulting a battery of cannon, quite alone, on foot. The gunners, naturally, were reluctant to surrender their gun to a lone madman. For gunners, as you know, are as proud of their guns and limbers as cavalry are of their steeds, or infantry of their colours. A number of these fellows surrounded the Prince, who held them at bay with his sword.

As we approached, we saw that the Prince had laid his czapka across the still smoking mouth of the cannon – the sign of capture! As he did so, one of the gunners stole upon him from behind, wielding an axe. I rode this treacherous fellow down, trampling him with my horse, and shot a second in the face with my pistol. Fortunately, the remaining gunners fled at the sight of us, conceiving that they were the object of a more general assault. But close by we heard the coarse shouts of the Cossacks, counter-attacking. We glimpsed their ragged beards and bloody lances through the haze of gunsmoke.

"We have them, boys!" cried Pepi, deluded in his despair.

80

"Indeed, Sire," said the high-born officer who had led us to the rescue. He spoke like a courtier, in a smooth and calm drawling voice. "Perhaps we might continue the chase by horse?"

I caught Pepi by the collar and hoisted him up onto his bloodied horse. Spatters of gore streaked its pure white flanks. The high-born officer took the bridle from me and led Pepi off without a backward glance at us. Then the Prince's shame-faced bodyguards reappeared from the mist, surrounding him with a thicket of friendly swords as he had lately been enclosed by the deadly blades of our foes. Pepi, thus ensconced, was carried from the battlefield. To what fate we knew not – to foreign exile? To hide in the cellars of ruined palaces? Or walled up in the tomb of an impenetrable gulag? We were left behind to cover Pepi's escape.

"So what do we do now?" Tanski spat angrily. "Those noble bastards have left us high and dry!" There were about one hundred horse remaining, with no officers, and the Russians closing in like the Red Sea over Pharaoh's chariots.

"Comrades!" I raised my sword, "form on me!" They needed no second invitation, for a drowning man cares not for the quality of the rope.

"Where the hell are we going, Blumer?" Sierawski demanded.

"Where else? To the arse of the earth, comrade!" I shouted back. "To Podolia!"

CHAPTER ELEVEN
PODOLIA, SEPTEMBER 1793

Thus I rode back to the wild land of my birth. I had dreamed of riding back as the chief of a regiment of cavalry. In my mind's eye I pictured it clear as a Canaletto. Bright flags, burnished swords, bands playing, girls flinging rose-petals under our horses' hooves... Be careful what you wish for, comrades. I rode home, a lowly warrant officer, at the head of a ragged band of defeated men. Our dirty and bloodied standards draped about us like funeral shrouds. Our horses limped, our swords were rusted, and our broken lances trailed along the ground. We no longer knew if we were deserters or patriots. We gazed at the black-earthed fields. The harvest was over, and they were fallow now.

We rode on by a walled village – a village of penniless nobles, the kind of place where they wore wooden swords, and pulled their ploughs by hand. My mother hailed from such a village as this. These noble brothers and sisters, fallen on hard times, degenerated to a condition of wretched destitution below even that of serfdom. Old Poland was studded with these rotten boroughs in those days, like maggots in a good cheese, spreading their rot. Each wretched hovel was distinguished only from peasants' huts by their wooden porch, proudly displaying their coat of arms. Everywhere, on every porch, was the double cross - the Pilawa.

These were Felix Potocki's clansmen. We would find no refuge here. A tattered militia of ragged scarecrows came out to meet us, afoot, dressed in threadbare crimson robes, armed with scythes, wheel-lock muskets, arquebuses that might have seen service at the crusades, wooden swords, and Cossack lances. My men, filthy and exhausted as they were, regarded them with disdain.

This Targowica rabble would lend us no aid, nor lift a finger to assist us, not even permit us to water at their troughs and wells. After fruitless hours of tense argument, conducted at swordpoint, we moved on, for we would not butcher or rob our own countrymen.

As we took our leave, however, we gloried in the visitation of angels. Two young women of the village ran after us. They were barefoot, and their cheeks were sunken with hunger, but their eyes shone at our sight. Both were tall, straight backed, majestic girls, one raven and one redhead. The raven haired girl pressed a wineskin into my hands, together with a hogshead and a bag of potatoes. The second, a haughty, tawny creature, her hair the colour of amber and Russian gold, had similar presents for Tanski and Sierawski. Greatly heartened, we kissed their slender hands and thanked them a thousand times. Then they melted away into the gathering dark.

A heavy sky hung overhead, the winter moon staring blank as a dead man's eye in the grey firmament. Twardowski's moon. We nodded our greetings, and crossed ourselves and rode on. It was almost dusk when I called a halt at the lee of a small river in the shelter of a stunted coppice of hanging trees. Mine was a savage country, ravaged by war, plague and famine. Yet it was also a fertile country. We Podolians ploughed our tears back into the black dirt and now it was growing rich and fat. So, naturally, cruel eyes and jealous hearts sought to wrest our land from us. It is not enough to be brave and true. If you wish to eat the fruits of your labours you must be strong and ruthless, comrades. Otherwise, you shall eat only hunger in the pit of your stomach.

Hunger was eating up my little troop, and would consume it whole if I should permit it. *An army marches on its stomach,* after all, as Napoleon said. My men – they were mine, for, in truth, they could be nobody else's now – had fallen into a shambles. Some lay on the ground, moaning, others sat

83

weeping with their heads in their hands. Weapons, uniforms, knapsacks lay strewn about in the worst disorder imaginable. Yet, with a start, I realised I could still have my homecoming.

"Tanski! Sierawski!" I roared. "Get off your skinny arses!" With a few clouts with the flat of my sword I stirred them into action. "Collect up all of the food and water and bring it to me. Have the men attend to their horses. Get a fire started."

Tanski blinked. "Won't the Russians see it?"

The land was as flat as a pancake, they would see us anyway. They would catch up with us sooner or later, but in the meantime, we would wash and eat and warm ourselves and water our horses. If they caught us now, in our disordered state, we were dead anyway. I did not relate any of this to Tanski, he could work it out for himself.

"You have your orders, Tanski," I barked, "I shall not ask you again." To my surprise, he obeyed without further question. I think it was a relief for both of us. It took a good hour, but I roused the exhausted troops to action. I posted sentries and then we unhitched our horses, drew water for them, pitched shelters, and lit fires. Sierawski even dug a latrine. After posting sentries and pickets I had the men swab their uniforms, polish their brasses and clean their weapons and their tack, bridles, and saddles, and so forth. The men worked painfully slowly, as if in a dream. Yet it had the desired effect. The exercise warmed our cold bodies and restored a sense of order and pride, and distracted our minds from the dire nature of our plight.

Oh, our poor, abused horses! My own horse was named 'Muszka' which means 'Little Fly' in our tongue, for he is a troublesome beast, always sticking his nose where it does not belong. As soon as I could I attended to my dear nag. I had sorely neglected him of late, owing to the lamentable end to the campaign. As I unhitched the saddle, Muszka blew out his guts with a great angry snort, tossed his mane, and danced on the spot, letting out a fart as loud as a gunshot. With immense relief and utter joy I saw that, by some miracle, there were no saddle sores.

I am no heavy-footed rider. I ride lightly enough, but I am a big heavy man, accoutered with heavy sword, musket, and pistols withal. We had been campaigning hard for months with little respite. When I removed the bridle from his mouth there was dried blood crusted on the bit, and I felt a deep pang of burning shame.

For all of the ill-treatment he had suffered at my hands, I apologised unreservedly to the nag, with an endless stream of soothing words in a soft, low voice. At first, he remained in ill humour, but permitted my examination of him. He did not attempt to kick or bite me as I examined his feet. One by one, I removed the clods of mud, and nicked the accumulated stones from his shoes, before wiping the nails of his hooves with a rag.

Running my hands over every inch of horseflesh, I found to my immense relief that he was scratched and filthy, and lousy with vermin, but otherwise whole and intact. His muscles were knotted from toe to tail, but the ligaments and bones of his legs rang true as a bell, and I rejoiced again.

By now, Muszka was stripping the grass from the earth with his long yellow teeth and so I ran the curry comb through the matted hair of his coat, pausing to cut out the worst knots with a pocket knife. I sluiced his sides with water, and the steam rose freely from his flanks, mouth, and nostrils like a smoking dragon. Throughout, I continued to talk to him in the most friendly and affectionate tones.

By the time I had finished, Muszka had forgiven all, capering about me like a colt, nuzzling at me with his great head, the huge brown eyes blinking with the kindest and most sincere goodwill. After draping a thick blanket over him, I found the remnant of a sugar lump in my saddlebag and he devoured it in the happiest and most contented fashion, all of his ill-uses and suffering at my heavy hands by now quite forgotten. At last the horse stretched himself on the ground to rest, and I did the same. Horses are the same as men. They can happily abide even the worst treatment as long as one speaks to them in sincere and soothing tones. If only women were so easy to please, then a man's life should be a bed of roses, rather than a crown of thorns.

Then, and only then, these labours ended, I allowed the men to finish their rations. We ate every scrap of mouldy bread and dried meat that remained in our saddlebags and we drained the last of the wine. I fell asleep with my head on Muszka's warm belly and my sword in my hand.

The next day I had the whole troop stand to morning inspection, *la diane*, as if we had been in the courtyard of the Poniatowski Palace, not skulking on the frozen steppe. Tanski rode up and, saluting smartly, presented the troop for inspection. Returning his salute, I passed up and down the line, as fastidious and petty as any blueblood officer. In the midst of the line was a boy with his arm shot away to the elbow, bound up with twisted strips of filthy cloth. Green pus ran from the bandage and the flesh stank of mortification. He should be lucky to live to see another day.

The headcount – one hundred horse. About a dozen carried injuries of various stripes, but all were able to ride. I took an inventory. We retained our arms but we had no food and little ammunition – hardly any musket balls and a few grains of powder. Sierawski was in a melancholy humour.

"My dear Blumer, I do so regret that your first command, and your first parade, should be in such circumstances as these," he said.

"Nonsense, my dear Sierawski," I replied. "We are alive. We have our honour, and our arms, with which to prosecute this war, and drive these invaders from our lands and our homes."

"For the love of Christ, Blumer!" Sierawski seized my horse's reins. "Are you blind? Are you mad? Can't you see that this war is lost?"

For a moment my temper flashed. Then we grinned at one another.

"True," I admitted, "this war is lost. But we have youth and strength to win another one, comrade," I replied, "and another still after that, if we must."

At this, Tanski rode back from the picket, brandishing his field glasses.

"Comrades, I have dire news to report."

Through the glass, I observed a pillar of dust on the horizon. Cavalry.

"Do we run?" Tanski asked. I shook my head as I looked at the exhausted and decimated brigade.

"Too late!" I replied. "We are run to earth, comrade. We shall sell our lives as dearly as possible."

At my order, the men formed up, the trees at their backs. The enemy would have to come up this low rise at us, and we could receive them at the charge, face to face. We were, as ever, outmatched by any number to one. Still, on the bright side, they had no cannon or infantry, so we could meet them in the field like men, and not be cut down like dogs.

"Grey bastards," spat a young sergeant, his face lined, his beard streaked with dust.

"Hold your fire!" I shouted. The men laughed, in spite of themselves, for we had scarcely a grain of powder to fire those scant few bullets we had. Yet they mistook me. I had observed that the riders wore Polish blue, not Russian grey. They were grey with the dust of the road. They were either our men or they were Targowican traitors.

The cavalry stopped at a good distance. There were several hundreds of them, far too many for us to defeat. A band of riders detached themselves from the rest and this small delegation advanced toward us under cover of a white flag across the open field.

It was somewhat tense. We had suffered so grievously from treachery in this war. We trusted no one. All around, the hackles rose on my men like angry dogs. Swords were drawn and muskets run out, and lances lowered for the charge. For Pilawa crosses glinted on those uniforms, like daggers, in the harsh dawn light. These were Podolian troops of the Targowica Confederation. Felix Potocki's men. They held a white flag on a lance.

"Hold your fire! No man to fire but on my orders!" I roared, brandishing my sword.

"Damn those treacherous Targowica bastards to hell!" Tanski hissed, levelling his lance at the riders. "It's a trick, Blumer!"

"Sir, that is a flag of truce. If anyone dishonours it, I will kill him myself."

Reluctantly, Tanski relented. The lead officer rode a black horse of great beauty and was equipped with fine and expensive weapons. He and his mount were caked in the grey dust of the road. He rode with a band of bodyguards. He was a huge bear of a man, in his forties, with a genial, round face. It could only be one man.

"Hell's bells! It's the Rottmeister himself! It's Brigadier Dabrowski!" Tanski exclaimed, but did not sheath his sword. This was a derogatory nickname in the ranks for the Brigadier, who had a Polish father and a Saxon mother. Dabrowski was educated in Leipzig, and started his career in the Saxon cavalry. There he attained the rank of Rottmeister, which is German for Captain. When the war drew near, he had come back to Poland, and been appointed one of our cavalry chiefs. Dabrowski had written our new cavalry manual, and he had trained our regiment for months. From the time he had spent among Germans, he sometimes mangled his Polish. To avoid this, he often spoke French with us.

Dabrowski saluted and bowed. With his courtly manners, and brave as a lion, he was more like a knight of olden days than a commanding officer. He was a fine officer, a good provider for his men, scrupulously honest, and no fool.

"Good morning, Tanski," Dabrowski saluted smartly. "Comrade Blumer – I assume that you command these men?"

"Warrant Officer Blumer," I corrected, but without taking my hand from my sword, nor my eyes off his. "You assume correctly, Sir. For my part, I assume from your colours that you command these Targowica scum yonder?"

Dabrowski nodded his great wise head sadly. "Indeed, Blumer, sad to say you are correct. I am cooperating with the Targowican military commission, since the war was lost. If I might enquire – where are your colours, Sir?"

I seized the red and white pennant on Tanski's lance that was fluttering close by.

"These are our colours!" I roared. "For shame, Sir! You led us! You trained us! You stood with us at Zielence – has it come to this? The Devil take you – say your piece and begone, and then we can go to it, pell mell. No surrender, no quarter asked or given."

Now this was a grievous insult. Little brothers did not speak so to their betters. It was possible that the Brigadier might demand satisfaction on the field of honour. Fortunately, Dabrowski did not take the point. He had too much wisdom. He listened to my outburst in silence, amiably enough, and nodded again. He gazed evenly at the line of cavalry, the pistols, muskets and lances aimed at his heart. Then he nodded towards the one-armed boy.

"A word, perhaps, Blumer?" Dabrowski asked, and we dismounted. We walked a little way and he placed his huge arm around my shoulders. I was a big man, but Dabrowski was a giant. He was a true Pole, and a cunning old fox. All at once I felt ashamed to have taken him for a traitor.

"My surgeon will attend to your wounded men, Blumer. After all, you will require every man you can muster to defeat us in battle," he smiled. "A fine affair it shall be too, Pole fighting against Pole, brother against brother, countryman against countryman, and the Russians the winners *in absentia*."

"I am sorry, Brigadier," I said. "I spoke in haste. Please accept my apologies."

Dabrowski smiled again and clapped me on the shoulder. We laughed at the ridiculousness of it all. Then we took a pipe of Dabrowski's tobacco (for I had none remaining) and he drank the last of my vodka.

"*He who turns and runs away, lives to fight another day*," Dabrowski said gently. "This war is lost, Blumer. Here in Podolia we can hide, lick our wounds, and prepare for the next one. I am hiding as many men as I can in this fashion – and better to hide here than in Siberia, don't you agree?"

"You are right," I agreed. "We must hide. But where?"

We looked at the serried ranks of Potocki cavalry, then at my own little line of Polish horse, then back again, and then I grinned at Dabrowski. The one armed boy would see another sunrise yet. Indeed, all of us would.

"As every peasant knows," Dabrowski said, "the best place to hide a tree is in a forest."

Thus we rode through the heart of the badlands, with an honour guard, all pretending to be traitors.

"Are these our allies, or our gaolers?" Tanski pondered.

"We have our weapons, our horses, and our lives," I said curtly, "be content."

Naturally, none of us could be content. We rode with our hands on our swords and our eyes screwed to the back of our heads. We had holstered our useless firearms, for we did not have enough powder to light a pipe, let alone fight a battle.

"What were the terms of your truce with Dabrowski?" Tanski demanded, wheeling his horse in front of mine. My horse Muszka pulled up short, his red eyes rolling, and bared his awful yellow teeth at Tanski's mare, in anger at having his path blocked.

"With the war's end, the Brigadier has joined the Targowicans, to organise the army. He is protecting us from being rounded up and sent to Siberia. Therefore, we are Felix Potocki's men now, in name, at least. When a suitable opportunity presents itself, we shall rejoin our own army."

"The Devil! So we are Targowicans, then?" Sierawski spat, enraged.

"In name only, Comrade," I said firmly.

"God's wounds, Blumer! In name or not, this is the worst disgrace conceivable to man!" Sierawski said, appalled.

"There is actually a worse disgrace," I replied, grimly.

"Worse?" Tanski roared. Heads turned. "How could it possibly be any worse?"

"Felix Potocki," I said slowly, staring into their angry eyes, "has, according to Dabrowski, been made a General in the Russian Army. Consequently you, I, and all the men here, are now *Russian* soldiers."

Nobody spoke. The wind howled.

"You mean to tell me, Blumer," Tanski said, "that we are hiding from the Russian Army *in* the Russian Army?"

"Aye," I replied, "that's about the size of it," I shrugged. "If it be any consolation, the pay is better."

Tanski and Sierawski exchanged amazed glances.

"I swear to God, I would shoot you if I had any bullets left, Blumer, you mad dog," Sierawski shook his head, unsure whether to laugh or cry.

As you may surmise, when the men did eventually find out, they were disgusted. Many harsh words and a few punches were exchanged, but by then there was nothing to be done about it. For their part, Dabrowski's lads eyed us with the same sullen and angry expressions that we reserved for them. Occasionally, one of us recognised old comrades from past battles, and we fell to bemoaning our fate together.

At noon we broke camp and Dabrowski had us retrace our old hoofprints. He had hunted us down and gathered us into his fold, like lost sheep. Whether we would end up put out to pasture, or skinned for the butcher's block, remained unknown. On the low horizon we rode back past the hanging copse of trees that we had passed two days hence. A murder of carrion crows wheeled and danced in the branches, fat as buzzing bluebottles. Something ill had befallen.

We three broke away from the rest, without orders, without words, beating our horses' hooves across the desolate rutted road. Under the hanging trees we found the raven and the redhead, their bodies swinging from the maiden boughs, their tiny feet circling as they turned and twisted at the end of a length of hempen cord. Their hands were tied behind their backs and their heads hung forward, like nuns at prayer. Shortly, Dabrowski arrived with his bodyguard. We stared at the ghastly gallows, as the wind blew russet leaves struck with dewdrops and blood about the broken bodies.

"This is Felix Potocki's doing," he cursed, and wept. We cut down the girls and we washed their bodies with the last of our drinking water. We had no choice but to bury them at that desolate unconsecrated copse, wrapped in our tattered flags. We sang the hymns and psalms, and gently tamped down the earth with our hands. We swore vengeance over the graves. Then we rode on, to Tulczyn.

CHAPTER TWELVE
TULCZYN, PODOLIA, OCTOBER 1793

Tulczyn Palace was the Potocki clan's ancestral stronghold. The old mouldering castle had been razed by the Cossacks, decades before, during their great rebellion, when they had massacred thousands of Poles, Jew and Gentile alike, here. Felix's father had the new Palace rebuilt on the same site. It was a modern fancy house, such as the Kings of France lived in – imposing buildings, like Greek temples. Three of these huge edifices had been erected here, on three sides around a gigantic courtyard. New and elegant as it was, it stood on the graveyard of a massacre, on pyramids of unquiet bones.

This new Tulczyn had no need of fortifications. It was a palace, not a castle. Felix felt so secure that he had no need of walls or ditches. This was his kingdom. His word was law, and he had the power of life and death over every man, woman and child in Podolia. Including us. We rode past a stretch of ground where workmen toiled with rocks and soil.

"Felix is building a park for his mistress, who is now his second wife," I told my comrades, for this was common gossip in Podolia.

"Whatever happened to Felix's *first* wife, then, Blumer?" Tanski asked sarcastically.

"Felix gave her a Podolian Divorce," I replied.

"Which means what?" Sierawski asked suspiciously.

"He threw her down a well!" I replied, for it was the truth. With that we rode into the stables, and dismounted. There was a magnificent *ménage* next to the courtyard, a place for training horses, as grand as one would find in Vienna or Madrid. It would have pleased me to have seen it, but I was given no time to tarry. Armed guards, dressed in Potocki's blue livery decorated with the Pilawa cross, ordered me peremptorily away from my fellows.

Vexed by this turn of events, I took stock, unsure whether to flee or fight. No one had tried to search or disarm me. I still had my sword and pistols, albeit neither of them was loaded, for we had long since run out of ammunition. So I girded up my loins, stuck out my chest, and marched into Tulczyn behind the guards. I was conveyed to a great study in the very largest and grandest of the three great palace buildings.

The sumptuousness of this room exceeded the Wawel, the Sejm, and Madame L's salon all put together. At the centre was an enormous fireplace, with a gilt and bronze mounted mantelpiece, which alone must have cost thousands of ducats. A stack of logs burned in the fire, casting a diabolical red glow over the face of Felix Potocki, the great krolik, who sat, wreathed in smoke, stoking the flames with a gold-handled iron poker in the shape of the Pilawa cross.

"*Gosc w dom, Bog w dom – when a guest enters the house, God enters also.* Good day, my young lord brother." He did not deign to get up.

"You do me honour, My Lord," I said, stiffly, in a surly fashion, and made a half-hearted bow. For my mother had taught me good manners with a leather strap, and I would not disgrace her here, before this loathsome man.

Felix Potocki had a long face like a horse, with curly grey hair greased and pomaded back from his forehead. He wore lace cuffs at his wrists and a lace ruff at his neck, like a fashionable dandy. A man of average height and build, or less, and scrawny in the shoulders and legs, I towered above him. With his feeble stature and dressed in those milksop's clothes, he could not have looked less the Warlord of Podolia. Yet such he was. For when Felix glanced up at me, he had the eyes of a wild beast – they were deep-ringed black pits, bloodshot and sunken. He was a man to be feared, after all. When he spoke, he was full of false kindness and concern, as if to a small and disobedient boy.

"Here you are, the prodigal son, young Blumer! I welcome you with open arms! By all accounts you fought well in that foolish rebellion you called a war. I can see that you have your father's talent for a fight! I have sent him word, he knows that you are safe."

Before I could reply, a lackey brought in a letter on a silver platter. Felix read it, grimaced, and threw it on the fire. We watched it burn.

"That damn fool Poniatowski has challenged me to a duel," Felix said, at last. "Can you imagine? How tiresome!" Clearly he meant Pepi, and not the Bullock. Now if Pepi were to kill Felix in a duel, then honour would be satisfied.

"Will you accept the challenge, My Lord?" I asked.

"Duelling? Barbaric! Out of the question," Felix said dismissively. At Felix's side hung a sabre with a solid gold handle, dripping with diamonds. For all the gold and jewels it displayed, it was naught but a dress sword, and I reckoned he could barely have opened that letter with it. He was not a fighting man – he was a man born for giving orders that others might do the dying.

"Then you do not hold with duelling, my Lord?" I said. There was no question of Felix fighting a duel with the likes of me, he was far too grand to even contemplate it. I was worth less to him than the horse dung beneath the feet of his grooms. Still, if it was beneath his dignity to duel with me, well, then I would provoke him as far as I dared, and have a little sport with him.

"No," Felix replied, offhandedly, as if swatting away a fly. "Of course not. The Empress has forbidden her subjects to duel – it lacks discipline."

"The Empress! Pah! A mere German whore!" I said with contempt, for Felix's mistress was the daughter of a Prussian soldier. "My father taught me only a coward would run from a duel," I said, mockingly.

"Your father!" Felix said, ignoring the slight on his mistress. Why, this devil was even smiling now. "What a great servant your father was. One of the old school! A great rent collector." He waved a hand at his enormous palace. "I need my rents. This place doesn't pay for itself, you know, boy."

My father was an extortionist, a slave driver, and a thief, and the peasants hated him more than they hated the Jewish moneylenders – which was a great deal. Still, I was not going to defame my own kin in front of this creature. A servant charged Felix's glass, then my glass. Felix called for his opium pipe, to which he was greatly devoted, and waited impatiently while another servant lit it. He smoked, breathing in deep, and great clouds of smoke billowed around the room. He did not offer me a puff, I noted, but kept all for himself. The smell was sickly sweet. I had another tilt at him as he smoked.

"I trust my father is well, my Lord," I said, "for his health has suffered from all of the wounds he has obtained in your service. My father never turned down a duel in his life. Most of them were fought on your account. If any man should call you a thief, a poltroon, a traitor, a Russian stooge, or a wife-murderer, why, my father would instantly leap to defend your honour! He took many cuts in that way – the damn fool."

Felix failed to stir. He merely raised an eyebrow and smoothed his sable cloak. Diamonds, emeralds and sapphires glittered among the folds. Felix – who naturally wished to change the subject away from his abject cowardice in refusing to fight Pepi – let out a great puff of smoke.

"Do not try my patience, boy – for I know what you are about," he said, and he smiled again. Still smiling, he went on to say, "you are trying to provoke me, my fine young lad. Well, if you continue with your feeble schoolboy taunts, I shall have you flogged around the courtyard with the knout – how's that?"

The hell with these rich cowards! I ground my teeth and held my tongue. He would not fight me, then, that was clear enough. Yet I might simply kill him – the thought took root in my mind. He stood before me, armed with only his dandified penknife, and I had my sabre, sharp as a razor, that had opened several heads in the war. But if I were to kill him out of hand, then it would have to be common murder. I had no stomach for that. I am no assassin – I am but a soldier.

Felix, having shown his teeth, spoke again. "Now keep a civil tongue in your head, and pray you silence, and listen to your Lord, young Blumer. I have never had such a good steward and rent-collector as your father, but he grows old, and tired. Why, he has not even the consolation of your mother's company in his old age. Such a fine lady!" This last he said through gritted teeth, for Felix and my mother loathed each other. "How many years has it been since your mother died?"

Long years had gone by, but I grieved her as keenly as if she had died that very morning.

"Three years," I said. "She would have wept to see what our nation has been reduced to."

Felix shot me an angry glance, and thumped the plump cushions on the arm of his velvet chair. "Yes! That is so! Reduced to a state of chaos! Our ancient laws tossed aside and trampled upon! The rights of the nobility stolen! A Constitution drawn up that was a pact with the Devil himself! The nation was beggared by Jews and Jacobins – and I have saved it!" he snarled. Then he calmed himself. With the young, Felix knew, you must try flattery.

"Enough of politics," he said smoothly, "the war is over. Since you mother died, you are all your father has left, my dear Ignatius. Your father has been in despair, with you riding out with rebels and traitors – an outlaw, no less. You have led us all a merry dance, and defied the Empress!"

"It was my duty to Poland," I retorted. My blood was up.

"Duty, indeed!" Felix snorted. "There is a list of names in Moscow," he said slyly, "and your name was on it. That is where your foolery has got you."

"Death warrants," I said, thinking of Pepi's letter, that I and my comrades had signed. Despite my anger at Felix, my blood ran cold. I began to sweat, and thirst for another vodka.

Felix shook his head. "Legal process, dear boy! All enemies of Russia will be lawfully punished. But fear not! For I have interceded upon your behalf, as I have on behalf of many others, who have also allowed themselves to be led astray. The Empress is persuaded that your actions were misguided – youthful high spirits, shall we say."

The devil! The snake! Smoke rolled from his jaws like the mouth of Hades. My very flesh crawled.

"I am grateful for your act of selfless kindness," I said sarcastically, "and my men and I will be on our way! I know you are too honest a Lord to expect anything in return."

I made to turn, but Felix clicked his fingers, as he would to an unruly dog.

"Not so fast! You have been granted amnesty by the Empress," he smiled, and stroked the arm of his chair, "but I would have you serve me, as your father did. You won yourself a fine reputation as a fighting man in that foolish rebellion."

He was eyeing me up like horsemeat. My old man was past his prime, and Felix wanted a new stallion – or rather a new gelding.

"I am flattered, Lord. I thank you." Although he had saved my life, all I could think of was taking his. Felix was a sword's length away. His damned servants were constantly in and out, but these were effete dandies in powdered wigs, armed with nothing more than hatpins, and I feared them not. It had not occurred to any of them that any person would dare to lift a finger against Felix, or touch a hair of his head. I pondered my predicament. To assassinate Potocki would guarantee my own awful death, as well as that of all of my men. It would make the Constitutionalists appear like brigands. My mother, I knew, would have told me to stay my hand. She would not have countenanced such a dishonourable act as murder.

Then I remembered the two dead girls, and instantly flew into a rage. I determined to kill Felix, and damn the consequences. He was wearing a sword, after all, and he could take his chances like the rest of us. If he would not fight like a man, why, he could die like a dog.

As my fingers closed around the hilt of my sabre, the door swung open. Two men walked in, and interrupted the murder before it had even begun!

The first newcomer was a great fat man in a full-length sable coat and a bearskin hat. He seemed familiar. The second was a tall, blonde man with a killer's eyes, in Russian uniform. Both were fully armed.

"Ah, excellent!" said Felix, turning to greet them, his eyes addled with opium and vodka, "there you are, Severyn!"

"My Lord," said Severyn Rzewuski, for it was he and none other. Rzewuski bowed to his master Felix, and swept off his hat. There was still a lump on his forehead the size of a quail's egg, that I had put there. He saw the murder in my eyes, for he had a murder of his own in mind – mine!

"Good day, young master Blumer, we meet again. All roads lead to Rome, as the proverb goes," he said. Then Rzewuski grinned evilly, and rested his hands on his pistols. The man next to him, dressed in Russian uniform, did the same. Four pistols between them. Armed with only my sword, I had no choice but to stay my hand. We stood and glared at each other. It was a stalemate. The air was thick with hate. In the grip of the opium, Felix was quite oblivious to the animosity between us.

"I see you already know each other?" Felix said cheerfully. "Excellent! For young Blumer will be joining our army. The Russian Army." Felix drew a packet from his armoire. It was bound in red ribbon and a wax seal bearing a double-headed eagle. He tossed it onto the card table, which was an elaborately inlaid and gilt-bronze mounted affair. The packet sat on it like a wager.

"This is for you, Blumer. A commission in the Russian Army. A captaincy, and in my regiment of cavalry, no less. I am going to St Petersburg shortly, to petition Her Majesty the Tsarina on various matters, for she has been tardy of late in fulfilling her promises to us. An oversight no doubt."

His face clouded over, and I guessed that all was not well between him and his dread patron, the Empress.

"Come with me to Russia," Felix said. "There are many opportunities for advancement in St Petersburg."

Rzewuski glared at me, his piggy eyes glowing like coals, full of hell and jealousy. Like a dog, he could not abide any rival for his master's affection. I guessed that this young man with him was his protégé, and that I was stealing his thunder. By God! I had walked into a fine crossfire, enfiladed from all sides!

I stared at the paper, which I dared not even touch. In front of me was the dotted line. I had only to sign, like Pan Twardowski, and the world was mine. I should be lying if I said that I was not tempted. I looked down. On my finger I saw the ring with the cross of rubies – my mother's ring. I shook my head. Felix's jaw fell in amazement.

"The Devil take your Targowica commission," I said. "I am a Pole, and I'll be damned if I'll be a Russian lackey."

"Fool!" Felix Potocki snorted with contempt. "You have tried my patience once too often. My Lord Rzewuski! Take this young upstart away out of my sight, at once!"

"As you command, my Lord Felix," Rzewuski grinned.

CHAPTER THIRTEEN
THE ABYSS OF DESPAIR

At midnight I was arrested and cast into the abyss of despair. A dozen armed men dressed in flowing black robes seized me and dragged me from my bed. We had been in Tulczyn for about one month, confined to barracks.

A black silk hood was thrust over my head and my hands bound behind my back. My tunic was torn open. The point of a dagger was held to my chest. A noose was looped around my neck. A gun's muzzle was prodded into the small of my back. Through my hood I heard the hammers of pistols cocked. Not one word was spoken throughout.

Then I was led, like a sacrificial lamb, into the courtyard of Tulczyn palace – the Abyss of Despair, as the Jews styled it. I assumed I was to meet the same fate as those who had perished there at the hands of rebel Cossacks, in the massacres of so many years ago. How awful to be hung like a dog, not shot like a gentleman! For the first time, fear gripped my soul. The wind was howling in the courtyard. I wondered at the strangeness of the hour, for it was customary to hold executions at dawn. Through my black silk mask I could dimly perceive the luminous glow of the moon. On either side I heard the heavy tread of armed men in hobnailed boots. Under my bare foot the slabs were cold as gravestones.

Dark rumours had spread across the land that the Targowicans were holding secret military trials. At the behest of their Russian masters, they were purging the army of patriots. There were dungeons at Tulczyn that never saw the light of day. There were gibbets and scaffolds. There were walls against which men were stood up and shot to rags.

Ahead of me, I heard shouts. Three resounding knocks sounded on a wooden door, and echoed in the cavernous chambers beyond. Three ominous knocks within sounded in answering echo. I heard the sound of another door yawning open and stumbled as I was led down stone steps.

"Welcome, brother," said a sardonic voice, which I imagined to be the gaoler, torturer, or executioner.

"What the Devil is the meaning of this? Unhand me, you bastards!" I shouted through the hood. "Give me a proper trial before I hang!" I had begun to panic, and was quite unmanned, and thoroughly terrified.

"Quiet, fool!" someone hissed under his breath. "Calm yourself! This is no execution! You have been proposed by Felix as a member of his Lodge."

I breathed a great sigh of relief, in spite of myself. I was glad of the hood, for my face had turned as red as a beetroot with embarrassed shame. For I was quite convinced that my time had come. This, I presumed, was Felix Potocki's idea of a jest. Now, if a man has not had quite his fill of foolery in life, then he can always become a Freemason. Through the hoodwink and cable-tow I perceived that I was in a great chamber filled with men. They were observing a silence, but now and then I heard coughs, whispers, the shuffling of feet, and the clink of scabbards and medals.

A stentorian voice demanded, "If you wish to enter, give me the password of the masters!" Abruptly, rough hands pulled the hood away. I screwed up my eyes against the light. A human shape stepped out from behind a pillar. We stood in the great hall of the temple, at the western end of the room. It was lit with oil lamps and candles. There were red columns around the walls of the hall. Three huge doors faced towards the north, the west, and the east. The Masons conducted me to the centre of the lodge, where, after first invoking the aid of the Deity, I was made to kneel and attend prayer, while the brethren stood, and repeated various incantations.

"Vouchsafe thine aid, Almighty Father of the Universe..."
it began, and I was suffered to listen to the master, the
chaplain, the deacons, the wizards and warlocks, and so forth,
droning on in this vein for many hours. Often their memories
would fail, and they would be obliged to begin a particular
passage again from scratch, or, worse, to consult their great
tomes, and thence bicker about the proper procedure like
pettifogging clerks.

All around me were the brethren of Felix Potocki's Grand
Lodge of Podolia. The Temple was hidden and set aside from
the profane world, buried within the vault of a huge
underground chamber with oak-panelled walls. Great banners,
bearing occult designs, hung from the walls – the circle and
the square, the sun and the moon, the star in flames, and the
All-Seeing Eye.

The scene was illuminated by the eerie glow of guttering
candles. A towering gilded throne was flanked by pillars of
lignum and surmounted by a golden canopy. The Worshipful
Grand Master, Felix Potocki, sat upon this throne, at the
eastern end of the temple, under a great canopy, as if he were
the Pope! Beneath his regalia he wore the black uniform of a
Russian General. He was flanked by the turncoat priest Bishop
Massalski, and my old enemy Hetman Rzewuski. The latter
had at his side the same tall, blond man, with piercing blue
eyes. From his insignia of rank and fine attire he was a
nobleman and a Freemason of a high degree.

This man, I had come to learn, was Szymon Korczak, a
serviceable villain, and Rzewuski's assassin. With hardly a
thought, Felix had tossed him the captaincy that I had refused.
It was well known that this blackguard Szymon Korczak had
ordered the killing of the two girls, the redhead and the raven,
for he boasted of it, openly, in the officers' mess. I had sworn
that I would kill him for it.

The other brothers, according to their degrees, were
arrayed along the stone columns, to the north and south. They

were adorned with aprons, medals, and jewels. Swords and pistols hung from their gilded crossbelts.

Hours passed in that infernal vault. Cold and draughty hours indeed, for they had neglected to furnish me with my trousers, and I was obliged to stand in my nightshirt, wearing but a single boot on my left foot. The marble floor was as cold as the dark side of the moon. With a lambskin apron around my waist, a chisel in one hand, and a set of compasses in the other, I stood in the centre of the Lodge, feeling entirely ridiculous.

Potocki's brethren made the appropriate symbols and gestures before the Sacred Altar, and thus I was initiated into the Freemasons. I can tell you nothing of the ceremony itself, for at the conclusion of it, I swore not to reveal the Freemason's secrets under no less a penalty than that of having my throat cut across, my tongue torn out by the root, with my body buried in the sands of the sea at low-water mark, so help me God.

Suffice it to say, it was a great deal of foolery and flummery, and uncomfortable in the extreme. There I stood, half-naked and trussed up like a Paris whore, while those lecherous old buffoons and traitors leered at me. The Bishop, in particular, was giving me the glad eye. I shivered, aye, and not only with the cold. It was better than being hanged or shot. But only just.

They taught me a secret handshake, a certain friendly or brotherly grip, whereby one Mason may know another in the dark as in the light. "May it protect you, Brother," one of them said, and the ritual was, at long last, concluded.

This foolishness ended, the Master called the Craft from labour to refreshment. 'Refreshment' signified but one thing – vodka. To a man, the Lodge drank, heartily. The brethren gathered around, clapping me on the back, and shaking my hand.

"Here, boy, drink this!" cried Bishop Massalski, producing a great foaming tankard of mead, in which something living was thrashing, "This will sort the apprentices from the craftsmen!" He leered at me with hungry eyes. I stared back.

"Bishop Massalski," I said coldly, "I have not seen you since the Third of May last year. *Sto lat!*" The priest stared at me with horror. He recognised me, at last, for I had been incognito beneath the hood.

"By God!" he hissed, "if I had known it was you, you young scoundrel, I should have blackballed you!"

I stared at him with contempt. "Blackballed me? You don't have any balls, you turncoat bastard."

The tankard contained a live frog, swimming in beer. A sea of expectant faces surrounded me. Without hesitation, I drank the beer in one gulp, feeling the frog's slimy legs kicking against my face. Raising the tankard to universal acclaim, I seized the front of Massalski's vestments, and tipped the frog down it. A great drunken cheer rose up as the priest ran crazily around the room, with the poor frog hopping and squirming inside his clothes. As the crowd parted to make way for the Bishop, who was jumping and cursing like the devil, I perceived the closing formalities of the day, as they closed the Lodge.

"Worshipful Master," called out a Mason, "Present the flag of our country at the Altar."

With that, they draped the Russian flag across the Altar. Some of the Brethren cheered – some were silent – some cried out, in anguish.

"In the Name of God Almighty!" I shouted, "This is not the flag of our nation! This is the yellow shield of Judas! This is the black beast of the Anti-Christ herself! But what more could I expect from a nest of Targowica vipers?"

Rzewuski roared with anger. "Beware your conduct, Brother! You violate the sanctity of the Lodge! Szymon – silence him!"

There was an uproar. The brethren were bitterly divided, for and against. Words were exchanged, and then blows. Tankards were thrown and fists flew. Amidst the chaos, the tall, blond man, with piercing blue eyes, came striding towards me across the Mosaic floor like an angry God. Sweeping off his hat, he bowed graciously in greeting. Without further ado, Szymon drew his sabre and made to run me through. I turned the blade aside with my chisel, wielding it like a poniard, for my blood was up, and I was glad of any excuse to kill one of these Targowica traitors. Roaring like a bull, I ran in to meet him, stabbing at him with the chisel like a dagger.

"Brothers!" came a vain shout, "the Lodge is holy ground! Put down your weapons!"

But we were not to be denied. Like dogs off the leash, we howled for vengeance, leaping at each other's throats, scattering the candles across the floor. My adversary executed an advance-lunge at my heart. I deflected this with a beat-parry, but Szymon Korczak was too canny for this, and our blades were too ill-matched – with a simple whip-over he disarmed me, the chisel spinning away into the darkness.

My adversary grinned. Flames were running up the banners and the wooden panels of the walls. Masons ran to and fro, screaming for water. Above the Altar hung the ceremonial sword. Unsportingly, Szymon had interposed himself between me and it.

Slowly and deliberately, Szymon prepared his coup de grace. He could not resist using the classic cavalryman's cut, the slow, deliberate, *par le moulinet*. It was his way of saying that he was cutting me down like a peasant.

This act of vanity gave me my chance. I ducked, and rolled under the flashing sabre, past Szymon and towards the Altar. Then I sprang up onto the Altar and wrenched the sword from the wall. My opponent, enraged, turned and ran in a mad charge, sweeping his blade at my ankles, to cut off my legs!

Leaping over the wild swing, I landed on the floor, my nightshirt flapping wildly, my bare backside gleaming in the light. I scrambled to my feet barely in time to receive My Lord Brother Szymon Korczak at full tilt, whereupon I dealt him a good cut to the body. My heart sang for joy. Oh, the cruel beauty which runs through all our souls, as it runs through the world! Squealing like a stuck pig, Szymon turned back and fell sprawling across the Altar. His blood spilled across the white altar cloth and his sabre clattered onto the floor. I made no move to finish him off. That would have been ungentlemanly.

By now, the Brethren and their servants had quelled the fires with buckets of water and snow. A thick, damp, acrid stink enveloped the chamber. A dozen Masons drew their sabres and levelled them at me, crying that I had killed him.

"Tis but a flesh wound, brothers," I said, sadly, and with great regret. "Fear not, Szymon Korczak will live to draw another treacherous breath."

From up high on his throne, Felix began to laugh, and then to cackle. We were all trapped in the hell of this little satan.

"Damn it, Blumer, that was good sport!" Felix said, applauding wildly, as at the theatre, and wiping vodka from his thin lips. "You've bested both Rzewuski, and now his finest sabre, Szymon Korczak! The door is always open to you, my lad!"

As I was led from the chamber, I paused and smiled with satisfaction. "Gentlemen," I said to the Masons, "I see that our flag is restored to the altar!"

The altar cloth was white above, and red with blood below!

CHAPTER FOURTEEN
THE BISON, NEW YEAR 1793

Felix Potocki celebrated the New Year by firing off ten brace of cannon. God knows, our poor country had little enough to celebrate. We had lost a third of our land and our populace to Russia, Prussia, and Austria, the Satanic Trinity. The Constitution was torn up. Our army was all but disbanded. Many of the regiments were taken into the hands of the Russians, or of kroliks such as Felix Potocki, to act as their own rent-collectors and jockeys.

Felix would not permit Szymon Korczak and I to kill each other like civilised men. Having declined to fight Pepi on the field of honour, he could not allow duels in his fiefdom, for fear of appearing a coward himself. Instead, my squadron was given unto Severyn Rzewuski's disposal, and he did all that he could to place us fellows in harm's way, by giving us dangerous and evil tasks.

That night, we huddled at the rail for midnight mass in the draughty Potocki chapel, making hurried confessions. "Bless me father for I have sinned. The day before yesterday we built gallows. Yesterday my men evicted serfs from land they had worked for generations. We dragged children from their hearth and homes, threw families to the wolves, extorted taxes from honest farmers, all in the name of Felix Potocki."

We trudged into the gathering dark of a Polish land under a foreign boot. Austrian, Russian, Prussian, it mattered not. After a hunter's breakfast of scrambled eggs we set off, freezing, at the crack of dawn, snow blowing in our faces, to hunt the deadly minotaurs that plagued Potocki's estates – bison!

Tanski was confident, hefting his lance with great bravado, twirling it like a choirmaster's baton, to great gasps from his adoring female admirers. The lads seemed to have warmed to the novelty of exile. Sierawski had filled out. No longer a gawky scarecrow, he had become a young adonis. His long hair shone. His skin was weatherbronzed. A veteran of the War of the Constitution, he rode with his czapka at a jaunty angle, with swooning girls grabbing at his saddle.

Myself, I was bereft of all soul and vitality. I sank into a bottomless melancholy. Not even the sweet wine of our fine Podolian girls, with their ebony hair and white skin, could rouse my mind from the black dog of lethargy. I was insensible to the charms of the girls. They took my ill-tempered brooding for the despair of a sensitive and tortured soul, and were greatly enamoured of me. Had I but cared, I could have cut a swathe through them as a scythe at the harvest. The more I spurned them, the more they coveted my glances. Such are women!

"Forget him, girls, all he cares for is bison-grass vodka!" Tanski said, waving his czapka on the end of his lance. We rode off into the forest. The snow was luminous in the darkness. Fire danced on the torches of the hunters.

"Cheer up, damn it, Blumer, you miserable hairy bastard!" Sierawski shouted, "we're better off here than in Siberia!"

Laughing, Tanski and Sierawski rode off. A shout came – the beast had been cornered. Cursing, I spurred Muszka mercilessly on, and gave the old warhorse his head. I should rather die than be last into any affair. Truth be told, at that moment I should have welcomed death, such was the depth of my despair.

Nearby there was a fusillade of shots, darts and arrows, that shook the very snow from the branches of the fir pines. The hunters and the hounds had caught up to the bison. They had drawn the beast round and round a great towering oak tree, with ancient spreading branches, like the arms of an old gnarled giant. As I drew nearer, hearing the cries and whoops

109

of the hunters, the crack of shots and broken branches, I saw red stains of blood on the snow.

Between the three of us fellows we cornered the great beast in an open clearing ringed by pine trees. Tanski was playing the great bison and teasing it until it dropped from its wounds. Darts and arrows stood out on the bison's great mane like broken crosses. Tanski raised his lance for the *coup de grace* – but missed. The spearhead sunk impotently into the snow, and the shaft shivered apart.

So Sierawski drew his pistol and pulled the trigger. A flash in the pan, a hiss – misfire! At that moment the great beast, wounded, angry, and blinded with rage, turned on Sierawski, goring his horse and unseating him. The bison stood over his prone, crumpled body. I spurred my horse between Sierawski and the bison.

The beast turned, finally, on me. My horse, God Bless him, stood his ground as a ton of bison-flesh bearing those wicked devil's horn points came charging at us. My breath running in ragged gasps, I shouldered my lance, and struck home. The bison swerved, barrelling down a hollow and careening away. I had but winged it. The broken lance hung from the bison's ribs, another bloody trophy.

As Muszka and I collected ourselves, blood and noise ringing in our eardrums, I saw, with mounting horror, the bison, mortally wounded but still bellowing, running down on a crowd of spectators who had gathered at the foot of the hill. At the centre of this small knot of horse riders was a lady, all in white.

Cursing, I spurred my horse after the bison, and with my free hand I drew my gun from my saddle holster. With scant yards to go, I drew a bead on the dying beast as it bore down on the damsel and a young man who stood, immobile, rooted to the spot. Placing my musket to my shoulder, I fired.

With a titanic gasp, the great beast expired at the lady's feet. Beside her the young man had drawn his sword, and brandished it impotently. Muszka slid to a halt. The branch of a tree had claimed my czapka. So I touched my fingers to the top of my bare head and bowed, full length, from the saddle, smoking musket in hand.

The lady, her eyes colder than the icy snows, colder than the diamond earrings she wore, regarded me with the most wicked dancing eyes I had ever seen, and placed her dainty foot on the bloody head of the bison. It was Madame L. Beside her was Elias Tremo, her young lover.

"There you are, Blumer, at last," she said coldly. "It has taken weeks to find you. Here, this letter is for you." She extended her hand imperiously and gave me the paper. Stunned, I took it from her. It bore the seal of the Republic. I broke open the wax. I should have been less astonished had the letter been delivered by Mercury himself, in his winged sandals. Flakes of snow drifted onto the white paper and blotted the words into inky tears.

"Blumer, Take Your Men to Krakow At Once. Dabrowski."

CHAPTER FIFTEEN
THE UPRISING, KRAKOW, 24 MARCH 1794

"Home at last!" Sierawski cried, waving his czapka in the air.

We saw two towers rising through the morning mist above the market place. These two square towers, of uneven height, like father and son, were crowned with domes, like onions. We rode on through the arches that ringed the market place, with the chimes of our horses' hooves ringing out on the flagstones. Our lances pointed at the heavens like a line of dragon's teeth.

"Your fame precedes you, comrade," I remarked. Sierawski beamed and doffed his czapka to the girls as they leaned out of the windows, scattering rose petals and blowing kisses at the soldiers. In his mad vanity, he fancied that their attentions were for him alone.

Word swept through the cities and towns, through every household, church and coffee house, through the fields and the forests. It flowed up and down the Vistula and the Varta with the spring tide, and climbed the peaks of the Carpathians – Uprising!

Krakow was buzzing like a beehive, with armed men of all descriptions converging upon it from every point of the compass – nobles armed with sabres and pistols, peasants wielding scythes, and veterans such as ourselves, in the tattered uniforms of the Republic. I ordered my troop to halt at a water trough. The horses sucked greedily at the water. Then, suddenly, the air was filled with strange music. A sad, silvery, plaintive clarion call from the cathedral tower, six simple notes that echoed hauntingly away into the blue. Then, abruptly, in the middle of a bar, the music stopped.

Tanski stood in his stirrups. "What the Devil?"

"Why, it is our Krakowian Hymn, the Hejnal," Sierawski, who as you know was a Krakowian, said proudly. "Five hundred years ago, the Mongols invaded old Poland. The Golden Horde flung themselves at the walls of Krakow – a hundred thousand warriors!"

Sierawski pointed to the higher of the two towers.

"A minstrel in that tower of the cathedral sounded the alarm. His trumpet called the city to arms. Battle was joined around the walls. An arrow from a Mongol bow cut short his signal and his life, but the barbarians were repulsed, and the city saved! Ever after, every single day, morning and evening, the same melody rings out over the city. It stops at the point where the herald died."

Tanski snorted with derision.

"Of course I have heard the story, but you have it all wrong, Sierawski. It was not the Mongol hordes, merely a small raiding party of Tartars that attacked this town of yours."

"Nonsense," I said, "it was the Turks, not the Tartars."

"All of them tried!" retorted Sierawski, "and we men of Krakow beat the lot!"

Thus we fell to bickering as earnestly and bitterly as any faculty of scholars of history.

"Harsh sounds the bloody trumpet of war!" Cyprian Godebski cried out delightedly, tossing back a glass of wine. We had met him on the way there.

"It's a fine story, all the same, comrades. No matter who they were, be they Turks, Mongols, Tartars, Cossacks, or Russians, here we are in fair Krakow, with the barbarians at the gates again! The stage is set for a grand encore of the same old song."

All around us the swarm of activity increased. Thick-waisted men of commerce, the keepers of inns and taverns, had run out to meet us, like flies after honey. They were rubbing their hands in sheer joy at the sight of thousands of thirsty soldiers, dreaming of the prices they could gouge and the profits they could make. Liquor doubled in price in the time it took to drink it.

A bristle-bearded fellow pressed a glass of wine into my hand. This avaricious fellow was going to be disappointed, for we had not a single zloty in our pockets between the whole brigade. Nevertheless, I drank it at a draught in any event, and made to tear a brass button from my tunic in token of payment.

"No charge, my lord," simpered this great toad. My lord, indeed – still, a man could get used to leading a brigade.

"On the house! God Bless you, my dear innkeeper," Sierawski grinned, "you are an honest patriot indeed, for this wine is of an excellent vintage."

"On the house in Krakow," I mused, "the Devil it is! Who paid for this, man?"

The innkeeper shrugged, shook his head and jerked a thumb towards a fashionable terrace lined with silk parasols. "His Excellency, yonder."

Now my mouth was dry and I could taste only the dregs of wine in it. For your nobles will only give away a sprat if they expect to catch a mackerel.

The square teemed with people. We made our way through the thickening crowd, drawing admiring glances from the women and envious stares from the men. Ignoring them, and brushing aside the protests of the waiters, we strode onto the terrace of the coffee house. It was a fancy place, with gleaming walnut tables swathed in white linen cloths, and red velvet cushions on the gilded chairs.

A man dressed in an immaculate blue uniform reclined at a table. He sat under a silk parasol, surrounded by a crowd of beautiful women, flitting around him like so many gorgeous butterflies. Any one of the women could have made a wife for a king. His Highness the Prince Jozef Poniatowski, for it could be no other, who was completely oblivious to their attentions (or at least affected to be so), sat drinking coffee and reading a newspaper.

"There you are, Blumer!" Pepi exclaimed delightedly, and he stood and greeted each one of us by name, shook our hands, and bowed as if each of us, and not he, were royalty. This simple gesture disarmed us completely. "Take a seat, my dear boys!" He held up the newspaper. The writing was clumsy and smudged, for it was an underground paper, printed clandestinely on a press of wooden blocks in a backroom or cellar.

THE SHARPER THE THISTLES,
THE SWEETER THE VICTORY.

The gist of it was this – the French had guillotined their King Louis, and Queen Marie Antoinette. Catherine the Empress, who saw Jacobins under every bed (and she saw many beds), needed no more provocation. Marie-Therese of Austria, the dead Queen's sister, cried revenge. Frederick of Prussia, third of the brigands, scented loot, and followed suit. All three declared war on France. So, while the cats were away, we mice could play.

We had quickly taken our leave of Tulczyn. Felix, the arch-traitor, had been betrayed in turn by the Empress, who had given him nothing for his pains, not a brass zloty. Treacherous German that she was, she had torn the Constitution up, all right, but she had refused to restore any of Felix's privileges – aye, and dismembered the country into the bargain. Thoroughly betrayed, Felix had gone off sulking to Vienna, and exile. There he sat and brooded alone in a vast empty palace, like a golden prison.

Naturally all this war and treachery had caused chaos in Tulczyn. So my men and I had slipped away, guided by Madame. Then we rode straight to Krakow as the crow flies, there to rendezvous with our comrades. We had ridden the very same road I had travelled five years before, when I had joined the King's cavalry.

And our traitor King? Well, he was with the Russian garrison in Warsaw. It was as well for him that he was, for had he shown his face in Krakow, we should have given him a drumhead court martial, King or no, and put his crowned head on the end of a pike. Nobody loves a traitor, it is well said!

But we all still loved Pepi. For the sins of the uncle are not to be visited on the nephew. The Prince clapped his hands and called 'Champagne!' and the champagne was brought, in buckets of ice. After a few glasses of that we were soon at our ease once more. We were warriors, not ragged vagabonds. We boasted, exaggerating our adventures beyond any shadow of the truth, and chasing the fine soft ladies around the chaise longues and gilt-topped tables. To our great surprise and delight, they seemed greatly pleased by our attentions.

In ordinary times such grand and dainty dames would not have spat on us had our moustaches been afire. Pepi poured another glass of the sweet French liquor. The comrades were flying higher than the moon by now. One of Pepi's gilded ladies leaned on my shoulder and another clutched at my elbow. Their gentle, high voices were sweeter than the sirens singing to old Odysseus, tied to the mast of his ship.

"He's here!" the crowd roared, "The Commander!"

Bowing to the ladies and doffing our czapkas, we took our leave. We formed up and marched across to the western side of the market square. There we took our place beside our Commander, and his officers, newly returned from exile. The Commander wore the national costume, a blue jacket, red trousers, and a white sukmana, with a peacock feather in his red czapka. He stood, surrounded by the blue and silver of the infantry and the green, black and gold of the artillerymen, at the centre of the market square. The banners of the guilds billowed in the spring breeze, beside placards proclaiming

'Equality and Freedom' and 'For Krakow and the Motherland'!

There the Commander took the solemn oath – the Act of Insurrection of the Citizens and Inhabitants of the Palatinate of Krakow –

"I, Tadeusz Kościuczko, swear before God and to the whole Polish nation, that I shall employ the authority vested in me for the integrity of the frontiers, for gaining national self-rule and for the foundation of general liberty, and not for private benefit. So help me, Lord God, and the innocent suffering of Thy Son!"

Here was the whole nation, or so it seemed, crowded together in one market square, and in arms. The Commander led us into the Cathedral, the Church of the Holy Virgin, with its bugler in the tower. It was a sombre, gothic church. Serried ranks of warriors processed solemnly through the doors with their lances, swords, and guns held up before them like holy banners. We passed over the threshold, tucking our czapkas under our arms, and making the sign of the cross in the air before us. Though plain and austere without, the church was richly ornamented within. All around were golden scrolls and scallop shells, red, black and golden seals, golden crosses starred with beams of light, mermaids, roses, and fleurs-de-lis. Stone columns of gold and black marble soared up to the heavens, glittering like spears. High above our bare heads the vault of the ceiling was blue as the Virgin's veil, studded with gold bosses. Thickets of guttering candles cast a golden glow over the gilded tombs and monuments of the saints and martyrs and kings.

We took our turn in line and knelt before the magnificent wooden altar. The priests blessed our sabres, lances, and guns. Rosary beads clicked against the hilts of swords. Holy water splashed our faces, mingling with the sweat. Above our heads the censer swung on black chains, and clouds of incense swirled through the air. Beside the altar and the host, the chalice gleamed like a silver sword. The bell was rung and we averted our eyes. We ate the body and drank the blood of Christ. The Lord Be With You.

A spectral company of angels and bearded apostles stood in fine array on that great wooden triptych. It seemed that their crooks and staves were golden lances, with fluttering golden pennants, that this heavenly army was rallying to defend our souls, as our temporal army rallied to defend our sacred soil, our families, and our language.

At last we found ourselves out in the square. It was cold dusk, with the Hejnal resounding once more, our heads dazzled with wine and eternity.

"Soldiers!"

It was the Commander. He was riding a white horse, with the feathers still flying in his cap. With him were Pepi and Dabrowski – who were now General Poniatowski and Lieutenant-General Dabrowski, at the Commander's order. Beside the three generals was an unruly mob of peasants armed with scythes.

"Orders, gentlemen," said the old lion, calmly. He pointed at Cyprian.

"Captain Godebski – Warsaw remains in Russian hands. You know what to do."

Godebski saluted, and departed.

"Comrade engineer – you will remain here and fortify Krakow."

Sierawski beamed with delight. "I will defend it to the death, Commander!"

"Blow it sky-high if you must," the Commander shrugged. Sierawski's face fell in horror.

"Next, Tanski – the best lancer in all Poland, so they say. Well, comrade, you have a chance to live up to your reputation. You will take Blumer's horsemen here and join Dabrowski's cavalry corps."

My cavalry brigade was gone! I was incensed. Then I saw the peasants, and I began to apprehend the extent of my misfortune. Well, as they say, one minute you're riding the horse, and the next minute, you're under it.

"Lieutenant Blumer – this is your new command. The First People's Brigade. If anyone can keep these peasants under control, it's you, son. You're wasted in the cavalry. Cavalry wins battles, but the infantry wins wars!" the Commander said to me. It had almost been worth leaving the cavalry to hear him say that. *Almost*. Lieutenant Blumer!

A promotion, and a command, by God. If you could call it that. But at what cost! I was now in the *infantry*. I cast a wary eye over my new brigade of irregular soldiers – that is, armed peasants.

"They're not exactly the grenadiers, Commander, but they will do," I replied.

CHAPTER SIXTEEN
THE SCYTHEMEN,
RACLAWICE, 4 APRIL 1794

It was a glorious morning. Our army was at Prayer on the redoubt. We sang the Bogurodzica, our battle hymn –

"Oh Mother of God, Oh Virgin,
Mary, blessed by God,
Your Son, our Lord,
Mary, chosen Mother,
Return to us, bestow upon us.
May the Lord have mercy.
For the sake of thy Baptist, oh Son of God,
Hear our voices, fulfil mankind's thoughts.
Hear the prayer which we offer
And grant us what we ask of him –
A prosperous stay on earth
And paradise in the hereafter.
May the Lord have mercy.

Amen!"

The Commander had chosen his ground well. We had marched south a few miles from Krakow to meet the first Russian army that was sent against us. Here, at the redoubt at Raclawice, we met them as they came at us from the east.

All across the field, ranks of soldiers and peasant volunteers knelt in the wet grass, jewelled with the morning dew. We crossed ourselves, and then we stood. The peasants put their red caps back on their heads and shouldered their war-scythes – scythes with the blades pointed up – and pikes. This rabble of a few hundred peasants (my rabble) were mostly dressed in the sukmana, and the traditional garb of Lesser Poland. Under their white overcoats they wore their Sunday best, as if they were going to Church.

The raddled old village Hetman shambled over and doffed his red cap from his bald head. His belt was on the last hole and his ample gut hung over his trousers, bulging out his kontusz. Neither he nor any of my men had swords, let alone firearms, only scythes and pikes. Many were barefoot.

I saluted the Hetman crisply, my back ramrod-straight. This parody of military discipline was entirely ridiculous, but my new peasant soldiers were greatly impressed by it. There had been a great deal of work to be done, in a short space of time. I had drilled them until their feet bled, and then we had marched out of Krakow alongside the Commander's regulars a week later. Three years ago I was a cadet. Now I was a veteran, a leader of men.

My ragged brigade had many shortcomings, but we had plenty of camp followers. Swarms of women followed the army to cook and fuss over us, like surrogate mothers – and, in some cases, substitute wives. Lambs lying down with wolves. One of them was the daughter of this sly old Hetman. She had set her cap at me, poor deluded creature. To these poor peasants, a lieutenant was a great man. Not a great lord, true, but a lord nonetheless – and a lord who, judging by his threadbare socks and empty pockets, was within the grasp of their matchmaking womenfolk. To be idolised made a curious change from being sneered at.

The old Hetman hawked on the trampled grass and studied the results intently, as if reading the outcome of the battle in his spittle. This done, he blew his nose on the sleeve of his sukmana and grinned up through a gap-toothed mouth. The old goat must have had prodigious loins. A third of my brigade seemed to be composed of his sons, and many of our camp wenches seemed to be his daughters. Tanski reckoned he had his crafty eye on me for a son-in-law.

I was caught between this prospect and the Russians. With any luck I would be dead by the end of the day, and that would be that. In the midst of these thoughts, our scouts came scurrying back to our lines. One of the old Hetman's infinite brood made his report to me.

"How many Russians?" I asked. He held up four fingers and grinned. Four thousand.

"The same as us, then – a fair fight!" I lied, loudly and confidently. My falsehood had the desired result. He and the men cackled with glee and drew their fingers across their throats, brandishing their wicked-looking scythes.

Of course it would not be a fair fight – it never was. I've never had a fair fight to this day, not in twenty years of soldiering. We had come to regard being outnumbered by anything less than three to one as a luxury. Yet this was to be the closest to a fair match I had ever known. Four thousand Russian regulars were coming. Our Commander had indeed gathered about four thousand men to stand against them, but only half of these were regular soldiers. The rest were peasant volunteers, like my men. These had been divided into People's Brigades, like mine.

My brigade was about two hundred peasants strong, but the numbers changed hour by hour. For every volunteer who came in, a deserter or a malingerer snuck out.

As for the Russians, here came their four thousand regulars, row upon row. They came marching up the hill in perfect order. Their great bulbous hats, shaped like tulip petals, were bobbing on their heads in unison. Above them flew the golden banner of the two-headed black eagle. Behind them, a row of black cannon, spitting smoke and flame like dragons.

"Here they come!" I called. Already my front rank was beginning to range forward, and lose their shape. I had to constantly walk back and forth up and down the rank, cuffing and collaring the men back in line. "Keep in line!"

Tanski came hurtling by on his charger, leading a string of lancers. My heart filled with pride and jealousy at the sight.

"Ho! It's Blumer the schoolmaster!" he called, and the insult stung. Then, in spite of myself, and in spite of the bullets and cannonballs that by now were whistling overhead, I had to laugh. For I did indeed look like a teacher struggling with a class of unruly pupils. "Are you teaching these villagers the mazurka, Blumer?" Tanski smirked.

With the most perfect timing, the Hetman's daughter darted out from the ranks. She was a pale, green-eyed creature, willow-thin, and clutching some gift for me. Her father, crafty as ever, let her go – he had plenty of other daughters should she be cut down by a bullet, after all.

Agatha (for such was the lass's name) gazed with awe at Tanski, on his horse, with his lance and pennant. She curtsied as if to a knight. Tanski doffed his czapka and bowed from the saddle. I could see her affections were wavering. Even though I had no great attachment to her, jealousy burned.

"Agatha," I said, with exquisite pleasure, "this is Warrant Officer Tanski. Salute when you address a Lieutenant, Tanski." Tanski blushed to his boots, and I delighted in his discomfort. He saluted, reluctantly, and said "Yes – Sir" through gritted teeth. Music to my ears! Bullets and bayonets were quite forgotten. Ears turning crimson, he wheeled away with his squadron towards the Russians.

Lead whipped over our heads. Eerie chants and drums followed the bullets on the wind.

"Get out of here, sweetheart," I spoke, softly for once. My throat was hoarse from bellowing orders. She pressed a bundle into my hand, and ran. I never saw her again. It was a loaf of bread, wrapped in a scarf. I wound the scarf around my arm. If

I could not ride to war on my steed, like a knight, then I should at least wear a lady's favours, like one. Before us was our foe. Endless grey-clad ranks of Russian soldiers. Black eagles glittered on gold flags. Behind me I felt the men's hackles rise. I heard their furious shouts as they beat their war-scythes on the ground. The old Hetman was at my elbow, begging me to charge. I sent him packing, before stalking up and down the line, pistol in hand.

"Stand your ground!" This was the order. It was simple. Beneath our feet, the ground slid down in a gentle slope towards the Russians. A gentle slope, until a man tried to run up it with musket in hand and a heavy knapsack on his back, that is. Our Commander had chosen this position well. Behind us, higher still, rose our redoubt.

At the foot of the slope I saw a Russian lieutenant – my opposite number, I presumed. With deliberate care the Russian conscripts drew up to face us, like partners at a dance. As a professional, I envied him his disciplined rank of surly slaves. Leading my men was like saddling cows. But as a man, my heart swelled with pride at the thought that I led free men, volunteers.

Respectfully, I doffed my cap to this Russian. I had not yet drawn my sword. Our eyes met. We were but a hundred yards away from each other. He sneered as he ordered his men to line up for the volley. He fully expected that we would break when they opened up, and scatter like a flock of birds.

I walked up and down the line again. My fear was not that the men would run. I saw their high temper, their murderous rage. They would not run, not today, not from all the devils in hell. No – I feared they would charge *too soon*. That would be a disaster. We had to charge after the Russians had fired, otherwise we would run into a hail of lead.

"Will you fire first, Lachy?" he called, sardonically, knowing full well that we had no muskets. All around him, his men were busy with ramrods and powder flasks.

"After you, Sir!" I bawled back, for I never forget my manners.

"Damn it, my lord!" yelled the old Hetman, brandishing his scythe. "Do we charge?"

"NOT YET! Stand your ground!" I roared at him. "Fire, damn you!" I implored the Russians, for I could hold this tide back no longer. Then at last, at long last, the Russians fired up the slope. The sky exploded with a great clatter of bangs, like hammers clashing on stone. A cloud of grey smoke hung over the grey jackets, like a pall of incense over orthodox monks. Bullets plucked at my hat and coat without touching me. All around, men were falling, cursing, weeping. Yet not so many. Perhaps only a dozen. Even of those few, some regained their feet. Cursing in panic, they ransacked their clothes to find the wound. A stain like wine was stretching over the old Hetman's white sukmana. He appeared oblivious.
"Bad shots," he muttered, shaking his head.

Muskets were poor things in those days, all sound and fury, signifying nothing. Guns were hopelessly inaccurate in my day. Even at short range, bullets flew hither and yon, like sparrows. They rarely came anywhere near their mark, except at point-blank range. If the muskets fired at all, that is, for misfires and half-cocks were common. This was why the infantry gathered together for a volley, for by that means at least some of the bullets should hit, by the law of averages.

My men roared like caged beasts, but still they held their line. With slow, deliberate care, not once taking my eyes from the Russian lieutenant, I drew my sword, and brought it chopping down over my head. Steel is surer than lead, comrade!

We charged across that hallowed ground at Raclawice, bearing down on our foes like the wrath of God. In the front rank, the grey-coated dogs were in disarray, frantically trying to reload. A musket is in excess of five feet long. Reloading is slow and cumbersome. First they had to clear their barrel of spent powder, then pour in fresh powder from their flasks, and finally the wad and the bullet. All this with tired, shaking hands, in the teeth of the wind, and with a mob of baying, armed peasants hurtling down the slope at you!

My scythemen tore into the dogs with great violence, as their pent-up fury exploded. Our foes did not run but stood and were butchered to a man. I saw the proud lieutenant cut to ribbons, his head struck clean from his shoulders. It rolled across the ground like a drum, eyes wide open. Scythes clashed against swords and bayonets. Screams rent the air. Dust and smoke rose up from the trampled soil. Guns discharged, haphazardly. On came the scythemen, yelling, wild, swinging their weapons, to and fro, and the Russian conscripts falling, clutching great wounds, calling on God, Mother –

"Onwards! On to the cannon!" came the cry. For these infantry were not our object. They merely stood between us and it. We surged for the cannon, our flag fluttering before us. My Hetman reached the cannon first, and laid his cap across the barrel.

"Mine!" he roared at the astonished gunners, who were cowering behind the gun carriage. A grey figure with an axe confronted him. I shot the Russian in the head at point-blank range – the only range you can trust a pistol at. His blood splashed my face and he crumpled to the soil. Moments later, the old Hetman and two of his cronies dragged a terrified Russian artilleryman from under the cannon's wheel. I watched as they cut him apart like a side of mutton, but I said nothing. Fortunes of war.

The men leapt jubilantly onto the cannon and planted a flag in the ground. All around was a scene of utter carnage. Upturned carts and caissons, disembowelled horses rolling around in their own entrails, dead men strewn about with severed limbs. Abandoned weapons, clothes, hats, medals, badges, blankets, and any number of discarded items were lying in the grass. All around and down the slope the Russian

126

dogs were running. With grim satisfaction, we watched them. They were tossing aside their muskets, hats, knapsacks, sabres, and even their greatcoats as they did so.

But where was our cavalry? Where was our pursuit? We, the victors, were as exhausted as the enemy. As the scythemen cheered, wild with bloodlust, all that I could think was – *can we afford another such victory?*

CHAPTER SEVENTEEN

WARSAW, 7 SEPTEMBER 1794

My little regiment, decimated in a dozen skirmishes, disbanded of its own accord. Most of the peasant volunteers were dead. The pitiful few who remained I sent home to the harvest. Madame L heard of this, God knows how, and she sent for me to stand as her guard dog. She said it would keep me out of trouble.

Thus I found myself in Warsaw, in September in the Year of Our Lord 1794. Our many enemies soon caught up with us. We were besieged from the west by the Prussians, and from the east by the Russians. Cannon bombarded us throughout the day. Barricades were raised across the streets. The citizens huddled in cellars and churches. It was the middle of the night, and beyond the city a thousand enemy campfires burned in the darkness. September was bleak. The crescent moon hung like a sabre over our heads.

Madame, as a Castellan, or Military Governor, supplied us with guns, bullets, food, shelter, and pay. She had spies everywhere, and she gave orders. Her grand mansion house was a fortress and a barracks. I had a nice perch on one of the lower floors, in a hallway. I had a plump leather armchair and there I sat, all day long, my gun across my knees, watching the street below. From this vantage point I could see everyone who came and went from Madame's house. There were some fine comings and goings, too, for the wives of many of the senior officers were billeted in the upper floors.

That night, stones skittered against the shutters. I cautiously peered out, keeping my face hidden in the shadows. Down in the street below, a poet proclaimed his love to a lady, and paid court to her. Warsaw was under siege, but in turn the suitor laid siege to his inamorata. A lot of this sort of thing went on at Madame's house. The war had changed much, but not everything. I listened as the latest besotted fool recited poetry beneath the window.

"Night, and in a serene sky the moon was incandescent amidst the fainter stars,
When you, about to flout the name of the great Gods,
Were swearing your solemn oath..."

"Bravo, Cyprian!" I clapped, leaning out of the window. It was my dear friend, the poet. "Much better than your usual drivel. Why, that was almost as good as Horace's poem, Epode Number Fifteen."

Cyprian glared up. The moonlight reflected on his balding temples. He had a dog-eared copy of Horace's Epodes in his hand, which he tried guiltily to conceal behind his back.

"Damn it! I've been serenading a great hairy-arsed Podolian!" he griped angrily. "No matter! Have you any vodka, Blumer? I'm bloody freezing!"

I ordered the servants to unbar the door. From my perch at the top of the stairs I watched as Godebski squeezed through the gate. As soon as he was within, the anxious servants threw the bolts and barred the door with heavy timbers. We embraced, for we had not seen each other since that glorious day in Krakow in the Market Square. To chase the cold away I produced a bottle of true water, and we drank. Our pistols lay beside it on the table.

"What are you doing here?" Cyprian demanded. "You're not after her too, are you?" he said suspiciously, for he was ever on the alert for rivals for his beloved's affections – real or imaginary. I merely laughed.

"Not a chance! She's as vicious as a she-wolf! No, you are welcome to her, comrade. I am but Madame's sentry. What about you? Are you here to woo the dread lady?"

Godebski grinned, "Why, yes, I am Madame's man, too, my heart and soul! I have the misfortune to be in love with my superior officer! I carry out her orders. It is all cloak and dagger."

"I'll wager there is more dagger than cloak where Madame is involved," I said.

"She is a formidable lady," Godebski agreed. "You should have seen her during the Warsaw Uprising, back in April. By God, she was in her element – the goddess of wrath!" He sat back in my chair, put his feet on the table, and lit his pipe. "Easter week was full of rumours of what the Russian garrison were going to do. It was feared they would murder the people while they were at prayer."

"Let me guess," I said, "Madame decided to act first."

"Indeed she did!" Godebski laughed. "Thus, on Easter Thursday[3] our men, and the city mob, led by the Guild of Slaughterers, took the Russians by surprise. Their spikes and axes lent a fine professional air to the business, I can tell you. We massacred every one of them we could lay our hands on."

"God rest their souls," I said facetiously, crossing myself. "Still, the Russians have a lot of people, I suppose, they won't miss 'em. What then?"

"Then we rounded up all the traitors we could find and hanged them on the spot. Your friend Bishop Massalski was dancing from a lamp post, the last time I saw him."

"*Sto lat!* Cheers!" We drank to a job well done.

"So you see, Madame drove the Russians from the capital," Godebski concluded. "But no sooner were we rid of them, than the accursed Prussians had laid siege to Warsaw, from the other side!"

"Now the Russians are back, as well," I observed.

"Aren't they always?" Godebski said, grimacing. Then he cast around him, as if Madame might be hiding in a cupboard.

---

[3] *17 April 1794*

"You must know everything that goes on in this house," Godebski said craftily. "Is she here, then?" he asked, eagerly. I shook my head.

"No, she is not. She is away with one of her, ah, officers," I said, and I coughed, trying to be as delicate as I could. Godebski's face fell. He buried his head in his hands.

"It's that infernal Tremo, isn't it?"

"I'm sorry," I said softly, placing a hand on my friend's shoulder. "She's infatuated with him. Why, she's even knitted him a pair of socks."

"Damn it!" Cyprian slammed his glass onto the table and flew into a rage. "She knitted him socks? A woman of her breeding, knitting socks for a lousy cook's son! Damn that infernal, confounded –" and here he said a great many more things, which I shall not repeat, pertaining to poor Elias Tremo and his ladylove. The gist of them, you will gather, was prejudicial and slanderous in the extreme. After a few moments, he pulled himself together.

"Look here, Blumer," he said, leaping up, "young Sierawski is in the trenches in Wola, and he needs some grenades. Could you lend me a dozen or so? I might as well get myself killed and be done with it!"

"Madame has some in the cellar. Follow me, Captain!"

We set off unsteadily down the stairs, having finished the vodka. Madame always provided plenty of vodka, so her men always fought like starving wolves. At the foot of the stairs were crates of bullets, and beside them, muskets stacked in a tripod. We passed by them and along a corridor to a drawing room.

"Quiet, here, comrade – this is our hospital. Don't trip up on any buckets," I admonished him. We tiptoed through a wood-panelled room with parquet floors. All around were sleeping bodies, huddled on the floor, lying on and underneath the tables. Injured men lay swathed in bandages, fitfully asleep. Some were missing arms or legs. Here and there were buckets for the large and small needs of the patients, who were too ill to venture out to the latrines. A lady nurse glared at us and we whispered our apologies and hurried by.

"It takes a lot of organising, this war business," I reflected. "Madame arms us, and feeds us, and she even heals us. I've learned more about war from that woman than I ever did at the academy."

"Yes," Godebski mused. "It's like the theatre – all the hard work goes on behind the scenes. All we poor actors can do is speak our lines and play our parts."

"And take our exit when the curtain falls," I agreed.

We set off down into the cellar. I took Godebski's pipe from him and placed it on a sideboard, and then opened the heavy oak door.

"Why, it's as dark as Hades down there!" Godebski complained. "Have you no lamp?"

"That cellar is no place for a naked flame," I replied. "One spark would blow this whole house to kingdom come."

We set off, cautiously, down the steps, fumbling at the banister. There was not a single light in the whole cellar. The glow from the open doorway cast a faint luminescence. At the foot of the stairs one could dimly perceive dozens of heavy wooden boxes. Gunpowder. We struggled in the stygian gloom, bumping into each other, tripping over, and barking our shins on the crates. At last, we found the grenades. With difficulty, we dragged them back towards the stairs.

"By God, this is thirsty work," I grumbled. I paused by the foot of the stairs to purloin another bottle of vodka. For this was the wine cellar, after all, and there was still some good liquor to be had down there. Even so, this powder magazine was not a place to tarry, and we heaved the box of bombs up the stairs as fast as we dared. With great relief, we shut the heavy door behind us, barred it, and put down the box in the hallway. There we pried it open and peered at the grenades, which were packed in straw. They were little metal balls, shiny and black. A few dozen of them were nestled amongst the straw, as innocent as hen's eggs or Christmas baubles.

"What a pretty bunch of little *pisanki*," I said, with a shudder. "Here," I said to Cyprian, passing him a leather saddlebag. "We can carry these bloody things in these satchels."

"*We?*" Cyprian asked, surprised. "But what about your sentry post? What about Madame's orders?"

"The hell with Madame," I growled, hefting one of the bags of grenades onto my shoulder. "What she doesn't know won't hurt her."

"Are you sure?" Cyprian stared at me doubtfully.

"Don't be such a milksop, Cyprian!" I said, "Madame can look after herself. Anyway, I told you, she's quite safe – she's with Elias Tremo. He's a bloody captain now, did you know?"

"To hell with her!" Cyprian agreed, angrily. "Let's go!"

A clock on the wall chimed. It was four in the morning. Cyprian picked up his czapka and his pistols, dusted down his book of poems, and stuffed it into his knapsack. Then he too hefted the other saddlebag full of grenades onto his shoulders. The servants unlocked the gate, and we were off.

"I was bored to death in that house, sitting on my arse," I told Cyprian. "A moonlit walk to Wola will be delightful."

CHAPTER EIGHTEEN
WOLA, 8 SEPTEMBER 1794

The walk to Wola was frightful. We had drunk plenty of vodka as usual, but the cold September wind wrung us sober all too quickly, and we struggled under our deadly burden through the deserted streets. I was beginning to think better of my bravado.

"I don't care much for this," I grumbled. "One spark, and there won't be anything left of us to bury. I prefer cold steel, myself, to these infernal devices."

I have never been fond of grenades. These crude bombs are metal flasks full of bullets, nails, scrap iron and gunpowder, with a fuse dangling like a ribbon from the top. Godebski grinned. Horrified, I watched him take out his pipe and flint.

"Stop grumbling and have a smoke!" Cyprian grinned.

"Damn it, Cyprian!" I snapped. He laughed and put away his tobacco. Despite the gloom, the moonlight lit up his lugubrious features. Much as I admired my dear friend, he was hardly an Adonis. His head was too large, for one thing. His receding, greying hair, which he fancied made him look distinguished, simply made him look old. His huge ears stuck out like saucepans. His big, fleshy lips spoke of passions too earthly for our chaste Polish ladies. Still, he had the heart of a lion, and he was a gentleman. I pitied him his plight, which was so hopeless as to make our impossible war seem a fair fight. For Madame had chosen the dashing young Captain Elias Tremo, who was aide-de-camp to General Dabrowski, and a man with a future. And that was that. Godebski was outgunned.

"I never stood a chance against that boy Tremo," Godebski admitted. "Madame L is a good Catholic. Very devout. She won't have anything to do with me, because I am divorced from my wife. I'm an outcast, my friend. No decent woman will have me."

I commiserated with him. "Plenty more fish in the river, old boy. Anyway, I shouldn't trouble yourself about decent women. We'll get you a French girl instead!"

I heard Godebski's mind ticking like the clock in Madame's hallway.

"What a fine idea, comrade! I may take you at your word!" Godebski rubbed his hands with glee and perked up immensely.

"Now then, come on, boy – let's chase these Prussian scoundrels back to Valmy Ridge, and then take our pick of the Parisiennes!"

Dawn was breaking as we reached Wola. Paris itself is a mere thousand miles further west, beyond Valmy Ridge, where the fanatical French Revolutionary army had kicked the Prussians arses up in the air for them, back in 1792.

"Here we are," Godebski exclaimed, "the Field of the Electors."

"Devil take this accursed place," I spat. The Field of the Electors was in Wola, a large and fashionable suburb at the west end of Warsaw. For the last three hundred years Poland had chosen Her Kings here. At our last election, Catherine of Russia had foisted her chosen candidate upon us – the Bullock. His election had been won with gold and lead, for where bribes fail, bullets prevail. Thus we had been saddled with our traitor king, and set on our road to ruin.

We stepped from the shadows onto the open field. A gentle incline ran downhill from beneath our feet. Where the incline ended one could see the outline of a wooden pavilion. Half of it had been torn down. The campfires of Prussian troops smouldered around it, for they burned our buildings to cook their sausages.

"I vote we do battle with these Prussians," I said. In reply, there was a colossal explosion from a battery of Prussian cannon. We hurled ourselves into a nearby trench, and kissed the dirt. Behind the trench was a handsome red brick townhouse. It had taken the full force of the blast. We watched as the facade began to crumble, with an awful, yawning noise, like the tearing of silk. A great cloud of black dust rose up in the air. Then I felt a knife at my throat. We were surrounded.

"Time to die, Prussian pigs!" an officer hissed. Then he grinned. It was Sierawski. He sheathed his dagger. "It's alright, boys, they're ours," Sierawski told his engineers.

In one corner of the trench was a pikestaff. Our flag, the white eagle, hung from it. There were a dozen of our comrades holding this trench and they were a sorry sight indeed. Sierawski himself wore rags barely recognisable as clothing, let alone a uniform. He was covered from head to foot in mud. His eyes were wild and he appeared to have a woman's nightcap on his head. He and his men had dug this earth rampart and they had been living in it for weeks, like human moles.

"Where are the reinforcements, Captain?" he demanded.

Godebski grinned and pointed at me. "Here we are!"

"What? Two of you?" Sierawski gestured wildly at the Prussian lines. "Out there," he raved, "is the most professional army the world has ever seen. They outnumber us more than five to one! I have no cannon – what am I supposed to do? Fend them off with my farts?"

"Your farts could clear a barnyard," I retorted. "Anyway, cheer up. We have brought vodka for you and your lads, and some grenades."

Abruptly, his demeanour changed, as I passed him the bottle. "Ah! Vodka! That's a different matter! Welcome to Wola, comrades!"

We handed out the grenades, and tapers to light the fuses. No sooner had we done so, than the Prussian bugles sounded. As if summoned by some evil magician, a cohort of Prussian soldiers, muskets shouldered and colours flying, stepped out of their trenches, and began to march across the Electors' Field towards us. On they came, marching in perfect order under their banner, red, black, and gold, with a black eagle. There was almost a battalion of them, perhaps sixty men strong, and they were a formidable sight. We could see their immaculate blue uniforms, the plumes in their hats, and the gleam of their swords and bayonets. We could hear the stamp of their leather boots and the beat of their drums.

Halfway across the field they halted. Their bugler sounded a signal and they aimed their muskets. They were forming up to give us a volley. We kissed the dirt again. Bullets whined over our heads like a thousand devils. Before they could reload, we lit our bombs and flung them into the ranks of oncoming Prussians. The grenades ignited with awful roars, blinding red flashes and plumes of thick grey smoke. It was a volcano of fire. The Electors' Field burned like the slopes of Mount Etna. The first rank died where they stood. The second rank of Prussians faltered, but did not break.

"To sword, comrades!" Cyprian roared, climbing up out of the trench – "Charge!"

We followed him, roaring like madmen. It must have been unbelievable for the Prussians. They stood facing us, their muskets discharged. Caught in the act of reloading – caught with their trousers down – the Prussian soldiers were struggling manfully with their clumsy ramrods, powder flasks, and wad cutters.

We hurled more bombs among them and followed up with a charge, bayonets and sabres swinging. Our bombs took a dreadful toll on our enemy, blasting them off their feet like skittles, tearing through the ranks like an iron fist. A stink of shit and sulphur filled the air. Grey coated soldiers lay all about, crumpled, in heaps. Wounded and dying men groaned and shrieked, shouted, whimpered, and pleaded. The ground was strewn with discarded swords, muskets, bandoliers, boots, knapsacks and kit.

Ahead, I saw Cyprian, bellowing like a bull, as he slashed left and right with his sabre. There was no time to help him. A knot of Prussians ran at me. I was amazed at their discipline, to have held firm after our devastating barrage of grenades. I had not yet fired my musket, and so I discharged it at them. I saw a man fall and then the others were spectres, fleeing through gunpowder smoke.

At last, they had had enough, and they fell back, but in good order, to their lines. Now it was our turn to retreat.

"Fall back, fall back!" Cyprian called, calm as you like. Our killing frenzy was over. It had evaporated as soon as it had begun, like a pan of water boiling over. So we fell back, snatching up a few weapons and cartridge belts as we did so. We scrambled back into our trench, the Prussian sharpshooters sniping after us as we went. Across the field we heard a bugle call. By now, we knew the Prussian signals as well as we did our own. They were calling 'Advance'.

"Out of this trench!" Sierawski called, "retreat! If we stay here, they'll catch us like rats! Go! Go!" he shouted, clouting us with the flat of his sword – for now he had a sword in his hand, and not a dagger, a strange German sabre, with a gold pompom hanging from it, like a curtain pull.

"To the house!" he called, pointing to the ruined house, the very same that had been wrecked by the Prussian artillery. At that time I had no experience of sieges and street fighting, but even I could see the sense in putting this ruined rampart betwixt us and the Prussian guns. Lead buzzed off the walls like angry bumblebees. We scrambled through the ruined doorway and into the hall of what had once been a grand townhouse, home of a rich merchant, doctor, or lawyer. A cockeyed crucifix hung in the hall, beneath it, a tumbled grandfather clock spilled its springs. God Bless This House, said a tapestry on the wall.

Heaps of broken bricks, masonry and stonework, and tangled beams spilled in all directions, as if the house had been poured down a hill. At the broken windows of the front parlour we paused. A walnut table was set with bread, ham, cheese and salt. On one wall was a portrait of a smiling old basia, with her husband beside her. Opposite and facing them was a picture of the Holy Virgin, the Black Madonna of Czestochowa. It stood above a long walnut sideboard decorated with trophies and ornaments. Crystal, fine china, gold and silver plate, all cracked, and broken, beyond repair. A fine shroud of white dust lay on everything, like a layer of icing on a cake.

Cyprian took up position next to the stern old wife. Above us the ceiling swelled alarmingly, like the sail of a ship in a storm. A chandelier hung from it like a bunch of golden grapes. Hurriedly, we swept the last of the broken glass from the lintels and the window frames with our swords.

Outside, the Prussians came on. Dread footsteps, like the golem, slow, implacable, never faltering. I could see their white faces streaked with black powder, their shining bayonets, their gleaming blue uniforms, hear the creak of their leather cross belts and boots.

I bowed to the Virgin, the Queen of Poland, and crossed myself. Godebski and I drew our pistols, like duellists.

"God bless this house," I said.

The first Prussian was a blond giant of a man and he came out of nowhere, clad in their damnable grey-blue. I desperately parried his thrust with my sword, his bayonet catching on the hilt, and twisted it aside. With desperate strength I struck him full in the face with the brass hilt of my cavalry pistol, like a club. He staggered, and Godebski ran him through the body with his sword.

"They are coming in the windows!" someone called. Another blue figure was crouched on the wide sill, armed with a pistol and a firebrand – they meant now to burn us out.

Godebski calmly shot the figure through the forehead with his second pistol, then roughly shoved the man's body back out, where it tumbled amongst his comrades in a chaos of shots and shouts.

But the brand had tumbled to the floor. A shower of sparks touched the parquet, the rugs, and the velvet curtains. Consumed by the fire's ardour, red tongues bloomed. Crimson mushrooms spread up the wood panelled walls, the curtains, the floors and ceiling. Black smoke billowed. Blue devils clambered resolutely through the smoke and into the inferno.

We ran back to the hallway, where Sierawski was holding off a Prussian soldier armed with an axe. Godebski swung a backhanded cut at the base of the man's spine, and he collapsed, with a scream of shock, like a girl soaked in cold water on Easter Monday.

"OUT!" Godebski ordered, unflustered, picking up the axe from the floor and hefting it. More of the dogs were at the door, running up the stairs, coming in the windows. Godebski flung the axe at them and we fled through the kitchen. I remembered the ham in the front parlour and sure enough, there was a haunch on a chopping block on the kitchen table, which I grabbed and shoved in my pocket. Eat, or be eaten.

We scrambled out of the back door and into the fresh air. We gulped it down like vodka and coughed like invalids. This was the house's stable-yard.

"Horses!" Godebski shouted. "We're saved!"

"A horse! A horse!" I cried, "The Republic for a horse!" and Cyprian and I fell into fits of giggles. For the horses were long gone, leaving behind only the evil savour of horse piss lingering in rotted straw. In front of us the ruined house folded up like a burning haystack, and collapsed in upon itself. I laughed, and took a bite of the ham. It tasted glorious. Sierawski and his men were reloading their pistols and muskets.

"Are you too grand to reload, Lieutenant Blumer?" Sierawski shouted, as he struggled to load an unfamiliar Prussian gun. "Or will you have your butler do it for you?"

"I have no bullets, Comrade Engineer," I shrugged, "and no musket either, come to that."

"Here!" Sierawski snapped, flinging me my own musket that he had somehow salvaged from the carnage. "You should take better care of that thing."

All around us we heard the Prussians gathering like wolves. We reloaded – a slow, clumsy process. At any moment I expected the Prussians to throw themselves upon us. That stable block should have been our execution yard. There were only five of us remaining.

"We are surrounded," Godebski said. "Gentlemen, it has been a privilege. Those of you who survive the first charge have my permission to surrender, with honour."

"For my part I intend to do the honourable thing and die," I said. I had finished the ham and it is very easy to be brave on a full stomach.

"Excuse me, Captain Godebski," Sierawski butted in, "these are my men! It is up to me to give the orders."

"What, these are your men, Lieutenant? Both of them?" Cyprian sneered, pointing at the last two surviving engineers. "Very well, then, what are your orders? How will you deploy your vast battalion, Lieutenant Sierawski? Shall we flank the Prussians, then?"

"Since when were you made a lieutenant?" I demanded of Sierawski, greatly piqued that I no longer outranked him. We began to bicker amongst ourselves.

Then we heard the chorus of angels. Bugles rang. God be praised."My dear Sirs," Sierawski said, "the tables are turned. It is our foe who is surrounded, and not us. It is our cavalry."

At that, two figures came thundering into the courtyard, elated with victory. One was a tall general with a moustache and tight, curly yellow hair, like a sheep. The second was our old friend, Tanski.

"Warrant Officer Tanski!" I cried, "So good of you to make it!"

"Lieutenant Tanski, of the cavalry, if you please," said Tanski, astride his shining grey mare, pirouetting and caracoling, twirling his lance like a wand. I cursed, silently.

"Who is this?" said the general.

"General Zayonczek, this is Lieutenant Blumer, of the *infantry*," Tanski said, grinning from ear to ear. I could have cut his throat!

CHAPTER NINETEEN
GENERAL ZAYONCZEK
AND GENERAL DABROWSKI

General Zayonczek's troop of cavalry had encircled the Prussians during the fight in the house, taking a few prisoner, and chasing off the rest. We searched the prisoners and relieved them of their guns. Not five minutes ago they had been trying with all their might to kill us. Now they were sullen and angry, for the tables were turned.

"This one's an officer," I said, regarding a tall, haughty Von Something, his face a patchwork of duelling scars, his barrel chest beribboned, his handmade boots gleaming like mirrors, except at the knees, where they were brown with fresh mud. He had a small rash of gashes over his forehead that he was allowing, ostentatiously, to spill red dewdrops of blood over his face and uniform, and to collect on his shirt and handkerchief. It was not much – the thump I had fetched Tanski on the Third of May was far worse, and he had slept it off by morning. The Prussian officer had been caught hiding under a privet hedge, while his men died bravely in droves.

"Your name, Sir?" I asked politely, for the forms had to be observed. Inside I was itching to give him a few good swipes across the jaw.

"I am Colonel Hermann Von Boyen," he replied sullenly. We could converse, this Prussian and I, for we both spoke French, as all gentlemen did in those days. Obviously I took his pistol from him. This he gave up without demur. It was an excellent pistol, too, with a carved handle and a barrel chased in German silver. I sold it later for a bottle of vodka. But the Prussian Colonel's wallet, watch, decorations, medals, and other effects were of course sacrosanct. Indeed, captured officers did not have to give up their swords, so long as they gave their word to behave themselves.

All nations – even the Prussians – abided by the Rules of War. Only Russia did not.

"You may retain your sword upon your parole of good conduct until the war is over, or you are released," I said, according to the custom.

"You have my word," he said sullenly, through gritted teeth, as he was led off with the other prisoners.

"You there – Blumer!" came a shout in a thick Podolian accent. It was the curly-haired General Zayonczek. He swung himself off his horse and strode over to me. He was chewing the stub of a cigar.

"Podolian, aren't you?" the General asked, for he was a Podolian, too. "I might have known! I've heard good reports about you, soldier. They say you held these Prussian dogs off single handed."

I began to protest. "No, Sir, humbly report, you are misinformed – "

"Silence!" Zayonczek laughed. "So modest! Don't worry, I'll write a proper report of this little affair. We Podolians should stick together." Then he winked. This was temptation! Comrades must stick together too, I thought. I threw my shoulders back, shouldered my gun, and clicked my heels.

"No Sir, I humbly report," I bellowed, so everyone could hear it, "CAPTAIN GODEBSKI and LIEUTENANT SIERAWSKI repulsed the attack! SIR!"

Zayonczek shook his head in disgust. "Have it your way, lad," he said, drawing on his cigar, and blowing smoke in my face. He pointed at the Prussian prisoners. "Dabrowski," he mouthed his rival's name with distaste, "wants to interrogate a few of these dogs. Speaks their language, you know. If you can call that vile babble a language. He used to serve with these Germans, in the Saxon army – he was Rottmeister Dabrowski in those days, did you know? Doesn't like to brag about it now, though. Dabrowski speaks German better than the mother tongue. I have to have all his despatches translated into proper Polish."

The general spat and pointed out the insolent Prussian Colonel and his men. "Get these scum out of my sight, before I do something I regret. Take them to Dabrowski, he can sit and drink schnapps with them for all I care. Dabrowski's man can show you the way."

He nodded at Tanski, who was, of course, Dabrowski's man. Zayonczek leant over close, and began to whisper conspiratorially. Smoke from his cigar billowed in my face.

"You want to watch that Tanski. He says he's your friend, but he's the one galloping for that German-loving Targowica traitor Dabrowski, and you're the one eating dirt and bullets in the trenches."

We stared at the line of prisoners. Insolent invaders in their pristine blue uniforms. We, by contrast, stood in our ragged and dishevelled clothes. But for our guns, a passing observer would have thought them the victors, and we the vanquished.

"If it were up to me," Zayonczek said, staring at the Prussians, "I'd put the fucking lot of them up against a wall."

"Amen to that, General," I replied, "but rules are rules. We are not Russians."

"True," he said. He spat out his cigar, and ground it out under his boot-heel, in the trampled dirt of the Field of Electors. As he mounted his horse, he called out to me over his shoulder. "Always room in my cavalry division for a good Podolian lad like you. Think about it."

General Dabrowski's great round face lit up as we herded the Prussian prisoners into the yard. He was surrounded by his jubilant dragoons. They too were leading lines of Prussian prisoners and were flushed with victory. Dabrowski's cavalry had lifted the siege from the north.

"Hermann!" Dabrowski bellowed, good naturedly, when he saw my prisoner. Dabrowski was a huge man. He towered over the Prussian Colonel and wrapped him a friendly bear hug with his massive arms. To our consternation they began to converse in German. They talked a good while. Dabrowski pointed, with exaggerated concern, at the Colonel's pathetic scratches, and the Colonel mimed musket shots, and they laughed, and clapped each other on the back. They were evidently old chums.

Dabrowski's dragoons took our other prisoners from us and we slumped onto our backsides in a corner of the yard, amongst the straw and trestles and upturned barrels. The place was flush with so many prisoners, no one took much notice of our small haul. It was like bringing grain to Grodno. We drank water to sluice the smoke from our parched throats and broke out the cards for a hand of whist.

After some time Dabrowski ambled over. He was in high spirits. Dabrowski was always a good provider for his men and there were canteens of vodka and knapsacks of bread and cheese for us. Disconcertingly, he called the Prussian Colonel over to join us. By now the Colonel's wounds (such as they were) had been dressed. His head had been ostentatiously swathed in yards of pristine white bandages, so that he had the appearance of a Turk in a turban.

"Colonel Von Boyen and I studied together at the cavalry school in Dresden," Dabrowski explained. We squirmed uneasily in our seats, with our unwanted Prussian guest, as if a spider sat among us. I cut the cards. We began to play a hand.

"Where are your famous Warsaw girls?" the Prussian asked Dabrowski.

"Hiding in the cellars from your ugly German face!" Dabrowski roared, good-naturedly. The Prussian Colonel laughed and poured himself a vodka. He coughed violently.

"I'd better get used to this vodka," he sneered, "I expect to be here awhile."

"Why? What happened to General Goetz's regiment, my dear Hermann?" Dabrowski asked

"Put to their heels, Henryk!" Hermann – the Prussian Colonel – laughed, and began to gobble every crumb of bread, sausage and cheese that he could lay his hands on, his bandaged head bobbing up and down.

"You don't seem too concerned," Dabrowski said gently.

"They'll be back soon enough, my dear Henryk. The Kaiser has ten regiments to the west to reinforce us. Your health, Sirs!" he raised his vodka in a mocking toast. "After the war," he said slyly, "there will be good commissions in the Kaiser's army. Plenty of marks. *Die Gelt*. Think on it."

Dabrowski slapped his cards down heavily. The table overturned. Hermann jumped.

"Do not mock us, Hermann. We are not traitors. The Good Lord may have dealt us a poor hand in this game," Dabrowski said, "but we'll take no cards from the bottom of the deck, and we'll play it out to the bitter end."

We all looked at him with deep respect.

"You have won, General," I said. Dabrowski had won the hand, and he gathered in his spoils. Abruptly, Elias Tremo came hurtling into the courtyard, on an exhausted horse lathered with sweat. He and Godebski exchanged a sullen stare, but no words passed. Tremo vaulted from his horse and spoke in hushed tones to Dabrowski. Our game broke up and we left the Prussian Colonel to play with a few of his fellow prisoners.

"Blumer," Dabrowski took me aside, "A message from Madame. Take your three comrades and go to her. She has need of you."

"At once, General," I saluted. I confess I was uneasy, because in truth I should never have gone with Godebski to Wola in the first place. If her message contained any reprimand, Dabrowski did not mention it.

"Wait a moment," Dabrowski beamed craftily, "be sure to tell Madame the dispositions of the enemy forces. General Goetz has five Prussian regiments to the north. The King of Prussia has ten regiments to the west, with six batteries of cannon. To the south, the Russians under General Fersen have thirteen regiments, and five batteries. We await Suvarov's army from the east. That intelligence may be useful."

"How the hell do you know that...?" I asked, nonplussed. Dabrowski was a crafty old fox. He grinned.

"Hermann Von Boyen is easy to flatter, and he has a big mouth. He told me everything. Remember that you catch more flies with honey than with vinegar, lad!" he said, clapping me on my shoulder, and sending us on our way.

CHAPTER TWENTY
THE OFFICERS' WIVES,
AND MADAME'S FURY

"That German had a point, though," Sierawski mused, as our cart rumbled over the cobbles, "where are all the girls?"

We had commandeered an apple-cart and a mule that was too old and stringy to be turned into mule-steaks, from Dabrowski's field kitchen and on this we made our way east from Wola. To the west, the Prussian guns had started up their fiendish music again.

"Warsaw's women are hiding in the cellars, and in the attics, praying for the siege to end," said Godebski, glumly.

"Well thank God for that," said Tanski, who was riding his glorious grey horse, a few yards ahead. "I'd be mortified to be seen in this company, you look like a bunch of beggars."

I stretched myself out in the straw on the back of the cart. I had found a bruised apple in one corner and I ate it. I thought of the plump girl who sold apples on the Third of May, whose hair smelled of cinnamon, and who danced the mazurka sweetly. I wondered idly if this was her cart, where she was, if she lived. I gazed up into the afternoon sky, glowing like a vault of amethyst. The white crescent of Twardowski's moon was faintly visible, a ghostly white scar amongst the blue.

"If you want women," I said, "a good few of them now seem to be hiding in Madame L's villa, which is playing host to the senior army officers' wives and sweethearts."

Suddenly the boys were all ears.

"Indeed! I should know, I've been there for two months." I bragged. "It's the greatest billet in Warsaw. Madame's house is a veritable boudoir, a seraglio, a harem. There are mistresses, courtesans, paramours and princesses, blondes, brunettes, redheads and ravens. It's a stable of thoroughbred mares and fillies!"

"Ridiculous!" Godeski cut me off. "You'll find nothing in that house but ungrateful old harridans."

"Aha!" Tanski and Sierawski laughed, "So the Captain remains unlucky in love!"

Godebski rounded on me angrily and drew back his fist to punch me on the nose. I sat, helpless with laughter, in the bed of the cart.

"God blast you, Blumer! You told these two swines!"

"I'm sorry, Captain, I confess," I admitted.

"Forget about Madame L, Captain!" Sierawski dragged him off, "what about *Madame Z*? That's the lady I want to know about!"

For the lady who aroused their most ardent interest was General Zayonczek's wife, Mrs Aleksandra Zayonczek.

"Comrades," I told them, "I have quizzed Madame L's parlour maid, who is an intimate of mine (although a gentleman does not say how intimate, of course) at great length on this subject. I have also had the opportunity to observe the lay of the land, and the two most prominent fortifications, at first hand."

I made an hourglass shape in the air and Sierawski whistled appreciatively.

"You lucky bugger. I've been in a mineshaft for three months smelling the farts and sweat of a dozen hairy-arsed engineers!" he wailed.

"While the Jacobin General is away at the front," I continued, "his fine lady fights her own tireless war with an implacable enemy – she fights to preserve her youth and beauty against the ravages of time. It is a battle that, in defiance of the laws of nature, she is winning. Her skin is the skin of a twenty year-old maiden."

"What, is she a witch?" Tanski snapped, cynically.

"An enchantress, my dear Tanski, not a witch! She preserves her body with the cold, as a butcher preserves the choicest cuts of meat. She will never so much as taste a morsel of a hot dish. She eats only raw vegetables and fruits. She drinks only milk. Each morning, she plunges stark naked into an ice bath of freezing cold water."

"I could do with some cold water right now," Sierawski muttered, tugging at his collar.

"She sleeps in an unheated room, always stark naked, with pots of ice under the bed, and will not even light candles in order to preserve her beautiful complexion. At bedtime, she sews herself up in roe-deer's leather for the night."

"She must be a bloody vampire!" Cyprian whispered, rapt, as he smoked his pipe.

"Well she can drink my blood anytime, Captain. So, each and every day, after her ice bath, she takes a half-mile walk at daybreak. During this cursed siege I have often served as her bodyguard, on these constitutional walks, within the city walls."

"Do you speak to her?" Sierawski said, his voice hoarse.

"Oh yes. One day we were walking down New World Street. My soul quakes at the memory. There were six inches of white snow on the ground, that crunched under her high-heeled leather boots. Crystals of ice gathered like diamonds in her lustrous hair. Her breath iced up as it passed between her coral red lips. She was wearing only the thinnest of Paris silk gowns, delicate as a butterfly's wing, and I could see the goosebumps rising on her snow-white skin. She drew close, so close I could smell the rosewater in her hair, and I said to her..."

"Yes? What did you say?"

My comrades gathered around, eyes wide, mouths agog, hanging on every word.

"I said... it's a bit bloody cold out today, love!"

"Lying bastard!"

The boys pelted me with rotten apple cores as the cart rolled into Madame L's courtyard. With a great shock, we saw three ladies there, and we scrambled to our feet, reddening with embarrassment, and trying to gain some semblance of a respectable appearance.

Of course the first was a tall pale lady dressed in a flimsy silk gown – Madame Z herself, who else! In all of our many meetings she had not, of course, said more than two words to me. She considered me no more than a guard dog, and should have lavished more conversation and concern on me had I been such.

The second lady was the equally formidable Madame Dabrowski, dressed in sable furs. I had never met her before, in spite of all my idle boasts to my comrades.

But most terrifying of all, was the third. She was armed with a cavalry pistol thrust through her belt. It was the stern, unsmiling figure of Madame L, the fatal lady, Captain Godebski's inamorata, and Elias Tremo's mistress. She was also, I realised with a start, my commanding officer, and I was returning from twenty-four hours absence without leave.

Madame L turned her medusa's glare on me. After I had passed on Dabrowski's message, she upbraided me for deserting my post, failing to follow orders, and for taking the bombs without permission, and so on. I stood, rooted to the spot, reddening. Her words stung like a knout.

It is hard to take such rebukes from a woman, as they are generally right in what they say, and one feels guilty. With a man it is easy, for he is generally wrong, and there is no shame in being hectored at by a fool. You may as well resent the wind blowing up your coat, or become angered by the windy farts of a horse.

"Indiscipline will be your downfall, Blumer," the lady concluded, "and your adventure at Wola was the kind of foolhardy enterprise that can only be justified by success. Next time you will not be so lucky."

Then she smiled. "Still, it was well done, boys," she admitted. "Come inside. I have work for you."

Inside, all was in uproar. A massive fire was burning in the grate. Great bundles of secret papers, roughly torn, were curling and blackening into thick ash. Soldiers, lackeys, and ladies came in and out, collecting muskets, swords and pistols, that would disappear into cellars and attics. Madame L swept through all of this pandemonium without a backward glance.

"What the Devil is going on? You are preparing to retreat!" Godebski spluttered, "but the siege was raised this very day, my dear lady! Rejoice! We have won!"

Madame L did not deign to reply. She and her two fellow ladies remained grim and silent. They swept on with their skirts flapping and billowing most becomingly around them. None of us could help ourselves from noticing the grace of the three women as they strode down the corridor.

No longer a blushing damsel, Madame L was entering her second youth, nearing her fortieth year. Her hair was long and wavy, running in dark curls down her back, the dark curls running to silver, which matched the silver ribbon in her hair. Her skin was not so pale as the ethereal Madame Z, who bathed in moonlight, nor had she the statuesque proportions of Dabrowski's wife. Madame was dressed simply, in a plain white gown and a red shawl.

What was arresting about Madame L were her intense dark eyes. Staring into them was like staring down the barrels of a pair of duelling pistols. I could not tell you what colour they were, I believe that they may have been blue, for I found it easier to stare at the Russian guns than into that gorgon gaze.

"Hey, Blumer," Sierawski nudged me in the ribs, "I'm hungry. Are we to eat? This is the old dining room!" We found ourselves in the same dining room where we ate on the Third of May, and where we behaved so disgracefully. No guns sounded in the distance. It was as if time stood still, and all was well, for Madame L's great walnut dining table still stood in the centre of the room. It was growing dark outside. We sank into the soft chairs and chaise longues that had served the learned posteriors of so many illustrious diners over the years, and that now served our thin, horse-aching arses.

Instead of a banquet, there were a number of great wooden boxes on the table. Instead of food, we found these to be filled with treasures. Silver rosaries, ivory boxes, gold watches and snuff boxes, filigree cutlery and crystal glasses. I should have swapped any one of those golden chalices for a loaf of bread or a glass of wine to ease the dust from my parched throat.

Resting along the length of the table was a flag wrapped around a long lance, tipped with a cross instead of a spearhead.

"These are Sobieski's trophies, and this flag was Sobieski's standard," Madame L told us. "This is a sacred relic. King Sobieski drove the Turks back from the very gates of Vienna, in 1683. Christendom itself had been hanging by a thread, for had the Turks taken Vienna, then Austria should have fallen, and had Austria fallen, then all Europe would have gone down with it, like a horse sucked into quicksand. But Sobieski lifted the siege, defeated the Muslim hordes, and saved Christendom from sure destruction."

"Aye," I snorted, "and one hundred years later, Christendom repays us by cutting our throats! We'd have been better off throwing our lot in with the Sultan! Who is here to lift our siege? I see no French armies hastening to our aid! I hear no word from the Pope for a crusade to save us! No hand is raised against our slaughter!"

Immediately we fell to arguing.

"Silence!" Madame called in a resounding voice. We obeyed, meek as infants.

"As God is my witness I despair of you men. Have you any conception of why these objects are here? Do you think that they are here for you to argue over, like boors in a tavern?"

We confessed we did not. Madame placed one weary hand on the table. At that moment she seemed tired, bent over with exhaustion and despair. Then she gathered herself, like an army rallying to the colours. Her back was like a ramrod and she stood before us like a general of the guards. Deep worry lines were etched across her face that her rouge could not hide. Crow's feet sat the corners of her dark eyes. Her hair was wild and unkempt. Still, she looked ravishing despite – or because – of all that. At last, I began to understand why Godebski loved her. She was a force of nature.

"Captain Godebski," she said, her eyes and her voice imperious, "I entrust this sacred mission to you and your men. The situation is critical. I fear Warsaw will fall. You will take these two ladies, and these treasures, and you will quit the city, evading capture. Then you will go to Pulawy, to await further orders. You will not engage the enemy unless attacked. I will not allow these relics to fall into the hands of our enemies."

"Madame," Godebski said, sweeping off his hat, bowing, and saluting, "I obey!"

"Thank you, Cyprian," she said, softly this time, and dismissed us.

"So here we are," I said afterwards, "risking our lives for tarts and trinkets! This is a foolish errand. God help us, if we are caught, they shall hang us for looters and rapists! Ah, well, it could be worse. I've had my fill of sieges. A good ride in open country – pursued every inch by the Cossacks – will be wonderfully invigorating for one's health!"

We stood in silence in the courtyard, smoking our pipes, and watching the leering moon. Whorls of white smoke from our pipes curled out into the night sky, and had Pan Twardowski but had a nose, then he should have smelled the sweet tobacco.

"Will Warsaw fall?" Sierawski asked, anxiously.

"It will be a hell of a battle," I said. "We have only five regiments to defend the city. We are facing fifteen regiments of Prussians and thirteen of Russians, with eleven batteries of cannon."

"Well," Godebski said after a while, "they do say the darkest hour comes before dawn."

"Fool! The darkest hour doesn't come before dawn," I retorted, "the darkest hour comes before everything goes completely black! Suvarov is coming!"

CHAPTER TWENTY-ONE
FINIS POLONIAE, OCTOBER 1794

One minute you're riding the horse – the next minute you're under it. On the 10 October, the Commander, outnumbered four to one, was defeated at Maciejowice, forty miles south of Warsaw. He was trying to break through the ring of enemy armies that encircled us. It was said by the Prussians that he shrieked – like a woman! – 'Finis Poloniae!' – *this is the end of Poland*! – as he was shot from his horse. Of course this story was not true, but what difference did it make?

We had lost.

Madame L gave us orders, coldly and quietly, at the crack of dawn. There were only ten of us – Godebski, Tanski, myself, and seven private soldiers. Sierawski had rejoined the engineers, and would not go with us. We stood in her courtyard by the stables. Our eyes fell to the ground. Our chins sank into our chests. Up above, in the heavens, only Twardowski bore witness as the rest of Europe averted its gaze. Poland might as well have been on the moon.

"Farewell, boys," said Madame L. We gathered up our bags, our few weapons, the trunks of gold and trinkets, and our reluctant passengers, for now there were not two but four ladies, the wives of important officers. Madame Z was wailing most piteously at the time. She was inconsolable. For her husband, the wild-haired cavalry general Zayonczek, was to stay behind.

"Hush, dearest," said Madame L, clasping the lady's milk-white hands, "God will protect him."

"What, as God has protected us?" she cried in fear and desperation. Madame L embraced her as she sobbed. "God has forsaken us all!"

"What the hell is the matter with her, the damned insufferable woman?" said Tanski, blunt as always.

"Have a care, Kasimir," I replied, "she is only a woman, after all. She may bathe her skin in ice, but not her heart. Zayonczek leads our army now, and we all know what that means."

We said nothing about this, in case she heard us, although judging by her anguished cries Madame Z was all too sensible of her husband's fate. It was, we all knew, a death sentence. Even if he survived, by some miracle, the Russians would take him to Siberia, whilst the Prussians would simply put him up against a wall – 'shot whilst escaping'. As a known Jacobin he would receive no mercy.

"Quite right too," Tanski retorted, insensitive as ever, "he is the commander now, it is his duty to die, and it is all exactly as it should be. A pox on that Huguenot harlot – will she not hurry up?"

There was fire in the sky. Suvarov was here.

"Why is it that women always take so long to get ready?" we sighed in frustration. If only I had known the trouble that would have been caused by Tanski and Zayonczek's wife, more than a decade later, why, I would have left them both behind for Suvarov.

"Hurry up!" champed Tanski. For it was the barbarian, the invincible, our nemesis, who came for us now. Suvarov had raised a new Russian army in the Ukraine and marched on Warsaw, destroying everything in his path.

We made haste to leave. Before I mounted I tightened Muszka's saddle. My horse! It was still a joy and a consolation to be back with my horse, even on that darkest of days. Muszka still sucked in as much air as he could to try to bulge out his belly, and loosen the girth. Before he could take another breath, I tightened the strap to its proper proportion, greatly satisfied.

"Why are you grinning, Blumer?" Godebski asked. "the Russians come, and yet you laugh!"

"Blumer is only happy when things are bad," Tanksi observed sourly.

"By God, it is good to be back in the cavalry, though, or near enough," I smiled, as I swung myself up into the saddle. We had lances, swords, muskets and pistols, but as ever, bullets and gunpowder were in short supply. We had long since exhausted the supply of grenades. We had wineskins and waterskins, bread and hard tack, only enough for seven days. Besides Muszka, I had a string of six remounts and pack animals. Each was laden with either supplies or a tearful lady refugee. These would encumber us mightily, but they were also our sacred charges, and we were ordered to defend them to the death.

"What makes her think we can get through, when the Commander did not?" Tanski asked me. "Ten of us, and a few women, against the world!"

Godebski began to berate us for cowards. I intervened.

"You misunderstand. We are simple soldiers, Cyprian," I said, "We do not fear bullets or swords, only the disgrace of the noose – that is, being hanged as common spies."

"Then fear not, comrades," Godebski smiled. This cloak-and-dagger business was not new to him. He had been doing Madame L's dirty work for years. "Where there is no room for a horse, there may be room for a sparrow. We will slip through their grasp, like water through a sieve."

"We'll be caught like flies in a web, more like," muttered Tanski, shaking his head. "See, how the spider draws near!"

Madame L's fine house lay on the west of the river. The west is the smart side, for the nobility and the fine folks. To the east of the river lies Praga. Praga is the poor relation. Dirty old Praga, on the east of the green, greasy old river. Happy years I spent living there. My old lodgings – a crumbling dilapidated boarding house, sawdust on the floor, small fire in the grate, a hard-faced old landlady. No cursing, no drinking, no house guests, no late nights, all rent in advance.

Over the months and years, I had won her over, walking her to church, bringing her shiny brass buttons and cambric purloined from the cavalry stores, mending the roof and stable. In exchange, she fattened me up on beer, pierogi and apple cake, and turned a blind eye to my nocturnal comings and goings, as I drank, danced and gambled away the days and nights.

In all probability my old landlady would not live to see the sunrise. The Russians came from the east, forced the lines open, and breached the walls. The day of the Slaughter of Praga was attended by the most horrid and unnecessary barbarities – houses burnt, women massacred, infants at the breast pierced with the pikes of Cossacks, and universal plunder. The whole of Praga was strewn with dead bodies. Blood was flowing in streams.

We saw the fire across the river. We heard the screams, the cannon, the musketry. We had seen enough of Suvarov to know what was in store for Praga, and with the same fate prepared for Warsaw. A plague of despair spread through us.

"This is the end of Poland!" came a desperate cry.

Madame L rounded on us. Her eyes shone with defiance.

"Poland is not dead, not as long as we live," she called. "Remember that! Now go, my boys! Godspeed, and may the Blessed Virgin protect you," she said, and made the sign of the cross. Godebski bowed from the saddle, doffing his czapka. He took her hand and kissed it. He had Sobieski's standard in his other hand, and he raised it above his head, the red and white colours whipping in the wind, the colours of blood and heaven.

We swept out of the courtyard of Madame L's villa, westwards out of Warsaw, leaving the city burning behind us.

Behind us the towers were falling. From that day forward Poland was dead, as dead as Troy or Byzantium. Nothing but a myth. These were to be the years of exile, of captivity, of wandering in the wilderness. Thus, we descended into the tomb.

We rode west, fleeing from Suvarov's army of savages. We quit the city unopposed and rode through the Prussian lines. Sparrows can fly where a hawk may not, and even the mouse can crawl through a hole to escape the cat.

After we had ridden west for a day, we halted in a thinly wooded forest to see out the night. The next morning we saw clouds of dust on the horizon– marching columns of Prussians – and grey lines of smoke. Now we were well behind enemy lines. Godebski and I spread a map over a tree stump, as if it were a tablecloth, and argued. Our ladies took the opportunity to pick mushrooms. Morning passed into afternoon, shadows lengthened. We lit no fires, but the smell of burning permeated the air. The Great Whore was dining on Warsaw, and its bones burned on her fire.

Tanski lay on the ground for much of the time. A worrying air of despondency had overwhelmed him. Eventually we made him guard the women – a pointless exercise, but at least it occupied his mind. In the gathering dark the ladies put down their baskets and took up their psalters and rosaries. Beads clicked softly like grasshoppers in the dark. Godebski doused the oil lamp and rolled up the map.

"We make for Krakow, which is held by the Austrians. They have a far more lenient and negligent disposition than our other enemies. If Sierawski lives, we'll meet him there."

We rode in a great horseshoe away from Warsaw, then back towards it, then away and southwards. This sweep took us, as we had hoped, behind the advancing Prussians. Now it took us back towards the Russian lines.

As we rode on, dancing flames lit up the night, near and far. Demented screams of pain and fear rang through the darkness. Our horses ran on, trusting our wisdom as masters. In that eternal dark my blind steed could easily break his leg in a ditch or a rabbit hole, and I my neck. We were all experienced riders, and singularly aware of this grave danger. Throughout it all, the crawling fear of running afoul of Cossacks, whose handiwork we saw and heard in the screams, the flames, and the desecrated bodies of the slain. As we rode, we rode through the very hell.

Each was alone with his thoughts, his terror, and the demons. My weapons could not help me now, this empty pistol and rusty sabre. I tried to put my trust in God, in the cross around my neck, but felt nothing but an empty angry hunger for murder and vengeance in my soul.

Help us, O God! In the hour of need, send your legions of archangels! Place the fiery sword in my hand! Heed my prayer! As God was my witness, as I rode through that awful blackness, I made a promise. I swore on my mother's grave that I would see Moscow burn, razed to the ground, and take the torch to it myself. I would avenge Praga.

Then I chanced to gaze up, in the depths of my despair, calling on Jesus and Mary. Up in the vault of the heavens was the silver globe of the moon. I saw, quite distinctly, a face. A face in the surface of the moon. His eyes were in the craters and canyons. His nose and mouth and crooked teeth were in the twisting rivers and canals of that white moon. It was, unmistakably, the face of the old man, Twardowski, with his spider perched on his shoulder, like a monkey, and a thread of silver silk hanging like a noose.

God can't help you now, boy, said the old man. Only I can. Twardowski's words were soft, and faint, but as clear as the priest in the confessional dark, lulling through the screen and the velvet. Around me, the smoke transformed into incense, but my horse's nostrils were full of the stink of brimstone.

Then help me, damn you! Lo and behold, the clouds of smoke evaporated, melting away like phantoms. The lines of Cossacks were gone. We rode out, every one of us whole and unharmed, but missing half of our mules and pack beasts, who had been lost along the way – including, to our horror, the one carrying Sobieski's precious flag.

We halted at a stream, near the village of Mogilinami, the crystal waters running clear. Sparkling diamonds of light reflected on it. Madame Z plunged into the icy waters, her gown billowing around her like angels' wings. She climbed out, unabashed, the gown clinging to her skin. We pretended to hide our eyes behind our czapkas and the women laughed. We broke bread, and we thanked God.

CHAPTER TWENTY-TWO
A SPLENDID STACK OF FIREWOOD,
NOVEMBER 1794

The manor house was single-storied with a grand colonnade flanking the massive iron-bound door. The door hung open, smashed from its hinges. From walnut floor to oak beams, every last splinter of that damned house was wood, aye, all save the glass in the windows. It was a grand nobleman's mansion, and a splendid stack of firewood at that. Nearby was a stone bastion, for defence, and the Russians swarmed over it, like ants.

"You can see them through the glass. Be careful! Don't draw down the light."

"How many?"

"A dozen, maybe."

"What are they doing?"

"What else? Looting, of course," Cyprian said, putting up the telescope, and passing it back to me. There were books scattered on the ground, like dead ravens in the snow. Soldiers ran in and out of the house carrying bundles of them. Beyond the entrance hall would be the library, the trophy room and the armoury, full of old muskets and the stuffed heads of wild beasts. The Russians were emptying each room in turn, and flinging their loot into a train of covered caissons.

"Damned if I know why they're stealing books," I said, "the ignorant bastards probably can't read." I knew not how truly I spoke. In the Blue Palace in Warsaw, by the Saxon Garden, was the Library. A serene labyrinth of rooms, adorned with marble statues, and with glorious books rising up to the heavens, it was my favourite place in the whole world. The oldest and finest library in Europe, I learned later that it was the first thing the Russians plundered when they took Warsaw. To this day, half a million volumes languish in St Petersburg, like slaves in the gulag, unread by their witless gaolers. Here was the same larceny, but on a pettier scale, as they robbed this blameless manor house near the village of Krzywacze.

"Ignorant or not," said Cyprian, putting up the telescope, "they stand between us and our escape."

We had been tracked for days by a troop of Cossacks, and now we were caught between hammer and anvil. In that time we had lost two men and another two horses.

"Madame said no fighting," I reminded him, laughing, and checking my pistols.

"What Madame doesn't know won't hurt her," Cyprian replied. We drew up a hasty plan as the Russians caroused, for they had found the vodka and the wine. They were pouring it down their necks as fast as the liquor would flow.

"Blumer will go behind the house," Cyprian said, "and I will clear out the bastion. As soon as battle is joined," he told Tanski, "you will take the other five soldiers, the ladies, and those blasted trinkets, whatever remains of them. Ride straight through these scoundrels, then ride like hell for Krakow. We'll cover your retreat. Don't wait for us – that is an order."

"Sir," Tanski saluted, and stared at us doubtfully. We shook hands, and he was gone. Cyprian and I drew our pistols and stuck our bayonets in our belts. Then Cyprian was gone behind the bastion. He was fleet of foot, and as stealthy as a ghost. I vaulted over a low fence, and trampled through a herb garden, as I traversed the house.

In the garden, I found three pathetic bodies crumpled in the snow, like broken dolls. A man, a woman, and a boy. A Russian soldier sat beside them, stupefied with drink, his musket lying against the wall. A bloody bayonet was fixed to the muzzle. I picked up the musket, thrust the bayonet into his belly, and moved on.

As I emerged at the front of the house, I faced a number of the Russians. They were preparing to raze the house to the ground, having broken the windows and tossed in bales of straw. It was an act of wanton destruction. Absorbed in their evil task, they took no notice of me. A fat sergeant flung a flaming torch through the front door. Then I heard gunshots, and many things happened all at once.

A Russian officer staggered from the bastion, blood pouring from his eyeless face. Tanski's horsemen hurtled past the front porch, wildly firing pistols. Several Russians, stupefied with drink, stood and gawped at them. They stared at the ladies, wrapped in white, as they hurtled by, full tilt. Tanski halted, and watched as the rest of his precious little convoy rode past. He counted them off, like a mother goose with her chicks. Then he tipped his czapka, caracoled his horse, and was gone.

"After them!" roared the fat sergeant, rousing his dumbfounded corps of arsonists. A column of flame blazed through the middle of the house, raising the roof. Heat scorched my face and burned the hairs from the back of my hands. I walked up to the sergeant, placed my pistol against the side of his head, and pulled the trigger. I wiped the sergeant's blood from my eyes with my sleeve. I remember the driver of one of the caissons staring at me. The traces were empty and the horses gone. His face contorted into a cry of fear and anger. He lashed his whip. I felt it kiss my cheek. Drawing my second pistol, and closing the gap with a few strides, I shot him through the liver at point-blank range.

Not a moment later, a young lad, crouched behind the caisson wheel with his pistol, returned the favour. It was as if I had been struck with an axe. All sensation passed from my body. With a groan I sank to the ground between the man I had lately shot, and the other man who had lately shot me. It was as if the very Devil had reached up from hell and struck me down!

I dropped my sabre, for I was fading fast. There is a hole in my leg, I thought. My belt and sash served for a tourniquet, and the bleeding staunched. I saw blood, dripping like tears. When I chanced to gaze up, the house was ablaze from end to end.

Curling claws of smoke rose from the chimney pot, the windows, the doors, and grasped up for the heavens. Coffers and planks flared out yellow tongues. The wood oozed and blackened, twisted and turned. Blizzards of sparks, like a snowstorm blowing in hell. Smoke and flames blinded us, Poles and Russians alike. Waves of heat seared our flesh. Horses reared, broke free from their fetters, and ran screaming into the dark.

I clung to the wheel of the caisson, and tried to stand, but my leg would have none of it. Thus I was obliged to watch the rest of the fight sitting on my backside. Godebski was grappling with the boy, and they rolled in the dirt, snarling like dogs. First one, then the other, took the upper hand. They fought furiously, raining blows on each other, biting and kicking, strangling, and gouging.

Behind them, the top of the roof lifted off one last time, as if the house were a man, doffing his cap. Then the great oak beams collapsed back in upon themselves in an agony of anguished groans and cries. At last the fire must have reached the library, for the books began to burn.

As I sat there, lightheaded, blood flowing from my leg, my mind drifted back to the Library in the Blue Palace, in Warsaw. I spent many happy hours there, for I am an avid reader. This library in that lovely manor house was not as grand as Warsaw's great library, but it contained many hundreds of books. It must have been a lovely little library, once. Now, as it burned, the books were taking flight, like the souls of the departed. With a great rustle of leaves, they burned, and fluttered, borne aloft on the scalding hot air. Ash and burning fragments rained down on me, blinding my sight.

When it was all over, the last man standing, sword in hand, came stalking towards me, silhouetted against the flames. I struggled in vain to hoist myself to my feet. The spectre emerged from the smoke.

It was Cyprian Godebski.

CHAPTER TWENTY-THREE
CALVARY, EASTER 1795

It was a Biblical Easter day. The room overlooked Herod's Palace. It belonged to a sweet and devout lady, Magdalena. In my hand, I held a letter from Judas.

> *"I can overlook what has gone before, but this is my final word. Here is an officer's commission in my regiment. Swear your sword to the Tsars, as your forefathers did. Serve with honour.*
>
> *Felix Potocki"*

Honour indeed! I scoffed. Kalwaria (or Calvary) Zebrydowski lies south of Krakow, between the Vistula and the Tatras mountains. It is a strange, melancholy place of pilgrimage, laid out as a replica of the Holy City of Jerusalem, built over a century before I was born. There are forty chapels, of which Herod's Palace was but one, set on the surrounding hills.

I had risen very early, and with great care, so as not to disturb my fellow sleeper. The girl was sleeping like an angel. Her golden hair curled in a halo around her head and threads of it spilled over her pillow. One tiny foot protruded from under the blanket. She slept so soundly that it seemed a great shame to tip a bucket of freezing water over her head, but I did it anyway. For it was Easter Monday, and that was the custom, and ever shall be.

"*Smigus dyngus*[4]!" I called out.

---

[4] *Easter Monday in Poland is still marked by this custom of throwing water over one another.*

I laughed heartily as I lit the fire with Felix's letter, barely listening to the wailing and shrieking from Magda as she flew about the room in a rage, crying "Damn you, Blumer!" all bared teeth and claws and wildcat hissing. I laughed on, like a wheezing donkey, for she was a fine sight with her yellow hair plastered to her head, water dripping from her nose and chin, and her eyes ablaze with rage.

"Stop laughing. You'll burst your stitches," Magda sneered, as she pulled off her sopping nightgown, and fussed with her petticoats. At first I had observed her stealthily at this, in the mirror, but over the last few months I had grown bolder and watched her openly and with great affection.

"Here," she said, "tie me up at the back."

I did as I was bid and drew in her ribbons and stays. From Magda's window one could see Herod's Palace, one of the stations of the cross of Calvary. Early morning light lit the red tiled roof, and the low spires. The walls were white, with the round windows, the doors and the colonnades framed in gold. I had been given sanctuary and dwelt here in Calvary since November, as my wound healed. Christmas brought no cheer from the outside world. No French army rode to our rescue. Our leaders were in exile, in the gulag, or dead. All save for Dabrowski, of whom we had heard nothing, and upon whose broad shoulders we now placed all our slender hopes.

"What's for breakfast, woman?" I demanded, rubbing my empty grumbling belly, for I was famished. "What about the eggs in that basket?"

"No! The eggs have not been blessed yet. We must go to Church first," said Magda firmly, and that was that. Then, more tenderly, she asked, "Will you need your walking stick?"

"I can manage well enough, thank you," I retorted, reaching for my sword belt. Magda began to protest but thought better of it. For I was a wanted man and even in this holy sanctuary I had to go everywhere armed.

"Did you read your letter?" she asked coldly. She picked up her basket of *pisanki* that we were off to Church to have blessed. She had steamed open the seal before I had read it, for she was an inquisitive creature.

"I did." I nodded to the grate, where the letter curled into ash, "and there's his answer."

"Good!" Magda smiled, kissed me, slipped her arm through mine, and we set off.

"It was a lot of money he was offering you, Ignatius," she said covetously as we walked, for women will always want to have it both ways. She quite forgot that she was not supposed to have read the letter.

"The wages of sin is death, my dear Magda," I replied. "Not all the salt in Wieliczka could tempt me to the flag of that treacherous son of a bitch."

"Not even for a general's hat?" she asked, wickedly.

"Not even that," I said, straightening my czapka. "Besides," I said, annoyed, "the stingy bastard only offered me a lieutenancy!"

Magda, God bless her dear sweet heart, was a lady, for she had hidden me, but she was also a woman, and the place where she hid me was in her bedchamber. She was a patriot, and she saw it as her duty to heal me, and care for me, and tender to my wants. Accordingly she performed her duties and offices ardently, passionately, and nightly. That she took great pleasure in her duty was a happy accident of fate. She told me her husband had died in the wars and I took her word for it, as she was a lady, she thus could not lie, as far I as was concerned.

At the crest of the hill we met a knot of pilgrims by the roadside. Then there was a hush, as the procession approached. It was the passion play. We watched it performed as it had been these hundred years past. Leading the procession was a man dressed as The Christ, and carrying an immense cross of wood. Flanking him were men garbed as

171

Roman soldiers, in red tunics and gold plumed helmets, with short swords, knouts, and lances.

We watched in silence, spellbound, as the familiar mystery played out, from cock crow to hanging tree. Torments and pain – the scourge, the whips, the crown of thorns. Wounds in His hands, wounds in His feet, the centurion's lance in His side. Mary weeps at the foot of the Cross. Then it is finished. The sky turns black. Mankind cries out in fear. We – Romans, soldiers, priests, the people of Judea – we all murdered Him. He died to wash away the sins of the world. We wept for a lost lord and a lost land.

Poland was gone, submerged by a deluge, obliterated from the map. Yet, like a great rock beneath an angry ocean, it survived, indestructible. Storks still nested in cartwheels on roofs. Old babcias still swept the Church steps. We still sang our songs, though we sang them in whispers.

Now the lead player struggled from the cross where he was merely tied, rather than nailed there with hammer blows. The other players took their bows, their armour counterfeit, their swords wooden, and all of us marched to Church, actors and spectators together.

We took Communion in silence with the others in the old baroque Church, the cold air redolent with the rich scents of incense. A priest blessed the Easter Eggs. In my youth the eggs were painted in every colour of the rainbow – pinks, blues, greens, yellows and browns, but mostly reds and whites. That day every egg was painted red and white, and crowned with eagles. Before the altar there was a sea of blood and heaven. At last, when the prayers had ended, the priest sent us on our way.

We took our last breakfast in Magda's little wooden house, eating the eggs that the priest had blessed, together with cold meats, bread, and salt, and little flat cakes covered with a paste of nuts and almonds, called mazurki, that she had baked. Magda saw that I walked without my stick and it was not lost on her that I had knelt at the altar rail unaided.

"My leg is healed," I said. We both knew what it meant.

"But you still have a limp," Magda said weakly, and began to cry, for it was no good, and at last she heard the thunder in the earth as the horsemen approached. Last night, while Magda had baked her cakes, I had gathered my few clothes and books, and cleaned my weapons. Outside, at the foot of the hill were two horsemen, and three horses.

"Madame sent us," Tanski explained.

"Where is Godebski?" I asked him.

"We meet him there," Tanski replied, tipping his czapka to Magda.

"Where is there?"

Tanski shrugged.

"How's your leg?" Sierawski asked, scratching his nose.

"There was a hole in it that big – big enough to put a tynf through!" I laughed, holding up a finger and thumb.

"That boy looks like a beggar, not a soldier," Magda snorted, pointing at Sierawski.

"By God, so he does," I said, for men scarcely take notice of such matters. My own appearance was good enough, for I had been well fed, and rested, and exercised. My uniform was old, but it was mended and cleaned.

Tanski was turned out immaculately, as always. He was dressed according to regulations in every particular, down to the last button on his tunic, and even carrying a lance, from which a pristine swallow-tailed pennant proudly flew the red and white. It was as if he had ridden straight out of the parade ground of the Poniatowski Palace on The Third of May.

Our friend Sierawski, by contrast, was in rags. If Tanski had ridden here from parade, the engineer had ridden here straight from his trench at Wola. He possessed no weapons save a sabre, which was scabbarded in the cut-off sleeve of a coat. This was secured to his waist by a cord, for he had not even the belt of his ragged pants to his name. His leather boots were worn down at heel, and caked with mud, the spurs lost.

An ancient woollen cap, bleached by sun and snow, sat limply upon his head. This he had set at what he considered a rakish angle, and we hooted at him and derided his woeful appearance.

In a short space of time Magda had turned Sierawski from scarecrow to officer. Her husband's clothes had been too small for me, but they fitted Sierawski, for he was a little beanpole of a man, too. For a finish, Magda produced an ancient gun for him, wrapped in an oilskin – a fowling piece, for hunting birds.

"That blunderbuss will do you good service if we make war on chickens!" I laughed. "Where the Devil have you two been, anyway?"

"We'll tell you on the way, Blumer," Tanski said tersely, for he seemed even more brusque and angry than ever. At the time I thought nothing of it, for it was a dark time. We Poles were at war with the whole world – and, as it turned out, with each other.

"Make haste. We were followed," Tanski snapped.

"Damn, I'd hoped for a few days' start," I cursed softly, so as not to startle the horse, for I was tightening the girth at the time. As ever, the crafty animal was blowing his guts out to stop me tightening it. A few moments ago I'd been tightening Magda's corsets, and I grinned at the thought. "Rzewuski's men?" I said, still grinning.

"The very same, comrade. What's so funny?"

"No matter, comrade."

I kissed Magda goodbye. Then I put my foot cautiously in the stirrup and gripped the pommel of the saddle. My leg buckled and would not take my weight, so I hauled myself up with the brute force of my arms. "Good as new," I lied, slapping my leg, and trying not to wince. Then I doffed my cap to Magda and bowed to her, full length, from the saddle. She clasped her hands around my neck and kissed me for the last time. "Fare thee well, sweet Magdalena," I said.

174

"Here," she said, "It is all I have." She pressed a small purse of money into my hand. As we rode away, I heard her sing a sad, bitter song –

"War, sweet war,
What a mistress you must be,
For you are pursued
By so many beautiful boys!"

Then we were gone. I never saw her again.

CHAPTER TWENTY-FOUR
THE EAGLES' NEST TRAIL

We rode across the boundary stones into what was now called
Austrian Galicia. This was the Hapsburgs' slice of the cake.
God knows how the pious Marie-Therese explained this
brigandry to her confessor. The Austrians shared our religion,
unlike the Prussians and Russians. Consequently, unlike them,
they rarely molested our worship or violated our holy places.

We rode north, for Krakow. Sierawski rode on my right,
Tanski on my left. Sierawski's eyes and cheeks were hollow
from a long winter of hunger. Tanski's jaw was set grimly, his
eyes blank and shining with hatred. It was fortunate for Tanski
that he was born and lived in days when we were at war with
all the world. For his natural humour was such that nothing
suited him better. Both rode in silence.

"What happened to you two? You look as if you've been
paroled from Hell, comrades!"

Sierawski said nothing. Tanski spat into the grass. We rode
on, through twisting forgotten paths and quiet woods to avoid
the Austrian patrols. This was not especially difficult. Of all
our enemies, the Austrians were the most negligent by far.
Night was falling as we forded the Vistula and slipped around
Krakow. It cost us all the money in Magda's purse, which was
all the money we had, to bribe the sentries. At first,
Sierawski's spirits grew at the sight of his beloved city. Even
in the darkness we could see the dreaming spires, the
twinkling lights of the houses, the dark hump of the Wawel
Castle, like a sleeping dragon.

An Austrian flag flew there above our slumbering kings. In
the taverns, coarse folk laughed and drank, their noisome din
carrying to us across the water. We rode on. Behind us the red

sun sank into the Vistula and drowned there, like Queen Wanda, who killed herself rather than marry a German prince. A whole night passed in this way. Sierawski, who knew this country, led us on, on a road he called the Eagles' Nest Trail. As Krakow dwindled behind us, so did Sierawski's spirits.

The Eagles' Nest Trail runs from a valley at the south, like a bottleneck, all the way north to the great monastery at Czestochowa. Krakow forms the cork of this upturned bottle, and a verdant valley the neck. This bottleneck is the Pradnik valley, a land studded with outcrops of limestone, like opals adorning a woman's green gown. For all its natural beauty, this is bandit country. Perched on rocky outcrops are the ruined castles that give this trail its name – Eagles' Nest. Once these were the strongholds of lords and kings, but since the Swedish Wars they had long since been ruined and were now fallen into the hands of bandits.

Vultures, not eagles, nested here.

This land brought the Swedish Wars to mind, and our great general from those old days, Czarniecki, of whom I had read. Finding himself outmatched by invaders, his small army waged a war of ambush, of hit and run, in places such as these. In the morning we stopped to rest the horses. Sierawski took a long pull of vodka with his breakfast as the sun rose, for his city was vanished and invisible behind us.

"Enough of that," I snapped, "we have a long ride ahead."

Sierawski ignored me and continued to drink.

"Tanski," I said, my nerves now somewhat frayed, "we must water the horses. We have no remounts so we must take good care of them."

"Damn your eyes, Blumer, and water your own stinking nag," Tanski said, dropping from his horse like a sack of hay thrown from a loft. There he sprawled in the grass and lay as if shot. His horse began to crop the wet grass, still wearing its saddle and tack. I hobbled my horse and undid the bridle of

Tanski's grey mare, cursing, for it had fouled the bit with a chewed cud of grass.

"You lazy swine," I chided him, "your beautiful horse could have choked."

At this, Tanski stood up. "I've had it with you ordering me about. You aren't even a cavalry lieutenant, Warrant Officer Blumer! You water the horses! I'm in charge here!"

"You couldn't take charge of a shithouse! What has become of you, comrade?" I asked him, aghast.

"I'll tell you what has become of me," he snarled, "I've watched my mother and father die, and my home burn. My uncle hid me in a grain cellar full of rats. Every day the Cossacks came, killing, raping and looting with impunity," he shouted. "while you – you've been drinking and living it up with a strumpet! In a bloody convent!"

"I grieve your loss, Sir," I said, "but don't refer to the lady so. She's a brave girl, and she hid me as your good uncle hid you, while I recovered from my wound."

"I'll call her whatever I damn well please," he shouted, "she's probably rutting with the Russians right this minute! What was your injury, anyway, comrade? Shot in the arse while running away?"

He was striking distance from me now.

"Another word and you die, Kasimir," I said, softly.

Tanksi stepped forward and knocked off my czapka.

"Draw your sword, then," he sneered, "you snivelling Irish coward."

This was sheer madness, of course. A mist of rage had descended on us. Impotent, angry, and defeated, we turned our teeth at each other's throats. All around us the spider was weaving his web, the threads drawing ever tighter. He spun his silken ropes like a hangman's noose.

"I'll not be called a coward, by God, not by any man, Sir," I said, and we drew our sabres, and took guard.

"Ahem," Sierawski coughed. He was sitting on a tree stump, loading his antiquated gun with powder and birdshot. "I hate to interrupt your duel, comrades, but we have been followed since Krakow."

"Now he tells us!" we exclaimed, lowering our sabres.

"I didn't want to worry you," Sierawski shrugged. At last, he cracked a smile! I never thought it would bring me joy to see his crooked yellow teeth, but such it did. We dragged our protesting horses to their knees and lay down behind them, putting the poor beasts betwixt us and the bullets that were liable to come whistling at us forthwith. I still had my grandfather's brass telescope, and I pressed it to my eye. The road behind us was long and plain and clear. On the horizon, apparitions danced in the glass. Horsemen, riding us down like the very Devil.

"Rzewuski's lackeys," I said, "seven of them." Dropping the telescope, I took my musket from the saddle holster, and began to prime it.

"Don't shoot until you can see their moustaches, comrades," I said, and we all grinned.

Rzewuski's men had caught up with us in the shadow of an immense rock that stood amidst a canopy of trees. It stretched against the blue sky like the stone pillar of a long-vanished temple. This was the famous stone named Hercules' Club. Now they were close, bearing down on us, the thundering hoof beats of their mounts throwing up clods of earth and echoing through the ground. They were Poles, in Rzewuski's service – that is, Russian service. They were dressed in black zupans that streamed behind them in the wind, and fur kolpaks on their heads. Sabres gleamed in the sunlight. Bandits or brigands, hired killers, but not soldiers, these. Some had pistols and they fired wildly, from too great a range to make the shots count. Wisps of smoke flew up and were snatched away on the wind. They closed with us. Man pulls the trigger, but God guides the bullet. My musket found the range and a man was plucked from his saddle.

"A hit! A palpable hit!" I cried, surprised and delighted, for I am a poor shot.

"Bloody assassins," Tanski hissed, and discharged his gun. A horse came crashing down but the rider rolled away, unhurt.

"Good shot, comrade!" we called.

"Damnation!" Tanski cursed, drawing his pistols, "I missed! I was aiming for the man, not his poor beast!"

Sierawski could do little more than make a noise with his hopeless firearm, but we had raised plenty of sound and fury between us, and knocked down a man and a horse, and it was more than enough to stop them in their tracks. The man I had shot with my musket was lying on the ground, screaming, clutching at his stomach – a killing shot. This traitor would suffer a long and agonising death, unless he was put out of his misery first. The rest of them fell back, lay down and cowered behind their horses, as we did. Here and there a shot was fired at us, but to no real purpose, as if to save face.

At the head of this band of cutthroats was a tall and handsome man in black, with a shock of blond hair on his head. He was rallying his men. Clearly their leader, he was made of sterner stuff than them. We were close enough now for me to see the Russian eagle on his chest, and the double-cross on his arm. It was Szymon Korczak.

"Shoot the blond man!" I roared. As you know by now, a pistol is rarely any use at anything but point-blank range. We carried four pistols between us, and we fired four shots at them. They scattered like bugs, burying their noses in the dirt, and hiding behind rocks and under stones.

"Let's go," I ordered, and we released our horses' necks, and sprang onto their backs, Tanski leading his grey mare by the mane, for I had of course removed the bridle. As we rode by, Tanski leaned out of the saddle and snatched the loose bridle up from the ground without his horse even breaking stride. That boy had a terrible temper but by God, he could ride. Sierawski rode ahead, for only he knew where we were going.

Lastly, I reluctantly turned to go. I burned to know if we had hit the blond man. Cursing, I saw him coolly stand up from behind his horse, a pistol in hand. Szymon stalked towards the wounded man, who was screaming pitiably. As I caracoled my horse and rode on, I heard a single shot, and the screaming ceased.

CHAPTER TWENTY-FIVE
SIERAWSKI'S ELEPHANT

"What do you mean, we're going the wrong way?" I demanded. Sierawski shrugged and took a pull at his water bottle, for it was a hot May morning.

"All you said was find a place to ambush them," he replied. "You didn't say it had to be on the way there."

"Hell's teeth! We need to be going north east to Pulawy!" Tanski shouted angrily, chewing a hunk of stale bread. "Instead, we are going north west, to Czestochowa!"

"By Mary and all the Saints!" I exclaimed, and sat down heavily on a log. My leg hurt as if the Devil was sinking his fangs into it. Cursing, I stood up again and began to saddle my horse. It hurt as badly at rest as at work.

"My plan was to skirt around Krakow and follow the Vistula north, perhaps catch a boat or steal a raft," Sierawski said mournfully, "but those boys behind us have spoiled everything."

"Damn it all," I cursed, studying the map. "We shall have to go the long way round, following the River Pilica, then. There is nothing else for it," I said. "Trust three Poles to do everything the hard way!"

We set off again.

"Have we any food for lunch?" Tanski grumbled.

"No," I shook my head, "you ate the last of the bread, you greedy bastard."

"Here is the church," Sierawski said. "This is the spot."

"An ambush at a church!" I spat, and shook my head. "Delightful! We're getting as bad as them. Still, I commend your cunning – they won't expect this."

"Fool! This is not the spot for the ambush!" Sierawski shook his head. "This is the spot for lunch! The priest will find us something to eat – I know him."

We dismounted and stood guard while Sierawski disappeared into the church. We heard the sound of a door being forced. He returned some time later with a basket full of apples, bread, hard-boiled painted eggs, and a bottle of communion wine.

"This priest is very generous," I said sceptically.

"He wasn't home," Sierawski admitted, shredding the brightly-painted shell from an egg and wolfing it down. "So I borrowed these."

"Body of Christ!" Tanski intoned, tearing the bread.

"Blood of Christ!" I laughed, swigging straight from the bottle. "The Lord be with you, comrades!"

"And also with you, Father Blumer!" Tanski and I laughed together, at long last, and his black cloud seemed to lift a little, until I could see the good heart of my old friend, like the sun through a storm. Sierawski, however, was still silent, but for the odd grunt and a few words. He ate as if he had never eaten before and feared never to do so again. It was as if the evil spider still hung over him.

"What the hell is that?" Tanski pointed out a green stone monument that stood by the wooden Church.

"It appears to be an elephant, comrade," I said, finishing the communion wine with a long glassy whistle, and tossing the bottle into the weeds.

"Why, so it is," Sierawski put in, the most animated we had seen him for days. His gloomy eyes brightened and he sprang to his feet. "It's my elephant!"

We were astonished to see him run like a schoolboy to this strange obelisk. He reached it in a trice, and to our further amazement he patted the pachyderm upon the tusk and trunk, petting it as if it were his dog.

"This," said Sierawski proudly, "is my elephant! The very one on my coat of arms! My lucky elephant!" He pulled a scrap of cloth from his pocket and showed it to us. It was his coat of arms. We had always wondered at this strange family emblem. Tears filled his eyes, but he was grinning.

"I never thought to see it again!" he wiped his eyes on his sleeve and drew his sword, pointing left and right. "I've changed my mind – this is where we'll make our ambush, boys. We'll cut them down as they pass between the church and the elephant. There is a hollow over there. You can't see it from the road, not until it's too late. I hid there many times as a boy, for my cousin lives hereabouts, and we used to visit in the summer. I used to leap out and fire my catapult at the girls. The priest would birch my backside whenever he caught me."

Without another word we went about our business with a will. We hid our horses in the woods and tethered them to a tree. We covered our tracks by sweeping them over with branches, and collected up all our mess, right down to the bottle I had carelessly tossed aside. After that, we lay down on the wet grass, still slick with morning dew, and hid. Sierawski's hollow was a shallow dip scooped out of the ground, and a perfect natural foxhole.

The day wore on. The sun lengthened and began to sweat the communion wine out of us. Our eyes and ears strained at the empty horizon for horsemen and hoof beats.

"Where have you been, Sierawski?" I asked, both to break the tension, and from genuine concern for my morose comrade. Sierawski took a sip of his half-empty water bottle, and told us.

"After I saw you boys last, at Wola, I returned to the engineers. We fought on until Kościuszko was taken prisoner. In November, we were ordered to go to Russia, and be enlisted into their army. Many of our regiments were conscripted in this way. We engineers were first. All armies are short of engineers, particularly the Russians. We are prized above all other soldiers for our skills."

"Enough of this idle boasting!" Tanski hissed peevishly, peering through my telescope, for we had but one, "anyone can dig a bloody hole."

"Ignore him, Sierawski – please continue," I said, softly. For Sierawski was like a skittish horse, and needed coaxing, not beating.

"Our General sent me to another General to talk some of his men into going to some place called Wysogrod, where we were to be housed in barracks and sworn into Russian service. Now these men were loyal sorts and not disposed to obey this treacherous command. So I was given a letter of passage, some men, and these despicable orders, which I abhorred with as great distaste as the lads I was to give them to. These angry men were as like to shoot the messenger as not, so the crafty generals sent me as their special envoy."

"They sent you on a suicide mission," I said.

"Precisely! When I rounded up these boys, they all still had their horses and their guns, and they were in a high old dudgeon, as you may imagine, with the Partition and all. So I proceeded to lead their mutiny myself, otherwise they'd have hung me from a tree anyway. We killed the guards and ran for it."

Sierawski took his turn peering through the telescope. "The steppe is a cruel old place, and I think we lost as many to the cold and hunger as to the Cossacks. We had hollow bellies and tight belts, I can tell you. It was a harsh Christmas, comrades. We sang our hymns out there in the Russian dark with a few mean fires burning and it felt as if we were at the end of the earth. We were free men, true, but we were still in Siberia, only without the leg irons. I told the boys enough was enough, and we rode down from the hills into a little place called Cycanow."

Sierawski passed me the telescope and took out a silver hip flask of vodka with a Russian eagle on it.

"The locals weren't too pleased to see us in Cycanow, for it is a Russian town. They don't get much by way of news there, so we told them that Old Poland had won the war, and it was the White Eagle, not the Black Janus, that was flying over the Kremlin now, as it had done in the days of Stefan Bathory[5], and so they had better behave themselves. Then we hoisted our tattered flag over their little town, and it was the last free town in Poland, except for the small fact that it was in Russia, and we bivouacked there.

"Well, in double-quick time the village hetman and the priest came to visit me. The hetman was a great fat old boy with his beard to his knees and his belt on the last hole, and the priest was the same, other than that his beard was longer, and he was even fatter, so that he needed an altar boy to carry his belly for him in a wheelbarrow. I shook my whip at them and told them that I was the Governor now, and the right royal representative of the Polish King, and they had better keep on the right side of me, or else, and they stood there quaking to their boots.

"At that the hetman fell to the floor and grabbed my knees, and wept, and said I could take their cattle, and their vodka, and that he would even give me his three daughters, on condition they could keep their religion. For he had been told all the usual lies about us in that regard."

As you will know, the Russians tell their serfs, falsely, that we Poles oblige all our citizens to take the Catholic Communion. This calumny has taken a deep root in the mind of their peasants. Nothing could be further from the truth – we hold that any man or woman in Poland is perfectly free to practise their own superstitions, however foolish, for there will then be all the more room in heaven for we true believers when the day of judgment comes. These same gullible peasants chose to overlook (or perhaps agreed with) the gross persecution of Jews, Catholics, and Uniates by the Tsars.

---

[5] *King of Poland (1576-1587) who conquered large parts of Russia*

"Well," Sierawski continued, "I said that sounded like a fair deal to me, and we spat on our hands and shook on it, and I said that he had better look lively about the vodka and the rest."

"God Almighty!" we whistled. "Only you, Sierawski, could do that."

"You might say I engineered the situation to my advantage," Sierawski said, twirling his moustaches. "It was all going very well, for a while, until the Russian Army turned up. Then it was all a bit of a fiasco, in the end, to tell you the truth. Lots of shooting and shouting, and cannon firing, and such, most unfortunate. Well, two of the hetman's daughters came at me with carving knives, and I had to take my exit through a bedroom window sharpish. It's pretty bracing out there on the steppe in December when you're wearing nothing but your boots and your sword, I can tell you. So I took some clothes off a scarecrow and cut up a horse blanket for a coat, helping myself to the horse while I was at it. Then I reckoned west by the sun and rode.

"A troop of uhlans caught me near Grodno, or Nowogrod, or some other damn place. They asked me if what I was wearing was the Polish fashion nowadays and I said no, these were French clothes from Paris. Thank God it wasn't the Cossacks so they saw the funny side. Their Colonel was a Polish lad in Russian service and I told him this story over a few vodkas. He offered me a commission in his uhlans on the spot, as he needed an engineer, but I said no, it wasn't for me, so he gave me back my sword and my horse and let me go. And that was it. Please pass me the bread, comrade? Damn it, I'm hungry."

He shrugged and passed me the telescope. Tanski and I shook our heads in wonderment. We had completely forgotten our ambush, the road, or what we were doing here.

Then a bell tolled.

"What the hell!" I peered through the telescope. "Your priest is back, Sierawski. What day is it today?"

"It's the Third of May," said Tanski.

"They are saying mass to celebrate," we whispered, our throats dry. We sighted down the barrels of our muskets at a line of horse-drawn carts and riders. Behind them came a long procession of peasants, men and women, with children and dogs straggling behind them. There were perhaps three dozen people in all, innocent country folks. Everyone was in their Sunday best – the men in bright red kontusz cloaks and fur zupans, the women in pink or lavender, or yellow kontusz, with slit sleeves rolled back and over the shoulder. Some wore more modern dresses in the French fashion. The men wore fur caps or czapkas. The peasant women wore bonnets, or turbans adorned with heron's feathers.

Amidst them all, right in the centre, riding on a pale horse, waving politely to the ladies, was the tall blond man, and his band of killers. At once we saw that this blond scoundrel was using these churchgoers as a living shield. The devil – he must have smelled us.

"Damnation," Sierawski snapped, "these people are in our line of fire."

"Then we need to scare them off," I replied simply.

"But that will give the game away," Tanski cursed, "and we are outmatched, five to three. Damn it all!"

"Being outmatched is nothing new," I said negligently. "We can still have our fight. Kasimir – run behind the church. Jan – get yourself behind the elephant."

"Now look here," said Tanski, pulling rank again, "I'm in charge here!"

I ground my teeth with anger.

"Do as I say, Kasimir," I said. "For you both need to run, to make your marks in time. I cannot run, I am as slow as a snail on this damn leg. Go!"

Tanski assented. With that they were away, fast as hares, and not a moment too soon, for the crowd was breasting the rise and would soon be upon us.

My blond friend was talking to the priest, and to a number of young ladies and some old babcias, who were riding in a two-horse carriage. He talked calmly and politely, but I could see him casting around for us, as if he had indeed smelt the ambush. As he rode, he was obliged to screw his eyes up against the sun, which was shining in his face. Around him, his hired killers were scowling and sweating in the midday heat.

One could see the unease in the faces of the wary townsfolk, their hands clutching their children and their rosaries, and their jittery horses, afrighted at their masters' fear. I felt a great pang of regret, for this had been the sweetest of hiding places, and we could have swatted the whole bunch of them like so many flies before they could have returned a single shot at us.

With that, after a brief whispered prayer, I stepped out of the hollow, into the open, and discharged a shot into the air. My shot frighted the birds from the trees and echoed through the valley. Polish guns had a voice still.

There was plenty of time to sit on a tree stump and carefully reload my musket and watch the scene unfold. Down below, the townsfolk imagined they were about to be set upon by the Cossacks, as so many other villages had been. They fled in terror. Carts upturned, horses reared, men shouted, ladies screamed, children shrieked, and dogs barked. Every rank of person, from the highest to the lowest, ran scrambling for cover in unseemly haste. Nor was there any differentiation between the sexes, for husbands elbowed their wives and mothers aside in a mad dash for ditch, hedge, wall, or tree to shelter behind.

Amid the dust thrown up by all this confusion I observed my blond friend. He remained admirably calm throughout. He and his men kept their horses reined tight in at the bit and under good control. After a few moments the avalanche of villagers had swept away, leaving behind a few pathetic remnants – hats tumbling in the dirt, spilled baskets of eggs, a child's doll. One of the blond man's party shooed away a loose horse with his whip, and then all was quiet again.

Now the field was clear for the combatants, although our element of surprise was forfeit. The blond man, Szymon Korczak, saw me straight away, as I had intended. Pointing me out to his fellows, he gave a great beam of delight and satisfaction, and then he doffed his cap to me.

"Ho there, Blumer!" he called good naturedly. "We are here to take you back to Podolia in chains! Hetman Rzewuski has ordered that you ride the whole way backwards, as befits a traitor, an outlaw, and a renegade. There, the flesh will be flayed from your back with the knout, and then you are to be broken on the wheel, drawn between four horses, and finally, as you beg for mercy, hanged like a dog!"

Evidently there was to be no trial. Sighting down the slope, I could see all five of them, bunched together from when the villagers had charged past in their headlong flight. It reminded one of stalking pigeons, lining them up to knock down two or three with one round of birdshot. In a moment, surely the same thought would occur to my antagonists.

"A Happy Easter to you too, you Targowica bastards!" I replied, raising my czapka, and then raising my musket. By now, I reckoned, my comrades would have enough time to be in position. I could see Szymon's crafty eyes judging the distance between us and the strength of the wind. His men carried pistols, which by now they all had in hand, and were training on my person. Despite the distance, for I knew them to be well out of range, it was an uncomfortable feeling.

"Where are your comrades, my dear Blumer?" Szymon called, casting around the horizon for Tanski and Sierawski, of whom there was no sign. Emboldened, he and his men began to walk their horses towards me, slowly, to close the range, before they charged. Good, I thought.

"Come up here and I'll tell you, you cowardly son of a bitch," I laughed, staring through my sights at the blond mane of hair. It was still somewhat of a range and I doubted the bullet would carry true, for as you know I am a poor shot.

"Very well then!" declared Szymon, and one could not doubt the cruel resolve in his traitor's heart. His men, I noticed, seemed far less sure of themselves.

"There are five of us, and only one of you," he chided.

"I will be happy simply to hit you alone, my lord brother," I replied, and this gave him pause for thought. Man pulls the trigger, but God guides the bullet. I squeezed the trigger, and the gun kicked like a mule.

Damnation! A miss!

"Unlucky, Sir!" Szymon called, "now it is our turn."

He and his men began to fire at me with their pistols. All around me the earth tore up with bullets and the bumblebees flew past my ears, plucked at my coat, and lifted off my hat. Miraculously, I was unhurt. They, too, were poor shots. Tossing my musket aside, I drew my pistols.

"Now we have you!" called Szymon. With that they drew sabres, spurred their horses, and made to charge. They closed the gap alarmingly quickly. In a few moments more they should have charged me down into my grave. Before they could do so, Tanski and Sierawski leapt from their hiding places, crying 'ambush!' and firing their guns.

This was all too much for the Targowicans, and they broke and ran, as fast as their horses could carry them. From the corner of my eye I saw a horseman tumbling dead from his mount. Then Szymon was upon me, brandishing his flashing sabre, for he was made of sterner stuff than his hired killers. His horse cast a great black shadow, blocking out the sun. At the last minute I discharged my pistol.

The horse reared and fell, with an awful scream, bucking and kicking, breaking its legs as it thrashed in agony. I cannot abide killing horses, and the sight was sickening. Killing men, however, no longer troubled my conscience. There he lay, my blond persecutor, his horse shot from under him. It now lay athwart, and he trapped beneath.

"Bless my soul, Szymon," I chuckled as I stumped slowly over, my leg dragging like an anchor, as I traversed the mound of bloody and mangled animal. "One minute you're on the horse, the next minute you're under it!"

My adversary was not finished. Nimble as a ferret, Szymon somehow slipped out from under the dead horse and away. I was at arm's length. I extended my second pistol to administer the *coup de grace*, for I had bloody murder and revenge in mind. At the last second, Szymon twisted desperately aside. The flash from my gun set light to his sable coat. The fine fur flared. He ran for the church, ablaze, and dropped his sword.

I trudged after him, grim as the golem. I stopped to pick up his fallen sword, and tramped on. Szymon pushed open the church door and fell over the threshold. His clothes were burning and tongues of flame licked at him hungrily, and he rolled desperately in the nave to smother them. No sooner had he put out the fire than I was upon him, sword at his throat. I stared down at him with contempt. His eyes were full of fear. My persecutor was unarmed, worn out, filthy, dejected, his burned clothes in rags. In short, he was thoroughly defeated.

"You were braver when it was five to one," I remarked, tossing his sword onto the flagstones. "Here, pick this up, and we'll finish this in the churchyard – I shall bury you where you die, or you me."

With one final terrified cry, he shrank back. "Sanctuary!" he cried, throwing up his hands before the altar. It was a pretty little church. Up above the altar, Christ and Mary had gazed down. Their sad faces quite took the murder out of my soul. My anger was quite gone, melted away like snow in a kettle.

"Why didn't you kill him?" Tanski asked, crossing himself as he stepped over the threshold.

"Rules are rules," I said simply, "he has sanctuary." I took a red cord from beside the altar, and proceeded to tie our prisoner's hands roughly behind his back and drag him out of the church into the spring sunshine.

"Then what are we going to do with this damn traitor?" Tanski said, snapping at my heels, and loading his gun. We were indeed presented with a problem. He was a traitor, and he meant to murder us, but he had claimed sanctuary. So we could not kill him, and we dare not turn him loose, but we had no means of taking him with us.

"You're the senior officer, aren't you?" I said to Tanski, coldly, "you decide."

Tanski pulled a glum expression as we walked out of the church, a strange band of celebrants. We might have been three centurions with Christ – albeit this prisoner was a Judas.

"I have the answer. Here's a good tree and a stout rope!" Sierawski chuckled, gleefully, "there are three of us – enough for a drumhead court martial! We can try and hang this traitor lawfully by the rules of war!" he cackled, capering around the worried prisoner with a noose. "Then both honour and justice are satisfied. And this bastard of a traitor will be dead, too."

"I'm no traitor!" our prisoner protested, "I am Captain Szymon Korczak, of Podolia, and I am a serving officer in the Russian army! Shoot me by all means, but you can't hang me! It would be quite improper."

"Hang him – the damned traitor!" Sierawski roared, "A Podolian in the Russian army indeed! He's Felix's man, a Targowica turncoat! A Russian running dog! I vote him guilty of treason. Let's hang him and be done with it!"

"I also vote him guilty of treason," Tanski said coldly, raising his pistol. "It is your vote, Blumer, and the casting vote. We must be unanimous, for this is a capital offence, and two votes to one will not do it. Quickly, now – let's hang him as a traitor and a coward, as he deserves."

"Untie my hands and you'll see how much of a coward I am!" blondie protested, with the false bravado of a chained dog, safe in his master's yard. Then he gazed at me, I who had been his terror a few moments ago, and who now presented his only salvation. A drowning man cares not the quality of the rope – a drowning man will clutch even at a razor blade.

With that, I cut the cord that bound his hands, and he fell silent, and took to rubbing his wrists and biting his lips.

"Veto," I said quietly. "I will not allow it – *nie pozwalam.* Captain Korczak is a prisoner of war."

Tanski and Sierawski howled at me with anger and rage. For a moment I thought they would turn their swords on me. Then our prisoner began to laugh.

"There is no war, Blumer!" the blond Captain said sourly, "It is you men who are the outlaws and traitors. The war is over, and you lost. Poland is dead!"

"Poland is not dead," I replied, "as long as we live."

Outside, two dead Targowicans that we had dispatched lay in the dirt, as if asleep. The wind ruffled the grass and their hair. By now, the peasants of the congregation had drifted back. They gathered, at a wary distance, to watch this strange trial unfold.

"One of us could fight a duel with him," Sierawski ventured, for he had not given up, like a dog that will not give up a bone.

"What cause have you to fight a duel, Sir?" Szymon said smugly. "Have I not been courteous in the face of your insults?"

"We cannot kill him," I said firmly, before my comrades could reply, "because if we do, the Targowicans will hang many of these good people hereabouts in reprisal." I pointed at the curious villagers, who had cautiously gathered, and watched us from a distance. There was a silence, as Tanski and Sierawski considered this bitter news, and Szymon exulted in his lucky escape.

"Then he gets away with nothing," Tanski seethed.

"Not quite," I replied. Drawing Szymon's sabre, I broke it over my knee, and flung it on the ground. Then I struck him a heavy blow with the back of my hand and he fell at my feet, quite crushed, for I am a big man, strong as an ox, and the stronger man by far. His proud face blushed crimson red at this disgrace, for to have his sword broken thus is the worst dishonour that can befall a gentleman.

"You have cause for a duel now, you treacherous coward, when we meet again. You and I have fought twice, and I have vanquished you twice," I said, "the third time, I will kill you, for you couldn't hit my arse with a handful of buckwheat, let alone a sword."

Szymon Korczak lay whining on the floor.

"Now, Tanski, Sierawski, tie his hands, blindfold him, and set him backwards on his horse, and let him ride where he will, the Devil take him!" I said.

When this was done, to the great merriment of the watching peasants, I said to Tanski –

"You are in charge now, comrade, for I am sick of it. You wanted command – now you have it."

CHAPTER TWENTY-SIX
THE HANGED MAN

As we rode on, we shared a full pipe every day. We had guns and supplies to spare now, that we had appropriated from the Targowicans. A week ago they had been hunting us, today we smoked their tobacco, drank their wine, and rode their horses. There are many that go out for wool and find themselves shorn.

We rode for a week into the Eagles' Nest Trail and did not seen another living human soul. We struck camp at the foot of a great rocky crag, where there was the ancient ruin of a small castle. Now there were only broken stones, lying like bleached bones on the green sward. We slept with our guns beside us under our blankets, like wives. There we lay up, like wolves with their bellies full of mutton, and their eyes full of fear of the hunters. It was a good stronghold, affording a tremendous vantage point. We could see the countryside for miles around. We sat around a blazing fire, one ear to the ground and two eyes to the horizon, waiting for hoof beats and horsemen.

After a further week had passed, there was still no pursuit. My leg began to heal and we breathed a little easier. Tanski took his new responsibility very seriously. One might have thought he commanded a whole regiment, not two forlorn fugitives. He spent his days hunting on horseback – spearing wild sheep, rabbits and pigs with his lance, or blasting game birds from the sky with Sierawski's ancient fowling gun. This gun had proved far more of a boon than we ever imagined, and we thanked Magda for it every night, as we tucked into the spitted flesh, roasted on the hillside amongst the ancient, fire-blackened stones of the dead fortress.

Of nights the fire threw our crazy shadows onto the jagged and tumbled walls. Out here only the wind whistled and whined and moaned. It seemed that even our enemies had forsaken us, disdaining to chase us into this badland, despising our blood feud as a mere nothing. Were we naught but outlaws? We talked of our many failures, the chances our generals had spurned, the comrades we had lost. We talked of our successes, which boiled down to only this – that we were still alive, and free. Sierawski and I have always been thoughtful sorts. We set ourselves to thinking about how we had recently beaten the Targowicans, though outnumbered by two to one. We talked this over for some time, pondering the reasons for this. For we should really have been head down over a saddle by now on our way back to Tulczyn.

"A disciplined body of men will always beat a rabble," I said, thinking of the histories of war I had read, for I had read everyone from Caesar to Czarniecki. "We are veteran soldiers, and they were jockeys, thugs for hire, good only for murdering peasants and Jews."

"Szymon is a soldier," Sierawski reminded me, unconvinced. "Perhaps it was our despicable and underhanded tactics of ambush, hit and run!"

"Perhaps," I laughed. "Cowards and backstabbers tend to win battles. *He who turns and runs away, lives to fight another day* – that was the Roman maxim, and they won a few wars, didn't they?" I drained a cup of our captured vodka to ward off the cold. "We Poles are too stubborn and brave. We should learn from the Cossacks, who hit and run. That was what Czarniecki did in the Swedish Wars, a hundred years ago," I concluded. Czarniecki had been the Polish general a hundred years ago, in wars we had fought concurrently with Swedes, Germans, Russians, Austrians, and Turks. Namely, unequal invasions by perfidious foreigners!

"Czarniecki fought the Swedes on this very ground," Sierawski said, pointing around us at the towering crags and hills, "in barren, godforsaken places like this. Fought them and won."

Why didn't the Commander let us fight like Czarniecki, we argued – like partisans? But Kościuszko had said it must be regular war, or nothing! So then we fell to bickering, as we always did, as to why we had lost the war.

"Not enough money," Sierawski said. "Not enough guns, not enough cannon, not enough men."

"Treachery and cowardice," Tanski spat, "damned Felix, and the damned king,"

"All that is true," I agreed, "but the real reason we lost, in my opinion, was General Suvarov. What we need, God help us," I concluded, "is our own Suvarov."

A chill wind fell across the hillside. We huddled in our cloaks and clutched our swords and guns, but these seemed naught but pitiful toys before the terrible name of Suvarov. We held up our crosses, and drank vodka, as if to ward off the curse.

"Blumer is right," Sierawski admitted, "he is a poor shot, and a middling swordsman, and he rides like a woman going to church, and he is a great oaf with a thick head, but he is right. We need our own Suvarov."

"In God's name, where in the world would we find a man like Suvarov?" Tanski asked.

"God," I laughed, "has no part in the begetting of men such as him. We will all have to pray to the Devil, boys! Amen!"

We stared into the flames as they danced. Up above, the moon glowed pale, fat, and unforgiving. When we stared up at the moon, we knew that the evil old devil up there had not forgotten us. We listened to the wolves howling in the wilderness, and the wood crackling and blazing in the fireplace, like laughter.

The very next day we rode on, and it was a good thing we did. We had seven horses now – three of our own, and four that we had taken from the Targowicans, and other spoils of war. We had their pistols, their powder, their victuals, their tobacco, their snuff, and sundry other trappings of good quality and quantity. The seizure of these articles was bittersweet. As ever, our enemies were better equipped than us in every particular. It would be preferable to receive supplies from a friendly quartermaster than to forever have to seize them, at great personal hazard, from hostile foes. Nevertheless Sierawski seemed delighted at something.

"Why, we have seven horses, and we are riding to war!" he exclaimed, for indeed we were, although how, and by whose command, was entirely uncertain. Still, we did not let that dampen our spirits.

Sierawski, as you know, was a Krakowian, and as we rode he bellowed out, very tunelessly and at great volume, a nonsense song that he knew, that did indeed fit the occasion perfectly. They have many such songs in Krakow, and they call them – with no great originality – 'Krakowiaks', which is also what the Krakowians call themselves. This was his favourite.

One man from Krakow
Had seven horses.
But after he went to war
Only one was left!

In seven years of war
He didn't draw his sword
So his sword went rusty
From no war!

As we rode, the valley narrowed and the flat plain turned to scrub and then to wood and the woods thickened to forest. Sierawski stopped singing and we drew our muskets, for this was bandit country still, and we with our four remounts laden with booty were a fat target. We saw that the trail rounded into a hairpin bend and we halted.

Up ahead we could hear wild shouts, and the neighing of Cossack ponies. We heard a shot, and smelled the faint whiff of powder.

"Damned Cossacks!" Tanski hissed, peering through a captured Targowican telescope, that had belonged to Szymon Korczak.

"This is as pisspoor as your ambush was, Blumer," Sierawski complained, "they've given the game away!"

"You stupid sod!" I laughed, as I peered through my own telescope, "they're not ambushing us! They're ambushing someone else!" Or rather, they had ambushed someone else, for we had arrived towards the end of the affair. About a dozen Cossacks had set upon three of our soldiers – fugitives like ourselves. Having overpowered them, and robbed them, they were in the process of murdering them. Intent on their villainy, the Cossacks were entirely oblivious to our presence, and had posted no pickets or sentries.

"To sword!" we roared, incensed, "to sword!"

One of the Cossacks had thrown a rope over the limb of a tree. The first prisoner had a noose around his neck and the Cossacks were hauling him up in the air. He kicked his legs, gasped helplessly for air, and grasped at the rope with his hands, which his tormentors had left untied. Every few moments, as his face turned red and blue, the Cossacks would release their grip, cackling as if this was the height of wit. No sooner had the poor man recovered his breath, than they would haul him up again, and repeat this torture.

The Cossack Hetman, which is their chief or sergeant, watched approvingly as he raised a bottle of wine to his lips.

A moment later, he was dead, run through with Tanski's lance, and the bottle rolled away into the dirt.

As we charged, I thought of the two girls hanged by the Targowicans. I was determined to prevent another such foul murder, and thus I reached the hangman first. Quickly I dispatched the drunk and unarmed Cossack with point-blank pistol fire, and without any qualms whatsoever. The rope flew from his hands like a whip and the hanged man fell to the ground, gasping for air.

"Lachy! Lachy!" the Cossacks cried, in despair, running for their ponies. All around, Cossacks were running to and fro. The three of us cut them down mercilessly like rabbits, blazing away at their backs until we ran out of shot, then slashing at the top of their heads with our sabres. For if you give no quarter, you can expect none in return.

Three of them made it out of the clearing alive and we took a man each, chasing them down on our horses. I caught up with my man near a stream and leapt from my horse, wrestling him to the ground, dropping my sword in the undergrowth. We rolled through a thorn bush and the barbs cut through my uniform and shredded the skin of my face and hands.

The Cossack was a stout, thick, round fellow, with a great bristling beard, dressed in filthy furs. We traded a few good punches, blacking each other's eyes and bloodying each other's noses. Then he sprang back and pulled a wicked dagger from his belt. My pistols were gone, in the mêlée.

Grinning, he began to circle me, feinting and jabbing his knife at my ribs and face, and cackling and cursing. It was, as you may imagine, extremely unpleasant, and I had to be on my guard to avoid being skewered. I had my own knife in my boot, but no leisure to draw it, for I was sorely pressed.

Then, from out of the trees, came another figure, wielding a huge Cossack cutlass, his neck still red with the rope burns, showing livid above his white shirt collar. He was, I noticed, a tall, handsome fellow with a great shock of shiny jet-black hair, and a black beard. I fancied that he looked a bit like a Jew, which struck me as an odd thought, and also appropriate. For the Cossacks have a great hatred of Jews, and would very well have tormented one in the base fashion that they had done, by strangling him with a rope.

As I was speculating on this, the hanged man struck the Cossack's head from his shoulders with a single vengeful blow of the sabre.

"*Dobry wieczor*, good day to you," I said, whistling with awe at this prodigious feat. "Warrant Officer Ignatius Blumer at your service, comrade. I am indebted to you, for saving my life!"

"Good day to you too, Sir," saluted the man, who was indeed a Jew, for he had the Star of David at his collar. He wore the same tattered uniform of the Republic as I did. The hanged man then rubbed vigorously at his throat, which was as raw as the meat on a butcher's block.

"My name is Private Karol Birnbaum," he said, still rubbing his throat, "and it is I who am indebted to you, Sir, for cutting me down from that accursed tree."

With Birnbaum and two of his comrades, who had also survived, there were now six of us riding, and not three. The three Jewish soldiers had recovered what the Cossacks had taken from them, and any of the Cossack weapons as were serviceable. Behind us we had a good few horses, both Cossack ponies and the thoroughbreds we had taken from the Targowicans. It is well said that they that go out for wool, often find themselves shorn!

In this way, across the nation, whole brigades of insurgents were gathering into companies and battalions and regiments. One day, we knew, into an army. Poland was not dead, not while we lived, at any rate.

Birnbaum now wore the enormous Cossack scimitar at his belt, black furs on his back, and a fur cap on his head. He was a striking-looking fellow, was Birnbaum, with his dark eyes and scowling brow.

"Damn it!" he laughed, as we rode through a terrified village, "these peasants think I'm a Cossack!" This Birnbaum had a fine sense of humour, and was a learned, bookish sort, and we found his society a pleasant change from banging our three heads together and being howled at by wolves.

"Tell us about the Beardlings," we said, for it was a subject that interested us all greatly. When the Commander had armed these Jewish volunteers, it had excited deep passions and prejudices amongst us Poles. Still, we had been desperate, and all hands were needed at the plough.

"Tanski here," I teased, "is, as you know, our superior officer, and he holds the esteemed rank of Lieutenant, from which he is hoping to be promoted to boot-licker or shit-collector."

"Go to hell, Blumer," Tanski exhorted me.

"Tanski is very keen to know about the history of his new Jewish legion," I continued, "for we see Tanski as a sort of Moses, leading his people out of the wilderness. Give him half a chance and he'll take away your golden calf, fetch you down ten commandments from that hill yonder, and part the waters of the Vistula with his farts."

"What the Devil do you mean by that – *his people*? I'm no Jew!" Tanski snapped, rising to the bait. He began ranting and raving about the times he had eaten pork, and the fact he had no beard, and so forth, until we fell about hooting with laughter. Eventually he shut up, his face crimson with rage, for by then even he saw the jest, and shrugged hopelessly. For if one commands, one must have skin thicker than a pig's, be it kosher or not.

Birnbaum told his story as we rode.

"I was a student in Wroclaw. After the Second Partition, Wroclaw fell into Prussian hands, as you know. Well, one day my tutor called me in and said that he was very sorry, but the Germans would not allow me to attend the university any longer, for I was a Jew, and therefore needed no learning but as could allow me to read the Talmud and to count money."

We threw up our hands and protested at this petty injustice, so typical of the Prussians.

"Now I was mighty put out by this, as you may imagine. For I was all set to make my way in the world as a fine lawyer or a doctor, or some such profession as tickled my fancy, and wear wigs and ride in a carriage and never have to labour for a living or want for a thing. That door to advancement being barred to me, I returned home to my father's business – he was a silk merchant – to put my shoulder to the wheel of honest commerce.

"My father was a hard working man, and he inherited his business from his father, and his father's father. We Birnbaums have been in Wroclaw since Sobieski's day, when our family sought sanctuary in Poland under the protection of the Polish kings. Polish kings have always been friends to the Jews – even when their subjects have not," he said, archly. "Anyway, our silks have always flourished, for we work hard, and we have the knack of turning a grosz into a zloty. We are a thrifty family, and we never waste a tynf.

"Yet our persecution did not end there. After the Partition, we found that a thousand new petty taxes and regulations had been inflicted upon us by our new overlords. It was bad indeed, for it was a hundred times worse than the torments inflicted upon us by our Polish masters. Truly, it is better the devil you know! For decades we had prayed for deliverance from Polish tyranny – if you fine officers will excuse me for saying so – and now we found ourselves delivered alright. Delivered right out of the frying pan, and into the fire!"

"Aye," I agreed, "be careful what you ask God for, in case you get it."

"So it goes!" Birnbaum laughed. "Anyway, between the customs house and the taxes and the fines levied on Jews, and the bribes that we had to pay just to open our shop in the morning, we were driven to the wall in short order, and to penury. A good business that had flourished since Sobieski's day, ground under the Prussian jackboot in less than six months. We watched as our creditors took our silks, our warehouse, and every stick of furniture in the house. Then the bailiffs gave us a good hiding with their truncheons into the bargain. They should have turned us out and packed us off to the ghetto, too, but for the fact that we already resided there. 'Well,' my old father said, as we dusted ourselves down and nursed our wounds, 'now we may have nothing, but at least we still have our good name.'"

"Your father was right," I said, "one's good name is the only possession that matters to a gentleman."

"Ha!" Birnbaum laughed, "My mother saw it differently. She scolded him for a fool, and said that in that case we had nothing but our lives, and like as not the Cossacks would be at our door for those presently. For we had all heard of the pogroms, of course. Then it took a turn for the worse, which I had scarcely considered conceivable. I woke up the next morning from this nightmare to find some Prussian gendarmes on my doorstep. They handed us a writ, or some such, and told us to present ourselves at the town hall on the morrow. There we were to be assigned a new name, and also to sign over our coat of arms, which was now null and void, nonesuch being permitted to be held by Jews. Now we really would have nothing – not even our good name!"

At this point, Birnbaum drew out a beautiful silk handkerchief, very large, embroidered with an elaborate heraldic design. This he tied to his lance and held aloft.

"Behold, the Birnbaum crest!" Birnbaum snorted with laughter. "Well, by now I'd had my fill of this. All of Poland was alight with rebellion. I resolved to join The Uprising. If all other occupations were barred to me, there was at least the profession of arms. We Jews all knew of a Jewish merchant named Colonel Joselewicz, from Kretina, who had raised a rallying cry in Yiddish against the invaders. This Joselewicz had worked as a financier for one of the magnates, and he had travelled to Paris, where he had learned French. Caught up in the revolution, with its spirit of liberty, equality, and fraternity, he was something of a Jewish Jacobin, and he found in the Commander a kindred spirit, and was made a Colonel."

"A Jewish Jacobin!" Tanski snorted, "saints preserve us!" Tanski, as you will know, was not fond of Jacobins, nor indeed of Jews, although he was always perfectly civil to our new comrades, except when in temper. Birnbaum continued his story.

"Well, in September last year the Colonel raised his own regiment of Jews, which I joined, named 'the Beardlings'." He pointed at his black beard. "It was so-called for we had been allowed to keep our beards, and eat kosher foods, and even to abstain from fighting on the Sabbath, when circumstances permitted. We were all volunteers, and most of us had been tradesmen or artisans, like my two comrades here that you also saved from the Cossacks. There we were, alongside the militia and the scythemen, when the Commander read the Act of Insurrection in Krakow Square."

"God's wounds, the Uprising!" we sighed, hearing the bells of the churches again, smelling the incense of the altars again, tasting Pepi's champagne on our lips. Krakow, and freedom.

It is a common slander that Poles hate the Jews. That may be so. Yet I never saw, nor fought against, nor even heard of, a regiment of Jewish volunteers under arms for any other nation. Not in twenty years of war. No Tsar, Kaiser, or Hapsburg ever had such a regiment as the Beardlings under their flag. But the Republic did. And it would have one again, in Italy, in our Polish Legion.

"There we stood with all free Poland," Birnbaum reminisced, "five hundred of us, the first regiment of Jewish warriors since the days of Masada!"

I laughed at this. "You Jews certainly know how to pick a fight! The odds we faced in The Uprising weren't much better than you Jews faced at Masada in Biblical times – standing against ten Roman legions!" The Jews of Masada, of course, committed suicide rather than submit to slavery.

"Alas," Birnbaum said ruefully, "you are right. We were cornered by the Cossacks at Praga. That must have occasioned those bastards great satisfaction, for their age-old hatred of us is unquenchable. As you see, a few of us Beardlings escaped, including the Colonel. We went into hiding in the ghettoes and synagogues, for our people sheltered us. We were making our way for Lwow, when a few of us were separated from the others, and the Cossacks caught up with us, and that is where my tongue catches up with my horse, so to speak."

"Why to Lwow?" we inquired, suspiciously.

"That is where the Legions are gathering," Birnbaum said cannily, "as everyone knows, and where you are bound yourselves."

"Soon enough, Birnbaum," I said, "but we have a rendezvous first."

With that, we all grinned, and spurred our horses.

CHAPTER TWENTY-SEVEN
PULAWY

Pulawy is south-east of Warsaw, not far from Maciejowice. We stayed well clear of that accursed spot where the Commander had his horse shot from under him, and was taken prisoner by the Russians. It took us until late summer, for the roads were thick with spies and soldiers. The harvest was already in and the skies were losing their lustre, like an old maid left on the shelf. In a few months' time it would be light enough to see the hand in front of your face, but dark enough not to see the knife as it was stuck in your back.

Cyprian Godebski had praised Madame L's beauty. He eulogised the tenderest and most beautiful eyes that nature had ever formed. Godebski would have appreciated her fine dress, her hat, her jewels, her glowing eyes. But they were also the cold, calculating eyes of a general, appraising newly arrived cannon fodder.

"Where the Devil have you been?" exclaimed Madame angrily, hands on hips, when we finally arrived. We vaulted from our horses and tied them up in the shade of a great round stone temple.

Madame was the lynchpin of our espionage network. She was a tigress. This lady did not lose heart now that we had been defeated. On the contrary, she had redoubled her efforts.

"All roads lead to Rome, my lady," I said, sweeping off my hat and bowing to kiss her hand. I had never dared before, but after our hard journey I was emboldened to kiss this beautiful gorgon. She stared back at me with the eyes of medusa.

"Sit down," she said, and clicked her fingers. Her lackeys brought us water, for it was still hot. We sat down on a bench in the shadow of the great stone edifice and drank. All around us were great boulders overgrown with moss.

"What, if I may ask, is this?" Sierawski piped up, indicating the great stone tower, which had a dome on top and columns around it.

"It's a tomb, you fool," I said, and cocked my head at Madame, "but whose?"

"This is the Temple of the Sibyl," Madame snapped, "and it is both a fortress, and a tomb. Inside the Temple we keep the flame burning. Here we will keep our culture, our language, and our history alive. It is a museum of our nation's treasures, those very same treasures that I salvaged from Warsaw, despite the best efforts of you gentlemen to foul it up, by losing half of them along the way – including the damned flag!"

At this we began to protest. We set to blaming the weather, the Cossacks, and treachery, for the disaster that had befallen our mission.

"Silence!" Madame hissed. We obeyed. "I see that you blame everything except your own negligence! None of you has exactly covered yourselves in glory in my service!"

We sat, gloomily, and contemplated her words. Workmen passed to and from the great tower with bricks and beams, mortar and marble, wood and water, loam and lime. There were a great deal of workmen, and as we watched them, we saw that they had the unmistakable walk of soldiers. After a time we began to recognise old comrades.

"This is an armed camp, in the guise of a building site," I said, doffing my threadbare czapka. "I applaud your ingenuity, Madame."

"When I need your approval, I shall ask for it," Madame snorted. "If circumstances were any different, I would dishonourably discharge the lot of you, or simply have you shot."

We hung our heads in shame.

"However," Madame went on, "I see that you have at least rescued these three good Jewish comrades, so perhaps you may redeem yourselves yet." She pointed at Birnbaum and the other Beardlings. They sat beside us, wisely keeping their bearded heads down.

"Also, I am desperately short of men," she admitted.

"Are things that bad?" I asked, quietly.

Her face was as grim as steel. "Indeed they are. The Commander is in a Russian gulag. A dozen of our generals are dead, including General Jasinski. Zayonczek is in an Austrian prison. Poniatowski has given up the fight – he drinks and gambles his days away in Warsaw."

"Hell's bells!" I swore, "Do all our leaders have feet of clay?"

"Not all, no," Madame replied. "General Dabrowski is in exile in Paris, seeking help from the French."

"With friends like the French, who needs enemies?" we asked, and began to laugh. For it had been discovered by now that a renegade Frenchman, spying for the English, had betrayed the plans of our Uprising to the Russians.

"So the Rottmeister really is our last hope?" Tanski cried, rolling his eyes. "Then we are indeed lost!" We fell to bickering. For Sierawski and I greatly esteemed Dabrowski, whilst Tanski did not. Madame silenced us with an imperious glance.

"Dabrowski has set up a Polish legion in exile. He has spent a year traipsing round the Courts of Europe, seeking sponsors. First, he went to the Prussians – a damn fool errand if you ask me, but then he is half-German by blood. As if those dogs would aid us after their treachery! No, they offered him a general's hat in their army instead, as indeed did the Russians. But our dear Dabrowski is no traitor, so he went to Paris instead. At first he was ignored by the French, but then he found a patron at last – Bonaparte."

"Bonaparte?" we asked blankly.

"Dabrowski has raised an army of Poles for the war in Italy against the Austrians, under the French General Bonaparte," Madame told us. By the end of the next year, that name would be on every pair of lips in Europe. Napoleon Bonaparte, the man of the age, who would shake the world like a wolf with a lamb.

"Then there is an army in exile? With the French!" we yelped, jubilant, capering about like children, "God bless this Bonaparte fellow! Hurrah for Dabrowski! When do we leave for Italy?" we asked, afire with new enthusiasm.

"You do not," Madame said. "A second legion is gathering in Lwow. Dabrowski has a spy in Turkey, in Constantinople, who is providing money and arms. You will go to Lwow, and you will take this with you." She called out to one of her lackeys, who hared off into the Temple at her command. A few moments later he returned, carrying Sobieski's standard, wrapped in an oilskin. Somehow this formidable woman had recovered it. Madame unfurled it. We cheered the sight of it, our poor threadbare flag.

"Poland is not dead, as long as we live!"

The six of us drew our swords, and pledged them to her. Madame raised her hands to the heavens. "Soldiers! Here are your orders. Do not fail this time. Go to Lwow. Go to Cyprian. He still lives – for now, at least," Madame said, her brow furrowed and careworn. "The Austrians have issued a warrant for his arrest."

We took to our heels at once. "Lwow is a big city. How will we find Cyprian?" I asked, from the saddle of my horse.

"You'll find him. All roads lead to Rome," Madame replied.

CHAPTER TWENTY-EIGHT
WIGILIA (CHRISTMAS EVE) 1795

All across occupied Poland, the Church bells were ringing, for it was *Wigilia*. We were crouched beside a forest track. A farmer drove by, and we watched him closely. His two horses had bells twined into their harnesses and the bells jingled as they trotted by. Behind them, his cart was heaped with food.

"He's getting away," Sierawski muttered, hand to sword.

"We're no thieves," I reminded him, "We'll pay him, even if it's by chopping wood and feeding the animals for our supper. Come on."

We were cold and hungry. Snow began to fall.

"Hail there, fellow!" I called, "*Wesołych Swiat!* Merry Christmas!"

Tanski was huddled in the shadows, sword drawn. We had no powder or shot left, from firefights with scattered patrols. Besides, steel is surer than lead. I kept my own sword sheathed, so as not to startle the man. If he ran, or raised an alarm, we should have to kill him. We had done it before.

"*Wesołych Swiat*," the farmer said, evenly, measuring the distance from the trees to the field with his eyes as we rode over. "What are you fellows doing out in this filth, on Wigilia? It's cold as hell!"

"Freezing our balls off!" I replied, and we laughed, and the farmer reached into his kontusz. As you can imagine, our hearts leapt. My own hand flew to my sword, but the farmer merely produced a bottle, and passed it around. Cautiously, I beckoned to the three Beardlings. Birnbaum and the others were wrapped against the storm, with only the slits of their eyes showing. We were all armed, and ragged. We must have appeared to be a band of the most vicious and desperate vagabonds. I watched the farmer closely. Fortunately, he was quite drunk.

"Follow me, boys, come on in out of the storm," said this ham-faced fellow, his cheeks flushed with good cheer. He was immune to the cold, for he was wearing an overcoat of one hundred per cent proof vodka. So we all drank ourselves cloaks of the same tailor who lived in that blessed bottle.

Gladly, we followed the farmer. Tanski did not show himself, but stepped in our footsteps, a ghostly shadow. For if we were betrayed, led into ambush, or overwhelmed, we should have a surprise up our sleeve.

"Visitors!" roared the farmer, as we trooped into his poor home. There was no porch – these were good honest peasants. As we stood, ravenously hungry, and dripping water like wet dogs, we glanced around the single room of the dwelling. Unthreshed sheaves of wheat had been placed in the four corners, for here the Christmas supper was about to take place. Heavenly scents of fish, cabbage and beetroot filled the air.

Sure enough, a redoubtable *basia* stood by the stove with a knife, her hands stained red from where she had been paring beetroot. Two tiny pairs of eyes peeked, terrified, from behind her apron strings. At the sight of us, of course the wife began to protest, but the farmer waved a hand.

"Five more places at table, Basia!" he cried, for that was indeed his wife's name. "When a guest enters the house, God enters also!"

The old basia, who was called Basia, scowled, and clutched her knife like a sabre. We stood there, wrapped up like Siberians, big as bears, with our rusty swords and empty guns. Thankfully, the farmer had recognised us for what we were. This was why he was not afraid.

"These are no Austrian scum, woman," the farmer spat, "these are our boys!"

Wise old Basia was unmoved, and stood her ground like a grenadier, knife raised. Finally I had the wit to pull out a red and white pennant, and handed it over, like a crumpled flower. At this, Basia smiled, put up her knife, wiped her hands on her apron, and then threw her arms around my chest. She put her hand to my whiskery face and I smelled the pink beetroot. It ran in my beard with my tears of joyful thanks.

"Thank you, dear *Pani*," I said, "we have a long road behind us, and a long road ahead."

"Who are these boys?" Basia said, peering at the Beardlings suspiciously. Birnbaum and the other two sat in their skullcaps, putting away the borsch as fast as they could.

"Are they Cossacks?" she said to me, warily. There were still a few loyal Cossacks, but even these tame Cossacks had a terrible reputation for drunkenness and wenching. Still, God alone knew what these people would make of a houseful of Jews at Wigilia. I decided not to put it to the test.

"Why, these are Poles, mother, from the west!" I said smoothly, and winked at her. "Soldiers of the Republic, like us. Birnbaum and his lads here are from Wroclaw. They wear their beards long over there, in the German fashion."

"Bloody Germans," the farmer said bitterly, tearing at the bread, without even glancing up from his borsch. Basia shrugged.

"Watch your money when you play cards with them – they are Jews, my lad!" Basia whispered to me as she passed. She went back into the kitchen. Then the moment passed, without any further disasters. I breathed a sigh of relief. At last I turned to my soup bowl.

Suddenly there came a fresh commotion. Tanski was at the door with a stout lad of fourteen, and a girl of perhaps sixteen. The girl was dark-haired and blue-eyed, and slender as a roe deer.

"Are you being murdered then, lads?" he laughed.

"Old Basia here will murder you if you don't get your hands off that girl," I said, disentangling him from the daughter, who was already making doe eyes at him, after scant seconds of acquaintance. By God, much as I loved Tanski as a brother, I loathed him sometimes! For his pride, his arrogance, and his foolishness. Most of all, though, for his success with the ladies.

After this stupid business was concluded, we found ourselves amongst friends, and not foes. Vodka was poured and 'Wesołych Swiat!' cried out in chorus. All of the customs were observed in this fine little house. We spread the hay under the tablecloth, to tell our fortunes. Even the Jews joined in, for they knew our customs, just as we knew theirs.

What luck awaited us? None good, we knew. Sure enough, every man pulled a blackened blade of hay, and we laughed heartily each time. For this meant bad luck, spoiled meat, spilled milk, broken bread, star-crossed love, unrequited ambition, cuckolds' horns, empty beds, grave goods, marked cards and shaved dice. Only the girl drew a green blade. It was the only blade I ever saw that frightened Tanski. For he feared but one thing – matrimony!

Then, the most blissful moment of the year. The farmer broke the wafer, and passed a tiny white piece of unleavened bread for each one of us. Kisses and greetings and best wishes were exchanged. All sins were forgiven. We were reconciled, all of us, even Tanski and I, our long feud at last forgotten. An empty place of honour stood at the end of the table. We cried and shed tears for those we had lost, tears flowing like blood. A great shared joy welled up within the tears. There, in our hearts, burned solidarity's eternal flame.

In those days, at Wigilia, all men and women, from highest to lowest, ate until their bellies burst. Supper commenced with red borsch and uszka. Next came a hearty dish of pike, a noble fish. We were served kutia with this, which is a sweet cereal dish. This was a custom in these parts, for we were now deep in the eastern lands of Poland – or what was once Poland, at any rate – on our way to Lwow.

Then, of course, the king of the feast – the royal carp! This was done proud with peas, green cabbage, dried brown mushrooms, and grey sauce. Basia cut the carp crosswise, and ladled on the grey sauce, which she had flavoured with pimento, horseradish, onions, bay leaves and salt. Besides this we had endless potatoes under chopped dill. Sometimes the carp is served with a glass of plum brandy, but instead we had vodka, and wine. It was not the Thursday Dinners. Instead of listening to the learned conversation of eminent men, I heard naught but the happy belching of my comrades, their gulps, snorts, and farts. They stuffed themselves like pigs, pausing only from their repast to gulp down a glass of wine or spirits. Aye, it may not have been the Thursday Dinners, but by God it was a fine, hearty, meal.

In those days we were not the milksops you are in these feeble times. There you sit, gnawing on leaves and stalks, like mice, whining temperance and moderation, God help you. So we fairly demolished the board between us, leaving only bones and gristle for the wolves. At length I was asked to take out these scraps, so observing the custom. This I did, slopping them outside the gate to appease the howling packs of wolves that roamed out in the ancient forest beyond. Icy fangs of the hungry gale gnawed at my face in vain. By now, I had drunk enough of the magic potion not to pay it any heed.

An idiotic custom, this – the invitation to the wolves is meant to appease them, so they will leave the house in peace. What foolishness! Our whole land was surrounded by wolfpacks, and over the years we had thrown out scraps at the gate for them. Treated so well, they came back for more. So we had thrown them more scraps. Still they were not satisfied. Thus we threw out the borsch, the uszka, the pike, the carp, and the pierogi besides. Then, when the food was all devoured, we had thrown them our silver, and gold, and lastly the lead from the church roofs! Of course the wolves had licked their lips, and, after eating all this, had eaten us whole.

I am not superstitious, but I always observe the customs, out of respect, and for good luck. I never cast bread on the ground, or set a place for thirteen guests. Hence, here I was, throwing slops to the wolves. I should have been throwing them to the good, honest, blameless beasts of burden who stood nearby, huddled together in the barn – horse, cow, pig, sheep, and dog. I saw the animals circled around in a wheel, huddling their heads together. They do this to keep warm, but in my fancy, I perceived them to be conversing.

Another foolish superstition that my mother always held firm to her breast was that, at midnight on Wigilia, the beasts conversed with human voices. To overhear them brought unspeakable, ruinous, damnable bad luck. As I stood, my empty bucket clanking in the wind, the animals raised their heads. They spoke to me, but thank God, they spoke in their own tongues. Sheep bleated and brayed, cows lowed, dogs barked. I laughed, and turned back inside to warmth, drink, and cards.

Then a cloud passed across the face of the moon, and all was dark in Twardowski's realms above and below. I did not run, to be sure, I walked away, but quickly, exactly as one does under musket fire. As I was crossing the threshold, I fancied that I heard the animals speak one single word, borne on the teeth of the wind –

"Bonaparte."

CHAPTER TWENTY-NINE
WOLVES, MUSHROOMS, AND WITCHES, JANUARY 1796

Before we departed our Christmas sanctuary, the young lad had begged to come with us, as a drummer boy.

"Out of the question – you have no military experience," Tanski said coldly.

"Besides, he's too young," Sierawski added.

He wouldn't last a week, I thought to myself. Basia, his mother, was torn by pride, and fear, throughout the exchange.

"Join the legions when you are of age, boy," I told him gently, "we will return."

It seemed a hollow promise, one that, even if fulfilled, was likely to augur doom. The clouds broke and we rode off in pouring rain. Of course, a day later we found the boy following us. We gave him a hiding, and sent him back to Basia. Finally we journeyed on from the plains, with their farmers and woodsmen, into the deep dark hanging groves of the forest. On we rode through a wall of towering pines and firs, like the masts of an enormous fleet of ships. On we rode over logs, roots and stumps, and pine cones scattered like empty cartridge cases after a battle. As if passing from this world into another, we rode into a realm of green.

This was a place of spirits and shadows, a realm of wood, trees yawning like great longbows being slowly drawn. At their feet, a thousand arrows of light were scattered about the forest floor. Our horses walked on a carpet of rotting brown leaves and pine needles, soft as sable cloaks, muffling their hoof beats to a whisper.

Above us the sky narrowed to a long trench of grey and blue, as it is glimpsed by a man peering through a prison window. Even in the heavens, there was warfare. On high, ranks of crows and ravens cawed, sounding their battle cry, until driven off by eagles and kites, which fell upon them like cavalry. These trees were as old as God, and they brooded on the secrets of ages. They closed ranks about us, and we rode in single file, meandering through lost tracks and forgotten trails, following streams and river beds frozen with snow.

At last, we began to relax our guard, for we were no longer being pursued. None but the wolves followed us here, in this ancient wilderness. A companionable silence fell among us as we listened to the songs of the forest. Sweet scents of pine filled our noses, our lungs, our daydreams. Yet the forest was not free of perils. Here were wild and dangerous beasts – the dread bison, the ferocious brown bears, and the wild boars, with their great tusks like ivory lances. Creeping in the thick carpet of sweet pine needles were rats, snakes, and wolverine. In the night, we fancied that we saw the gleam of yellow eyes beyond the circle of our campfire. But it may simply have been the fireflies, or the spirits. All of us had heard tell of the other things that haunted the forest – fell creatures of the night. Werewolves. Vampires. Rusalka. Witches.

After a few months Wigilia was but a memory. We saw not a living soul in that time beyond our own small party of partisans. Each day, two of us would gather food, while the others rested and tended to the horses. One strange day, Tanski and I went out to collect mushrooms. Sierawski had shot a stag, and while the others were roasting and smoking the meat, we hunted the noblest and rarest jewel of the forest – the noble boletus. The real mushroom.

There were rows and rows of mushrooms, silver, gold, red and white. Some with scalloped edges, some as round as plates, some like upturned goblets, and yet others, funnel shaped, slim as champagne flutes. This pretty display reminded me of the cups and plates on the sideboard of that ruined house in Wola, where dear Cyprian led us against the Prussians. Alas! Was Cyprian alive or dead?

Now, some years are fat, and some years are lean. This proved another lean year. We picked not a solitary boletus. But we found the famed orange agaric, almost as tasty as the boletus, and good both fresh and salted for our journey. As we strayed still further into the dark and uncharted beyond, we found, in abundance, a fine staff of pretty colonels!

"Aha!" Tanski cried, "here is another Vixen – that's the Lithuanian name – to add to my collection! A virgin, too, I'll be bound – not a single worm or beetle has befouled her virtue!" Tanski held the luscious brown-capped mushroom aloft, like a trophy. He had a string of them in his czapka already.

"Damn, this place is quiet!" he called out, "What a shame that it wasn't Basia's daughter who followed us, instead of the boy! This place needs a woman's touch," Tanski remarked, idly, twirling his moustaches, as we picked amongst the logs and leaves and shrubs and ferns and fallen stumps.

"That it does," I agreed. "I'll bet there hasn't been a woman in this forest for a hundred years," I laughed, flinging a toadstool at him, "unless you count the Rusalka, of course!"

The toadstool was an ugly plug of poison, virulent enough to kill a barracks full of men. Tanski laughed, caught it, and lobbed the black knob away into the darkness, like a grenade. I followed the graceful arc of the deadly fungus with my eye as it spun down a ravine and watched where it fell. Beyond it, a lazy black finger curled up into the air, as if it was the flash after a shell burst.

"Smoke," I said. At this, Tanski dropped to his knees, spilling his maidens onto the forest floor. He was ever careless with female hearts! We drew our sabres, and set off down the slope towards the smoke. At the end of the ravine, there was a lopsided hut, leaning like an evil grin. Around it were slick bottomless quicksands to swallow a horse whole, dead pools gleaming with rusty bloodstains. A steaming vapour clung about, stinking of suphur and damnation.

"Perhaps it's the Rusalka's house," I said. Tanski grinned, but despite himself his face was pale, and his sabre shook in his hand. The Rusalka, you will know, is an evil spirit that takes the form of a delightful, charming, captivating and beautiful young maiden. She dances naked in the woods, and lures unwary foolish men to their deaths. Suddenly unnerved, we touched the crosses at our throats. Overgrowing grass spilled over in the pools, like strands of long brown hair. The twisted trees hunched over the bottomless pool like witches over a cauldron. Bald of leaves and bark, they grasped with wormy fingers into the rich black soils, like a miser after gold.

The wooden hut was clothed in a coat of green moss that crawled over every inch of the rough-hewn planks. There was no chimney, and no door. Smoke rose through a hole in the roof. A blanket hung across the threshold. Tanski rapped on the wooden wall with his sword hilt. It swayed. No answer came. Inside was a raddled old crone, a storybook witch. Her nose curled over her chin like an ancient bird's beak. She wore a patchwork of filthy clothes. Her feet were bare and black as a beast's, with horny toes. A long cable of thick, matted hair hung down to her waist. Her rheumy old eyes, though, were as bright as a crow's. Childlike, she hid them behind her bony hands. She said nothing, yet she did not shrink from us.

"If she's the Rusalka," I remarked, somewhat unchivalrously, "I'd say she's seen better days."

Cautiously, so as not to startle this strange lady, we ventured into the hut, and, removing our czapkas, we sat down on our cloaks. The hut stank of damp, and dried herbs, and all-pervading woodsmoke. All the while, the woman – who must have been as old as God – sat and watched us, peeking over her long talons of fingernails. A battered copper kettle, sitting on the fire, began to whistle, and the pair of us nearly jumped out of our skins! At this, the old woman cackled, and began to mutter incomprehensibly to herself, to us, to the air, or, for aught we knew, to her familiar spirits. Then she scuttled away, spiderlike, and began scrabbling bunches of herbs together.

"I have been expecting you, my brave boys," crooned the Witch. She spoke in Old Polish, in an archaic accent, but she was quite lucid. "You are late," she scolded us, which was damned peculiar. We shrugged. We even apologised.

"Here, drink, and I will tell your fortunes," she croaked. We watched as the woman began to pour us what appeared to be tea, sieving the brew through a rag.

"You are from these parts," Tanski whispered to me, "is this a five-nippled Witch?"

I was, of course, not from these parts, but it was close enough. I knew the countryside and its ways better than he.

"This woman is – or was – a Goralka, a hill woman," I told him. "An outcast, no doubt, from those wild folk. Perhaps she has a deformity, as you say, or perhaps she bore a child outside wedlock, and was thrown out by her family. Who can say? I doubt she remembers it herself. Look at her – she's probably been here since the Swedish Wars."

The old woman set cups of evil-smelling liquid before us. It was reminiscent of the stagnant pool outside, with its rusty bloodstained surface and green mantle of muck. We choked down the scalding tea. It tasted of fennel and mandrake, wormwood and aniseed, and the woody tang of mushroom. A brackish, metallic taste remained in my mouth, like sucking on a bullet. After we had drunk, the crone snatched away our teacups and held out her wizened claw for payment. I had a few worthless coins in my wallet and handed them over. The old crone simpered, a corpse's smile through a mouthful of gravestones, her lips as parched and cracked as dried worms. She stared at the coins, transfixed by their gleam, then bit into them with her few remaining teeth. Satisfied, she hid the coins within her stinking and ragged robes.

Then, with a wild grin and a cackle, she rooted around in a corner, scattering weeds and rubble, then levered up a rotten wooden board.

"What fresh madness is this?" Tanski snapped, "Clearly, the woman's mind has gone. Let us be off."

From under the board she produced, to our immense surprise, wrapped in a filthy cloth, a silver chalice, carved all over with strange symbols. This she filled from a pitcher of water, and bid us look. She set herself on her knees, as if in prayer, and bent over this divination bowl, and stared into it.

"In the water," she hissed. We all stared into the cauldron. We stared hard until white spots boiled before our eyes. Still, stare as we might, we saw nothing but our own ugly mugs peering back at us, as if from the bottom of a well.

"What is in the water?" Tanski grumbled, "your sanity?"

"Silence!" she cried. "See what is written in the water."

Abruptly Tanski bent over and was violently sick.

"To hell with this," he muttered, storming out of the hut. I sat awhile longer with the Witch. We stared into the water. Sweat ran down my forehead in rivulets. My head spun and my sight blurred. I tasted the vile tea, and thick vomit in my belly, and choked back bitter bile. Pictures took shape in the water, or perhaps in my head. I saw our Legions marching into Vienna, into Berlin, and finally, into Moscow itself. I saw the Kremlin ablaze. I saw the three Black Eagles scatter, in full flight before the White.

At last, I tore my gaze away, triumphant, and stared at the Witch. She met my eyes.

"So we win, old woman?" I demanded.

The woman said nothing. She merely gathered herself into a ball, and rocked on her heels. Then she laughed and laughed, and laughed again, laughing fit to split her corsets, as if this were the greatest joke in all creation.

CHAPTER-THIRTY
LWOW, FEBRUARY 1796

Lwow, in those days, was a great bustling place. From the top of a hill, we saw the streets spread out below us like wings. With her fine brick houses of red, pink, yellow, green, and brown, she was a bird of rare plumage. Down below were the streets, the bridges, the aqueducts, and green parks full of trees. Spearing up to the heavens were a phalanx of spires. From left to right it was girt with seven great towers, the farthest left being a squat, rotund fellow, the others being variously square or round and with points, crosses, and domes. These stretched away to the right, where there was a huge windmill, spinning like the very devil. Today, this rare bird was a white raven. All was dusted with a shroud of snow. It was February. We were well into another New Year, but we faced the same old enemies.

We stopped to let a cart pass, and it rumbled by, wheels groaning, carthorses' hooves padding in the snow. Our own horses blew hard from their thin flanks, where their ribs were showing.

"Who is this Godebski?" Birnbaum asked. Snow was falling now, great fat flakes of it like moths. The Austrians were negligent, but even they might notice six armed men. So Tanski, Sierawski and the others were shivering in a barn. Birnbaum and I, alone, had ridden on ahead as outriders. We were freezing on this wind-blown hill, while below us in Lwow, they sang and drank.

Lwow, like Krakow, was now in Austrian Galicia, which was what the Hapsburgs had renamed the province. This so-called 'Galicia' was a creation that had swelled like a blood-bloated tick, swallowing Podolia. So this was another bitter homecoming for me! Black Austrian eagles flew from all seven of the spires that I had spied from the hill.

This city, though, was an unruly horse. The trade route here runs through Bar and on to the wild lands beyond, as far away as China. A hundred nationalities pass through the inns and staging-houses of Lwow. Here jostle Poles, Jews, Germans, Austrians, Czechs, Slovaks, Hungarians, Cossacks, Zaporozhians, Ruthenians, Tartars, Turks, and many others besides. In this chaotic swirl, conspirators may come and go freely enough. This was another fine forest for we hunted wolves to slink through. A forest of stone.

"Cyprian is my dear friend," I said, "and we must be careful not to bring ruin upon him. He is a great soldier and a spy, and he will have been as careful as a fox in covering his tracks."

"So how will we find him?" Birnbaum asked, reasonably enough, shouting to make himself heard above the roaring gale.

"All roads lead to Rome!" I shouted back. Then I cast behind me for the hundredth time, like a hunted animal. No one was taking the least notice of us. We were swathed in cloaks against the wild weather, but then so was everyone else. The customs house had been closed, the Austrian guards were snoring in their bunks or drinking in the taverns.

The two of us wandered the streets for many miserable hours. In all the houses the lights were burning. Smells of food and snatches of songs raced by on the blizzard's wings. A long fruitless afternoon had run out of the hourglass. Evening was soon pouring into it. We were dripping wet. Snow and ice rimed every inch of our clothes, with only our red raw wind-whipped faces above.

"Hell's teeth," I said at last, "let's have a drink."

The tavern had an enormous white eagle hanging above the door. The wooden beams were painted red and the plaster was whitewashed. As so many others in our land, the inn was named '*Rzym*' – 'Rome'. If it was a trap, it was a fairly obvious one, but by now we were long past caring. All roads lead to Rome!

We stabled our horses ourselves, for the servants were nowhere to be seen. After we had seen our horses aright, we shook ourselves like dogs. Great slops of slush and snow fell at our feet and into the straw. Lastly, I slung my musket over my shoulder and we marched up to the door.

It was barred. We thumped on it with our fists. Inside we could hear the sounds of laughter and merrymaking. Glasses and tankards were being clinked, and heavy plates of food clattering down on trestle tables. A heavenly scent of food and mead seemed to permeate through the very oak of the ironbound door. Inside they were singing. A slit in the door opened and suspicious eyes peered out.

"No room at the inn!" jeered a voice. "Piss off!"

"Devil take you," I roared, shoving my gun through the slit, "what kind of welcome is that for a good Polander? There's gold if you let us in – and lead if you don't!"

At this, there was a great commotion, and the sound of chairs being loudly scraped back across the floor. Then, dead silence fell. The singing ceased.

"Sweet Jehovah," Birnbaum hissed, "what have you done now, you crazy *pistolet*?"

After a moment the bolts were drawn. "Better come in then, boys," the voice said mockingly. The door swung open and we stepped over the threshold, hands on our swords. Inside was a typical inn – a great blaze in the hearth, with suckling pigs turning on spits above it. Gobs of fat dripped off the meat into the fire and spat and fizzed like grenades. The glorious smell of roasting flesh wafted out.

A host of men and women were gathered in a horseshoe around the door, facing us. Each and every one, the women included, held a gun, a sword, or a knife. We heard the familiar click of hammers drawn back on flintlocks. I walked through the thicket of blades and barrels straight to the bar. The barman was a great lugubrious fellow with a huge domed head and silver whiskers, armed with a blunderbuss, and laughing like a horse. I recognised him at once.

"Two vodkas, Cyprian, and be quick about it," I snapped, and then added, "on second thoughts, bring the bottle!"

Cyprian Godebski set the vodka before us, and sent a boy to summon our comrades, who were still huddled in a barn. They sneaked through Lwow to avoid attracting attention, not that the Austrians seemed to care in the slightest. A short while later, the four of us – Godebski, Tanski, Sierawski and I – sat down together at a table, reunited for the first time in a long, dreadful year. This was the first of two joyful reunions that day.

"Thank the Lord!" Godebski cried, clapping us each on the back. We introduced our new comrades, including Birnbaum and his two fellow Beardlings. Then we all of us, Jew and Gentile, cast longing eyes at the roasting pigs on the hearth. Our stomachs gave a volley of rumbling.

"Hey, sweetheart," I said to the cook as she passed, "get some fish! These boys don't eat white beef!"

"Yes we damned well do," said a ravenous Birnbaum. As it was, he was spared the sacrilege, for the girl was a fine hostess. She could turn her hand to kosher as well as any rabbi's wife. When she came back from the kitchen it was with several fish for us to eat along with the pigs, and we would have eaten her, too, had we caught her. Instead, we watched her frying the fish three times. For a fish must swim three times – in water, in butter, and in wine. We regarded these fish with great interest. There were several of them, of different species. It made a fine allegory.

"Here we have Poland!" I exclaimed, "for here are both pike and carp, and both of them are roasting on the fire."

The girl took a shine to Birnbaum – he was, as I have said, a wickedly handsome villain – and made him pike in grey sauce, a favourite Jewish dish. This pleased me greatly, for it annoyed Tanski immensely. He was a jealous soul, was Tanski. The womenfolk of Lwow seemed to prefer Birnbaum to him. So Tanski seethed at Birnbaum and we set about the food and drink with a will, like jackals. This tavern had a fine wine cellar, seemingly bottomless, and I could see the wheels of Birnbaum's mind turning like clockwork.

Birnbaum asked the girl whose tavern this was. It was hers, she said. Her father, a volunteer, had died at Maciejowice, leaving it to her. She would not take payment for our lodge and board – "Sooner you boys drink the place dry and burn it down," she said, "than let the invaders take a drop of mead or a bite of fish." If only others were as faithful!

Thereafter, she collected our dishes. As she bent over the table, Birnbaum watched the crucifix bobbing on the girl's bosom. There he sighed, defeated, for that immovable fortification was most likely the end of his campaign.

"Pike do not swim with carp, after all," he said sadly, but he still ate every drop of his grey sauce, until his black beard ran with it. No sooner had we finished, than the church bells tolled.

"Time for mass!" Cyprian exclaimed, wrapping himself in a great fur cape. "Come with us, lads," he said to Birnbaum and the other Beardlings. Birnbaum's face fell, as did all of the Beardlings, thinking themselves ill-used by this.

"When in Rome, do as the Romans do," I said. After some dark mutterings, they tucked their skullcaps under their hats and we all set off, pike and carp together. That day there were two reunions. Cyprian and I went off, arm in arm, to midnight mass. We had drunk somewhat of the vodka. Our drinking was medicinal, for it remained ferociously cold, and I was suffering from a fever. Drink stilled the pain. Even so, I ran with sweat even in the cold, such that the snowflakes steamed from my body as if from a hot anvil.

We trudged off to mass, a few at a time, to avoid suspicion. Had the Austrians but eyes to see, it should have been quite manifest as to what we were about. Yet no one molested us. The little stone church was heaving with a congregation of armed insurgents, such that they spilled out into the graveyard that stood beside it.

As we passed over the threshold, and doffed our czapkas. I dipped my hand in the freezing water bowl and made the sign of the cross. The holy water stung my brow, for my skin was burning hotter than gunmetal. By now I was fading fast, my head steaming and my nose and eyes streaming, so Godebski conveyed me to the front of the church. A few men recognised me and there were muted cries of joy and concern. For I read in their faces that I was in a bad way. My limp had returned now. A cold burning fire was spreading from the old wound in my leg.

"So you command all these men?" I asked Godebski, between coughs and increasingly violent sneezes.

"No," Godebski shook his head, as we reached the front of the church, "here is our commander – Lieutenant Colonel Jablonowski."

At the front, the wounded were seated, or kneeling, according to the severity of their injuries, and the strength of their piety. In the centre of the pew, swathed in bandages and sitting amongst the other wounded, was as a tall black gentleman. A handsome fellow, to be sure, but a black man all the same, with a head of hair of tight black curls swept back from a wide brow. He wore a bushy cavalryman's moustache above full lips. His skin colour and features were all distinctly African. Who was this? To confound me even more, he wore the uniform of a lieutenant-colonel of the Republic. Could this blackamoor be Cyprian's commander? Impossible! Still, I kept my mouth firmly shut, to avoid placing my boot in it. For the second time in our acquaintance, Birnbaum came to my rescue.

"Sir! I thought you were dead at Praga!" Birnbaum cried, in delight, much to our surprise. He raced forward and embraced the black colonel, who warmly embraced him in turn.

"Karol!" replied the black man, delighted. In spite of his injuries, he hauled himself to his feet, with some difficulty. Swaying on crutches, he and Birnbaum embraced. The black officer shook his head and pointed at his wounds.

"It was close! No, as you see, I escaped – along with your Colonel of the Beardlings."

"Is the Colonel here?" Birnbaum asked eagerly.

"No," the black officer shook his head. "He has gone to Paris, with Dabrowski. Perhaps they will raise another Jewish legion there!"

"Certainly there are enough moneylenders in Paris," someone muttered unkindly.

The black officer grinned, his white teeth gleaming against his dark skin.

"But what is this – here you are in church! Have you converted, my dear Birnbaum?"

Birnbaum grinned back and shook his head vehemently. "No, Sir, I have not, but your Christian God has given me a great gift this day!"

When they mentioned Praga, my addled mind began to work at last. This unfortunate officer had been in command of Praga when it fell to Suvarov and his Cossacks, and given up for dead. This was Jablonowski. Everyone knew who Jablonowski was. For there was only one black officer in the Polish army, after all. Jablonowski was a rare bird – as rare as a white raven, but black, of course. He was known to all as the Little Negro.

Then the bells rang, and the singing began, and the priest walked in, swinging his censer over the huddled bodies of his congregation. After Mass was ended, we picked our way through the dark, some limping with wounds, others with drink, back to the tavern called Rome. Birnbaum lent his shoulder to the Little Negro, who had been shot to ribbons by the Russians, and was slowly healing his wounds. As we walked back to the tavern, we heard the wolves howling in the hills. So after they had serenaded us, we sang our cavalryman's song back to them –

> *"O sacred love of the beloved country,*
> *For thee, 'twere nothing to live poor,*
> *'Twere nothing to die!"*

This had been the anthem of our Corps of Cadets, and a great favourite of the army. Now our corps was gone. I thought many times of the dear old academy, ruined. Standing empty, the roof caved in, the doors barred, the armoury looted, spiders spinning webs in the halls. Worse, I thought of the classrooms full of Russians and their lackeys – a weapon of war to be turned against us, a school for murderers and torturers.

"*Sto lat!*" we cried. We shut the door on the dark and drank the first of many toasts.

"Damn it all," Jablonowski said, throwing himself into a chair, "these wounds give a man a thirst," and he filled his wineglass. At a draught he drained it, and drew another. This next he threw down his throat without it touching the sides. We were all heavy drinkers, but Jablonowski was prodigious. He drank like a priest.

There were no girls to be seen now. Our friends Tanski and Sierawski, who were in fine fettle, and full of beans, were dancing in the back room with them. Birnbaum's comrades, like so many Jews, were apt musicians. In no time they were playing a storm of mazurkas and polonaises, and from time to time, their own mournful songs.

But we four sat apart – Cyprian, Birnbaum, the black colonel, and myself. For we had deadly serious business. Ostensibly, we were standing guard at the doorway, but our affair was far more important than that. As the wolves of the forest scent each other out, men of our stamp know each other instantly, without a word, merely by glance. We were card players.

"The game is whist, as always," I said, pulling out a pack of cards. The deck was greasy, cracked, blacked with dirt and campfire-soot.

"I'm not playing with your lucky deck!" Godebski sneered, producing a fresh pack from behind the bar, and tossing it onto the table, together with another bottle of vodka.

"My dear Captain," I said, in tones of mock horror, "are you implying that my deck is marked?"

For an accusation of cheating, even in jest, is not to be borne by a gentleman.

"Certainly not," Cyprian said quickly, holding up his hands, "I meant merely that this particular deck of yours is especially favoured by the gods of chance."

"Good," I said, "now shut up and deal!" Then I let out a thunderous sneeze. Everyone called "*Na zdrowie!* Bless You!"

From time to time we heard Sierawski croaking out a Krakowiak, his dreadful voice keening like a crow. This was greeted with a gale of derisory laughter, and not the storm of acclaim that he expected. I did not see it that night, but I had seen it a hundred times before, in every village or tavern where Sierawski inflicted his atrocious singing. But otherwise our game was not interrupted. It was blissful.

"Here, Blumer," said Godebski, cutting the cards, "the Beardling and I shall play together, and you shall play with the Little Negro."

Thus my partner for the first hand of whist was the Little Negro. This epithet was the name by which Jablonowski was universally known. He seemed heedless of this usage by

Godebski, but for myself I was very careful to defer to him as 'Colonel' at all times. For Jablonowski was an exceedingly dangerous man, quick to temper, and a fast blade. He had fought any number of duels and killed or wounded any number of men. Scarcely less dangerous in peace than in war, one should know better than to cross him.

At length, the Little Negro said to me, "Blumer – I have never heard this name. Have you foreign blood, by any chance?"

"That I do, Colonel," I said, piqued, "although I'd wager I'm not the only one at this table that does." Then I cursed myself for my impudence, but to my relief Jablonowski fell about laughing.

"*Touché,* my boy! Tell me, where are you from?"

"From the provinces, Sir," I replied, "Podolia. Not so far from here."

"Aha!" said Jablonowski, stealing a point, "then thou must be used to Turks, Tartars, and blackamoors, then, for they abound in these parts, as we are so near to the Ottoman lands. How fortunate for you that your mother did not have one serving in the house, like mine, or we might be blood brothers!"

We were all very drunk, and we roared with laughter. For this was how the Little Negro had been conceived, outside of wedlock. Everyone in the army knew it. For Jablonowski, his mother a Stuart princess, and her husband the inspector of the Royal Mint at Krakow, was the bastard son of a Negro footman. Black footmen were very much in vogue in Paris, and Polish ladies were wont to follow French fashions, as always. When his wife returned from a visit to Paris, pregnant, the cuckolded inspector found that his own marital treasury had been raided, and his coins clipped, and his stamp defamed! No man in Poland wore such huge horns as poor Prince Konstanty Jablonowski. For the boy wore his mother's treachery on every inch of his skin.

The Prince, casting his eyes on the newborn baby for the first time, saw it black as a lump of Wielice coal. In consternation, he demanded to know where on earth the 'Little Negro' had come from. The lady coolly replied that in Paris, she had stopped in front of a tobacconist's shop, to examine the wax effigy of a Negro holding a pipe in his mouth.

'That's fine, my lady,' thundered the cuckolded Prince, 'but where is the pipe? I don't see anything in the infant's mouth!' This was the story. With such royals as we had, it was hardly a surprise that Poland was fallen! Catamites, cuckolds, cowards, and card sharps, all of them!

"Trump!" Godebski called, and Jablonowski the Little Negro, cursed, and slammed his purse on the table, and counted out the wager.

"Damn it all, my wallet sags like a widow's tits. Lend a hand, my dear Blumer," he said, blithely appropriating the last of my coins. I watched it go with sad heart, knowing I should not see it again, for without my lucky deck, Godebski was routing us all. The poet was a bold player, and that cautious cad Birnbaum complemented him perfectly, like musket and bayonet. The Little Negro, by contrast, played a wild and reckless hand, and the fates were against him that night. My heart was in it, but my head was swimming with a fugue of drink and sickness, and I could not keep up.

"Trump! Bad luck, there, fellows!" Cyprian crowed again. "I fear that you have no stomach for another hand!"

"Nor any gold, neither," Birnbaum snorted.

"I'll write you a promissory note against my arrears of pay," I said solemnly. This was a remark that always brought a hoot. Our arrears were as dead as our state. It was said that the Prussians had even melted down the crown jewels.

So we played on, for paper. That night Godebski and Birnbaum won enough fortunes from the Little Negro and I to ransom the Pope. The sums were scrupulously written down, to the last zloty. Like a national debt, they were obviously never repaid.

"Tell me, Colonel," I asked the Little Negro, feeling entitled to it, having paid so dear in my purse, and now being saddled with debts that would have made even the Bullock blush, "how goes Dabrowski with this Frenchman Bonaparte?"

For Bonaparte was the coming man. At this, the game was forgot, and the players clamoured for precious news. The Little Negro shrugged and drained his glass. He had been on many courtier's missions to Paris. He knew the names of all the great ones, all the generals and officers of both the Polish and the French armies, and all their gossips and intrigues. The Poles and the French were alone in Europe – outcasts. Thrown together, we were unequal allies and uneasy bedfellows. We fought the same enemies – the Satanic Trinity of Prussia, Austria, and Russia. Or so we were led to believe.

"Ah, yes," said the Little Negro, "my dear old friend General Bonaparte."

"You know him, then?" I asked, avidly. The Little Negro chuckled bitterly, "I know him all right. We were at school together, in France. There, as you may imagine, I had to endure the taunts of my schoolmates, among them a short-arsed Corsican named Napoleon Bonaparte."

"What is he like, this Bonaparte?" I asked.

The Little Negro's eyes darkened. "A fine officer," he replied, draining his glass. He was holding something back.

"Excellent! But what kind of a man is he?" I demanded.

"Put it this way," Jablonowski replied, "better to be a Negro with a white heart than a white man with a black heart!"

CHAPTER THIRTY-ONE
WOMEN'S FASHIONS , LWOW, JULY 1796

Around the time we reached Lwow, in February, Bonaparte was appointed commander of the French Army of Italy. The same day of his appointment, he married Josephine Beauharnais, the future Empress. Then he marched over the Alps to face the Austrians, who occupied Italy. What the hell were the Austrians doing in Italy, you may ask? Well, I would answer, what the hell were those Hapsburg bastards doing in Poland?

We were sitting in a café in Lwow, kicking our heels. It was July. Bonaparte and Dabrowski were kicking the Austrians up and down the boot of Italy. We had nothing better to do than read of their exploits in the censored Austrian newspapers. For that year began Bonaparte's miraculous string of legendary victories – he routed the Austrians at Montenotte, Dego, Mondovi, and Lodi. News took weeks or months to reach us here in Lwow. Thus, by the time we read in the newspapers of Bonaparte's latest victory, the dead corpses would be long buried in the ground, and the French had marched on. Onwards with their Revolution! Liberty! Fraternity! Equality! And all of that nonsense.

"Where is Bonaparte now?" we asked Godebski, breathlessly. He sighed and rolled his eyes.

"Bonaparte is besieging Mantua," Godebski replied, peering through his spectacles, and scouring the newspaper with his face screwed up. We could only read it with the greatest difficulty, for it was in German. As gentlemen, we spoke little German of course, for we were really only fluent in the civilised tongues – Polish, Latin, and the lingua Franca.

"Mantua!" Godebski repeated, "a great city, and the birthplace of Virgil, of course. I should like to go there."

"So Bonaparte's odyssey continues!" Sierawski grinned, delighted, and ordered another round of coffees which we laced with vodka.

"Virgil wrote the Aeneid, you buffoon, not the Odyssey," Godebski snapped. "Besides, Mantua is defended by a strong Austrian garrison. A French victory is far from assured."

"Bah!" Tanski sniffed at his glass of wine, "the Austrian papers would say that! Let us have another drink to toast the latest victory! To Bonaparte!" he shouted.

"The war will be over by the time we get to Italy," I said, glumly. We had no victories in Lwow. Here we brooded and plotted in the shadows, conspiring in cellars by candlelight. We followed Bonaparte's victories avidly, for they fell on us like shafts of light in the dark. In truth, it was merely the rays of the sun falling through prison bars. Cyprian perceived this, for he grew terse and angry.

"Damn it all, we are nothing but armchair generals," he snarled, "sitting here in a coffee shop, idling away the days, while the Frenchmen trounce our enemies for us! This Bonaparte has shown us how it is done – France will win all the glory."

It did rankle that we had been defeated, while Napoleon's barefoot army had marched over the Alps and, in a matter of months, driven the Austrians out of Northern Italy. These same haughty Austrians who now lorded it over us, who made us take our coffee in German, and hoisted a filthy black buzzard where the White Eagle should be flying on the spires across the square.

We glanced up and out of the window, and, sure enough, the carrion crow flapped on the flagpole in the spring breeze. The sun was high overhead, and we had dreamed and drunk much of the day away. Godebski threw down the newspaper, and I took it up. I carefully refolded it in the manner of one who has spent too long folding newspapers.

The others took the opportunity to watch the local girls through the window as they promenaded down the street, which always cheered us up. The richer girls rode by in fine carriages. At that moment a particularly lovely pair of doves walked into the cafe. We stood and bowed and doffed our czapkas respectfully. As they retired to a suitable table in the corner, we cast curious glances after them. For in spite of our years in the saddle, and at the wars, and all our many casual liaisons, hurried amours, and brief affairs, women remained a mystery to us all. As strange and mysterious as the surface of the moon. An enigma to us all, except for Cyprian, of course.

"Not all of the men fighting in Italy are French," I said, at length. "It says here that good old Dabrowski fights alongside Bonaparte, commanding a *'foreign legion'* of deserters."

"A foreign legion, indeed!" Godebski grinned, and slammed his fist on the table, scattering cakes, coffee cups, glasses and bottles. "The Austrian press is censored. Our very name is proscribed. That is no foreign legion, comrades – that is the *Polish* Legion! For Austria, Russia and Prussia – the Satanic Trinity – have sworn to suppress the very name of the Republic of Poland, as from the present, and forever. Thus they call our men *'the Foreign Legion'!* More drinks, there, barman! Let us drink to The Foreign Legion!" Godebski called, gleefully, his eyes gleaming red, and his cheeks flushed a livid scarlet. "By God, we have been shown ways to victory by this Bonaparte!"

It was then that I realised he was entirely inebriated. With that, Godebski swept the bunch of flowers, vase and all, off the table, and presenting them to one of the two very lovely girls, importuned them both to dance. The older girl glared at him angrily, with a stare that could have frighted a horse.

"Who on earth are you, Sir?" she said coldly.

"Why, allow me to present my credentials, my sweet!" he said, "I am the famous outlaw, Captain Cyprian Godebski!" he cried, in a most charming manner. He bowed to the waist, one hand on his sword hilt, the other he extended in a graceful gesture almost brushing the boots of the blushing maidens.

"Won't you dance with me, ladies?" he asked, "for tomorrow the Austrians may have me dance upon the scaffold!"

"If they did, you'd deserve it," snorted the older girl, but hiding a smile behind her hand.

"I will dance!" cried the younger, gladly. They set to a merry mazurka among the tables. Protesting that it was against her will, the older sister – who was very stern faced, but much the prettier by far – was conscripted into the dance. Soon she and her sister and the other three lads were lurching and spinning around the place. Tanski vaulted over a table heaving with a full hearty lunch, so low that he knocked the heads off the drinker's beers, to howls of angry protest.

For me, I took a place with the minstrels – for the place had a string quartet – seized a violin, and we struck up the mazurka, in double-quick time. Our old friend, the mazurka of the Third of May! Someone ought to put words to this melody, I thought to myself.

Sierawski slumped down by my side after a few turns of this wild dance had thoroughly disordered the place. Upturned chairs and tables and broken crockery littered the floor. As Godebski swept by with one of the girls, he almost upturned another table, and I caught a carafe of wine and hugged it safe before it was shattered on the floor.

"He seems to have forgotten Madame," Sierawski said.

"Plenty more fish in the river," I grinned, and we agreed this was all for the best, for the further we were from that lethal lady, the less likely our necks were to be stretched.

"A thousand pardons, My Lord Brother!" Godebski was saying to a large gentleman, for he had knocked over his table.

It was a Polish nobleman, of great size and girth, wearing a sable cloak and a sabre. The nobleman was sitting at a table with four hatchet-faced jockeys. By the expression on his face – for he had the look of a bull about to charge – he was not pleased. He seemed like a good trencherman, and fond of his food. The spilled cabbage stew on his breeches was, alas, Cyprian's fault.

"A thousand pardons," Cyprian repeated, merrily, "won't you take a drink with me, my dear sir? We are celebrating General Bonaparte's latest victory over the Austrian scoundrels."

The other fellow almost exploded like a cannon of rage. He dashed his glass to the floor in a fury. "Go to the Devil! Bonaparte is a French Jacobin dog," he spat, reaching for his sword hilt, and his lackeys formed up in a phalanx behind him. "My son is in the Austrian hussars. The Empress Marie-Therese is our sovereign. You are a traitor, and you talk treason!"

There was a hush.

"A traitor, am I?" Cyprian smiled thinly. "If my honour is to be impugned, with both ladies and gentlemen present, then I think perhaps we should settle this outside?"

"Good! After you!" grunted the great beast.

"Oh no! After you!" Cyprian insisted, bowing. His adversary – a man who was used to being obeyed, and going first, assented. As he walked by, Cyprian grabbed him by the seat of his breeches, hoisted them, set his shoulders, and hurled him bodily. They both did meet in the street, although they did not fight their duel. For although Cyprian later departed through the door, he had thrown his opponent out through the window. Unfortunately for him, we were on the second floor of the café!

At this, the nobleman's lackeys were in uproar. The whole place was in chaos. Waiters, musicians and patrons ran to and fro, pell mell, cowering under tables, and running out of the doors. Tanski and Sierawski, grinning, grabbed the two screaming ladies and held them tight – for their own protection, no doubt.

"Our Master!" the angry lackeys screamed. "You'll pay for this, brigands!" They leapt to their feet. Hands went to sabres. I placed my gun under the table, for I had no intention of this becoming a massacre, and waded in to meet them. The first of them made for Cyprian, to exact revenge, and came charging across the room. He was a stout fellow, but short, so I swatted him over the head with my chair. The chair shattered in my hands, and the man uttered a single surprised cry before tumbling to the floor with a crash. Then someone gave me a good swipe across the jaw, which stung somewhat, and I felt blood on my nose.

"Why, you little weasel!" I exclaimed to the second bodyguard, rocking on my feet, but not falling. There was a peach of a look on his scabby little face, a joy to behold, as he realised that he had tweaked a wolf by the tail, for he was no match for me. So he drew his sword, but I did not. I disdained to honour a man such as this with my blade. Stepping inside his clumsy lunge, I caught him a good left-and-right, to pay him back for the slap he had fetched me, cracking the bones in his nose and jaw. This sent him staggering across the room, over the bar, and into a stack of bottles. A dozen bottles broke, showering the room with wine, champagne, and shards of broken glass. Corks popped like gunshots. The little weasel lay amongst the wreckage, insensible, unmoving, covered in blood, and dead for aught I cared.

The other two lackeys held back. They had witnessed this fight with some trepidation. Terror-struck, they fled. I walked over to the bar. Amongst the wreckage was a single unbroken goblet of red wine. Picking it up, I drained it at a draught. "By God, this is thirsty work, comrades!" I bellowed to the others, for my blood was up. Tanski and Sierawski also in their cups, and quite drunk, were in fits of laughter, rolling around in the wreckage of the café.

"That was well done, Blumer," Godebski declared, making his way unsteadily through the carnage. "Is there any more drink?"

"I think the bar is closed," I said, staring at my shattered reflection in the broken mirror. Shards of glass fell tinkling from the wall. Bottles rolled across the floor. The rugs and carpets were sodden with spilled wine. A strong wind blew in through the plate glass window that was shattered from top to bottom, with a hole in it the size of a door. Even the chandelier swung crazily from the ceiling, for we had somehow contrived to destroy it in the brawl, I know not how.

We said our goodbyes to the ladies and paid for the bill, and the damages, with a promissory note, to be drawn against our arrears of army pay. I collected my gun from under the table and then gathered up my drunken, rowdy companions. We set off into the breezy afternoon, with a fine sun blazing in the sky. Outside, Godebski stared up at the Austrian flag with hate-filled eyes.

"Blumer – cut down that fucking blackbird before the garrison arrives," he snarled.

"Yes, Sir!" I grinned, drawing my sword.

CHAPTER THIRTY-TWO
WE LEAVE LWOW, AUGUST 1796

We left Lwow on a black dark night for unknown shores, our mouths filled with the taste of our mothers' tears. Not long after we had retired to bed, the girl who kept the tavern burst into our rooms. We didn't know whether to reach for our pantaloons or our pistols.

"Fly! Fly!" she shrieked, "you are betrayed!"

At this, we heard the crack of muskets. Sierawski stuck his head out of the window, but he was too crafty to return fire and give away our position. Besides, it was so dark one couldn't have hit the side of a barn with a handful of grain.

"Our friends from Tulczyn?" I asked, wearily, burying my head under the pillows.

"No," Sierawski replied, shaking his head. "I hear German. It's the Austrians."

"Have we not enough enemies in this cursed world!" I lamented. In truth we had not exactly ingratiated ourselves during our sojourn in Lwow. The incident at the café had been the final straw. Downstairs, Cyprian was drinking coffee and eating bread and jam. His gun lay on the table beside him.

"You look terrible," he said, offering me the coffee.

"Thanks!" I laughed, wishing myself back under the warm blankets, but the gunfire sounded closer at hand now.

"Nobody has shot at us for six months," Sierawski said jovially, stuffing his bag with food, "it couldn't last."

"Yes," I agreed, rubbing my eyes until I saw stars, and splashing water on my face, "I was beginning to miss it!"

Tanski scowled and stalked out to the stables. We always kept a few horses saddled. Hunted as we were, such a day

would always come. We had little enough by way of baggage
– rusty sabres, guns, a handful of bullets, a knapsack, a
saddlebag or two. Besides this I had my bundle of books,
Sierawski had his engineers tools, and Tanski had the flag.
Tanski vaulted onto his horse theatrically and caracoled it,
flashy as always. His hands were empty.

A line of horsemen were already hurtling away into the
distance. We watched as the night swallowed them up. Our
comrades were heading east, and we with them.

"The flag, you damned fool!" I roared at Tanski, as soon as
I had sat my horse. "Where is it?"

"It's here, Blumer," Godebski replied, walking across the
flagstones. He tossed the flag to Tanski, who caught it, and
unfurled it. It fluttered in the breeze, antique talisman of our
long dead king, Sobieski. A hundred years ago Sobieski had
chased the Turks out of Austria. Now the ingrate Austrians
were chasing us out of Lwow, out of our own country, and
into exile beyond.

A crack of shots, like the crash of cymbals, rent the air.
Austrian bugles sounded – mere minutes away.

"The bloody trumpets of war!" Godebski laughed,
checking his pistols and grenades, and slinging a musket
across his back.

"This is madness! They'll arrest you," I protested, "they'll
put you in a dungeon with Zayonczek! They'll kill you!"

Godebski shook his head. "No they won't. Good luck,
boys," said the poet, saluting, "follow the Little Negro, he'll
see you right. See you in Italy."

"Good hunting, Captain," I cried, clasping my friend's
hand. "See you in Italy."

"See you in Italy, Blumer!" Cyprian smiled, tossing a
grenade up in the air like an apple. Turning on his heel, he
walked back into the inn, whistling the mysterious mazurka of
the Third of May. Then he was gone.

There were no more bugles thereafter, only gunshots. A heavy moon hung overhead, with a big gleaming belly. Pan Twardowski was mocking us. The old sorcerer was lighting up the fields, like a ballroom is lit up with candles, with an eerie silvery glow. We rode hard for the tree line. As we did, a line of Austrian cavalry made to cut us off, swinging like a stable door on a hinge. It was a quite beautifully executed manoeuvre, for which they were to be commended, and moreover carried out at night. I watched it all with a professional eye – I felt strangely detached and unafraid. It was as if I were watching an opera.

I quite forgot my sickness, and my mind was lucid and clear. Austria was the third deadly enemy to be reckoned with. She was slow, but she was implacable. Like a giant mill, her wheels ground slowly – but they ground small. These, her cavalry, were excellent, the very best in the world. Strong men on heavy steeds, cuirassiers with gleaming metal breastplates and great plumed metal helmets, like Roman centurions. Moonlight glinted on the steel, shining like quicksilver in the dark. This heavy armour, magnificent in aspect, weighed them down mightily. Thus, we were faster.

We six – for the three Beardlings still rode with us – we too were horsemen, down to our boots. We dug in our spurs until the rowels ran with our horses' blood. The ground and the heavens hammered in a wild tattoo, the roaring wind stinging tears from our eyes. Our horses, sensing the danger, set their ears against the sides of their heads and foamed at the mouth. It was good ground, thank the Lord God. Not one of their hooves found a furrow or a rabbit hole to fall into.

As the noose closed, we shrank to a single file, and spurred our horses until their flanks ran red. Shots sounded, the reports snatched away on the wind, sounding like cloth-wrapped hammers beating on stones. Tanski lowered the flag like a lance.

We split their line like threading the eye of a needle, and then a cloud passed across the moon, thank God. Darkness at last veiled the earth, and we vanished.

We spent an ill-starred Christmas out on the steppe. The wind howled down as if the very devils of Siberia were calling us home to their gulags. I was huddled in the shelter, wrapped in a blanket. The blanket was as cold as iron, and seemed to have been drenched with icy water. Dusk had fallen, and the moment the evening star appeared, we sat down for supper – for it was Wigilia again. Reluctantly I stuck my head out of the shelter, which was a rough stockade of piled branches. One end of the shelter was propped up with Sobieski's antique standard, the old soldier pressed into service yet again.

"Sierawski! Birnbaum!" I called, "Get your bloody arses in here! Merry Christmas!"

Tanski and I huddled over a battered pot that sat on a heap of mouldering grass. It gave off few flames and little heat, but vast clouds of acrid, evil-smelling smoke. The smoke stung our eyes and chafed my throat. I coughed until there were silver stars in front of my eyes and Tanski clapped me on the back. We had some old dry beetroot, and were boiling it up with snow to make a broth that could perhaps be called borsch.

"Fish!" Sierawski cried triumphantly, as he came into the tent. "Fish!" for as you know, no good Catholic eats meat on Christmas Eve.

"You should see the net and line Sierawski rigged up," Birnbaum enthused, "the boy's a genius, the greatest engineer of our time!"

"Spare us the engineering claptrap!" Tanski shouted. He had fallen out with Sierawski. "If the honoured Lieutenant Sierawski were any sort of real engineer, he'd magic us up a balloon, so we could float to Italy!"

"God's blood," I roared, staring at the fish. "Is that your bait or your catch? It's tiny!"

"Piss off and catch you own, then," Sierawski retorted, "you pair of tits!" He clutched two small pike in his hands. They were dangling from hooks and still bloodied where their heads had been beaten in with a rock.

"I already did, comrade," I replied, pointing to a fat, ugly carp I had caught earlier that day. My fish sat among the embers, its eyes already swelling up white, and red blood congealed around its gills.

"*Touché*," Sierawski admitted, and we set his catch beside ours. Here we had another fine allegory of Poland, I shivered, for we had both pike and carp, and both of them hanging from the gallows! I kept this pretty thought to myself.

"Grey sauce for us, quartermaster, and quick about it," I ordered Tanski grandly, snapping my fingers. He growled angrily back, like a dog. The rest of us grinned, and we watched him cook the fish. The smoke made me cough again and I had to leave the shelter until it had subsided, the wind beating my bones like a rent collector's knout.

"*Sto lat!* Cheers!" we cried, each taking a small gulp of vodka. The bottle was running light as air, a few more sips and it would blow away on the wind. We looked at the meagre food. We had some ragged strips of bread, and a few dried mushrooms, and the fish. Birnbaum stared at this gentile repast with suspicion.

"Remember the old days!" we all said, dreaming of Christmases and Chanukahs.

"I thought last year was bad, but by God! The Devil take this year!" Sierawski lamented. The fish took an age to cook on that feeble campfire. We were so hungry on that Christmas Eve, our stomachs could have burst like empty bladders. At last, the fish was ready. It smelled so heavenly, I cannot think that even the legendary Thursday Dinners had such a grand aroma. It was such a consolation to anticipate the borsch, the fish, and the sacred wafer.

"Now, boys, who has the wafers?" Tanski asked. Sierawski looked at him blankly.

"Not us," Birnbaum said indignantly. "We are Jews!"

"Then we have none!" went out a pathetic cry over the steppes.

"Hell's teeth," I said to my Christian comrades, "you miserable sinners would be lost without me!"

"What, Father Ignatius," Tanski sneered, "you have some wafers in your chasuble, then?"

"That I have, my son, that I have!" I laughed, pulling an old army biscuit from my bag. It was dried bullet-hard. I could have fired it from my musket. Very solemnly, I turned my back. Then I laid the biscuit on a saddlebag, and, wrapping myself in a blanket and imitating the unctuous actions of a priest, blessed it as best I could. I blessed it with a prayer, and a sprinkling of water that was holy to me, for it was from the rivers of our land.

"Praise be for the Podolian Pope!" Tanski laughed, and the others capered about, laughing, bowing and genuflecting.

"The Lord be with you," I said, unctuously, tracing a cross in the air, and they gave the response – "and also with you!" – and then we fell about laughing. The newly blessed 'wafer' was so hard I had to break it into pieces with the butt of a pistol.

For dessert, we dreamed of delicacies. A confection of air and dreams, of smoke swirling from the towers of an imaginary castle.

"Oh for hot coffee," Sierawski moaned.

"Oh for poppy seed cake!" Tanski muttered, eyes closed.

"Oh for Chanukah!" Birnbaum whined, wrapped in his cloak.

"Oh for another glass of vodka," I said quietly.

That year we left no slops for the wolves, for they ate well enough. Wolves sat at high table, in regal attire, with silver knives and forks, the length and breadth of our country, from the Wawel Castle to Krakow Cathedral.

Over the new year, we departed from Christendom. Mark you, the way our fellow Christians had treated us Poles of late, we may as well have worn turbans. There was not a living soul for miles. The towns and the markers had run out weeks ago. We pushed on into the blank uncharted regions of the map. In Poland we had been driven into hiding. Now we had been driven off the very edge of the world.

"Where the hell are we?" Tanski demanded.

"This is Romania, a dominion of the Turkish Empire," I told them. Of course, there was absolutely no sign by which to tell where we were, or who the ruler was. In every direction the trees were exactly the same, regardless of which sovereign they belonged to.

"How I miss Krakow!" Sierawski moaned, "the girls and the taverns! Hell and devils, I even miss lousy Lwow and pissing Podolia."

"There's no girls and taverns here, comrade," I laughed, "only bears and trees!"

Row upon row of trees, an army of them, brigades and divisions, marching for a thousand miles. It was January, and these trees wore a uniform of winter white, crowned with snowy czapkas. Shafts of sunlight through the trees cast shadows like long black lances on the snowy carpet of the forest floor. The grand army of trees even had its own company of musicians. The birds sang like heaven's own orchestra. They called *la diane* at dawn and played all day and long into the night.

Up and down the mountains these trees ranged. At night, as the trunks swayed in the night breeze, and snow shook from their boughs, it seemed they were marching, swaying in step. If only we could have recruited those stout fellows, with their hearts of oak, to lay siege to Vienna, Berlin, and Muscovy, to burn out the vile nests of the black eagles, cuckoo birds and vultures that they are.

"What about Szymon?" Tanski asked at last, after some days immersed in the forest. Dear Szymon! We had quite forgotten him, what with our other troubles. For we were caught between the Austrians and starvation.

"He will follow us even here, and to the ends of the earth," I replied, "but hunger is our enemy now, comrades, not that upstart boy."

We had ridden for day after day until our bellies hung inside out. Now we would have to pierce new holes in our belts. At the foot of the Carpathians we forded an angry stream, the white waters gushing like the River Nile over Pharaoh's chariots. We had no Moses to part the waters, and one of the Beardlings was carried off to his death, and drowned. Thus the Austrians had hounded the poor fellow to his death. We were but five.

Until then, we had kept pace with the last of the Little Negro's rearguard. Now, we had lost track of them. Swallowed by the forest, we wandered blind and lost in this wooden labyrinth. Our progress was now measured in days, not miles. In this measureless wilderness there were no roads. Paths meandered crazily as if God had scratched them there in a drunken fit. A gentle incline would, without warning, terminate in a ghastly vertical cliff, obliging us to retrace our steps. Agonising days were wasted in such fruitless effort. Of nights we sat shivering amongst the tall trees and the dead trunks, lying like fallen soldiers, listening to the reveille of howling wolves.

One morning, yet again, we had followed a path that terminated in a dead end. We stood atop a huge rocky escarpment, falling off on both sides like a vast *glacis*. We were in desperate straits, trapped, lost, and starving. Still, had we but known it, compared to the months ahead, we would consider our time in Romania a sojourn in paradise.

"Do you still have your compass?" Tanski demanded.

"I do," I told him, passing it to him for the hundredth time, "but in this uncharted vastness without maps, this empire of nothing, inhabited by bears and werewolves, what meaning has left or right, east or west? Or up or down, come to that? Face it, Tanski, we are lost. Put your faith in God, and be patient."

Tanski frowned. Then he tried another tack. "Do you have the telescope?" he demanded of Sierawski, who shrugged and passed it to him. Undeterred, Tanski clambered atop a great heap of fallen trees, lying side by side in mossy slumbers, and began to survey the horizon. It was a hazardous climb, for the wood of these trunks was shiny and slick with ice. Still, on he climbed, undaunted. The man was a whipcord of angry energy. In a trice he reached the top. From there we could see him peering through the telescope.

"I see it!" Tanski cried, triumphant, nearly falling from his precarious nest. We swarmed up the trunks after him, and crowded around, jubilant, peering one by one through the eyepiece. In the distance, we spied the fires of the Little Negro's camp, and, among the tiny pillars of smoke, the red and white flying from the spear of a lance.

CHAPTER THIRTY-THREE
DENISKO'S CAMP, APRIL 1797

"God is Great, and Allah be Praised!" we joyfully blasphemed. When in Rome – or even when in Romania – do as the Romans do. The Little Negro sat in splendour in a vast Turkish tent, filled with wooden crates and saddlebags stamped with French insignia. It was like the cave of Ali Baba and the forty thieves. There were uniforms, boots, guns, powder and shot, sides of beef and lamb, but no pork of course, and bottles of wine. We sat down on a woven rug decorated with splendid patterns and broke our fast.

Guided by the invisible hand of Madame L, several thousand men had now crossed into the safety of the Ottoman Empire. We patriots had no intention of taking the Tsarina's thirty pieces of silver, or the long walk to Siberia. Far better the ride to exile, sword in hand.

Despite the bundles of equipment and chests of money, it was a shambolic place. There was no single uniform. Many men wore the pattern of the national cavalry, like us. Others wore navy blue trousers, and red jackets, and a diverse mix of headgear – czapkas, sheepskin hats, desperado hats, and others. There were men from all over Poland and Lithuania – from Danzig, Warsaw, Krakow, Lwow, Vilnius, Podolia, Poznan, and anywhere you cared to name, from greater or lesser Poland, and beyond.

Besides these, there were those who were not Poles, but who made common cause with us – Jews, loyal Cossacks, Serbian partisans and rebels from Russia. There were all manner of men – cavalry, artillery, infantry, refugees, volunteers, politicians, and priests. There were peasants and there were princelings – for was not the Little Negro himself the son of a princess? – and everything in between. It was as noisy and chaotic as the market in Krakow.

"The Turks and the French have given us shelter and aid, at long last," said Lieutenant-Colonel Jablonowski – alias the Little Negro. "Unfortunately the French cannot spare any troops, for they are sorely pressed in their war with the Austrians, and as far as I can tell they want us to fight them on their behalf."

"Sir," I said facetiously, "with the greatest of respect, and I am but a simple soldier, but I had envisaged that in a Polish-French alliance, the French would be helping *us*, not the other way around." Tanski kicked my shin to quiet me.

The Little Negro smiled. "Quite true, Blumer. But still there are two thousand men under arms out here in the forest – a formidable force. Welcome to the Legion of the Danube, comrades."

Our band was the latest and alas, it seemed, the last, to take this road. For Madame's secret organisation had been paralysed. Her conspirators had been betrayed. Rounded up for the dungeons and gulags, or shot out of hand. A warrant had been issued for Cyprian Godebski's arrest, and there was a price on his head, but our friend's own fate was unknown.

We were fed with chunks of lamb in a hot spicy sauce, and boiled rice. After we had eaten our fill, we wiped our mouths on our sleeves, sat back, and belched contentedly. Although we felt like kings at the time, we spent the night in agony, crouched over the latrines. After months of living off the land, our hungry bellies could not cope with this rich food.

"Good health, men! Wine from our Turkish friends, although I am told they do not drink it themselves," said the Little Negro, as we drained a glass or two together. This place he told us was called Jassy. It was the dirtiest of all the fly-blown one-horse towns in Europe, but after our time in the forests, it felt like a palm-thronged oasis in the middle of a desert, with crystal waters, sherbet, and dancing girls. Oh, woeful days. For this would prove to be another mirage.

"Our Turkish friends?" Birnbaum said suspiciously. The Turks have always been Poland's enemies, since long before Sobieski's time.

"The Turks have a saying, 'My enemy's enemy is my friend,'" said the Little Negro, tossing back a glass of the wine. "They will help us if it will hurt the Russians and the Austrians."

"They are not to be trusted," I said, for we lived close enough to them in Podolia to know their treacherous ways.

"Perhaps. What do you think of the wine?" the Little Negro asked.

"Dry as sticks and sawdust," Tanski grinned.

"Not fit for a Russian to swill," Sierawski grinned.

"It's bloody delicious," I grinned, and it was all three, for we had not drunk a drop for months, "for beggars can't be choosers."

"That," said the little Negro, clapping me on the shoulder, "is exactly why we are stuck with these treacherous Turks, and the fornicating French. Beggars can't be choosers."

At the back of the tent were crates marked with the French cockade. The Little Negro sat up from his rug, for we all squatted on the floor, in the Turkish style. He groaned, and flexed his legs, for his wounds pained him greatly. Besides that, he was greatly troubled by the gout.

"How are you boys for supplies?" he asked. We snapped like hungry dogs, for we had nothing but the clothes we stood up in. Our bare arses hung from our threadbare pants, and the soles of our boots were worn paper thin.

"Open that trunk, would you?" he asked Sierawski, who fairly demolished the wood in his eagerness. Inside we found a cache of uniforms. Delighted, we grabbed clean, fresh clothes, and pulled them on. Amongst the clothes were Polish czapkas and French cockades.

"The latest French fashions?" I inquired.

The Little Negro nodded, and laughed. "Why, yes! Two French generals have inspected this camp already, and the French admiral shipped these supplies over the Black Sea. We have some friends after all, Blumer! Now, boys, about your back pay," he added, lifting the lid on a strongbox. It was full to the brim with silver coins. We gasped.

"I can't give you much, I'm afraid," he said, apologetically, handing us fifty piastres each, which he said was ten months' pay, reckoned at five piastres a month. This was far less than our due, but we were so amazed and delighted we could have kissed his ugly black noggin. For we had given up every penny of our arrears for lost many years ago. This pay seemed to us not the pittance it was, but a miracle. To us, these small purses contained the untold riches of Croesus and Midas.

Upon receiving this bounty, we roundly congratulated the Little Negro at once upon his appointment as head of this Legion. He was a fine fellow, and a first-rate soldier. We esteemed him enormously. To our dismay, he demurred.

"I am not in command here. That honour belongs to Brigadier Denisko," said Jablonowski. His brow furrowed. This boded ill. One day, the Little Negro did command one of our Legions, and a damned good leader he was, too. Sadly for all of us, and for the many brave lads who died, it was not Denisko's ill-starred legion.

"Is this Denisko a good officer, Sir?" I asked, cautiously.

"Depends how you reckon it," the Little Negro scowled. "On the strength of the zoldu he pays himself, Denisko considers himself worth his weight in gold, for he pays himself five hundred piastres a month."

"One hundred times ours!" I whistled. "That's his pay, then, but what's his worth?"

A few months later, in late June, we awoke to the familiar sound of gunfire, shaking the summer birds loose from the trees. All had gone badly wrong. This was how.

Denisko was a worthless fool, the camp a shambles, and his strategy insane. Our funds had dried up. Rumours flew. It was said that fifty million piastres had disappeared into Denisko's pocket. At the same time, hundreds of Poles were escaping to Turkey. Many of them passed through our camp. From there they were taking ship to join Dabrowski's Legion in Italy. The Little Negro was all for following them to Constantinople. By June half of the men in our camp had already struck their tents and gone. In disgust, the Little Negro went to Bucharest, seeking orders from the French Ambassador there.

"To Arms! He who loves the Fatherland, will not go to Turkey!" Denisko proclaimed. About two hundred men remained stubbornly with him. The other eight hundred of us had decided that enough was enough. It was a bloodless mutiny, but it was a mutiny all the same. We were at arms all right, for we were at daggers drawn with each other. Denisko's men cursed us for cowards, and we cursed them for fools.

The Austrians, naturally enough, had got wind of Denisko's legion. They gathered eight thousand troops to do away with us, and they made no secret of it, in the hope that we might simply quit their empire and cause our trouble elsewhere. So we were vastly outnumbered, as usual. Denisko, who clearly could not read a map, or count, had nevertheless decided to seize the insignificant border town of Bukowina with his two hundred men – in the teeth of these eight thousand Austrian soldiers. Why Bukowina, for the love of God? The place had no military value at all. Perhaps Denisko kept a mistress there!

"Here they are!" Sierawski called. It was a year almost to the day since they had chased us out of Lwow, and here were those damned Austrians again.

"How many?" Birnbaum asked, as we bundled up our belongings.

"How should I know?" Sierawski shouted, hauling at his horse's girth, as the animal bucked and snorted. All around us was chaos and pandemonium. Loose horses and oxen hurtled about. Three men were striking a huge Arab tent, the canvas painted with red and green stripes. It swirled in the wind like a genie struggling out of a bottle. A rider careered into it, and both man and mount crashed to the ground.

"Damn it!" Tanski cursed, "what a bloody shambles!"

"Business as usual, then," I sneered. We set about our work, knocking heads together, saddling horses, and loading up our pack animals. We ran through our familiar routine – loading up our possessions onto the back of our horses. I had only three horses remaining. The others had been lost, stolen, or eaten. Onto these good beasts I loaded my trusty English musket (which I still had), several cartridge belts (courtesy of our French patrons) my blankets, my victuals, a few bottles of wine, and my small bundle of precious books. All of the silver piastres were gone, of course. The whole exercise took a shake of a mare's tail.

Soon we were in the saddle and away, and the Devil take the hindmost. Tanski rode ahead with the flag. At our heels we heard the clap of shots, like hammers being struck against stone. We could easily guess that in the hills and forests beyond our camp, outside Bukowina, Denisko's doomed legion was fighting its first – and last – battle.

Sure enough, there were the Austrian dragoons, streaming out of the tree line and chasing after us. They were riding down our stragglers, smoke rising over the plumes of their hats, having discharged their pistols. Dragoons are light cavalry, fast, and without armour. We cursed, because they could chase us all the way to the gates of Rome without breaking sweat.

"God Almighty!" Sierawski cried, "we are riding north! What madness is this? Are we going back to Poland?"

We had no time to ponder this, for the dragoons were hard on our heels. Serbs from the Bukowina garrison. A subject people of the Austrian Empire. Hard men, dirty fighters, but poor stuff to be running from, truth be told. Denisko should have been hanged for this negligence! I thought, but as the dragoons charged us, it was our necks on the gallows, not his.

Naturally our Polish horses were better than their Balkan carthorses. But laden as we were with gear, the dragoons kept pace with us. Try as we might, we could not outstrip them. Mile after mile we rode north, on the south side of a filthy river that dragged its way through Bukowina. We thundered straight through a fly blown village and the peasants watched us as if spectating at a horse race.

It was bleak country, this, to my eye, ragged and wild. The roads were so rough as to make our Polish mud-tracks look like ancient Roman highways. Our horses, though, after months in pasture, were fresh, and flew over the boggy ground that kissed the feathers of their hooves with great sucking gasps.

By now one of the Serbian lads was close enough to touch my pack-horse's tail, close enough that its hooves were throwing mud in his eye. His sword was drawn, and he was reaching out to cut the line – he meant to steal my horse! It occurred to me to cut the beast loose, like a sacrificial goat. With booty, these boys might well give up, satisfied. A cavalryman earns little enough, when he is paid at all. A good Polish horse, pack, and tack, would bring a year's wages, and make the taker cock of the barrack room, to boot.

I had, you will gather, conceived a great hatred of the Austrians over the years. It pained me greatly to do this. Nevertheless I released the pack horse. The Serbs fell on it like a bunch of jackals, clubbing at each other with the flats of their sabres. The poor animal was torn to pieces in the struggle for possession. They entirely forgot about us. Before I had even drawn my pistol, my own swift horse carried me away over the hills, and we were gone.

Some miles on, we forded the river at a place where it turns sharply to the east. We rode north, along a narrow corridor of open land through a wood. Walled in by trees on both sides, it was a perfect place for an ambush. Thankfully the Austrians were far behind us. We snatched a few moments to rest and water our exhausted beasts.

"Damn it," I said softly, "my wine was aboard the horse I lost! A shame, because we need a drink now as never before."

"Why? Where the hell are we going?" Tanski demanded.

"At the end of this bottleneck is the Dniester River," I told him, laughing bitterly.

"What?" Sierawski cried, sinking to his knees. Birnbaum wailed, gnashing his teeth and tearing his hair. Tanski roared with rage like a caged lion.

"The Dniester? But that means..."

"Russia! Don't worry, comrades," I laughed, "I'm sure our beloved Slav brothers, our kind liberators, will welcome us warmly!"

CHAPTER THIRTY-FOUR
WE FORD THE DNIESTER, JULY 1797

"God," Sierawski said, "is an engineer, however you look at it. He is the creator of the universe, according to the Priests, and the divine watchmaker, according to the Atheist French philosophers."

This was a favourite theme of his. We were riding point, the other fellows in our group bringing up the rear. My musket did not leave my hand.

"Take the horse, for example," he continued, "what a marvel! A sublime engine of propulsion! A ton of muscle perched on four needles! So delicate, so precise. Yet the creature is strong enough to endure all manner of hardships," he patted his animal's neck. "They have character, too, for they are loyal, faithful, and brave. Unlike women, they never complain. Is this not the Supreme Being's gift, to have provided us with such a blessed companion?"

"My dear Sierawski," I said, "at last you see why only the cavalry is fit for a gentleman!"

As we rode, the trees narrowed, and thinned, to a gentle grassy slope, which led down to a greasy brown bank, terminating in a shallow valley, and there, a ford.

"These brave steeds of ours have carried us halfway across Europe, through endless forests, and over mighty rivers."

Below us lay the latest of the many rivers we had to cross. The mighty Dniester was boiling like an angry cauldron, running swifter than even our swift steeds. Summer sun shone on these swirling silver waters. Waves cut the surface like green sabres. It was as if the Rusalka's hands were reaching up at us from the depths. We peered at it doubtfully. It might as well have been the river Styx, the boundary of the underworld. Beyond it lay Hades itself – Russia! It was not an enticing prospect.

"Those fellows have made it," Sierawski said dubiously, and indeed they had. For the riders before us had forded the torrent and now stood on the other side, their horses shaking themselves off like dogs, before pressing onwards.

"Let's go, comrade!" Sierawski grinned, relieved, raising his whip and spurs. "We can't wait here for the ferryman!"

"Fools rush in where angels fear to tread. Hold hard, comrade," I said, sweeping the other bank with my telescope. There I saw a line of dragon's teeth glinting on the horizon.

"Damn it, what now, Blumer?"

"Why, it's the ferryman – waiting to take us to Siberia!" I said, as we dropped from our horses and took shelter. The bank on the other side was lower, and from our vantage point, we could spy them out. Horrorstruck, we watched as they emerged from the trees, at a slow walk, sabres drawn. There, from an ensign's flag, flew the double-headed black eagle, on its familiar yellow banner. We took count.

"Thirty-six horse!" Sierawski whistled. "Russian cuirassiers." We could see that they were massive men, on huge horses. The horses were magnificent, heavy, gigantic beasts, their black bodies gleaming like ebony. From the tips of their tails to the feathers of their hooves, every inch of them was parade-ground immaculate. The riders were dressed all in black, except for their silver breastplates, which now gleamed quite distinctly, flashing like the waters of the Dniester. We admired them enormously, they were a stupendous sight. We watched, spellbound, holding our breaths, as the Russians let our men pass by unmolested. Our men rode on, unharmed, and in ignorance of the sword that had hung on a thread over their very heads.

"I don't understand! Why did they not fall on those other fellows of ours?" Sierawski hissed, tugging at my sleeve.

"They must have seen them! But they just let them go, like a stockman counting cattle! What are those Russian bastards waiting for?"

"They're waiting for us," I answered.

I had recognised him at once through the telescope. Down below, at the head of the cavalry, the cavalry's captain had taken off his black feather plumed Russian helmet, lined with bear's fur, to drink from his water flask. As he tilted his head, we saw the unmistakable shock of blond hair, gleaming in the summer sun like a golden halo.

Our dear friend Szymon Korczak.

When he rode down the slope, Sierawski was, as he so often did, singing a Krakowiak at the top of his voice. I have never understood a word of this childish rhyme, but I have heard him sing it so often, that I can remember it word for word.

"One man from Krakow
Had seven horses.
But after he went to war
Only one of them was left.

He was at war for seven years
He didn't draw his sword
So his sword went rusty
From no war!

I'm a Krakowiak
With a Krakowian nature
Anyone who gets in my way
I'll jump on him!"

Sierawski rode carelessly down the bank, swigging from a vodka bottle, and singing at the top of his voice. It echoed down the valley, even over the tumultuous roar of the Dniester. His rusty sword swung carelessly from his hand, and he swished at the flies with it. His head was bare, his shirt open, and he carried no firearms and led no packhorses. The cuirassiers saw – and heard – him at once. He sang on –

"Vistula, my Vistula
Sky blue river
Krakow bows down to you
And Warsaw bows down to you."

"That lad really is a *mensch*," Birnbaum whispered, for that was the Yiddish term for a '*meszczyzna*', a man.

"He's a hero," Tanski agreed.

"He's mad!" I averred, quietly.

From our hiding place, we sighted down the barrels of our muskets. We had proposed drawing lots to be the decoy, but Sierawski was having none of it – it was his plan, and he would not ask another man to do what he would not do himself.

The rest of us had doubled down a rocky bank nearby that led to the ford. Our horses hooves were hastily muffled with rags, their snouts gagged, their eyes blindfolded. There was but one ford, but there were, fortunately, two paths down to it on the Austrian side. We made our way down the second, hidden path. In a wooded copse at the foot of the slope we huddled, still on the Austrian side of the Dniester. The cuirassiers, being on the Russian side, thought that they had the trap closed tight.

We watched as the Russian cavalry watched Sierawski. The sergeant was angry. It seemed that he was piqued to have waited here for a straggler and a drunk, while dozens of other riders had escaped. Szymon silenced him and bawled orders.

At this, about twenty of the cuirassiers advanced down the bank, rolling like a great black dragon. Szymon and the rest stayed behind, champing at the bit.

Sierawski halted at the water's edge and let his horse drink. As it did, so did he. He swigged from a bottle of vodka that was full of water. Sierawski swung crazily in the saddle, grabbed at the pommel to steady himself, and dropped the bottle into the waves, where it was snatched away by the river. The cuirassiers were laughing at him now, and calling out. They began to wade their horses into the foam.

"Not yet," I said to the boys, whose fingers were whitening on their triggers. Now the horsemen moved close enough for us to make out their shouts, quite distinct above the roar of the water.

"Halt! You there, boy!" the sergeant bellowed. Downstream, Sierawski began to curse at the cuirassiers.

"Russian dogs!" he roared, "heretics! Sons of bitches!"

"Easy, lad!" came back the sergeant, in a calm voice, seeking to reel in his fish, "no need for that!"

"Kiss my arse!" Sierawski threw back. "You bloody Russian bastards! Sons of bitches! Murdering, thieving, illiterate, ignorant, lying, pig-fucking pagan shits!"

This oration very quickly taxed the sergeant's patience. He ordered his men on through the bubbling waters.

"I spit on your whore of a mother!" Sierawski screamed at him. The sergeant, angered, drew his pistol, and his men followed suit.

"Come along quietly, son. We have orders to take you alive."

"Take *me* alive! That's a laugh!" Sierawski shouted, "I'll kill the fucking lot of you!" he bawled, riding his horse back and forth, up and down the bank, and brandishing his sword. A chorus of jeers came from the cuirassiers, who by now were up to their horses' shoulders in foam. A few of them, though, began to look doubtful, for the water here was darker than it was elsewhere. They fired off their pistols at him, one by one, as if shooting at a squirrel.

A dozen pistol balls cut up the stones on the river bank by Sierawski's horse's hooves. It shied and almost reared, but he held it. Then we saw him ride up to the water's edge and gaze down. At that spot, the water was as black as night. From our vantage point up on the hill the black spot glared up at us like the eye of the Devil himself. Down by the river's edge it was nigh-on invisible.

"Missed, you syphilitic bastards!" he shouted, triumphant, before riding back again.

Beneath that spot, the river must have been a fathom deep. Sierawski, with his engineer's eye, had spied out this gift from God – or Satan. A treacherous hole. So fearsome it rendered Charybdis and Scylla, the sea monsters and whirlpools of antiquity, about as dangerous as a chamber pot. Beneath that spot dwelt the Rusalka, the witch of the waters of the forest.

"Put up your sword, and surrender!" the sergeant shouted, oblivious to the peril. But by now his horse was up to its neck, and the water was around his waist, and he had to hold his pistol above his head. Again he shouted, but now it seemed that the torrent was rising, and his words were snatched away by it.

Sierawski said nothing but pulled a hidden gun from his saddlebag. It was the same ancient fowling piece that Magda had given him, back at Kalwaria Zebrydowski. He had kept it in good order. He had cleaned, oiled, and renovated every part of it by the dim light of campfires and candlelit cellars, until his eyes were red and sore. It had ridden with him, this harbinger of this sergeant's death, for all of these hundreds of miles.

Sierawski rode his horse right up to its knees in the water and fired at the sergeant's horse, quite cold bloodedly. With a terrible scream it collapsed. Both beast and rider were swept away and drowned in the blink of an eye, dragged away by the cold hands of the Rusalka into her icy embrace.

Immediately after that we burst forth from hiding, and gave a volley to the rest of them. Struggling as they were up to their waists in the freezing, raging waters of the Dniester, they panicked. Horses reared and plunged, and whinnied in terror. Riders screamed pitiably as they were swept away, and dragged under by their heavy armour. Tonight the Rusalka would have many suitors.

We forded the river easily, further upstream in the proper spot, where a sandbar ran barely a yard under the water. One could cross there hardly wetting the tops of one's boots. I slipped my musket back into its saddle holster, and drew my pistols. My comrades drew pistols or raised their lances.

There were about fifty of us, and we wound across the river like a snake. Szymon's men stood dumbfounded, having lost half of their comrades at a stroke. Across the river, Sierawski calmly reloaded his gun before trotting his horse along the bank, and carefully crossing at the proper place, behind us.

"There's many that go out for wool and find themselves shorn, Szymon!" Tanski shouted.

"We have a rope here for you, Szymon!" I called, "for he that swings cannot drown!"

Tanski led the line, and we formed up in three ranks, the first armed with lances. They couched their spears like winged knights, the pennants hissing and fluttering in the breeze. Along this narrow bank there was no room to manouevre, and it would be a brutal and bloody charge. Cuirassiers they may have been, heavier and stronger than us. But we had them three to one, and we had our lances. So they turned and ran, back to their Russian masters, with their tails between their legs.

We rode on, south and then east. As we rode we clapped Sierawski on the back, and pressed gifts of tobacco and vodka on him. This drowning of the cuirassiers was a great moment of ingenuity and courage. Had he been a princeling, or the son of a karmazym, with a father who wore scarlet boots, they'd have written songs about him. Why, he would have had a score of medals for it. As it was, the affair made him our hero. His fame quickly went to his head – of course.

CHAPTER THIRTY-FIVE
THE VOID

About fifty of us made it across the ford. We followed the
Dniester east for a week, doubled back, recrossed it, and
headed south, across immense steppes and almost inaccessible
citadels of stone. There we sought sanctuary in the great
sweep of wasteland that curves like a dagger down into the
Ottoman realms. It was as desolate as the surface of the moon.
Below our horses' hooves grew not grass but stones.
Innumerable stones! The debris from gigantic cities not yet
made – or perhaps long since destroyed.

There was no shelter. A wild jackal wind that could pare
flesh from bone drove great columns of biting grey dust into
the sky. Dust as black as the Devil's cape. We and our beasts
did great penance under these accursed storms, which chafed
the skin like a hairshirt.

This void of rocks was naked of trees and of all vegetation
save bristly tamarisk and great crowns of razor-sharp thorns.
A huge outcrop of rocks thrust out of the dusty grey earth.
Steep, sheer sided rocks. We marvelled at them, and ran our
hands over their smooth faces. Some were as shiny as glass,
and the mass of them was quite impassable. I expected to see
the Devil on that outcrop, offering us our souls in exchange
for turning the flat stones that lay at our feet into bread. We
were sorely hungry.

We took a long detour around the outcrop, down into the
belly of a great crater. It ran for many leagues across the plain.
Our horses slid sideways, like crabs, down the edge of this pit.
There, my last packhorse, a pretty white mare, took a tumble.
She dragged old Muszka, my stallion, down with her. We
three rolled down the slope in a chaos of crashing rocks,

stones cracking against my head like musket balls. I felt as Twardowski must have done, falling from the Devil's claws through empty space onto the moon.

"Are you alright, Blumer?" someone shouted. The little column halted. We were still about fifty men strong. The men sat heavily in their stirrups and waited.

"I'm alive," I called back, "but what of my poor horses!" I shouted, in despair. Amid a crop of thorns I found old Muszka, sitting on his backside like a dog by a fireside, and blinking. Ignoring the pain in my jolted bones I dragged him, growling, to his feet, whereupon he bit my arm. He stood easy and unlamed on all four hooves. I braced myself, sickened, for the shock to come.

In a fever of fumbling, I ran my fingers over every leg, from fetlock to shoulder, over every bone, muscle and sinew. Nothing. No injury. Next I counted every rib of the great barrel of his fat belly. At each I gave a tearful prayer of thanks, still awaiting the inevitable mortal wound. I ran my hands over his backbone, his flanks, and neck, his ears and eyes, and into his mouth. He had a thorn stuck in his foot, which I plucked out, and deep cuts in his shaggy hair, from which blood flowed freely, but these were mere flesh wounds, and soon staunched.

"Thank God!" I shouted at the top of my voice, and danced a mad mazurka around my bemused horse, with the void echoing to my words. By some glorious miracle he was unharmed, and whole. My stallion stood staring at me patiently as if I were an idiot, as he always did. Then he turned his huge head. I followed his gaze, and saw Tanski standing by my poor white mare. She lay stricken, soaked in sweat, her flanks heaving, and panting as heavily as if she were in foal. Her leg was completely shattered.

"I'll do it, if you like," Tanski said kindly, clapping hand on my shoulder.

"Thank you brother, but no. It's my horse," I replied.

The pistol shot illuminated a tiny corner of that desolate place, and put an end to the poor creature's suffering. Her burden of baggage we divided up between us. Then we swiftly butchered the dead beast into steaks with our knives and bayonets, and collected the warm blood in our canteens.

A halt was called, and we struck camp for the night. In truth, one could not tell if it was night or day, so dark and desolate was what passed for the day in that endless void. Down there, in the crater, the contours of the land were like beggar's cupped hands. It gave us shelter from the gnawing gale, and we were thankful. Yet still we froze in the eternal black of the miserable gloomy place. Desperate for warmth, we found a thicket of thorn scrub and painstakingly cut it up, with frozen fingers. Our hands were lacerated and the flesh hung in shreds. We suffered such torments in those thorns as would have tested the patience of a saint.

"Well, we have made it out of hell, at least," I said grimly, for the fire was made, and we ate strips of meat from the mare, and drank the last of the blood, mixed with wine. "Now we are merely in purgatory!"

Tanski said nothing, but glowered. We thought that this was because he was jealous of Sierawski's fame. How mistaken we were! Our comrade was gravely ill, but he said nothing. He merely shouldered his share of our burdens without complaint.

"Let's hear the Proclamation!" Sierawski said, and we all listened, for his fame glowed stronger still than the miserable fire, all smoke but no flame, and precious little heat. All of the company hung on his word, including the lads who had never clapped eyes on him before the affair at the ford. Whatever he said, we did, for he had earned it back there. So I dug the Proclamation from my saddlebag. We were sorely in need of its consolation now, it was our prayer. My comrades urged me to my feet, and obligingly I stood up. I declaimed it in near total darkness, for by now I knew it by heart.

"Proclamation to Poles!

*I, Dabrowski, the Polish Lieutenant General, faithful to our
Motherland, am forming a Polish Legion in Italy! We
struggled for freedom, led by the immortal Kościuszko. We
saw our flag victorious at Dubienka, Raclawice, Warsaw
and Vilnius. But our nation fell through violence, and the
blood of innocents flowed in the soil that belonged to our
forefathers.*

*Poles, fresh hope has come from France! Victorious
France has come to our aid, so that we may fight our
common enemies! France will give us shelter, to await
better fortunes for our own country. We shall fight under
her Tricolour flag, for these are signs of honour and
victory. The Polish Legion, formed in Italy, the Holy
Temple of Freedom!*

*There are many brave soldiers and officers, your comrades
in hardship, here with me. Battalions are forming. Those of
you who are conscripts – desert from the enemy armies!
Join us! All nations who love liberty are fighting together
as allies, under the brave Bonaparte, Victor of Italy. Our
only hope to save our nation is the French Republic.*

*The Legion's Headquarters in Milan, the First Day of the
Month of Pluvoise, Year Five of the French Republic."*

Dabrowski's Proclamation had been made in February of that
year, 1797. The strange dates were from the French
Revolutionary calendar. It seemed that not even time itself
was safe from the Revolution!

At the end, the men fell to discussing Italy, which was to
be reached by ship from Constantinople, and how we would
get there.

271

"Do you know, Blumer – I think that we have taken a most terrible detour under your inept guidance! We are lost!" Sierawski said, chewing a hunk of horsemeat, savouring it, and savouring the way the men now hung on his every word. The engineer's head was getting too big for his czapka, I feared.

"I think," the engineer continued, "that this is not Turkey at all. We must have journeyed to the moon! You and your damned Podolian maps!" he laughed, clapping his thigh with glee. They all laughed at this, and I frowned. It is not good to hear fifty men laughing at you like damned hyenas. Had my hands not been wrapped in rags, hurting like the very devil, and dripping blood like tears, I should have knocked out every last one of Sierawski's teeth for him, and seen how well he chewed my horsemeat then. So instead I laughed, too, and Sierawski handed me his flask, and I drank, and calmed myself. For I was a real *pistolet* in those days, a hothead. It landed me in no end of trouble, I can tell you. My temper had brought me naught but an empty purse and the tarnished badge of a warrant officer, after six long years of toil.

"Blumer is a good lad – for a Podolian," Sierawski expounded. "He has the maps and the compass, and he even has Dabrowski's Proclamation in there. We'd be lost without him. Why, he carries the entire Warsaw library in his saddlebag. Blumer is as organised as our general staff!"

"I hope not," I retorted, "or we really are fucked!"

The others all laughed at this, and they passed me another drink. It occurred to me at last that one catches more flies with honey than with vinegar.

"Well, anyway," Sierawski said, generously – as only a man who is cock of the walk can be generous – "we all agree that we'd be lost without you, comrade."

"So tell us then," Birnbaum put in sadly, "where in the world are we now, Blumer? Are we in hell, or on the moon?" Birnbaum was desolately sad. For he was the last of the

Beardlings. His fellow Jewish cavalryman had been cut down by the Austrians, or taken, we knew not. At any rate the poor fellow was lost. We were all Birnbaum had now, and even pig-headed Tanski was kind to him in consequence.

"We are halfway to Galatz, Comrade Birnbaum," I replied, "for I have reckoned it by the stars, and by my compass and maps."

"Galatz!" Tanski spat, "What negligence is this? We are supposed to be going to Constantinople, Blumer, damn your eyes! Why the hell are we going to Galatz?" they all demanded, angry with me again.

How fickle is the mob! I explained it to them all, yet again, very wearily. My comrades knew little and cared less for geography. I had told them a dozen times already.

"We still have many miles to Constantinople. It is three months' journey over land from here, hard riding across the mountain passes of Bulgaria and Greece, which are infested with bandits. But from Galatz it is a mere three weeks plain sailing by sea," I told them.

"Galatz is the biggest port in a hundred miles. Finding a ship there will be easier than finding a priest in a whorehouse!"

CHAPTER THIRTY-SIX
GALATZ, SEPTEMBER 1797

It took us another month to reach Galatz. I reckoned the time by Twardowski's face, which waxed and waned, and curved into a silver crescent, in honour of our Turkish hosts. We were armed, and strong in numbers, so the roving bands of Tartar raiders and the bandits let us be. But word of our coming would have spread.

After emerging from the void we crossed Moldavia, where we encountered naught but marshes, gypsies, and carrion birds. When we reached the River Prul we followed it south. Three rivers drain into this Turkish sinkhole – the Prul, the Siret, and the mighty Danube. The Danube is the Austrians' sewer, of course, which endeared it not to us. Still, the prospect of sailing to Italy on the Austrians' own waterway was quite poetic.

Galatz had been burned down by the Russians in the Turkish War of 1789, eight years before. Judging by the state of the place, it may as well have been yesterday. Even the Danube shared this state of dilapidation, for it ran brown and reeking here, not shining blue and emerald. But there were boats in Galatz, just as I had promised the lads.

Boats! Hundreds of vessels of every kind and every size, from tiny fishing canoes to vast three-masted merchantmen bristling with cannon. We marvelled at the huge ships as they drifted lazily along the vast, placid river, dozens of them, one after another. We had to find but one. Still, none of us had any experience of anything larger than the grain-rafts of the Baltic grain trade to Danzig.

"I'm fairly certain we can't row and punt our way to Constantinople," Sierawski said, doubtfully. "We need something with sails."

"Thank God we have an expert engineer with us!" I sneered at him. "Four years of training were not wasted, I see."

Galatz harbour was a filthy and degenerate hole. Toothless old men tried to sell us their young daughters. When we refused, they tapped their hooked noses knowingly, cackled, and brought out their sons, instead. We tried to shoo these scoundrels away but nevertheless a crowd of them gathered. A veritable swarm of bawds, pimps, pederasts, water-sellers, cut-purses and hawkers. They trailed in our wake like the gulls trailed after the boats.

"Damn it all," I cursed, "this commotion will bring out the Janissaries." Well, speak of the Devil, and he will appear. Sure enough, a party of evil-looking brigands came out to greet us. Splendid-looking devils, mark you.

The Janissaries – the Turkish Army. Bronze-skinned Arab fellows of fierce aspect, with drooping moustaches, pointed beards, and betel-stained teeth, riding magnificent horses or stink-spitting camels. Their finery was splendid to behold. Some wore flowing robes of white, green, or gold, embroidered with bright colours in exquisite geometric patterns. Others wore armour – spiked bronze helmets, breastplates, and chain mail, like fish-scales.

All their weapons had jewelled hilts and scabbards of exquisite workmanship and beauty. They were armed with great scimitars, up to half a man's length, and curved daggers, ancient firelock muskets with intricately carved stocks, or spears with silk tassels. Amongst the number of this exotic, fantastical host were massive bare-chested Nubian warriors wielding axes and half-pikes. They looked like executioners from the tale of the Arabian Nights.

Most incredible of all, the Janissaries brought with them two docile elephants trailing a huge antique brass cannon, of the vintage of the siege of Vienna in 1683. This amazing sight, fearsome as it was, filled my heart with joy. I felt like applauding.

"Blumer can talk to them," Sierawski hissed, "Podolians are practically Turks anyhow."

"I will, then," I said, "damn your eyes. Keep calm, lads," I called out to my comrades, "this is the Turks' land. Their ways are no doubt strange to us."

I raised a white handkerchief on a lance, and rode forward, alone. It was a tense moment – our men shouldered their arms and raised their lances as a mark of respect. But we would charge or volley if the need arose. Our hearts were beating a triple-march. I flew a flag of truce and so the Janissaries did likewise. We breathed again. Two men, a petty official, a vizier or suchlike, and a great barrel-chested Janissary officer of fifty years rode forward on white Arab chargers from the Turkish lines. Their harnesses shone and jingled with gold rings. Our men watched in disgust as the Janissaries dispersed the crowd with whips, and we politely ignored the resultant chaos.

It was the old Janissary who took charge. He wore a jewelled eye-patch and his long beard ran to grey. He wheeled his horse and grinned grotesquely with a gap-toothed smile. He began to leer and bawl a challenge at us. At me, I realised. The Vizier translated into French, for we had fewer words of Turkish than the old Janissary had teeth in his jaw.

"The Austrians say Poland is dead. The Russians say Poles are weak," he declaimed. "What are you, Poles? Are you the strong sons of Sobieski, or bastard catamites of the Bullock?" The old Janissary made a set of obscene gestures with his hands that could be universally translated. I turned back to Tanski and Sierawski.

"Whatever happens, don't fire on them, and don't draw blood. We are strangers here – they will have the whole country on us. More than that, we need their help. Wait here, and be calm. I will show this old fool who is strong and who is a milksop."

With that, I got off my horse, and the old Janissary did the same. His men cheered him to the echo, while jeering at me. Our little legion of fifty men did the opposite, beating their lances on the ground, and waving their pennants, which made the Arab horses buck and shy in fright.

Between the two sets of troops was a set of stone water troughs and a smithy. The blacksmith had wisely run for cover. His furnace roared untended. Beside it were a set of iron horseshoes, fresh-forged, glowing white- and red-hot. I unbuckled my sword and guns and cast them aside.

The Janissary grinned and followed suit, and began flexing his arms and cracking his knuckles. His arms were huge and brawny, with thick sinews like whipcords. Although his skin had been burnished dark as teak by the burning Turkish sun, he was a white man by blood. I guessed that he was a Greek, or a Serb, or even a Cossack. For the Janissaries conscripted slaves from all across their vast empire, and not only Turks.

At first he made to wrestle with me, but I shook my head. For I knew he would put his thumb in my eye, his elbow in my groin, or suchlike chicanery, and I would not brook it. Besides, if he did not maim me, I might kill him, and either way it would end badly.

"A trial of strength," I said, picking up a horseshoe in a pair of tongs, and plunging them into the water trough. A great hiss of steam blazed forth. I tossed a second into the cauldron, a third, and so on until six of them lay at the bottom of the water. The Janissary eyed me, warily. Taking off my coat, I fished the horseshoes out of the water, and laid them on the anvil.

Intrigued, the Janissary made for me to continue. Thus I picked up the first horseshoe in my bare hands, and with a grunt, bent it straight between my hands. My adversary nodded, and grinned his ragged smile, for now he understood the contest. Negligently picking up a horseshoe, he bent it straight, and cast it aside.

Now the game was on. I smiled, for I had him. So I picked up two horseshoes. I held them up to my men, and then to the Janissaries. I clinked them against each other, like a conjuror. I struck them against the anvil and drew sparks. Chimes rang out across the dockside. Our men began to cheer and stamp at my back, and waved their lances. Before me, the Janissaries waved their arms and let out wild yelps like dogs and eerie, ululating cries. My adversary watched me with a keen eye, wary, but still confident.

I put the two horseshoes together, doubling the thickness. Tensing my arms, I set my strength against the two horseshoes. Sweat burst out of my temples. My head throbbed and my sinews groaned. Then I felt the metal give, and they bent, straight as an arrow. A hush fell, and then my fellow Poles cheered me to the rafters.

Angered, and sorely afraid that he was outmatched, the old Janissary set his gap toothed jaw, and strained his hands against the metal. Great cords of sinew stuck out on his neck and arms, thick as ship's ropes. A river of sweat ran down his brawny back. His massive arms shook with the effort. Suddenly blood ran from his nose, for he must have burst a blood-vessel with the effort. Wiping his dripping nose on his hairy arm, he raised the straightened horseshoes in triumph.

"A draw!" he roared, in Russian.

"A draw!" echoed the Vizier, greatly perturbed, for he clearly feared the wrath of this burly brute.

"Like Hell," I shook my head. "Not yet, *friend*."

Then I bent the doubled horseshoes back again, into a 'U'.

Our little legion cheered this to the rafters, and had there been any glass in the windows of those rude houses, why it would have been broken loose. The docks shook to their stones. With a grunt, the Janissary hawked a bloody gob of spit on the ground, and tossed his unbent horseshoes into the river, conceding defeat. His sunburned chest still heaved, for he had not yet recovered. Blood bubbled from his nose. A lackey passed him a silk kerchief. This he tore into strips, and stuffed them up his nostrils. Squaring his shoulders, he made for me. I myself was quite calm. I set my feet and chest against his blow. It never came. Instead, he held out a hand.

"I am Hassan," he said, "General of the Janissaries. I am a strong man, Allah be praised," he said, with some grudging admiration, "but you are stronger! Strong as a lion!"

"I am Blumer," I told him.

We shook hands. We exchanged signs, to knuckle and thumb. He was a brother Freemason. Then he held my hand aloft to his troops, and they all cheered, before doing the same to our Polish ranks. To my great surprise, he spoke fluent Russian, so we were able to converse freely. For he was indeed a Cossack, sold by his mother to the Janissaries at the age of five, and converted to the Muslim faith.

"Welcome!" he grinned, throwing his arms around me, "for my enemy's enemy is my friend!" We salaamed and bowed, and then embraced. He crushed me against his great chest as hard as he could, in a bear hug. Beneath his sweet perfume he smelt as rank as a bear, and sweat ran freely down his back. When he spoke, he held his face up to mine, and he roared, and flecked my face with spittle and stale fumes of garlic, cloves, tobacco, and coffee. I could not flinch, for to do so would show weakness, and so I stood there, subjected to this torrent, and I pretended it was raining.

"I know there is a price on your heads," he whispered into my ear, like a lover, "but you are safe here, effendi. I have been waiting here for you. I have an arrangement with your General Dabrowski."

One of Dabrowski's men, Rymkiewicz, and the French Ambassador, Du Bayet, had bribed this unscrupulous brigand to escort us, and others, to Constantinople. A ship of the Turkish navy was paid to take us. I was indeed stronger than Hassan, so I bore this vile embrace with a smile, and then hugged him back stronger, until his ribs cracked, and he gasped for air. I released him, and we sat on the stone bench, laughing. Then he clapped his hands. In the blink of an eye his slaves pitched a green tent there in the dusty earth beside the harbour.

"Come, Blumer!" he said, motioning the tent, "take a sherbet with me." His manner had served to put me ill at ease, for the Turks were infamous for their perversions. I was heartily glad of Tanski, Sierawski and Birnbaum and half a dozen legionnaires beside me in the tent. I had no idea what depredations this strange Hassan intended.

We sat cross-legged, after the custom of that nation, on a Persian rug, under a silk awning hung with carpets. Opposite us Hassan sat with the Vizier, and a dozen bodyguards armed with halberds and arquebuses. This rank of splendid looking fellows stood scowling at us, impassive as statues. Half a dozen slaves in golden collars ran back and forth with coffee and sherbet. It was deliciously cooling, and we swilled away the dust and sweat of the road.

"Blumer, my friend," Hassan said in Russian, producing a flask of vodka, "these are your men? You lead them?"

I shook my head and pointed to Tanski. "He leads us."

Hassan grimaced and looked affronted. "No? The pretty one? Why, he is but your flag-bearer, Blumer! Surely? Ah, but when I look at him close, he has a killer's eyes! Like a hawk."

Of course Tanski could hear every word of this exchange, but Hassan spoke as if he was not there, for he would only deign to converse with me. It must have been some protocol amongst the Janissaries.

Hassan cast his eyes over us as if appraising horses.

"So we have the lion, the hawk, and this one – (he indicated Sierawski) – this one is the fox! The cunning one! The three of you – the strong, the skilful, the cunning – you are like the Trinity of the Christians! And as for the fourth – you even have a Jew returned from the dead – he wears the mark of the scaffold on his neck, does he not?"

Hassan indicated his own neck, which was also scarred with rope burns, and laughed, and Birnbaum grew pale and fretted at his musket. I stilled him with a glance, and Hassan saw this with his good eye, and winked at me.

"Ah," he said, "my men are good, but my officers are dust! I should say they are women, but women fight harder than they do! Turkish officers are eunuchs and catamites, worse than women. What I would give for officers such as you! Trained men, hard men, white warriors, like me!" and he thumped his chest, belched, and sighed. Beside him the Vizier began to importune, and cajole, and the two of them fell to bickering in their impenetrable tongue, which sounds like snakes and daggers. As the argument became heated, the Vizier made the palms-out, money-grubbing gesture.

"My friend, the Sultan's man," Hassan explained, "wants you to pay a toll if you want to reach The City." By this he meant Constantinople, which the Turks call by many names, but mostly it is referred to simply as 'The City.'

"What toll?" I said, suspiciously, for Hassan had already told me that Dabrowski had arranged for him to be paid.

Hassan smiled. "The Vizier says you must forfeit all your horses, guns, and swords. This, he says, is the Sultan's law. What say you, Blumer? Will you stand for this insult?" Hassan grinned, and made a secret sign to me. Drastic action was called for. I took a chance. With that I leaned forward and slapped the Vizier full in the face. The blow sounded loud as a gunshot. The Vizier fainted dead away, blood pouring from his mouth. Two of the Nubians carried him out. Hassan spat and a slave caught the spittle in a silver salver before it hit the carpet. I held my breath. No one moved. Hassan did not bat an

281

eyelid. My comrades stared at me, aghast. Hassan's men began to reach for their weapons and Hassan stilled them with a wave of his hand.

"That was well done, Blumer," Hassan observed, blandly. "My friend the Vizier insulted you, my dear guests, and he has dishonoured me. I apologise to you, Blumer, and I apologise to your men," Hassan bowed to me, quite delighted by what I had done. Breathing a great sigh of relief, I bowed in return from where I sat.

"Apology accepted, Your Excellency," I shrugged.

"You do me much honour," he inclined his head. "As you see, Blumer – we Janissaries rule in Turkey," Hassan grinned, tapping his antique pistol, with a hilt chased in silver and studded with jewels, "and not the Sultan's eunuchs. It is good to be a Janissary."

"That," I said, "seems to be very clear."

Hassan laughed again and a slave poured my coffee. What he said next astounded us.

"Tell me, what news of Pepi?" he asked, as if we were sitting in Madame L's salon, back in Warsaw, and not in this Godforsaken fly-blown hole.

"The last I heard," I replied, "the Prince was living in exile. You know him, your Excellency?"

"Know him!" Hassan laughed, pointing at his scarred face and jewelled eye patch, "why, he took my eye, at the Siege of Sabbatch! Ah, good old Pepi! What a warrior! Tell me, will he join your Legion?"

I shrugged. "If God wills it."

At this, the Arab exploded with laughter and slapped his knees with his heavy, ringed hands. He asked me of the wars, the Uprising, of the Commander, of our adventures, of Poland, and of the fall. We talked long, and smoked the tobacco in the water pipe down to the ashes. It was now or never, or we should be sitting by this harbour until doomsday, with this evil old fellow.

"The tide turns," I said, pointing to the water. "We must take ship, Your Excellency."

"Go with God, Blumer," Hassan said, and we all stood, our stiff knees shooting out a volley of cracks. "My man will take you to your ship – pride of the Turkish navy."

After thanking our strange benefactor, we took our leave as fast as we could. Beside the road the Janissaries lounged in the sun like dogs, with the hawkers and peddlers circling them like flies. Hassan clapped a huge hand on my shoulder.

"Fight for me, Blumer," he cackled, making the money gesture, palms out. "Much gold!"

I laughed, for I was flattered, but not tempted.

"I'll think about it, Excellency."

Hassan watched us go through hooded eyes.

"I will see you in The City yet, Blumer, my son! Go with God!"

"Go with God? We will both go to the Devil, you and I!" I replied, and grinned, as I climbed onto my horse.

CHAPTER THIRTY-SEVEN
THE CRAB BOAT

"These are damn strange sailors," I said sceptically, staring at the mass of crabs crawling across the deck. One of them began snapping at my boot and I flipped it over on its back. "I don't think the English Navy has much to worry about," I added.

"This is no battleship!" Sierawski said, needlessly, "this is a bleeding fishing boat!"

"Thank God we have an expert engineer to advise us on these matters," Tanski said sarcastically. He was breathing heavily and leaning on his lance, and appeared unwell. "What do you think, Birnbaum?"

Birnbaum stared at the mass of crabs. There were crabs writhing in pots, wriggling in great baskets, clacking their claws in nets, crawling in buckets of water, and scuttling sideways across the decks. There were loose crabs battling vainly with predatory seagulls. Here and there a lucky fugitive crab would escape, and abandon ship, dropping over the side and hitting the water with a plop. Their pink, red and yellow shells shone wetly in the sun. Above all the rest, an astonishing, overpowering stink of fish assailed our nostrils.

"This ship," Birnbaum said wryly, "is not kosher."

Pride of the Turkish navy, my horse's sainted arse! You will have divined, as we did, that this was a mere crab ship. Old Hassan had no doubt pocketed the excess fare, and substituted this cheaper vessel. Instead of an escort of marines and sailors, a dozen raddled and tattooed old fishermen worked the sails and oars.

Still, we met another group of Polish lads on the way, about a dozen, and it was good to swell our numbers for once. Our masters had been bilked and shortchanged by Hassan, but at least we had not been robbed blind and stripped naked by the rapacious Vizier. No doubt, as soon as he had our weapons, we should have found ourselves auctioned off in the slave markets of Constantinople!

The boat itself was of a fine enough aspect, if one overlooked the cargo of crabs, and held one's nose against the stench of fish. It was similar to a galley – a long, slim brig, of a type they called a chebec. It had a long narrow hull, like a lance, and was fitted with both oars and sails. It had two large triangular sails at the front, and one small sail on the rear deck, which was a raised box, like a wooden castle. A castle piled high with baskets of writhing crabs for battlements, of course. These chebecs, we discovered later, were coastal craft. Fast and manouevrable, but vulnerable on the open ocean, and prey to bad weather. More of that anon, for it was almost our undoing. None of us knew anything of ships at the time, and there was naught to be done about it.

Our horses liked this not, so we held czapkas and blinkers over their eyes, and dragged them aboard. Some would not budge, and had to be winched aboard with block and tackle, and slings under their bellies. We watched anxiously as the poor frightened horses took wing like birds, hoisted up into the sky, and were deposited, whining piteously, on the deck. The horses were not enamoured of the crabs. They sniffed suspiciously at them, and the angry crabs nipped at their noses with their pincers. So the horses huddled together at one end of the deck, and the great wooden yard yawed and heaved unsteadily. Greatly alarmed by this, for the sea was as calm as a millpond, I spoke to the crew. It was hard to make myself understood, but eventually I did. As the boat set off, I had the men and the crew spread out the horses, and tether them below the decks, at intervals, as ballast.

Of course, this process took hours of threats, and cajoling, and hard sweat and toil. Eventually, the boat reached a sort of equilibrium, a balance, and steadied herself somewhat. The number of men running to the rail to vomit began to diminish accordingly.

"Damned Turks could have laid on some food," Tanski muttered, "my stomach hurts like hell, I'm so hungry."

"What the Devil do you think this is?" I said, grabbing a pair of passing crabs by their heels and slinging them on to a brazier. Unlike the horses, the men were greatly enamoured of the crabs, the Lithuanians amongst us fondly remembering the crayfish of their homeland. Soon the deck was turned into a kitchen, as the men cheerfully boiled buckets of crabs alive. The delicious scent of cooking fish and the sound of cracking shells filled the air, and we ate our fill of the sweet white meats. The sailors were outraged. We were eating their catch.

"We will pay them," I said curtly. "Pass the hat," I ordered, filling my hat with worthless coins, brass buttons, and a few old trinkets. All I had left to my name was my mother's ring, but that would only be taken from my dead body.

"What?" Sierawski moaned, "we have already been robbed once! Are we to robbed again by these Turkish scum? We are armed, and they are not, remember?"

"We are ignorant of seafaring, and they are not," I replied, "and that is that. Pay up."

So we paid for our meal, and ate, out on the water. The wind and sun made us ravenous, and we butchered hundreds of crabs, and tossed mounds of spent shells into the sea.

"Not eating, comrade?" I asked Birnbaum.

Birnbaum looked at us with envy. "Not hungry, Sir," he replied, licking his lips.

"Here," I said, taking some worm-eaten hard tack and biscuits from my bag. It was about as appetising as a length of ship's rope, and took as long to boil down, but Birnbaum thanked me graciously, and ate it without complaint. Still, the

Jew had the last laugh, for he was the only member of our whole company who did not spend a goodly part of the voyage praying over the ships rail, and giving the contents of his stomach to Neptune and the mermaids as a watery offering.

By the time we crossed the estuary at the mouth of the Danube, and entered the open sea, Tanski had turned a brilliant white, flashing with green, like some exotic fish. He alternated between squatting in the heads and vomiting in a bucket, not even having the strength to lean over the side any more. He was in no fit state to command, not even being master of his own bowels. Arms wrapped over his chest, he lay curled up, head down in a corner, moaning balefully. Sierawski, too, though not as far gone, was devout in his prayers to the mermaids, and swayed on his feet. So at last I was in command again. It was a real case of dead men's shoes – or rather dead men's stomachs.

"Look at that English bastard," Sierawski said, enviously, for I had only vomited once or twice, "seafaring must be in the blood."

"Polish bastard, if you please," I said cheerfully, "and my forbears were Irish, not English."

"Same difference," Sierawski said, and puked in a bucket.

I alone found the ship invigorating, the swell of the sea, the deck rolling beneath me like a wooden horse. I watched, fascinated, as the sailors climbed the ropes like monkeys, adjusting the sails that grew empty or full-bellied on the wind, as the occasion demanded. As we sailed, I talked to the captain, the mates, the tillerman, even the oarsmen. I had set off from Galatz entirely ignorant of seagoing, but I was learning fast. Because we had paid for our suppers, they were happy to speak to me. They grew garrulous, and boastful, and delighted in showing me the tricks of their trade.

We passed a good few days like this. Many comrades joined in with the crew, hauling ropes, and scaling the rigging.

Still, we made poor time, for the water was becalmed, and the breath of the wind fell from a lusty bellows to a feeble whispering breath, such as would scarcely upset the feather in a lady's hat. So I set a team of the lads to pulling on the oars, both to take their minds off the sickness, and to hurry us along. Besides, the Devil makes work for idle hands.

Abruptly, the crew's manner changed. They grew anxious, angry, and restive about something. I thought at first that we Poles, in our ignorance, had offended their customs or religion somehow. I racked my brains as the Turkish sailors ran about, yelping like mad angry dogs. Then the storm blew, and a curtain of darkness fell, with driving rain, like a wall of icy daggers. A white light lit up the sky, and there came a roll of thunder so loud that it was as if all the cannons in every battle we had ever fought had been discharged at one stupendous volley. On the coat-tails of the storm came her attendants, the wailing winds, and the driving rains.

We gazed, transfixed, at the sky. Mother of God! Such rain! Such a deluge! Such waves! Such a sea! Oh, the weight of water! To draw a pitcher of it is hard enough, but to be on a boat, struck by hills, mountains of the stuff! The poor slim boat reeled and heeled, pitched and hawed. All manner of things were hurled overboard and lost – weapons, spars, ropes, hats, and several men. They flew through the air before my very eyes, like sparrows. Great strips of the sails were torn off, as a child tears the petals from a flower.

"We are lost!" I heard a cry. "Save yourselves!" Fortunately, I had sent Tanski below decks, for he had been a liability, what with his groaning and his constant voiding of his bowels. The others cowered below decks, or clung as best they could to the deck, the masts, or the rigging, holding on with strength born of terror.

"Sierawski!" I shouted. "Our Lord walked upon the waters, and so can we!" For I saw the root of the problem – these slim chebec ships were too unsteady for these waters. They carried too much weight, too high. It was those damned crabs.

Sierawski was losing his footing, and struggling. I grabbed him by the heels as he flew past me, hauling him to his feet like a rag doll, for he is but a slight fellow.

"What desertion is this?" I laughed, "come, Sierawski! To the crab nets! It's them or us!"

Drawing our daggers, we held them between our teeth. Grabbing a rope, we hauled ourselves bodily across the deck, like mountaineers. She rolled wildy, bucking like a crazy horse. One moment the deck was as flat as a field, the next it was as steep as a hillside. Somehow we made it to the heavy box nets full of crabs. Rain lashed our faces, endless droves of icy arrows. Now the very air had turned to water. As we stood on the deck, waves broke across our bodies, drenching us to the core.

"Cut the ropes, damn you!" I roared, my voice lost in the storm. But Sierawski saw my frantic slashes at the ropes that lashed the boxes to the deck, and he understood. We cut one box free. The ship lurched and it was pitched over the side, snatched from our hands by the greedy ocean, and we very nearly went with it.

"Now the other side!" I cried, for we had to keep her level. We repeated our awful journey to the other side. By now we were thoroughly drenched, our hands red raw. Our lungs heaved, our eyes streamed, our teeth chattered. The stentorian roar of the sea, the angry voice of Neptune, was louder than the sounds of any battle. One after another we cut the heavy cargo of crabs loose, throwing them over the side, first from the left side of the ship, then the right. Soon they were all gone. If the crabs were pleased at their liberation and reprieve, it showed not in their black, beady eyes, as we returned them to the deeps from which they had so recently been abducted.

Thus lightened, the ship ran on a more even keel. It hurtled off, like a cork from a bottle, a flying bullet, or a loosed horse, out of the path of that diabolic storm. Later, we learned that several boats like ours had been lost, with all hands. Thankfully we knew it not then.

"The rocks!" Sierawski wailed. We had been caught between Charybdis and Scylla, for the storm had driven us towards the shore.

"At least we can be buried on land!" I laughed. Huge boulders loomed into view, like enormous teeth. The ship, by some miracle, swept by the rocks, missing them by a hair's breadth. It hurtled towards a low yellow beach at an alarming rate. Still the ship lurched from side to side. The shipwreck, when it came, was like a bodyblow. Our poor boat, that had been travelling so fast, struck the sandy bank, slewed across it, and ground to a halt. Every timber of the ship rattled right down to its splinters. As if I had been fired from a cannon, I flew. I knew what it was to be a musket ball. When I landed, I was buried in soft yellow earth, praise God. I was utterly exhilarated and elated.

"It was as if all creation turned upside down, on its head, and the world spun on its axis! Still, I have had worse in drink," I said to Sierawski, elated. For Sierawski and I were lying in the sand, on the beach. All around us were broken barrels and shattered spars and wooden planks. We had been hurled bodily completely from the deck of the ship. It lay beside us on its side, like an exhausted lover.

"Ha ha!" I laughed at Sierawski, "you still have your hat!" Even after all this, his sodden czapka, leaking water like a sieve, was still jammed onto his head.

It carried on raining after we had run aground, which seemed like the act of a spiteful God. We huddled together under the sodden canvas, without even a fire for comfort. The men pined for the happy days when they were seasick! We would be back to eating horseflesh, for a sad number of the beasts had died when the ship capsized. It was a wonder that any survived at all, but the majority, including my dear indestructible Muszka, had made it. Now we had learned the hard way how unstable these slim chebec ships were on open waters. It was a bitter lesson, but we learned it well. A cold night we had of it, but in the morning the rain ceased, and we surveyed the damage, and the death toll.

"How many dead?" Tanski asked. He was sitting in a chair on the beach, wrapped in a blanket like an old man.

"A dozen overboard, and twenty dead horses," I replied bitterly, frozen to the core. My soaking rags stuck to my bones, and seeped icy water. None of us had known cold like it – not in the steppes, not in the snows, nor even in the icy void. Not for nothing was it called the Black Sea. It was as black and cold as the Devil's heart. We knew now something of how those Russian Cuirassiers had suffered, when they were swallowed by the whirlpool of the Dniester.

"A dozen men and twenty horses! I lost less at Raclawice!" Tanski groaned, and struggled to his feet. He was clutching his stomach, for he was in agonies of cramp and sickness.

"Drink this comrade, for God's sake," I said to him, "you look like hell."

He drank the water I offered him. "Still," he said, rubbing his belly, "you did well, Blumer. But for you and the boy Sierawski, we'd all be dead."

Tanski turned aside and was sick, bringing up the water immediately. He wiped his face, grimaced, and turned back to us. "What about this damned ship?"

"Well, it isn't too badly damaged, considering," Sierawski said, "all the masts are still there. The oars and all the boats though, have been smashed to matchwood."

"Not too bad?" Tanski said incredulously. "The bloody boat is upside down!"

"Come now, Tanski," I said scratching my aching head. "The boat is not upside down, she is merely lying on her side."

"Oh well, that's nothing, then! Lying on her side with her damned skinny arse sticking out of the water! What say you now, you salty sea dogs? We are a bunch of Jonahs, only without the whale!" With that he sat back in his chair on the sand, and sulked, and clutched at his stomach.

"He has a point," I admitted to Sierawski, "but we have plenty of rope, still, and if we could but right the vessel, we could heave her back into the water."

"Enough rope!" Tanski gnashed his teeth, "I'll give you enough rope to hang you both! That is, if I could find a tree strong enough to bear the weight of your fat Irish carcass! So we get the accursed floating coffin back in the water. Then what?" Tanski snapped. "How do we get back out to sea with no oars?"

I shrugged. "I suppose we wait for a passing zephyr to waft us on a gentle breeze all the way to Constantinople. A mere triviality."

"Ha ha ha!" Tanski laughed, at last, and wept, although whether tears of laughter, or real tears, I dared not ask. "All right then, Admiral Blumer, how do we right this bastard of a boat?"

I had an idea. "Let's ask an engineer!" I said and we both turned on Sierawski.

"Easy," said he, negligently, "we ask the crew for a windlass and ropes."

We found the surviving crew some way off. They had set their prayer mats on the sand, and, after orienting these towards their holy city, were praying. We had to wait until this was finished, and then we found the captain. He was a short fellow, with thin strong arms, like whipcords, his skin tanned like leather. We followed his barefoot steps back across the sand to the stricken ship.

"He says we have a windlass, Allah be praised," Sierawski said, as we retrieved a bulky wood and metal contraption from the hold. It was a great winch that turned on a horizontal axis. Apparently this was a 'windlass'. This, as you may imagine, was an awkward and hazardous business, but we had plenty of strong men, and carried it off without incident.

"What now?" I asked Sierawski, who was taking charge.

"You set a company of men to making oars," said Sierawski, "for there is plenty of wood on the boat. But touch not those trees yonder, for I have need of them."

Hard by the beach was a low copse of hanging trees, with vast round bellies thick as houses, and black as the ace of spades. They must have been a thousand years old when Christ was a boy.

"I doubt that I could cut those down with anything short of ten barrels of gunpowder," I observed.

"Precisely," Sierawski said, "they will be my anchors."

It took all of the morning, but Sierawski's men, under his direction, secured the windlass to the largest of the trees with a tangle of ropes. They ran the line around a second tree, to make a pulley, and secured the other end of the ropes to the hull of the ship, fore and aft, and to the tops of each mast.

"Like a spider, running the angle of a web," I said, wonderingly. "With the right lever, a man can move the whole earth!"

It was a long, slow, process, and the sun was at its zenith by the time they were done, and the ship's crew was back to noonday prayers. A pile of new, rough-hewn oars, made of broken spars and ship's planks, was growing on the beach. Tanski stood apart, with the horses, for this seafaring business was not for him. His health was worsening again. His bowels and belly were voiding frightful amounts of soil and brackish water. To be in his element amongst the equines consoled his soul, and the company of the horses calmed him somewhat.

When the ropes were secure, Sierawski bid the men wind the handles of the windlass. The machine resembled a great mangle in a laundry, and the men laughed, and complained that they were not washerwomen.

"Silence!" Sierawski ordered, and I saw him now as he was at Wola, deadly serious and professional. "This is an important business, gentlemen, and dangerous. Fail now, and like as not we die here, on this beach."

So they put their shoulders to the wheel. At first, the ropes were slack. The windlass turned easily, but to no apparent result. Gradually the screw tightened. The ropes tautened. The ship seemed to come to life, as the wood began to strain, and groan. Suddenly, it rolled in the sand, and began to rise.

"She's moving!" cheered the men, and heaved on the ropes with renewed vigour. Sierawski had placed men on the seaward side, with props of wood, and they hammered these into the wet sand, to steady the vessel. With a great crack, like an enormous whip, one of the ropes snapped. It flashed across the sand like an angry serpent. We dived for cover. Sierawski stood quite still, and the end of the rope knocked his czapka from his head, and it rolled in the sand. By a miracle, the rope did not touch a hair of his head. The man did not even flinch.

"Steady there! Steady you bastards!" Sierawski roared. "Not too hard! Pull, don't jerk! Ease her up! Imagine you're stroking a woman, not plucking a chicken!"

Incredibly, awe-inspiringly, against all the laws of God and nature, the ship rose. Reborn, she turned on her axis, writhing like a living beast. As the sun set, the masts pointed up to the heavens, like church spires. Then we put our bare shoulders to that great rotten argosy. We fifty men heaved it, bodily, across ten feet of sand, into the sea. There it sat, in a couple of feet of water, flat bottom flush to the ocean floor. Now all we had to do was wait for the tide to turn, and with a kindly breeze, and another heave on the windlass, we would be off.

The men capered about the sand, dancing wild mad mazurkas. We had no more vodka to break out, but for once we cared not. We canonised Sierawski by dunking him in the sea, then lofted him on our shoulders. We scattered the seagulls with our cheers. Amid it all, the crew fell to their prayer mats again, thanking Allah for his timely intervention.

At midnight we loaded the surviving horses and the remaining gear back aboard Sierawski's cathedral. When the tide came in, at around four in the morning, we set her afloat again. Exhausted as we were, still we did not wait for our kindly zephyr but put our shoulders, one and all, to the oars. Sierawski sat in state on the quarterdeck, our undisputed captain and saviour. Anointed and beatified, sanctified and lauded. Relegated to first mate, running back and forth across the deck, I contented myself with the actual running of the ship.

We landed at a place called Czeligra, in Bulgaria, and then another fly-blown place called Warny. At each, we picked up supplies, and a few Polish stragglers and refugees, to replace the men we had lost. At each, Sierawski's boasting, and his legend, grew. I held my tongue, said nothing, listened, and learned. Two days out of Warny, another black wall fell across the heavens. Rain fell hard. The horses grew restless, and panicked, their hooves thudding muffled against the lower decks. I smelled a fresh thunderstorm like sulphur in my nostrils.

"What now, Admiral?" I said to Sierawski, who was in his cups in the captain's chair, with a tricorn hat on his head, holding forth to some of the men, and the ship's crew, on the finer points of seamanship and navigation. Subjects on which he was entirely ignorant.

"That?" Sierawski said, "Tis naught but a shower, Blumer. Have the men collect rainwater," he said airily. At that moment, a great finger of white fire struck a resounding blow on the topmast. We cleared our blinded eyes and looked up to see the mast and sail ablaze, lighting up the sea like a beacon. It must have been visible for twenty miles around, like a lighthouse.

"Aye aye Captain Sierawski," I replied blandly, "and shall I collect the lightning, too, while I'm about it?"

CHAPTER THIRTY-EIGHT
CITY OF THE WORLD'S DESIRE, CONSTANTINOPLE, OCTOBER 1797

By some miracle that rickety old crab-boat, bursting at the seams, finally rounded the Horns of the Bosphorous. We sailed into the greatest city in the history of the world, at last. We cheered and flung our czapkas in the air. The sight of the city took our breath away. It was bigger than Warsaw, Krakow, and Lwow rolled into one, and multiplied a hundred times.

This place, as you know, had once been Byzantium, the eastern capital of the Roman Empire. When Rome fell, the double-headed eagle flew here for another thousand years, and they still called themselves *Romanii* – Romans. Yet their degenerate empire had eventually crumbled, and three hundred years ago had been conquered by the Ottoman Turks, a race of virile warrior nomads.

The Russians had adopted the old redundant symbols of Byzantium for their own, for they had always coveted the City, even before the Turks took it. A dozen Tsars had sworn that one day they would lay their bones in the Hagia Sofia, having first restored it to the Orthodox Church and conquered the City. None had succeeded.

There we saw the great dome of the Hagia Sofia itself, surrounded by minarets. Once the greatest Church in Christendom, now the greatest Mosque of the Caliphate. 'My enemy's enemy is my friend,' as the Turks say, and thus it proved. We did not share their religion, but we shared their enemy, and thus they gave us refuge. True, our Polish King

Sobieski had defeated the Turks way back in 1683, but times had changed.

One half of the city stood in Europe, and the other in Asia. Through the Dardanelles – the great channel of water that runs between the two – passes half of the world's commerce. Among all this bustle our tiny crab-boat went unnoticed. We had never seen such a press of humanity, in all its infinite shapes and colours.

We landed with great jubilation and thanked God. We saw the vast land walls that ringed the city and the harbour. By the side of the harbour was an immense chain, curled up in a heap, with links as big as a man. We tethered our horses to this great metal leviathan and gaped at it. None of the locals paid it any heed.

"What the Devil is this?" Sierawski demanded, intrigued.

"The Romans strung this chain across the harbour," I said, in amazement, "to keep out enemy ships. It must have lain here ever since! Think of it! Just three hundred years ago, Roman legionnaries walked those walls! A Roman Emperor still ruled in this place!"

"Such a strong position, a natural fortress – those walls, this harbour! If only we had such advantages in Poland!" Sierawski enthused.

"Didn't do the Romans any good, though, did it? That chain, this harbour, those huge land walls?" Tanski sneered, weakly, from his seat, for he was riding in a wagon beside us. Although he had recovered somewhat, he could barely walk, let alone ride his horse. He was wrapped in a blanket, and taking badly to being an invalid. His mood was even more foul than usual.

"Where are the Romans now, eh?" Tanski castigated the dead Romans. "Stupid bastards! Gone! There are no Churches here. I see only mosques and minarets! Byzantium sank beneath an Ottoman tide, and was obliterated. Erased from history, like Troy and Carthage, and ...!"

His head dropped, and he wiped his eyes. We all fell silent. Would the same fate await Poland? Annihilation? Genocide? The Ottomans had usurped the Romans, driven them from Byzantium, and made it their own. We too had been driven from our homes by a tide of barbarians and savages. Would we ever return to our motherland?

A Polish courier, acting as our guide, collected us and led us off, in column. In the great chaotic swirl of the harbour, whole camel trains, thousands of people, and hundreds of beasts came and went. Like the great chain, no one paid us any heed whatsoever. Impassive Janissaries watched us go by.

Heathens or not, the Arabs treated us with great respect, and we spent one month enjoying the hospitality of the Sultan. We soon learned why – they meant to ensnare as many of us as they could for their army, which was sorely short of good officers. For they knew well that you catch more flies with honey than with vinegar. Here there were sirens to trap the unwary. We needed to plug our ears with wax, blind our eyes, and tie ourselves to the ship's mast, to resist the temptations of the City of the World's Desire.

We were quartered in the old diplomatic mission buildings and embassy. These lay empty, as we had no ambassador, and no nation. So General Dabrowski's chief spy, Rymkiewicz, his man in Constantinople, had taken them over, and now they swarmed with soldiers. Every day another company took ship for the Legions in Italy, but there were many men to carry, and we must wait our turn. We were told this by Rymkiewicz himself. It was this spy who had arranged our safe passage here with Hassan. He was a tall, handsome man, very able, and a great soldier. He was a close friend of Cyprian Godebski, but when I asked him for news, he shrugged, and said there was none. Cyprian's fate was in God's hands. This same spy Rymkiewicz was dumbfounded when, after three short weeks, we received an invitation to dine at Hassan's palace. The wily old one-eyed Sheikh had not forgotten us, it seemed.

"Try not to get killed, and don't convert to Islam, if you can possibly help it," Rymkiewicz said drily. "But you cannot refuse the invitation – it would be a mortal insult, and there would be blood. Enjoy yourselves. That's an order."

In truth we had no intention of refusing. We were itching to explore this celebrated den of iniquity. For Constantinople was well known as the most depraved city in the world, as well as the richest, for the two things always go hand in hand. It was the Sodom and Gomorrah of the age. Decadent Paris was but a Sunday school by comparison. We had been provided with a small allowance – one hundred piastres each – and we meant to spend every last tynf of it on debauchery. Even Tanski had rallied, and dragged himself from his sickbed, proclaiming between coughs and constant trips to the latrines that he was completely recovered.

So off we went together, in a tiny boat, that drew us across the water to our destination. Hassan's grand abode was the size of one of Warsaw's city blocks. It stood hard by the water, and the dappled light shimmered on the sandstone walls. A small skiff with liveried servants bore us to the Palace's private jetty. Armed guards patrolled the walls. We stepped ashore and were led by a perfumed eunuch through a vast iron-bound door, wide enough to admit an elephant. A huge iron portcullis studded with garnets hung overhead. Slaves fawned on us as if we were the sons of the crimson ones.

"In what manner of army," I said to my comrades, "does a General have such a Palace as this?"

Hassan wore a curved dagger and curling slippers to match. The dagger had a huge jewel on the end the size of a hen's egg, and was stuck in a belt that was also studded with huge jewels. His grey beard was dyed black, and was oiled and tied with ribbons. Although he had obviously bathed, still he smelled like a rutting ox, beneath the wafting clouds of perfume that he had been doused in. The Old Janissary greeted us all warmly, as if we were his lost sons – even Birnbaum. It turned out that this was how he viewed us all – as prospective sons. But he began with a lamentation.

"Every day the Sultan still asks where the Polish Ambassador is," he said, "and every day the Vizier replies that the King of Poland regrets that he cannot pay his compliments. An empty echo in eternity!"

A water pipe was brought and set before us, with a great bubbling glass globe, and eight arms like an octopus. Hassan and we Poles smoked, and the tobacco smelt sweet as honey. It was the fruit of the lotus flower – hashish. After a few bubbling pulls on the pipe, the room was suffused with a warm happy glow.

"We will restore our land, and our eagle," I said quietly to Hassan, "our Poland will rise again, like Our Christ."

"As God wills it," Hassan said. Steaming food was brought on silver platters. Hassan scooped up a great handful of curried lamb in his massive paw. We did likewise. The dinner was delicious, and strongly spiced, but it burned like hell on the way in – and indeed on the way out.

"Flags and names matter not. You are Poles, I am a Cossack. So what? Everybody must serve somebody. I have fought eighty-five battles, and given my eye to the Sultan. I serve the Janissaries, and it serves me well! What does it matter who you serve? It matters not! What matters is the reward for service!" he laughed, pointing at the opulence that surrounded him. Then he thumped his barrel chest, rattling his gaudy gold finery.

"I am well rewarded! I, Hassan! A humble Cossack, born in a tent on the steppes, born the son of a whore, no less! I had no fame, no name, why, not even a father! Yet here I sit, a Sheikh and a General. I have one palace, three wives, four daughters, and a harem of concubines," he bragged.

"Where are your dear lady wives?" Tanski asked, interested. Indeed, there were a dozen glum-faced Turkish lads in attendance, flunkies, bodyguards, servants and soldiers, all wearing Hassan's livery, but not a single female.

"I see a great deal of swords here, but not many spear-carriers, Excellency," I said, for I too was curious, and I craved women's company. "In Poland, a man has but one wife, but she and his daughters may sit at table, and speak their minds, and sing to his companions. Why," I said sadly, "we even have women warriors in Poland," and I thought of Madame, the courageous Castellan, lioness of Poland.

Hassan grinned. "Blumer, you have much to learn of our ways! Decent women do not consort with men outside their family. Decent women go veiled out of doors, if they leave the house at all. My daughters stay confined in their seraglio. Until it is time for them to marry, that is." He said this last very meaningfully, and we all sat uneasily on the floor. Particularly Tanski, who dreaded matrimony more than death, for he lived only to kill men and chase women.

"Are all the women in the City decent?" I asked Hassan, with a grin.

"No! They are not, Allah be praised!" Hassan replied, and clapped his hands. With that, we heard silken rustling, jangling bells, giggling, and footfalls. This was the garden of earthly delights indeed. These were the famed houris of the east, belly-dancers, courtesans, slave girls. A whirlwind of beauty!

In swept a pair of willowy Circassian girls, to dazzle and entice Tanski and Sierawski. A dusky, busty girl flung herself on Birnbaum's lap. All of the girls writhed as supple as snakes, undulating their bellies, wiggling their backsides, tossing their long shiny hair with their slender fingers. All of them were naked save for jewels and wisps of silk to save what little remained of their modesty, and barely covering their womanly charms.

Before me, like a dream of beauty, were a raven and a redhead, no older than seventeen years apiece. They were as

301

supple as acrobats, stretching up their long slim legs, to make their silver anklets touch to their golden earrings. It was said that Bullock used to buy girls from Constantinople's slave markets, and these were slave girls. Here we were, wallowing in the same filth as our traitor king.

And yet, and yet – the gleam of their skin, the warmth of their flesh. A man is only blood, and blood runs hot. We had spent so long without the company of women. Still the girls writhed, their breath hot on my neck. Still I did not resist.

"What rank are you in your Legion, Blumer?" Hassan said to me slyly, "a captain?"

"A warrant officer. Not even a lieutenant, Hassan," I replied, tearing my eyes from the intoxicating beauty of the two girls, and back to his ugly old face.

"What?" he spat on the priceless Persian carpet. "Infamy! I will make you a Colonel of Janissaries this very day if you swear yourself to me. A regiment of five hundred Cossack cavalry at your command. I shall give you my eldest daughter, too, Blumer, a thousand ducats for her dowry, and these two girls for your harem. What say, you, lad? Is it a bargain?"

He spat in his palm, and held out his hand. "Here you may have your heart's desire, Blumer," he said.

"What of my comrades?" I replied, shaking my head.

"By Satan's beard, that's why I want you! Because you look after your men. Have no fear, *Colonel* Blumer - I have another three daughters, after all! One for each of your captains, here! Each of your comrades will captain one of your companies!"

Now I'll be damned if I won't say it wasn't tempting. If Felix Potocki had tried this on me, why I doubt I should ever have left Podolia. But damn it, Blumer, I said to myself, your blood is as cold as a lizard's, you are a man of steel and slaughter. You cannot fall for this old trick. Yet there we sat transfixed, like the lotus eaters, transformed into pigs by this stinking Circe and his siren slaves. Hassan sought to made us into golems. Killers to do their master's bidding.

"Of course you will all have to convert," Hassan was saying, "and that means no pork, and no more vodka."

Sierawski looked up from between a girl's thighs. "No more pork? No more vodka, you say?"

Hassan tapped the water pipe. "The lotus is better than any drink, and the harem tastes sweeter than any pig's flesh."

Birnbaum tried and failed to get the girl off his lap. "Convert? This Jew will die first," he said, unsteadily, his jaw slack, his eyes glassy.

"Be still, sweet Jew," Hassan crooned, "you have already had the unkindest cut, what more have you to fear from me?"

Tanski looked up from his stupor. He had hardly looked at the girls, he was so out of sorts. He was hardly moving. It was most unlike him, for he loved to chase women above all things. "Wives, you say? The Devil take that," Tanski muttered. "I'll not give up my freedom!"

"Four wives and ten concubines is enough for any man's appetite," Hassan laughed.

Then one of the girls took my hand, to lead me off to the dark of a nearby chamber. Hassan sat on his cushion, wrapped in wreaths of smoke, grinning and laughing. All the earth spun around the room. The second girl took hold of my other hand. She saw the ring, and cooed at it, covetously. My mother's ring. One hundred ducats of gold, rubies and diamonds. She saw my drowsy drunken eyes. She made to slip the ring from my finger and spirit it away.

"Damn it!" I shouted, wide awake from the evil dream, pushing the slave girls away, roughly. They cowered, and cried. At last I looked at them, and the scales fell from my eyes. I saw them for what they were, through the haze of smoke. I saw the hanged girls from Podolia, the women that Szymon Korczak had murdered. Then I saw them again for what they were, two poor whores, slaves to the Janissary. I shoved them roughly away, and the redhead shrank back, and tripping across the carpet, kicked over the great pipe. It shattered on the ground with a crashing hiss, like a huge angry serpent.

The spell was broken.

"Comrades!" I called, dragging the nearest to his feet, and rousing the others with sharp kicks, "a guest stinks like a fish after three days! We have outstayed our welcome!"

"We've only been here for three hours!" Sierawski whined. I seized him by the hair and hoisted him to his feet. Tanski was lying on the floor, out quite cold. I grabbed him and hoisted him over my shoulder. There was a great commotion, as you can imagine, and a great deal of wailing and gnashing of teeth, and angry girls demanding their fee. Hassan sat among the broken pipe, as his slaves hastened away the shards and debris. He gazed at me as we struggled into our kontusz, and away from the chamber.

"Fare thee well, General," I said, with the insensible Tanski slung over my shoulders, head down, "we will all long remember this night. I thank you for your hospitality. I thank you for your offer. But my heart's desire lies not within your city."

"Then go with God, Blumer," Hassan said, and bowed, his face immobile as stone. I dragged and carried my reluctant comrades out of Hassan's palace back onto the jetty.

"What the hell did you make us leave for?" Sierawski complained as we made our way through the cold dark moonlight back to the boat. "I was just starting to enjoy myself!"

"Tanski is ill," I said, by way of excuse. "Wake up, Kasimir," I said to him, slapping his face gently, and pouring water on his lips. He stirred somewhat, and cursed, and called for his mother. The next moment he was quite insensible.

"It is surely the drink," I said, concerned, but Tanski had barely touched a drop that night.

Tanski was gravely ill – his malady had returned. Abruptly, he awoke from his deep sleep, and fell into a delirium, half asleep, half awake, shrieking and crying out. When we were some distance from shore he thrashed weakly about in the boat like a fish, and tried to climb out of it. I held him fast in my arms and whispered to him until he calmed himself. There was scarcely more strength in him than a rabbit. He drifted in and out of consciousness. When we reached the embassy, he fell to his knees, and vomited. There was blood in his soil.

"What is the matter with him?" Sierawski whispered.

"It is the plague," someone said, and we crossed ourselves.

CHAPTER THIRTY-NINE
HE WHO SWINGS CANNOT DROWN

Two days out of Constantinople, in the Mediterranean, bound for Genoa, we were attacked by pirates. They were waiting for us. Four galleys. Black flags.

We had three brigs. The first, a quarantine ship, carrying the wounded, flew under a yellow flag – quarantine, infectious diseases. Leprosy, yellow fever, cholera, plague. Aboard was Tanski, lying helpless as a babe in his hammock, bleeding out his life from every orifice. Not surprisingly, the pirates let them go.

Our second brig was a swift merchant vessel, with a complement of only seventeen. It contained a vital passenger – the French Ambassador, Du Bayet. He had been visiting us, and inspecting our troops. When told of Sierawski's exploits – his bravery at the sieges of Krakow and Wola, his cunning at the ford of the Dniester, and his ingenuity during our shipwreck – he had appointed Sierawski his personal bodyguard. Sierawski was to be promoted, and paid in gold. I could scarcely credit it.

Sierawski's brig was fast. It sailed south, as we had agreed beforehand, with three of the pirate galleys in hot pursuit, stretching every stitch of canvas to catch their quarry, a fine prize for ransom. Soon they were gone.

With a pang, I felt the loss of my friends. The loss of Cyprian Godebski – disappeared. The loss of Tanski – mortally ill, for all we knew. The loss of Sierawski, caught up on a fool errand protecting a damned Frenchman, bound for a fate unknown.

"Hassan sold us out," I said to Birnbaum, who was loading a blunderbuss.

"Do we run?" Birnbaum asked.

"No need," I laughed, "Tis a fair fight – one to one."

"You should raise the white flag. They will ransom you in Tunisia, you will see. You cannot win. The pirate ships always carry big crews, for boarding merchant ships," one of the Turkish sailors said. It was the ship's helmsman, a craven fellow indeed.

"So do we, you damn fool," I replied, "we have twenty Legionnaires aboard."

Through the glass, I took in the pirate ship. Algerian, flying the flag of the man in the moon – like Pan Twardowski, I thought, with delight. How apt. I swept the decks, saw what I expected to see, and snapped the telescope shut.

I was well used to the sea now. My body ducked and rolled like a boxer, swaying with the wild heaves and gentle lurches of the ship. I had my sea legs, and I fancied myself alright – as a pirate captain, the same as these pirates on the horizon. I had no nation. I was bound by no laws. I was hunted by all.

"Aha!" I said, with delight. "There he is. Birnbaum – break out the sabres, have the men load every musket and pistol, but tell them to keep their weapons out of sight. Assemble them on deck."

"What about me?" said the cowardly sailor.

"You were absolutely right, sir," I said to him, with a wicked grin. "Raise the white flag, and lower the sails."

The Turk quailed, and ran off, hastening to raise the traitor flag, and save his skin. I gathered the men. My men.

"Comrades!" I said, "Silence! No one must cheer, or shout, for such noises carry far across the water. Commanding that ship is Szymon Korczak, a Targowica man, and now a Captain in the Russian army. He has been sent to kill us. He will offer no quarter. Neither will we."

I took out my mother's ring. I had nothing else. I showed them the rubies, the diamonds, the gold.

"This ring is worth a hundred ducats. I will give it to the man who takes Szymon Korczak. Dead or alive."

Then the white flag snaked up the mast, and the men stared at me angrily. I held up a hand. "The white flag is a ruse. Otherwise they will turn their cannon on us, for they have four guns, and we have none. In a moment we will be boarded, and I will raise the red flag. Then, under our flag, our own dear flag, the old red and white, we will fight to the death."

The men grinned, and went about their business. I touched the ruby and diamond ring to my lips for luck.

A roar of cannon, a shot across the bows. Roundshot churned the depths. I ordered us to stop and weigh anchor. I gripped my rosary under my shirt. Hail Mary, full of grace, the Lord is with thee. Pray for us sinners now, and at the hour of our death. Had I miscalculated? We would find soon out.

"Surrender or die!" came the cry.

Szymon's galley drew near. The man himself stood by a second cannon. He was swathed in a black cloak that flapped in the wind like a vulture's wing. He held a lit cigar in hand, and with a wild, melodramatic gesture, put it to the touch-hole. The blast blew out a section of our rail, hurling wood splinters and debris in all directions, cutting a man in two. Then grappling hooks and lines flew through the air, like fishing lines. Pirates, rough handed Algerians, with burnished skins, and Russian marines in blue capes, swarmed across the decks of the pirate ship.

"Surrender or die!" Szymon roared.

"Will our lives be spared if we surrender?" I yelled back through the bullhorn.

"They will," he lied.

"Have I your word of honour?" I asked, grinning at Birnbaum.

A pause. "Yes."

"Then we surrender!" I replied, "You have my word of honour, too!"

Szymon looked sceptical, but his hired men relaxed, and stared at our white flag. Some fools even sheathed their weapons.

"Prepare to be boarded!" came the shout. Our ships clashed together with a violent crash, and a great spray of water flew up from between them. Bearded figures with silk scarves around their faces, armed with scimitars, pikes, axes and cutlasses vaulted over the sides, their bodies casting demonic shadows on the water.

"Now raise the red flag!" I called, and Birnbaum hauled up the colours. There, under the old red and white, my men drew heart. They met the pirates with a good volley, then fixed their bayonets and moved in for the kill. They were poor stuff indeed, these pirates. Although we were outnumbered, it was by the barest of margins. We made short work of them all, for their stock in trade was killing innocent sailors, and women and children. They were rapists and murderers, not soldiers. Rarely have I killed so many men in my life at one time, nor took such pleasure in it. After mere moments, the deck awash with their blood, the pirates were on the run.

"Mercy!" said one of them, a young lad barely sixteen, falling to his knees, hands clasped in prayer.

"God will have mercy, for I will not," I replied, cleaving his head from his shoulders. Barely had I done so, than I turned on the next man. Brushing aside his feeble guard, I knocked his sword from his grasp, and dispatched him with my bloody sabre. Only the Russian marines, of whom there were but half a dozen, put up much of a fight, killing two of my men before they were butchered and bayoneted to death. Birnbaum lead the charge. He ran amok, blasting a group of fleeing scum with his blunderbuss, then swinging his scimitar wildly. Heads and limbs rolled across the decks. Since he had run out of men to kill on our ship, grabbing a rope, he swung over to the pirate vessel.

The rope swung back across. I gazed for a moment down into the deep dark depths, running black with blood, churning with foam like gnashing teeth. For a moment my stomach heaved as the deck lurched beneath my feet. Then the rope was in my hand, and I was swinging through the void. Szymon, my quarry, was but yards away.

As you know, I am a heavy man. As I swung, a line snapped, or a spar broke, with a crack like a knout. My momentum carried me across the water, and I landed heavily on deck. My ankle cracked. The wound in my leg seemed to tear open. But I had made it, with sword in hand, and a great length of rope in the other. I fell to the deck in a heap as Szymon ran for the other deck, Birnbaum hard on his heels. A Russian stepped between Birnbaum and his cowardly quarry, but I drew my pistol and shot him down from where I sat on my arse. We heard a splash from the other side of the boat. Birnbaum cursed, leaned over the side, and drew his pistol.

All was quiet. It seemed as if everyone was dead except for our men, and Szymon. And indeed, they were. No quarter. We were true to our word. I limped over to the opposite side of the boat next to Birnbaum. Down below was a pathetic lifeboat, a coracle, a dinghy, with oars no longer than lances. We were a hundred miles from land. The dinghy was still tethered to the pirate ship by a rope, which Birnbaum was reeling in, like a fishing line. Szymon Korczak sat in it, desperately and pathetically pulling on the oars. I turned to Birnbaum.

"This is yours, comrade," I said, taking off my ring.

"Nonsense. It was your mother's," Birnbaum replied, immediately returning it to me. A hundred ducats!

Sitting in the dinghy, soaked and terrified, was the traitor Szymon. He had drawn a knife, and was attempting to cut through the rope.

"Put up that knife, and fear thee not, Szymon." I said. "He who swings cannot drown."

CHAPTER FORTY
TWO DEATHS
MILAN, 13 FEBRUARY 1798

"So the war is over?" I said, aghast. We had discharged our mission, and handed the old flag over at headquarters. No one even said as much as thank you. I was given a receipt, and a boot up the arse. We sat in the barracks, penniless, unrewarded, and unremarked.

We had ridden our old nags from Genoa to Milan. In Milan we discovered that we had missed the whole damned war with the Austrians. In October of the preceding year, 1797, Napoleon had signed the peace of Campo Formio. France was, damn it all, at peace with Austria, Prussia, and Russia. We cursed our ill-luck.

In December, Bonaparte, as if to oblige us, started a new war. This time it was with the Pope, of all people. We missed the best of that, too, for by the time we arrived, Dabrowski's men had stormed the Pope's prison fortress at San Leo. Thereby he had broken the Pontiff's earthly power, if not his spiritual influence.

When we arrived in Milan everyone was drunk and happy, for it was nearly Christmas and we had all heard that the Tsarina had died, in carnal congress, copulating with a horse. It was the talk of all Europe, and an occasion of great rejoicing in all civilised lands.

Birnbaum and I found a garret in Milan and every day petitioned headquarters for commissions. The weather in Italy was new to us. There we shivered through the blackbird days of January, and the short and accursed month of February, and waited for orders. Every day we watched as the legion grew. A trickle of men quickening to a flood.

Both of us spoke Latin, which is the mother tongue of Italian, so we found the language easy enough. Birnbaum prevailed on the Jewish merchants of the local ghetto for charity. I did likewise with the Church, the local priest apparently ignorant of the Legion's disagreement with his chief, the Vicar of Rome. So we made the best of it. We caulked up our draughty attic room and the leaking roof. We repaired our uniforms and weapons so that, despite our lowly status, we looked like cavaliers.

We received our zoldu regularly throughout. Dabrowski was a damn good provider, it had to be said. Regular pay was a novelty I had never known before, not even in the Bullock's army. Even so, it was not much to live on. I was still a warrant officer and Birnbaum a private soldier.

It would all have been easier had the Italians not insisted on living on lettuce leaves, like rabbits. Where was the meat? we wailed, as our landlady fed us soups clogged with greens, macaroni, and watered wine. She took a good few solidi for it, too. The meat fell off our bones and we stayed as lean as winter wolves.

As for the girls, though, they were a delight. We glimpsed angels, but their men folk kept them tight behind doors. As we soon discovered, their chaperones were armed with daggers. Many a night we had to leap from a bedroom window or a balcony for our very lives, laughing furiously, pursued by some formidable old black-clad Italian babcia, with no teeth in her head but clutching a stiletto in her hand. By the Devil's horns, the women of Constantinople's seraglios were less tightly guarded! Our wealthy officers had no trouble making the acquaintance of high-born ladies, though, at the theatre, in the gaming houses, or in church. This gave us hope for the future.

"Just you wait until we are Captains," I told Birnbaum.

"When hell freezes over, then," he retorted.

In short, we needed advancement, a regiment, and funds. March, the Italians say, is crazy. The weather changes from day to day and hour to hour. One day we sweated like pigs on the butcher's block, the next, our hands were studded with chilblains. So we changed our tactics and swallowed our pride. I begged an old friend for help.

"This is my only friend at headquarters, and our last hope," I told Birnbaum. "If this doesn't work, we will be back to Turkey to fight for the Sultan!"

Thus we spent another stultifying day in suffocating corridors, waiting. Our boots shone like mirrors, our brass buttons gleamed like brilliant stars, and our hair glowed with powder and oil. We waited all day. By the time we were let in to see the General, we had wilted like winter straw.

Before us sat General Jozef Wybicki – rebel, warrior, and judge. We had first met on my mother's farm, when I was but a lad, and last seen each other on the Third of May, at Madame's celebration dinner. His hair was white now, not grey, and his face was flushed red with the sun, and lined with deep creases.

"General Wybicki, Sir!" we shouted, saluting, bowing, scraping and all but licking his boots!

"We meet again, lad," he said, shaking my hand. He sat in a dusty office, surrounded by overflowing piles of parchment wrapped in red ribbons, great heavy books of accounts, pots of ink and quill pens. "Move some of those papers out of the way and sit down, comrades. So much paper! I have to organise everything from the latrines to the Courts Martial," he complained. "It wasn't like this in the good old days," he said to us sadly, looking at the bulging piles of paperwork, "Back then I was a fighting general, not a glorified clerk! I might as well be back in my law office in Warsaw. All I'm good for nowadays is jawing and paperwork. Ah, well, *tempus fugit*, I suppose," he grumbled.

Too old for fighting, Wybicki still worked tirelessly for our cause, organising the Legions. He was Dabrowski's right-hand man and assistant, and he kept the wheels of our Legion turning as best he could. He had hundreds of things to do and organise. Amongst his many duties was handing out officers' commissions. This was why we went to him.

"Now then, what can I do for you lads?" Wybicki asked pleasantly.

"General Wybicki, Sir! We humbly request a commission, and a regiment! We want to fight, Sir!" I toadied shamelessly. Birnbaum and I sat down, and leaned forward eagerly, like anxious schoolboys. "We have been kicking our heels in Milan for months, Sir!" I added.

"My dear Blumer, there's no need for all this "Sir" business, do call me Jozef!" Wybicki insisted, "we've known each other, what, twenty years now?" he took out a pipe, and offered it to us.

"Aye," I said, sensing an opening, "twenty years since you hid in my mother's barn. And how long since we last met, on the Third of May?"

"Good God, my boy!" he exclaimed, as we shared the pipe. "Almost seven years! Seven years next month since the Third of May! How time passes!" he exclaimed. Those hard years were writ on his face. On ours, too.

"You've a fine record, Blumer," Wybicki said. "Zielence, Dubienka, Markuszem, Raclawice, Wola, that damned Denisko business..."

"Seven years is a damned long time to still be a warrant officer," I reminded him.

"Well, there are not many places, you know," he vacillated, for he was still a lawyer, after all. "We have so many officers like you, exiles, and so few men to go around. Too many Tsars, not enough Cossacks! Five captains for every dragoon, as they say! Not that we have any cavalry yet – it's all artillery and infantry. General Bonaparte started his career in the artillery, don't you know?"

"I'll do anything, General. Put me in the grenadiers, or even the artillery," I said quietly, "anything except the engineers, obviously. A gentleman must have some standards."

"Good God, no! Quite right too," Wybicki agreed.

I changed tack. "A lot of good officers are volunteering on ten per cent of their zoldu, and running here and there as gallopers. Let me do that, Sir, I implore you."

Wybicki shifted uneasily in his chair. I was losing him. "Have you heard the news?" the kindly Wybicki said, changing the subject. "The Bullock is dead."

"Good bloody riddance," I snarled. "Damned traitor!"

On 12 February 1798 the Bullock, the Tsarina's former lover, and her prisoner, had died in St Petersburg, shortly after the Great Whore herself. He passed away without mourning. Nobody loves a traitor.

"Is there any word of Pepi – I mean the Prince Poniatowski?" I asked. Wybicki shrugged. "The nephew follows the uncle. Living drunk and dissolute in exile, a typical idle princeling, the last I heard."

Pepi, years later, went on to redeem himself. Of course, we had no way of knowing that then. By God, that was a dark time! I was desperate now. In a moment Wybicki would usher us out, empty handed, and we would be back to our dreary purgatory in our dingy lodgings.

"I have heard that the Commander is to be pardoned soon, and will join us," I said, staking on one last turn of the cards, for I had been struck by an idea.

"Ah!" Wybicki exclaimed, his face brightening up, "God grant us Kościuszko!"

"Indeed!" I said, "Did you know, Sir, that the Commander himself made me a Lieutenant of foot, during the Uprising, in Krakow, before Raclawice?" I suddenly remembered it, with a jolt of triumph. "If we are all in the infantry now, perhaps I might have that rank back, at least?"

Of course, I had no papers to prove this, they had all been lost, but Wybicki took my word for it as a gentleman.

"Why the Devil didn't you say so!" Wybicki beamed. "Of course! If the Commander ordered it, then who am I to gainsay him? I shall write out the commission forthwith. I can give you a platoon, but you'll have to find yourself a sergeant."

"There he is," I said, quick as a flash, pointing at Birnbaum. Wybicki nodded and smiled and wrote it all out. He cared not a jot that Birnbaum was a Jew.

"Congratulations, Lieutenant Blumer, Sergeant Birnbaum," Wybicki said, shaking our hands. He offered us cigars, and lit them with a match. This was a new invention, and a marvel of the age. Fascinated, we watched him strike it. We sat back and puffed on the cigars until a fug of companionable smoke filled the room, and drank a small toast.

"We were speaking of the Commander," I said to Wybicki. "Are the rumours true?"

"They are! Since the Tsarina's death, and the Peace Treaty with the French," Wybicki told me, "The new Tsar, Paul, has pardoned the Commander and given him parole. General Dabrowski hopes that the Commander will join us soon – he is talking to Bonaparte about it."

"Excellent news indeed!" we rejoiced. Falsely, as it turned out.

"Tsar Paul has proved himself a wise, kind, and merciful ruler," Wybicki went on. "He rarely executes anyone, and has never even ordered a pogrom," he nodded at Birnbaum, who was as stunned as I was by this revelation.

"Are you sure, Jozef?" I asked, wondering if the General had become senile. "This Paul sounds an unlikely Tsar to me," I said dubiously. "I bet the Russians hate him, at least."

"Naturally the Russians hate him," General Wybicki agreed. "They call him 'Paul the Mad', and are spoiling to murder him." We shook our heads, bemused. Not long after that the Russians did indeed murder 'Paul the Mad' as a punishment for his singular failure to execute, torture, rape, imprison, massacre, or persecute anyone at all, which are all the things one expects of a normal Tsar.

"Yet they mourn the odious Catherine as if she was a dead saint." I reflected.

"That vile woman," Wybicki said bitterly. "What a way to die!"

"Nonsense! It's what she would have wanted!" I laughed, and we drank the first of many toasts, "To horses! Let us have our cavalry soon!" I said, downing the vodka at one gulp.

CHAPTER FORTY-ONE
ALL ROADS LEAD TO ROME,
FIRST OF MAY 1798,
FIRST BATTALION, SECOND LEGION

We were on the march, at last!

"How do you know this road leads to Rome, *Lieutenant* Blumer?"

"Because all roads lead to Rome, *Sergeant* Birnbaum," I replied with a grin.

We had rank, and money in our pockets, and we were at war! We were happy. May is the month of roses in Italy, when travellers begin to flock to see the sites – the Colosseum, the Catacombs, the Forum – and the signoras. It was said that their skin was finer than the marble of the statues. Well, we would see for ourselves. Here was the nation of Poland, ten thousand men under arms, and another ten thousand camp followers, taking the grand tour!

Although both Birnbaum and I still had our horses, we slogged on foot. It would hardly do to ride while the men walked. Instead we piled our warhorses with baggage, and made pack-mules of them, much to their disgust. We were all in the infantry now. I had never thought to sink so low again. The infantry! The ignominy! For the Legions had no cavalry to speak of – yet. It could have been worse. It could have been the artillery, or God forbid, the engineers.

We marched in the shade of olive trees where we could, and in blazing golden sunlight where we could not. The soil here was a scorched umber in colour. The pitiless Italian sun heated it like a clay oven. We marched past rugged hillsides and groves of olive and cypress. We marched past vineyards and terraces. White farmhouses gave way to smart marble villas.

After another few days march, the road was lined on both sides by a gigantic cemetery. Thousands of graves, as far as the eye could see. A calvary of crosses, urns, reliquaries, and weeping angels. This necropolis must have contained all the tombs of antiquity, and it took us a full day and a night to march through it. I did not ask my men to stop, for they would not have done. Not for all their arrears of pay in solid gold. We tarried not in these shadows of Hades, this land of the dead. We quickened our step, and sang Wybicki's song. The Song of the Legions –

"Poland has not died
As long as we live
Our lands, that the invaders have taken,
We, with our sabres, will retrieve!

March, march, Dabrowski,
From Italy to Poland!
We'll reclaim our nation
Under thy command!"

On the other side of the cemetery, the men marched on, drowsy with heat and red wine from their canteens. Waves of heat shimmered and rippled from the road. At every mile post the villas became larger, more opulent, and more magnificent. Villas gave way to mansions, mansions to palaces. Above us hung a sky of pure amethyst. Light and beauty burned our hungry eyes.

Well, if we had not earned a rest, we had one anyway. Many leagues from the cemetery, and beside a water trough, I ordered the men to sit in the shade. We watched as our horses drank the water. I always had them drink first, as a matter of course. This was a precaution, in case of poison, or bad water.

As the horses showed no ill-effects I had the men fill their skins, and drink their fills.

Then we sat in the shade of an ancient olive tree, and smoked. It was an ancient, gnarled old trunk, the branches like cannon barrels, the base as thick as a house. As venerable a tree as any of those silent sentinels we sat under in the heart of the forests of Poland. Julius Caesar might have marched past this very tree, on his campaigns, two millennia ago.

The men took off their czapkas and rested. These were worn by all of the infantry, but with different colours for rank and regiment. Beneath, we all cut our hair in the style *a la Kościuszko* – long hair to the middle of the collar, for both officers and the rank and file.

We officers wore epaulettes on the left shoulder with the traditional Polish insignia. Thus I wore a badge of rank in the same style as I had at Raclawice, for I was an infantry Lieutenant again. On the right shoulder was another epaulette with a strap in the Italian colours of red, white, and green. The white band of this strap bore embroidered on it the words "*Gli uomini liberi sono fratelli – All free men are brothers.*"

Any man of ability could become an officer, not only the rich and noble, as long as he could read and write. Dabrowski was trying to build a new nation, where a man might rise by merit, not birth. Naturally some of the *szlachta*, those officers from our old nobility, had mutinied against this already. Dabrowski had put down their revolt with some force.

We sat and smoked. Birnbaum, and some of my other men, as was their wont, began to talk politics. For we were men of principle, volunteers, not conscripts or mercenaries.

"Lieutenant," Birnbaum said snidely, "begging your pardon, but why are we at war with the Pope? As a Jew, I have no personal qualms about it. If the Pope wants a bayonet, then by my beard he can have it! But you boys are all good Catholics, are you not?"

"We are at war with the Pope because he badmouthed Bonaparte," I said flippantly, and the men fell about with laughter. As it was, I was not far from the truth.

"So what if he did? What's that to us Poles?" someone piped up.

"The Pope is a Hapsburg puppet!" came another.

"An arrogant Austrian arsehole!" someone snarled.

"The Tsar kisses his ring!" came a final lewd shout.

"That's all true, no doubt," I said, "but we have our own score to settle, remember? Those of us who were at the Third of May have not forgotten this Pope[6]. He condemned the Constitution in '91, and he blessed the Targowica traitors in '92! Damn it, he even blessed the Russian invasion, and the great whore herself! Now he can join her – in Hell!"

"The Pope will pay!" roared the men, good naturedly. They were convinced, or at least satisfied, and marched off with renewed vigour.

"Is any of that true?" Birnbaum asked, with a mixture of shock and admiration.

"True enough," I replied. "Besides, it will be good to be on the winning side for once."

As we marched, I remembered what Wybicki had told us. 'There are two Legions now,' Wybicki had said proudly, 'for we now have so many men. Most are deserters or prisoners of war from the Austrian army, sent to us by Bonaparte.'

At first, we were delighted to discover that we had two Legions. Then we discovered that the Second Legion – our legion – was the least fashionable of the two, by a considerable margin. The Second Legion was sneered at as 'the Algerians' by the First. Most of the men of the Second Legion had taken the hard road through the Turkish Empire that we had. But the gentlemen of quality had ridden their

---

[6]sadly Pope Pius VI did do this, see for example Norman Davies God's Playground Vol II page 156

carriages through France, and taken their ease in Paris along the way. Glamorous émigrés with beautiful wives wearing sable cloaks, and money in Paris. These nobles had fought in the First Legion, alongside Napoleon Bonaparte, in his glorious and victorious war against the Austrians.

We, the men of the Second Legion, had been defeated, caught up in Denisko's catastrophe. You will recall that Denisko had pitted two hundred men against eight thousand Austrians, all for the worthless hole called Bukowina. Two hundred men missing or dead! It could have been worse – it could have been the entire Second Legion. A bad business, Wybicki had said.

A cloud of dust. A rider approached. Speak of the Devil!

"Look sharp if you value your necks!" I roared. "It's the Head of the Courts' Martial!"

This trick worked better than any amount of cursing or cajoling. By the time he arrived, my men were on their feet, in a perfect column, not one of their white buttons out of place, and marching fifteen paces to the minute. Amongst his many other duties, Wybicki was responsible for our code of military discipline. For we were a regular army, not a rabble of mercenaries. Thieves, deserters and rapists were all shot. After a fair trial, naturally, over a drumhead.

"Hold my horse, there, Blumer, I'm an old man!" Wybicki said to me gleefully, "by God! It's good to get out of that damned office at last! What beautiful country this is!"

Wybicki was covered in the dust of the road, but his face glowed with elation as he wiped the sweat off it with the braided cuff of his general's uniform. The General dismounted, and we walked side by side, next to the men as they marched along the quiet Roman road, echoing with their boot-heels.

Quite suddenly, and in spite of their fear of the Court Martial, my men cheered at the sight of Wybicki. They knew him as a true patriot, and they loved him for his song. Wybicki had forged this weapon for us, a weapon of words – the Song of the Legions. It was the song of the *New* Poland, rising like a salamander from the ashes.

"Would you care to take the salute, Sir?" I asked, for he seemed quite affected by it.

"I will!" said the old general, wiping at his eyes with a handkerchief, "this damned dust!" he cursed, "it makes my eyes water," he lied. "I'm an old man, you know, Blumer!" We grinned, for he was weeping with joy.

My men marched past, in perfect order, arms at the slope, bayonets fixed. I drew my sword – it flashed in the sun – eyes right! Salute! – and Wybicki watched them. Our uniform was as close as we could make it to the traditional Polish uniform. The French had tried to dress us up in their colours. We were very sensitive to such impositions, and resisted them vigorously. We were Polish soldiers, not French mercenaries.

On our heads, to keep off the sun, we wore the czapka, with bright feather plumes, and cockades of red and white. The uniform was a dark blue jacket, piped with the battalion colour, which in our case was black. This jacket had red turnbacks, a white collar, and green cuffs. The breeches were dark blue, skin tight, with no stripes. As for our trappings, everyone wore a tricolored belt, with red, white and blue stripes – French colours. A bullet pouch, of standard French issue, was hung from a white belt that was hooked over the left shoulder. Our haversacks too were standard French issue. In fact, everything from boot-heel to bayonet was French issue, albeit we were paid in Italian solidi, and not French francs. Bonaparte meant the Italians to foot the bill for their own liberation.

We stood for a moment as the men marched by under our strange new flag – an Italian Tricolor with a silver Polish Eagle perched atop it. The French, famously, had silver eagles on their standards. Our Legions had the same, but with our distinctive crowned eagle on it. Emblazoned on the Tricolore

Flag were the strange words 'The Second Auxiliary Polish Legion of the Cisalpine Republic'.

"Forgive me for asking, Sir," I asked, "but the men were wondering, what the Hell is the Cisalpine Republic? None of us has even heard of it. And more to the point, why are we not simply in the French army?"

Wybicki shrugged. "By French law, Bonaparte is forbidden from raising foreign troops for the French army. So he got around this prohibition by *inventing a whole new country* – the Cisalpine Republic – from territory captured (or rather liberated) from the Austrians, in October last year. He's a better lawyer than I am!"

As we talked, the men finished their march past, and we fell in step behind them.

"I have never heard of a general who created nations and provinces out of thin air," I said, "not since the days of Julius Caesar. Plenty of generals destroy them, mark you, but none build them! General Bonaparte! A man of destiny indeed, as celebrated in your fine song."

"Oh, yes, my song!" Wybicki said bashfully. "Tell me – do your men like it?"

"Why, the men are hungry for this song of yours!" I replied. "We shall have it this instant, General!"

So I gave the order and we sang it, loudly and passionately, for its author to hear it. It was, of course, sung to the tune of the wonderful, mysterious mazurka of the Third of May. What else? For a fond moment, we imagined it was seven years ago, marching through Warsaw with the Bullock, and Pepi, and the Commander, and Dabrowski. We were cheering with the crowds outside the red walls of the Royal Castle. Dancing with the girls around King Sigismund's statute, in a sea of red and white, and kisses, and cheering. Tears of joy, flowing like blood. Dabrowski had given us hope. Good old Dabrowski!

"Poland has not died
As long as we live
Our lands, that the invaders have taken,
We, with our sabres, will retrieve!

March, march, Dabrowski,
From Italy to Poland!
We'll reclaim our nation
Under thy command!

Like Czarniecki to Poznan
Returning across the sea
To free our fatherland from chains
Fighting with the Swedes

March, march, Dabrowski...

Across the Vistula and Warta
And Poles we shall be
We've been shown by Bonaparte
Ways to victory!

March, march, Dabrowski...

Germans, Muscovites will not rest
When, backsword in hand
Peace will be our watchword
And the motherland will be ours!

March, march, Dabrowski...

Father, in tears
Says to his Basia
Just listen, our people
Are beating the drums!

March, march, Dabrowski...

All cry out as one
Enough of this slavery
We've got scythes from Raclawice
And God will give us The Commander!"

"We'll sing it louder still for Dabrowski himself," we shouted, "In Rome!"

CHAPTER FORTY-TWO
ROME!

Such a day! The Third of May, 1798. At one in the afternoon, to be precise, Dabrowski's Legion marched into Rome. It was a fine, sunny day, and curious people lined the streets. First came the drummers, then the orchestra, then the artillery, and finally the infantry. My company was fortunate to be there. As you will have expected, the honour of taking Rome fell almost exclusively to the bluebloods of the *First* Legion.

We entered Rome through the Porta del Popolo – the Gate of the People – near the Piazza del Popolo. We entered the Eternal City unopposed. This was storybook war, as played out by old men in armchairs, and boys with lead soldiers on tabletops. Rose petals, not bloody rags, were trampled beneath our feet. The air was alive with scarlet and white flags and blossoms. There were no dead bodies or screaming horses. Only pomp, victory, and girls.

Along the length of the Via Del Corso to Santa Maria we scoured the balconies and rooftops for riflemen. We needn't have concerned ourselves. The only powder expended that day was on squibs and fireworks. The Pope's men had broken and run at San Leo. So our suspicious gazes turned to gleeful, lusty stares.

From the window of every villa we were watched, and we drew amorous fire. We returned it! At every window, Italian beauties. Roman ladies dressed in white flowing gowns, drawn low over the bosom, and tight in beneath it, for such was the fashion of the day. Some few peered coquettishly from behind wooden shutters, or fluttering fans. For the most part, they sat quite brazenly at balcony and terrace, sipping noonday wine, or biting into apples. These Roman wenches gazed down at us with greedy eyes. We watched them appraising us as if we were beasts at market, or gladiators at some slave-auction of bygone days.

We called *ciao bella, belissima*, at the tops of our voices, and they called back, *ciao*, and *Dobra Pologna*! Favours, silk scarves, and love-notes rained down on our heads. There was precious little decorum, and no modesty in their conduct, which was brazen, unchristian, and quite immoral. Thank God! It was, in short, a splendid and glorious day! We vied to see who could score the highest in roses, billet-doux, and wisps of chiffon. I swear that I saw one lady throw her silk undergarments to a captain of grenadiers. We strutted like kings.

Military discipline that had held through slaughter and steel, and every imaginable disaster and privation, broke down after a few moments of this amorous onslaught. On that day I determined to take one of these Italian beauties – preferably a Contessa – to be my wife. This I did, eight years later. But that is another story.

Dabrowski's column halted on the Capitoline Hill, at a monumental staircase, like a huge glacis. Atop this great Jacob's Ladder sat the grim face of the Church of Santa Maria. It resembled a bastion as much as it did a church, with its high, thick stone walls, and tiny loophole windows. This fortress of God was built to commemorate the victims of the plague. Had the Pope chosen to defend it, why, he could have inflicted a new plague of casualties on us – but he did not. The Pope's spirit was well and truly broken, and he feared to spill the blood of the populace by enraging us. Thus our conquest proceeded in a stately fashion, like a society ball.

There, at the foot of the staircase, sheltering under silk parasols, were our generals and officers in dress uniform, and their wives arrayed in all their finery. For the Legion travelled as a wandering nation, or a crusader army. We travelled with our women folk, our camp-followers, our sweethearts (and indeed other men's), and the old, the young, the crippled and the infirm. Those who had wives and children brought them, for we had no homes to go back to. Our houses and estates were burnt, or stolen and given to traitors.

We counted those wives and officers we knew. We recognised the Little Negro instantly, for he gleamed like a black pearl. He stood arm in arm with a pretty blonde-haired, blue-eyed Frenchwoman. She professed to be his wife – although they were not married. As we esteemed him so highly, no one ever mentioned the fact they lived in sin, although it was an open secret.

A Jewish officer was standing near to Dabrowski. Birnbaum told me this was Colonel Joselewicz, who had inspired him to join the Beardlings, and who had survived the Slaughter of Praga.

Lastly, we spied, next to her husband, Madame Dabrowski, and beside her, the Junoesque Madame Zayonczek. Splendid as any statue, the white ice queen outgunned not only the other wives, and the Roman women, but the glories of antiquity itself. Raphael and Michaelangelo would have duelled to carve her marble figure!

We saw not Madame L.

Pius VI, the beaten pontiff, met Dabrowski here. We watched as our leader ascended the stone staircase, like a bear ambling up a mountain. Dabrowski clutched Sobieski's flag in his great paw. That standard which had caused us such trouble since Madame had entrusted it to us. Dabrowski was a giant of a man, strong as a minotaur, able to bend two horseshoes in his hands. He wielded the double-tailed flag as easily as a toothpick. General Dabrowski himself was indifferent to religion. Yet he knew its value to the men, and accorded the beaten pontiff all honours, such as showing him Sobieski's flag. Dabrowski and the Pope greeted each other like fellow pilgrims, as if the one had granted a plenary indulgence, and the other had paid for a cathedral to purchase it.

We Poles did not loot churches, as the French notoriously did. So perhaps the Pope's joy was real! At any rate, we attributed his good humours, and the city's kind favours, to this fact. Girls waved, boys brought us water, old men asked us about our battles. Priests blessed us. One and all commiserated our fallen homeland. Like Italy, Poland was a land divided, and under the evil yoke of foreign rule. So we stood in the sun awhile, drinking in the scenery and the signoras, and sharpening our thirsts like blades.

"That was my idea of a battle!" Birnbaum and I laughed as we fell out, when we were eventually let off the leash to wander the city. "Now let's have a drink!"

We wandered through the Piazza del Campodoglio, full of smart cafes. Beneath our boots was a geometric paving laid out by Michaelangelo himself, who also scribbled the designs for the pretty pink facades of the ice-cream coloured buildings surrounding the square.

Cyprian Godebski was sitting in a cafe in the Via Calvi, with two ladies. These he introduced as the Duchesa and the Marquisa. Oh, to be a captain!

"Tanski and Sierawski are here already," the poet said, offhandedly, and offered us wine. We had not clapped eyes on each other for a full year. Godebski was greyer and gaunter, but otherwise unchanged. If he was still heartbroken over Madame, he was doing a damn good job of hiding it. He wore the facings of the Second Legion, and Captain's epaulettes, and a lady's red silk drawers were knotted around his neck. Whether these belonged to the Marquisa, the Duchesa, or a third lady, I never established. But both the ladies were vigorously contesting the trophy. At the ladies' insistence, Cyprian regaled us with tales of his miraculous escape.

"I was the most wanted man in Europe," he boasted, or rather lied, "I rode through the heart of the Austrian ranks, cutting a swathe through them like a scythe through corn! Then my swift horse carried me across tyrannical Prussia, that foul police state, where spies and gendarmes lurk in every shadow! I made my way to France, the home of Liberty, and in Paris I found Dabrowski and the Legion." He lit cigars for us all, including the ladies, who blew smoke rings in our faces.

"Dabrowski has given me your Battalion to command, boys, to whip it into shape," Godebski said, raising his eyebrows. "I've heard some pretty damned rum things about your Battalion – they say it's full of Podolians and Jews!"

"Damned impertinence!" we laughed. To our immense delight, Tanski and Sierawski appeared, laden with bottles.

"Where the hell have you two bastards been!" I roared at them. "You, Lazarus," I said to Tanski, "risen from your grave! How come you aren't dead of the plague? Someone must have said a few prayers for you!"

Tanski shrugged. "It was naught but a touch of dysentery. I spent twenty-eight days in bed, living on water and rusks, and then I was as right as rain." His brush with death had sharpened his appetite, unless it had been that diet of rusks, for with that, he turned to one of the black-haired ladies nearby at the next table, bowed, introduced himself, kissed her hand, and began wooing and pursuing her with a will.

"What about you?" I asked Sierawski.

"The French Ambassador and I were captured by pirates, and taken to Tunisia," Sierawski said sheepishly. "The French ransomed us after a few months. The food was good, although they had no strong liquor there, only beer and wine."

"My heart bleeds!" I snarled, "it sounds like torture!"

"It was all quite civilised," Sierawski admitted, downing a stiff drink. "We won a lot of money at cards, and smoked a lot of tobacco. They have very strong tobacco in Tunis," he said casually, slurring his words.

"By God!" I cursed. I was by then very refreshed myself.
"You're as lazy as a bloody horse! Some of us have been
busy, settling old scores! But no matter! Who is this drunken
bastard of a priest?"

Tanski and Sierawski had with them a man dressed in
Cardinal's scarlet vestments. A lit pipe hung from his mouth.
Two Legionnaries with muskets followed at a respectful
distance. The priest, who was drunk, dropped his crook and
mitre, and the guards picked them up. Their faces wore
long-suffering expressions.

Sierawski, who was also blind drunk by now, laughed, "It's
the Podolian Pope, Blumer! Bow down before His Holiness!"

"Sancta Piva i Vodka!" the Priest said, casting a
benediction over us all. The ladies sniggered and tittered, and
primped their bosoms, and the priest leered at them with an
expression that was entirely sinful, and not at all spiritual.
Then he slumped over the table and passed out.

"Who the Hell is this priest of yours? If Podolia had a
Pope, he'd hold his drink better than this!" I laughed, as we
propped up the old goat in an armchair to sleep off the
communion wine.

"In fact this is His Grace, Cardinal Testaferrato," Tanski
explained. "He is the Pope's henchman, and a very valuable
prisoner. I am his gaoler. As you can see my regime is very
humane. We charge all of his expenses to his Diocese. It is a
very blessed arrangement indeed. And the old fellow is catnip
to the ladies – they can't get enough of him. He never gives a
penance of more than three Hail Marys."

With that, came three Hail Marys and Three Graces. The
Marias were fair ladies in waiting, and the Graces were
black-eyed Contessas. Their long hair shone ebony-black, in
glorious waves. All wore dresses in the Greek style, white like
Doric Columns. Rome still aped Greece in all things after all
these years – just as we Poles aped the French. One Contessa
and her lady swarmed to my side, and Birnbaum and I felt

quite delightfully besieged, or perhaps boarded by amorous amazon pirates. We hoisted the white flag, and drank deep of the scarlet wine.

Sierawski grabbed the cardinal's mitre, rammed it on his head, and capered about the tables, waving the jewelled crook in the air like a lance. Great ironic drunken cheers went up all around as the engineer ran wildly by.

"Our engineer is very highly thought of by Dabrowski, and a great favourite," Godebski told me, "the French Ambassador passed on an excellent report, saying that he owes him his life. Mark my words, the lad will go far."

I felt a great pang of joy for my friend – for he deserved it – and a great pang of jealousy, also. With that, the mitre fell over his eyes, and Sierawski stumbled on the crook, fell, and landed on his arse in a fountain. We dragged him out, soaking wet. Ah well, one minute you're on the horse, the next minute you're under it! We propped him up next to the Cardinal, and the pair of them gave drunken benedictions to passers-by.

Birnbaum, being a dark and swarthy cove, favoured pale white blondes with blue eyes. Vice versa, I, with my pale freckly Irish skin, was attracted to dark-eyed Latin girls, who reminded me of the sharp cheeked Tartar girls of Podolia.

"Is your Sergeant really a Jew?" the Contessa asked, amazed, as Birnbaum charmed her lady-in-waiting.

"That he is," I replied, "a fighting Jew, like King David himself!" Birnbaum proudly displayed the rope scars and told the story of his rescue, painting me in a most flattering light. I returned the favour by describing the Cossack he slew, and pointing to the great scimitar that he still carried at his side.

Overhead, the sky blazed a glorious blue. Luchina – for such was the Contessa's name – told me of her homeland to the south of Italy, a place called Calabria.

"It is a fertile land of wine and olives. To the South, near the toe of the boot," she said, wiggling her leg by way of a delightful, if gratuitous, explanation. Her calf was milk-white and shapely under her silk stockings.

"Intriguing," I said, studying her map closely. As she described it, this Calabria sounded like Podolia by the sea. It was dirt-poor, rife with war and banditry, and ruled by petty chiefs and kroliks, of whom her elderly father was one. Peasants toiled in the hot sun, or shivered as the winds flayed their skins. Meanwhile Luchina sat on her plump backside in Rome, boasting about the vast estates she had never visited. She pouted prettily, and fanned away the sweat of the road from my brow.

"My dear father is old and infirm," she said, fretting on her inheritance, "bad men and bandits roam my estates, and take my – forgive me, his – rents." Gorgeous emeralds and diamonds glistered at her pale, heaving bosom. She fluttered her fan and lashes coquettishly. "There are so many bad men in Calabria," she sighed, "what is a lady to do?"

"I am a bad man, too," I grinned.

"Exactly!" she smiled a gioconda smile, and brushed my thigh with her fingers, "I need a *bad* man, not a milksop! Those rents do not collect themselves, you know," she confided. Ah, me! Here was another Felix Potocki, in corset and stays! Another tempting siren voice to divert me from my quest. Although, it must be said, the Contessa Luchina's offer was tied up in prettier ribbons than surly old Felix's, with his shaking hands and bloodshot eyes. Still, Luchina's eyes were every inch as black as her soul, and as bewitching as the Rusalka's whirlpool.

"My house is on the Via Faustina," she said, quite boldly, "be there tonight, after Church."

It was not so much invitation as command!

We all spoke French together, for the ladies knew but two words of Polish – '*Dobra Pologna*!' which they called out whenever they saw a Legionary. This new-found popularity was incomprehensible. We were the pariahs of Europe –

334

outcasts, renegades, terrorists. There were two reasons for this. It transpired that this excited the Roman ladies. They adored bandits and desperadoes – what we call *bandyta*. There was a second reason – their disdain of the French.

"Atheists! Jacobins! Robbers! We fear to go to vespers," said the Marquisa, "we fear the French, for they are looters and," she crossed herself, "violators of virtuous women."

"Then you, my dear, have nothing to worry about," catted the Duchesa from behind her fan. We all fell about laughing, while the Marquisa burned hot as hell with fury.

"We had better be off to Church shortly," the Marquisa fired back, "for it is sunset now, and you will scarce have time to confess all your sins before midnight."

The sun was setting on the Eternal City as it had done untold times before. From Capitoline to Palatine, from the Colosseum to the Tarpeian Rock, seven shadows of seven hills fell over the filthy Tiber. The Tiber was foaming not with blood, but with the boiling effluent of Roman kitchens and sewers. No guns fired. Dogs barked. Music played. Wafting from the door of every cafe we heard the strains of the Song of the Legions, hastily improvised on harpsichord and accordion. Invader and occupied danced through a fog of vino. Godebski and I walked together to vespers through the bemused city, taking it in turns to carry Tanski's drunken priest.

We took the giggling ladies – all prim and proper now behind their veils – into a beautiful tiny church, a true glory to God. We gave thanks to Him, and His Son, and to the Virgin. Gave thanks and praise even after all the wars, the treachery, the defeats, the deaths and suffering. Inside, in that blessed sanctuary of the Church, it was calm serenity. A haven of cool silence after the dusty hell of the road. Yet not for long.

"What the Devil is that?" I thought, rising from my pew. The Priest halted his Latin and turned from the altar.

There, at the back of the Church, were four or five leering French soldiers. I had not seen any Frenchmen until now. Les

Crapauds, Les Bleus, Les Galles, our friends – allies – masters. All of them had bootlace moustaches, and their hair tied back with ribbons in long queues. They wore a blue uniform with a brilliant white front, tricolore cockades in their hats, and white gaiters. These were the Sans Culottes, Revolutionaries and Jacobins, in uniform. Stinking of drink, and stinking of trouble. Militants, atheists, persecutors of religion, the Scourge of God. Sweepings of the gutters of Paris. They spouted revolutionary slogans at us.

"Vive The Revolution!" they shouted. "Death to God!"

They jeered the priest. Their coarse shouts echoed off the Church walls. They hooted at the ladies, made lewd gestures, and grabbed at their crotches. They drank the holy water and spat in the font. They broke the collection boxes and crawled drunkenly across the marble floors after the spinning coins. Then a thin Frenchman stuck his bayonet in the eye of the Virgin.

At that point that my fist connected with his jaw, spilling teeth and blood. He went down hard. The other lads were close at my heels, fists and feet flying. The next Frenchman was a big man, as big as myself, and so I picked up the fallen soldier, and flung him bodily at the head of his comrade. The fight was over quickly enough. Outside, we heard the whistles of the gendarmes, the military police. The beaten Frenchmen lay on the church floor, bloodied and groaning. The big fellow raised his head to get up, and so, I am ashamed to say, I gave him an angry kick with my boot. The black Madonna on the wall gazed down at me reproachfully.

"Moja wina, moja wina, moja bardzo wielka wina!
My sin, my sin, my very grievous sin!"

"I'm sorry, Mother," I said, as we ran, "forgive me!"

CHAPTER FORTY-THREE
THE INVASION!

When we entered Rome we were admired and lauded – but soon we found it completely empty, with deserted streets, shuttered houses, and the inhabitants closeted away in hiding. They were afraid. French malice had inspired this fear, for the Romans had been told by the French that the Poles were a race of savage barbarians, of a cruel and fierce nature.

The French themselves were unconcerned by the ill-will they had created. They marched off to Civitavecchia, a port that lay close to Rome. This they did with a vast amount of fuss, for they were setting out on an expedition – to invade England, it was said. Thankfully we were not to accompany them on this insane adventure, for Dabrowski had wisely kept us out of it.

To rule Rome, Dabrowski had to convince the citizens of our true conduct and character. We had to show that we were better than the French, more decent and honourable. So Tanski, in the First Legion, with his pet cardinal, was hobnobbing with priests and bishops – and their sisters and mistresses – and having a high old time. As the priests were so powerful, a great deal of money and effort was spent on entertaining them. He was making friends. It was said that Tanski was being groomed for a cavalry division, as soon as we had one, that is.

Cyprian Godebski was at first enraged to discover that *Major* Elias Tremo was his commanding officer. Yet this was only a temporary state of affairs. For Tremo was soon to be transferred. General Dabrowski wanted us to have a cavalry regiment, and his man Tremo was to organise it. With Tremo gone from the infantry, the way would be clear for Cyprian to take over our division. So Cyprian awaited the happy day when his rival would be out of the way and he would be promoted. Meantime he merrily penned his own operetta, using the rehearsals as a pretence to chase the lady sopranos.

Even Sierawski was destined for higher things. The brass considered him a genius, a prodigy. They had made him adjutant to a major, no less, and were grooming him, also, for a division. His skills as an engineer were greatly in demand, and highly esteemed. Whilst, on the contrary, we had no shortage of junior cavalrymen with bad disciplinary records.

As for myself, then, I was the odd man out. Stuck in the infantry, and under suspicion after the affray at the church. My old friend Wybicki summoned me to his office.

"The French are furious," he said darkly, disappointment writ all over his face. "I have promised to investigate for them, to keep the French gendarmes out of this. You'd best take a few days leave, Blumer," Wybicki said, furious. "Dismissed!"

Of course, he was too polite to say anything, but I had let him down, and the whole Legion, too. I had behaved like a *pistolet* – a stupid hothead. I had behaved exactly as the rumours said we Poles did – like a fierce, savage barbarian.

Luchina, though, was greatly taken with savagery. She had a cannibal heart and wild lust for blood. Well, any stable in a storm. Disheartened, and chastened, I frequented the Via Faustina. Her house there was as large as a small palace – a palazzo, she called it – and inside it shone as gaudy as a heaven fashioned by magpies. A boudoir of pink, green and gold. Every wall glittered with decadent mosaics. Forests of crystal glass and gilt furniture glowed and sparkled amongst guttering candles. For a few deluded days, lying under cracked ceilings with faded painted angels, I tarried with that wicked little painted devil. There, in the Via Faustina, I discovered that Luchina's jewel's were paste.

"Hell's bells," I cursed, pulling on my boots, and glancing at the clock, for it was gone midnight, "who calls?"

"It is my husband!" Luchina cried, delighted, letting the bedclothes fall from her uncorseted bosom. Down in the hallway below all was chaos. A carriage arrived. Dogs barked. Servants ran hither and thither. Doors slammed. Boots marched up the stairs.

"You must challenge him!" she demanded, flashing her ivory teeth, thrusting my sabre into my hands. In the moonlight, one could see the pocks and blemishes on her powdered skin. I had no stomach for this painted harlot any longer, and had rather take my chances with the military police.

"Upon my soul!" I laughed, "what, end a man's life, for the sake of a strumpet! What do you take me for, madam – an assassin?"

"Damn you, treacherous seducer!" Luchina cried, eyes dark as daggers. She screamed, and hurled a stiletto at me. It wedged in a window frame. I bowed, pulled on my kontusz, and strolled out to the balcony. Outside, the moon glowed. Pan Twardowski laughing at me again, the son of a bitch.

After scrambling down the curtain-ropes and vines I met Birnbaum in a nearby inn, where our horses were stabled. As we were leaving, we ran full pelt into a figure with dark curly hair and moustaches, swathed in billowing smoke and cloak, silhouetted against the eerie glow of the fire, like a cameo of Satan. We thought it was the Devil come to collect our souls, so I prayed to the Virgin, and Birnbaum called on Jehovah, but it was worse than that –

"General Zayonczek!" we said, saluting. After a few brief seconds, I recovered my senses.

"What a surprise! That is, a pleasant surprise! We thought you dead, Sir! How the Devil did you escape?" I asked, nonplussed.

"My wife pulled some strings and got me out of that stinking Austrian gaol," Zayonczek replied. Zayonczek's wife was of course the beautiful ice-maiden who we had escorted out of Warsaw, before it was taken. She was wealthy and well-connected. She had freed her husband, by hook or by crook.

"So here I am!" Zayonczek said, "and here you are too – in the nick of time! Well, get your horses, and let's be on our way, comrades!"

We collected our horses and then we lost ourselves in the backstreets. Scant moments later, as we rode out onto the highway, we became sensible of a great commotion, a vast noise of hooves in the darkness, and then a great body of horsemen were upon us. Zayonczek's men.

"A strong wife," Zayonczek boasted, gloating about his gorgeous spouse, "is the greatest treasure a man can have."

"I've not had much luck with women recently," I admitted.

"Well, you must get yourself a wife, lad. We shall get you one when we conquer England!" Zayonczek laughed.

"Indeed, Sir," I replied, having not the faintest idea what this wild lunatic was raving about. England? I glanced at the stars. We were riding north. North to Civitavecchia. The port. Hills and forests whirled by, dark shapes on the horizon, black trees on a low sky, silhouetted in silver by the light of Twardowski's moon. Behind me were gendarmes and a vengeful medusa. Ahead of me was the devil-knew-what. By my side, was, well, a madman!

"I'm glad you could make it, Blumer," said Zayonczek, "I need good Podolian lads, especially those with English blood, and the English tongue."

"I have Irish blood, Sir," I averred, "but I speak the language tolerably well." Still I was in ignorance.

"Better yet, boy!" Zayonczek declared, greatly delighted. "That will be invaluable. The English oppress the Irish as the Russians oppress us Poles. We will find many Irish allies in England! This morning we set sail with General Bonaparte – for the invasion!"

"By the Blessed Virgin!" I whispered, appalled. "I thought Dabrowski had kept us out of this – ahem – splendid plan?" I asked, horrified. Dabrowski had fought like a lion to keep us Poles out of this mad adventure, which would do nothing to free our Motherland.

"Well," Zayonczek replied, "I had a word with Bonaparte, who is a most splendid fellow. My battalion have been made into honorary Frenchmen, and transferred out of the Legion, for this campaign. Dabrowski can go hang, the miserable cowardly fool!"

God help us! I thought. Birnbaum and I had been taken from Dabrowski's wise leadership, into the arms of this ambitious and unscrupulous lunatic! But there was nothing to be done. By now we were at the port, surrounded by Zayonczek's men.

"Damnedest thing," Zayonczek said as we boarded the ship, "have you heard what happened to Felix Potocki?" And he told me the story. Felix had been cast aside by the Russians, for they had no further use for him. Then he discovered his new young wife taken in adultery with his own brother. Humiliated for all the world to see, Felix eked out his days, alone, in an empty palace in Vienna. Nobody loves a traitor.

As we boarded the ship, I thought of the faithful friends and comrades that we had left behind in Italy. Proud Tanski, wily Sierawski, brave Godebski. I thought of Madame, back in Poland, carrying on the struggle, her life in danger at every moment. For seven long years she had guided us and kept us safe through the disasters that had befallen our sad land. A deluge of fire and sword, the plague of the barbarian Suvarov.

From that glorious day on the Third of May, when the Bullock had signed our great Constitution, we had been through the torments of the damned. Our nation was hurled into a tomb of destruction. Waves of invaders had annihilated our armies, imprisoned our leaders, burned down our homes, and stolen our treasures. We had fought desperate battles and escaped the slaughter of Praga. Betrayed by our King, our nation destroyed, we were forgotten by the world. Our very name was forbidden to be spoken. Yet still Dabrowski and the Legion fought on, against impossible odds.

Poland was not dead, as long as we lived!

Later, as the other men puked at the ship's rail, I stared up at the moon. I reckoned the direction we were sailing in by my compass, and the moonlight. England was north, but we were sailing south. We were sailing to Egypt.

Twardowski was still up there on the moon, laughing fit to burst. He, and Felix too, had made their bargains, and look how it served them! We of the Legion had made our bargain, too, for good or ill. For seven long dark years we had prayed for a saviour. Bonaparte had answered our call.

But was he sent to us by God – or the Devil?

KONIEC
(THE END)

HISTORICAL NOTES
GENERAL DABROWSKI'S LEGION

The story of General Dabrowski's legendary Legion is one of the most tragic and heroic in military history. But although there are hundreds of novels set in the age of Napoleon, there is not a single novel in the English language about Dabrowski's Legion. If mine is not the definitive work in English, it is at least (as far as I know) the first. In Napoleonic novels, Polish soldiers crop up as stage villains (or staunch French allies), but certainly not as heroes. There was never any portrayal of their desperate fight for freedom, their immense courage, or their capacity for drink, gambling, womanising, and wild adventures.

Historians disagree as to the contribution of Dabrowski's Legions to the Polish cause. Some argue that they had a propaganda value and nothing more. Yet it is generally accepted that the Legions were as good as the best French army units, at a time when the French were universally agreed to be the best soldiers in the world.

Napoleon recognised the military value and bravery of the Poles, but he used them with great cynicism. The Poles were not unique in that. Napoleon considered all soldiers, including French, to be expendable. The Legion itself was subjected to frequent changes of name and organisation by Napoleon, sometimes for sound military reasons, sometimes for dubious political ones. Even so, it remained recognisably Dabrowski's Legion.

Ironically, although their enemies referred to Dabrowski's regiment as 'The Foreign Legion', the French themselves did not use the term until after the Bourbon restoration, and Napoleon had been exiled to St Helena. Nevertheless, Dabrowski's Legion was the direct forerunner of the regiment that still serves France today, called the Hohelohe Legion in 1821, then renamed The Foreign Legion in 1831. Both contained many Polish soldiers who had fought for Dabrowski.

The late Professor Jan Pachonski wrote the seminal Polish textbooks on Dabrowski's Legion. I am indebted in particular to his masterwork "Prawda I Legendy" ("Truth and Legend"), now sadly out of print. A bibliography of English and Polish reference works is included for those who wish to read further – and whose Polish is up to it!

As far as possible, my descriptions of the Partition of Poland and the formation of Dabrowski's Legion, are historically accurate. But as I discovered, and as Professor Pachonski himself admitted, there were often gaps in the records, or contradictory accounts. Dabrowski was putting together the Legion from scratch in difficult circumstances after the Polish Republic was destroyed by violent foreign invasions. For a writer, though, this is a gift. It gives me the excuse to put my characters in the thick of the action. Occasionally there is a total gap in history, or an inconsistency. I have therefore sometimes had to invent or alter the facts for dramatic purposes. Out of respect for the Legions, I have included a set of notes at the back of this book showing where I have done this. Often what I have invented was less strange than the real history.

I needed to enlist a hero of Dabrowski's Legion, and in my research I found a real person more extraordinary than any character I would have ever dared to invent. This is Ignatius Blumer, the half-Irish, half-Polish gentleman soldier. Blumer fought at a score of legendary battles from Zielence to the Berezina, and was awarded both the Virtuti Militari and the Legion D'Honneur, the Polish and French equivalents of the Victoria Cross. He was a controversial man, with many enemies, happy to bend the rules, and involved in a lot of political skulduggery. He would have heartily approved of Pepi's strong arm tactics on the Third of May.

Blumer is buried in the Powazki Cemetery in Warsaw. His opulent marble tomb, which I visited on the 177th anniversary of his death, in the November snows, is a national monument. He lies in the crypt beside the love of his life, his first wife, the beautiful and vivacious Countess Marianne Cecciopieri. Blumer's friend, the martyred poet Cyprian Godebski, is buried a few yards away. In this book I have narrated only the first seven years of Blumer's eventful career, which was full of bizarre adventures, triumph and tragedy. Next year I will follow Blumer to Egypt, and beyond...

MICHAEL LARGE, ESSEX, 2011

HISTORICAL NOTES YEAR BY YEAR

1778

Ignatius Alexander Blumer was born in Oleszyce, in Austrian-occupied Podolia, on 31 July 1773, a year after the First Partition of Poland. His mother was called Angela and his father Peter. His grandfather was an Irish colonel in the British Army who subsequently served as Peter the Great's artillery instructor before retiring and settling down in Poland. Blumer's large physical stature and his fiery temper are well-recorded, although exact accounts vary. He was nicknamed 'Blumerowski' and later, 'General Pistolet'. He is known to have had a dry, sardonic sense of humour. Blumer's home village nowadays stands within the borders of a free and democratic Republic of Poland.

I am not aware that Blumer's father served Felix Potocki although I have seen unverified comments that he did, or was in Russian service – effectively the same thing. I am also not aware that his mother was an ardent patriot, but Blumer presumably got his patriotism from somewhere. There is a portrait of Blumer (from later life) in 'Poland's Caribbean Tragedy', by Pachonski and Wilson.

Blumer's childhood 'initiation' is invented but based on an account in 'God's Playground' by Norman Davies. The other biographical details of Blumer's childhood are also invented. However, Blumer did indeed choose to serve the Polish King as I describe, although he did not have to. He could have joined the Austrian, Prussian or Russian armies, as many others sadly did.

All of the details regarding Felix Potocki are accurate.

Jozef Wybicki did indeed write the Song of the Legions, Dabrowski's Mazurka. He was a lawyer by profession and a leader of the Confederates of Bar, and later became General Dabrowski's assistant. I have invented his association with Blumer and his mother, although Bar is in Podolia and Wybicki and his comrades did have to hide there.

The original words to The Song of The Legions can be found at (for example) http://en.poland.gov.pl/the,Polish,National,Anthem,7060.html.

The words have undergone a number of revisions and changes over the years. I have used Wybicki's original as far as possible, with some minor changes in my translation. There is an interesting discussion of this in Norman Davies 'God's Playground'. For obvious reasons the changes over the years since 1797 are not dealt with in this novel. Suffice to say that the major change is that some found the original version's "Poland is not dead (umarła)" unacceptable, on the basis that Poland might have died of natural causes, rather than being murdered. Over time the modern version was preferred, which begins "Poland has not perished yet (zginela)" which is how it stands at the present day.

1791

The irascible Tanski (who later became a Colonel in the Polish Lancers of Napoleon's Imperial Guard), the crafty engineer Sierawski, and the poet Cyprian Godebski, were all friends or comrades of Blumer's. I have tried to stay true to their biographical details wherever possible.

The descriptions of The Four Year Sejm, Third of May, King Stanislaus-August, his nephew Prince Jozef 'Pepi' Poniatowski, and so on, are all accurate. The description of the King as "poor, foolish Poniatowski... reeking of macassar" is by Thomas Carlyle. The Poniatowski Palace is today the official residence of the Polish President.

On the Third of May the Sejm was only about half to two-thirds full. The signing of the Constitution was carefully timed to take place when hostile delegates were on holiday, and was actually supposed to have been on the Fifth of May. Pepi used drastic measures similar to those described to solve the terrible problem of the 'Liberum Veto'. Many of those who opposed the Constitution were basically traitors in the pay of foreign powers, and later found guilty of high treason. My sympathies lie with Pepi. Blumer and his comrades were actually present at the Third of May, according to Pachonski, and although I have invented their participation in the 'political debate' that went on, it is quite plausible. The encounter with Hetman Rzewuski and Bishop Massalski is invented but all of the details about those two rather despicable persons are sadly accurate.

The formidable Madame L is based on the real-life Castellan of Polaniec, Madame Marianne Lanckoronska, although there are elements of other people in her character. She was in charge of a resistance network called 'Lwow Central', as described in the book. She arranged for Blumer and the others to escape into exile through

Lwow, and she was Godebski's superior while he was making trouble there. As well as being a military governess, Madame did indeed have a fashionable salon where there were political intrigues, as I have described. Dabrowski was a regular visitor and a picture of the salon appears in Pachonski's biography of him.

The love affair between Madame and Elias Tremo, and Cyprian Godebski's unrequited passion, are all invented by me. Nevertheless the dashing Tremo was indeed the son of the King's cook, Pawel Tremo. Elias Tremo also visited Madame Lanckoronska's salon regularly, as Dabrowski's messenger... As for the Thursday Dinners (cooked by Tremo's father) I am grateful to the excellent 'Old Polish Traditions' by Lemnis & Vitry for the details, and for most of the meals and culinary details that appear in this novel, as well as for various customs and practices of the home and dinner table.

The fight scene with the 'Podolian Pope' is inspired by the fight in Jan Chrystostom Pasek's Memoir 'The Polish Baroque', which I highly recommend. It is from an earlier era, the days of King Sobieski, but the spirit (and the vodka consumption) were the same.

1792

The details of the Targowica Confederacy are all too sadly accurate. The exchange of correspondence between Pepi and Rzewuski happened, although I have abridged their letters.

Jan Nepomucen Potocki, Felix's nephew, and the legendary author of the classic novel 'The Saragossa Scrolls,' is known (amongst many other things) for the first flight over Warsaw in a hot air balloon in 1790, and fought at Zielence for the Republic.

The Polish nobility claimed descent from the Sarmatians of ancient Persia, wild warrior horsemen who fought the Romans. This romantic belief is supported by some archaeological evidence.

Blumer, Tanski and Sierawski were present at the battle of Zielence, according to Pachonski, although I have invented the details. The course of the battle was broadly as I described, and the Poles did capture the Russian flag, as later celebrated in a famous painting by Wojciech Kossak. There is no evidence Blumer captured it, here I have taken a liberty. I understand that the flag itself was taken from Morkov's division, who the old boyar tries to rally.

The great Tadeusz Kościuszko's biographical details and description are well-known. Blumer and his comrades were at

Dubienka, although I have invented the precise details. The outline of the battle was as described and the Russians had to go through supposedly neutral Austrian territory to outflank the Poles, who then fell back to Warsaw. General Kochowski was in command of the Russian forces at Dubienka.

As for the betrayal by the King, sadly the defection of Stanislaus-August to the Targowicans was real, and something he will never be forgiven for. Pepi vacillated in overthrowing his uncle and the chance was lost. Pepi did then seek death at Markuszem and was saved by one of his aides, another Prince called Sanguszko, rather than by Blumer and his comrades. However, according to Pachonski, they were indeed among the die-hards at the battle, so again it is plausible they were used for the dirty work as I suggest.

1793

All Pachonski says about 1793 was that Blumer's men "broke through the Russian cordon" but were then later captured and spent the year "in the Russian army".

I have therefore had a free hand, and I have Blumer return to Podolia for a confrontation with Felix Potocki. The encounter with Felix is of course invented. Blumer describes Felix as a Russian General. Felix was given numerous meaningless titles such as 'Field Marshal Imperial' by the Tsarina to fob him off, and was buried in the uniform of a Russian general. Potocki almost certainly murdered his first wife, either by using his Cossack bodyguards, or, as was commonly said at the time, throwing her down a well. Tulczyn Palace (which still stands) is accurately described. A fireplace from Tulczyn was offered for auction at Sotheby's in 2008 with an incredible guide price of 100,000-150,000 US Dollars. The card table was in the same auction. This gives some idea of Felix's vast wealth.

The Targowicans were basically criminals and traitors and did carry out numerous rapes and murders. Dabrowski did however collaborate with the Targowicans in order to save soldiers and regiments from death and deportation, as I have described. This he did very successfully, as I have shown him do with Blumer's men in this invented encounter.

Dabrowski's actions were held against him later by his Polish rivals, mainly Zayonczek. The Legions were sadly bedevilled by infighting, petty rivalries and duelling, as indeed were all armies of the time. I have tried to reflect this in the novel. Dabrowski himself was indeed half

German and had served in the Saxon Army before 1791. That may well be where he learned to be such a fine and disciplined soldier. It has to be said that the armies of the Republic, although undeniably brave, were underfunded and not very well organised. They placed far too much emphasis on cavalry and not enough attention on drill.

Szymon Korczak is an invented character who is an amalgam of two Targowica henchmen, Hetman Szymon Kossakowski and Hetman Szymon Branicki, of the Korczak clan. The manner but not the place and time of Korczak's death are those of Szymon Kossakowski.

The duel in the Masonic Lodge is of course invented, but the details of Masonic practices in 1793 are taken from 'Masonic Quarterly' magazine. Practically every man of note in the Napoleonic era was a freemason, although oddly scholars have never been able to agree if Napoleon himself was. The author (a non-Mason) would be very grateful for any help regarding the history of freemasonry for the next novel, where this will be a major theme.

A similar bison hunt in Podolia to mine is related in Norman Davies 'God's Playground'.

1794

I have tried to be as faithful to the history of the Uprising as possible. The line 'The Sharper The Thistles The Sweeter The Victory' is taken from Norman Davies.

According to Pachonski, Blumer and his comrades were in Krakow for the Act of Insurrection, but only Tanski and Sierawski were at Raclawice. However, Blumer was made a Lieutenant in command of a 'People's Brigade' of volunteer infantry, exactly as I described. It was a small leap to place him with the scythemen in the front rank at Raclawice and I hope I may be forgiven for it.

Sierawski did indeed defend his beloved Krakow using a powder mine and other fortifications – sadly I had to omit this for reasons of space. During the siege of Warsaw, Sierawski was also called upon to defend Wola, and seems to have performed heroically. I do not know that Blumer and Godebski were involved in the siege of Warsaw at all, let alone at Wola, so I have invented that part, again, for dramatic purposes. However, I have tried to make amends, as I have Blumer do to Zayonczek, by giving Sierawski the credit.

Zayonczek did lift the very same siege of Wola, a suburb, by charging cavalry through the streets, as I described. A brave fighter, he was unfortunately a completely unscrupulous man (see Nafziger, for example) and plotted endlessly against Dabrowski, his rival. The details of Madame Zayonczek's beauty regime are taken from no less and authority than the official webpage of the President of Poland: www.president.pl/en/presidential-residences. The lady herself was a Protestant, a Huguenot, as Tanski refers to her.

Dabrowski was also initially successful in counter-attacking against the Prussians, as I describe. He was often criticised (particularly by Zayonczek) for being too well-disposed towards Germans and Prussians. My descriptions of Dabrowski have been as accurate as possible, and taken from Pachonski. I have had Blumer playing cards with Dabrowski in Warsaw, and this is not entirely implausible – Blumer regularly played whist with Dabrowski in Italy, a few years later – but this scene is invented.

Madame's house probably was used for the war effort, but this is conjecture. The Lanckoronski family have been fighting for Poland and her culture for generations, and The Lanckoronski Foundation is very active at the present day. This inspired the invented sub-plot to save a number of historic treasures, including Sobieski's Flag, which Blumer and his comrades almost ruin. Although this is invented, there are tantalising hints about 'Sobieski's Flag' contained in Godebski's poem 'Poem of the Legions'. The extract from Horace is Epode Number 15, which was known to Godebski as he quotes from it in the same poem.

The Slaughter of Praga was one of the worst atrocities of the whole Napoleonic Era. It remains very contentious. Suvarov argued at the time that it was a reprisal for the killing of Russians during the Uprising. However, the argument is fairly feeble – even he was appalled by it. I have deliberately chosen descriptions by the British Ambassador Colonel William Gardner, and by Suvarov himself, to avoid any accusations of bias.

"It is with regret I inform your Lordships that the day of the forcing of the lines of Praga was attended by the most horrid and unnecessary barbarities – houses burnt, women massacred, infants at the breast pierced with the pikes of Cossacks and universal plunder, and with the same fate prepared for Warsaw" – the words of the British Ambassador, see Norman Davies, 'God's Playground', page 410. Suvarov *himself* said "The whole of Praga was strewn with dead bodies. Blood was flowing in streams." (Isabel de Madoniaga, "Russia in the Age of Catherine the Great"). Needless to say the Tsarina was delighted with the massacre, sending the famous message – 'Hurrah!' – and promoting Suvarov.

351

The comrades' flight from Warsaw with the flag, the treasures, and the army wives, is invented, but similar scenes obviously occurred after Praga. The incident with the burned manor house is invented but reflects accurately what was going on at the time. The wholesale theft of nearly half a million precious books of the Warsaw Library – the House of Kings – has been well documented and did take place: see for example Norman Davies page 384-5.

1795

Kalwaria Zebrydowski was built between the years of 1605 and 1632 (see www.kalwaria.eu). There are forty chapels, including Herod's Palace, set on the surrounding hills. After being wounded in the leg, in a skirmish at Krywacze, Blumer did indeed go on a pilgrimage to Kalwaria. There he met up again with Tanski and Sierawski at Easter 1795, before setting out for Krakow, and then Lwow, where they eventually met up with Godebski.

Wieliczka contains world famous salt mines.

Magda's Song at Chapter Twenty-Three is based on one quoted by Norman Davies at Volume II, page 200.

Sierawski's incredible story and Tanski's sad tale are both taken from Pachonski and are in outline true. The Generals who sent Sierawski on his suicide mission were Wojczynski and Grabowski, according to Professor Pachonski. Sierawski did have an elephant on his coat of arms. The descriptions of places and customs are accurate, although the pursuit of Blumer and his comrades by the Targowicans led by the fictional Szymon Korczak is of course invented.

Birnbaum was Blumer's sergeant later but probably did not know him at that point. The story of the Beardlings is however entirely true and well-documented. It makes an interesting addition to the story of Polish-Jewish relations. This was of great importance to the society of the Republic and something I felt was vital to deal with in the book. I have not really done this theme justice (due to constraints of space) but it would have been a great shame to omit it altogether.

Princess Isabella Czartoryska, who does not appear in the book, created the Temple at Pulawy and preserved cultural relics in the museum there (see www.muzeum-czartoryskich.krakow.pl). Pulawy was under construction at the time I have the comrades visit it, as I describe.

The renegade Frenchman who betrayed the plans of the Uprising was General Dumouriez, who had been a friend of Kościuszko's.

1796

Cyprian Godebski was a resistance leader in Lwow and the comrades were reunited there.

Also in Lwow the same time was Jablonowski, 'The Little Negro', who is mentioned in Pan Tadeusz, the Polish national poem. I have no idea if the comrades met him, and the encounter is invented, but all of the details (including his not very politically correct nickname) regarding this extraordinary man are taken from Pachonski, 'Poland's Caribbean Tragedy'. There is a portrait of him (and of Blumer) in the Appendix to that book. Napoleon and Jablonowski were classmates at the exclusive French military academy at Brienne in 1783. Napoleon, whose prejudices are well documented, never liked him. During their school days Jablonowski is said to have retorted to Napoleon's racial jibes in exactly the manner Blumer relates. By all accounts (even Napoleon's) Jabolonowski was an exemplary soldier and physically fearless. He does not appear to have suffered any racial prejudice from Dabrowski, as he was repeatedly promoted by him, and ultimately commanded the Second Legion, although that takes place after this novel is set.

'The Beloved Country' was written by Ignacy Krasinski in 1774 and was the anthem of the Warsaw Corps of Cadets. The comrades sojourn in Lwow was interrupted by a warrant being issued for Godebski's arrest, so they presumably made a nuisance of themselves. Although their time in Lwow is fictionalised, the accounts of the French campaigns that I have them reading (in frustration) in the Austrian newspapers are accurate, including Dabrowski's involvement. The Austrian newspapers referred to Dabrowski's men as 'The Foreign Legion' because they were not allowed to use the name 'Poland'. The Partitioners had agreed that '...the name or designation of the Kingdom of Poland... shall remain suppressed as from the present and forever...' This was contained in a Secret Protocol to the Treaty of 15/26 January 1797 between Prussia, Austria and Russia. See (for example) Norman Davies 'God's Playground' at page 408.

Dabrowski's Proclamation had a hugely positive effect on a shattered nation, and drew émigrés and deserters from the Austrian army to Italy. I am very conscious that General Dabrowski does not get a huge amount of time in the novel, even though it was his Legion. We encounter him only three times – on the run in Podolia, at the raising of the Siege of Wola, and in Rome. Dabrowski spent much of this period outside Poland, in exile, putting together the Legion, travelling to Prussia and France, and fighting alongside Bonaparte in Italy.

Details of Denisko's shambolic camp are taken from Pachonski, and from Zamoyski's 'Holy Madness', page 121. Although Denisko used the funds badly, much of the French silver had been stolen by the Sultan of Turkey, according to Pachonski. Blumer and his comrades (and many others) took their leave to go to Italy via Turkey, around the time of 'Denisko's Catastrophe' which occurred around 25 June – 4 July 1797. Dabrowski conceived the original plan, and intended to send relief to Denisko, via Bukowina and the Leoben pass. When a truce was signed between Austria and France. Dabrowski rescinded the order, but in the fog of war, Denisko carried on with the original plan, with tragic results.

At the Dniester, Sierawski was again the hero of the hour, leading the comrades against 36 Russian Cuirassiers, although I have fictionalised the scene, including the involvement of Szymon Korczak.

The description of 'The Void' at Chapter 35 is taken from Tanski's diary (see Pachonski). Blumer and his comrades' dreadful journey to Constantinople was by crab boat, although they were shipwrecked twice, not once, as I have it. Hassan is a fictional character, but the Turkish Janissaries did conscript Cossacks and others as I describe. The Turks were short of officers and did their best to recruit Polish émigrés.Some did defect and converted to Islam.

Rymkiewicz did commandeer the embassy buildings in Constantinople, and the old Roman chain was left lying beside the harbour right up until the early twentieth century!

Before the journey to Italy, according to Pachonski, Tanski did contract an unpleasant illness, probably dysentery, from which he made a complete recovery. Sierawski was the bodyguard to the French Ambassador du Bayet, although he was not very successful at this and they were taken prisoner by pirates. Blumer's journey was uneventful so I used the opportunity for a final showdown with Korczak. Here history catches up with the traitor. His fictional model, Szymon Kossakowski, was captured by the Lithuanians in Vilnius, trying to escape in a boat during the Uprising in 1794, and hanged under the slogan 'He Who Swings Cannot Drown'.

<u>1798</u>

Dabrowski's headquarters were in Milan, where the aging Wybicki was in charge of various administrative issues. Blumer was given, or restored, to the rank of Lieutenant there.

The short reign of Tsar Paul 'The Mad' was as I describe. Stanislaus-August died a prisoner in St Petersburg and his nephew Prince Poniatowski, in despair, spent his time in a dissolute fashion.

Bonaparte declared war on the Pope for his own nefarious reasons. Dabrowski captured Rome for him but in a peaceful fashion as I describe – see Pachonski. The Pope showed Dabrowski the captured standard of the Ottoman Sultan, taken by Sobieski at Vienna in 1683 as a trophy, and presented to the Pope of the day as a present by Sobieski.

The comrades did end up in Rome, and according to Pachonski, their fortunes were as I described. Tanski was assigned to guard Cardinal Testaferrato by Dabrowski – I have not painted a very flattering portrait of the Cardinal, but such behaviour was fairly typical! As far as I know Godebski did not arrive in Rome until later in May, so I hope I may be forgiven for stretching this small point.

The staircase I describe, where Dabrowski met the Pope, is the Aracoeli staircase, which can still be seen in Rome today. Blumer married an Italian Countess and Godebski a French aristocrat, so their alliances are plausible.

There was a brawl in a church between Polish Legionnaries and radical French soldiers, as I describe, although I am not aware that Blumer or his comrades were involved.

Blumer has an Egypt-sized hole in his CV, and a large inscription of the Egyptian Sun God Ra on his tomb. Napoleon did originally intend to invade England, but changed his plans. Many of the invasion force were ignorant of their destination until well after departure. The Legions did not officially take part in Napoleon's Egyptian expedition, as it was rightly frowned on by Dabrowski. However, a contingent of Poles under Zayonczek, from the Second Legion (Blumer's Legion) did take part...

CHRONOLOGY

1764	Election of King Stanislaus-August Poniatowski, the Last King of Poland
1768	Confederacy of Bar
1772	First Partition of Poland
1789	French Revolution, Storming of the Bastille (14 July)
1791	Polish Constitution of 3 May
1792	Targowica Confederacy (May) and War of the Constitution, Battles of Zielence and Dubienka
1793	Second Partition of Poland
1794	National Uprising begins in Krakow, Battles of Raclawice and Maciejowice
1795	Third and Final Partition of Poland
1796	Napoleon Bonaparte marries Josephine Beauharnais and is appointed commander of the French Army of Italy in the war against Austria (March)
1797	General Dabrowski's Proclamation (30 January) Polish Legions created in French Army Treaty and Peace of Campo Formio (17 October)
1798	Polish Legions under General Dabrowski enter Rome (3 May) Bonaparte sails for Egypt (19 May)

GLOSSARY

Babcia	Grandmother or old woman
Basia	Polish for Barbara, can also be used for 'old woman'
Boyar	Russian nobleman
Caisson	Two-wheeled ammunition carriage
Caracole	Single half turn to left or right on horseback
Drumhead	Carried out at speed according to military regulations
	A Drumhead Court Martial is a Summary execution!
Glacis	Sloping defensive fortification
Hetman	Chief
Jacobins	Extremist French Revolutionary political party. 'Jacobin' was also used as a term of abuse as 'communist' is today
Jockey	Hired thug on a horse. The modern meaning is obviously different
Knout	Vicious Russian whip, also used in Poland
Kolpak	Brimmed or brimless high-crowned hats of the period
Kontusz	Horseman's long coat
Krolik	Petty king or warlord, also means 'small rabbit'
Mamusia	Mummy (Mother)
Pan / Pani	Mr / Mrs
Pierogi	Polish dumplings
Pisanki	Easter eggs
Pistolet	Pistol or gun, but it can also mean 'hothead'
Sto lat!	'May you live a hundred years!' (Cheers!)
Sukmana	Man's overcoat, part of the national costume
Szlachta	Polish nobility
Tynf	Polish coins of the time were tynf, grosz, and zloty
Uhlans	Hussars (cavalry)
Zoldu	Soldier's pay
Zupan	Long, colourful garment worn under the kontusz

NOTE ON PRONOUNCING POLISH WORDS

A full guide to the Polish names and words found in this book, their alternative spellings, and to Polish pronunciation, can be found on the author's website www.songofthelegions.com.

Polish pronunciation is tricky. In brief, where Polish words and names are used in this book –

'c' is pronounced 'ts', so the villainous Felix Potocki's name is pronounced 'Pot-ots-ski'. (Fortunately most people called him Felix.)

'sz' is pronounced 'sh', so kontusz (a horseman's coat) is 'kont-ush'.

'w' is pronounced 'v', so Dabrowski is 'Dabrovski', Krakow is 'Krak-ov' and Lwow is 'Lvov', Poniatowski is 'Poniatovski', Sierawski is 'Sieravski', Twardowski is 'Tvardovski', and Wigilia (Christmas Eve) is 'Vigilia', and so on.

'i' is usually pronounced 'ee'.

So Targowica and Targowican are therefore 'Targoveetsa' and 'Targoveetsan'.

Lastly, 'Kościuszko' deserves a note all of its own. It is pronounced 'Kosh-choo-shko'. There are numerous towns, villages and even hills and mountains in Austrialia and the USA named after Tadeusz Kościuszko, and one wonders how these are rendered in the local dialect!

BIBLIOGRAPHY

IN ENGLISH

God's Playground, Norman Davies, Oxford University Press 2005

A Concise History of Poland (Second Edition) Lukowski and Zawadzki) Cambridge 2006

Tactics and Experience of Battle in the Age of Napoleon, Rory Muir, Yale University Press 2000

Memoirs of the Polish Baroque, Jan Chrysostom Pasek, translated by C.S. Leach, University of California Press 1976

Poles and Saxons of the Napoleonic Wars, George Nafziger, Emperor's Press 1991

Holy Madness, Adam Zamoyski, Phoenix Press 1999

The Manuscript Found In Saragossa, translated by Ian MacLean, Penguin 1995

In the Legions of Napoleon, Heinrich von Brandt, translated by Julian North, Greenhill Books 1999

Memoirs of a Polish Lancer, Dezydery Chlapowski, translated by Tim Simmons, Emperor's Press 1992

Old Polish Traditions, Lemnis & Vitry, Hippocrene Books 2001

Napoleon's Mercenaries, Guy C. Dempsey, Greenhill Books 2002

Reveries on the Art of War, (De Saxe) translated by General Thomas R. Phillips, Dover Publications 2007

Poland's Caribbean Tragedy, Jan Pachonski and Reuel K. Wilson, Columbia University Press 1986

IN ENGLISH and POLISH

Pan Tadeusz (1832) Adam Mickiewicz (translated by Kenneth R. Mackenzie) Hippocrene Books 1986

IN POLISH

Jan Pachonski, Legiony Polskie, Prawda I Legenda (Polish Legions, Truth and Legend), Volumes I – IV, (Ministry of Defence, Poland) 1969

Jan Pachonski, General Jan Henryk Dabrowski, (Ministry of Defence, Poland) 1981

Jan Pachonski, Slownik Biograficzny Oficerow Polskich (Biographical Dictionary of Polish Officers) and Korpus Oficerski Legionow Polskich (Officer Corps of the Polish Legion) 1796-1807, both published by Biblioteku Centrum Dokumentacji Czynu Niepodleglosciowego 1998

Wiersz do Legiow Polskich (Poem of the Polish Legions), Cyprian Godebski, 1805, Ossolineum

Grenadier-Filozof (Grenadier Philosopher), Cyprian Godebski (1799) Universitas Krakow 2002